Praise for *Sisters i*

"*Sisters in Arms* is heartwarming but fier̶ camaraderie and fire, starring women you'd love to make your friends. Prickly, musical Grace and bubbly, privileged Eliza may not make the most natural allies, but it's fight or die when they're thrown together in the Army's first class of female officers—and the first Black women allowed to serve their country in World War II. Grace, Eliza, and their sisters in arms battle prejudice, Army regulations, and enemies at home and abroad as they serve in the only all-Black female battalion deployed overseas, and it's a fight to make you stand up and cheer. Kaia Alderson's debut is a triumph!"

—Kate Quinn, *New York Times*
bestselling author of *The Rose Code*

"This is not just another World War II story; this is a stirring and timely novel about the only all-Black battalion of the Women's Army Auxiliary Corps, a group of women who had to fight resolutely against countless obstacles in order to be permitted to serve their country. Grace and Eliza stole my heart with their spirit and their resilience, and the ups and downs of their tumultuous friendship made me laugh and cry. Poignant and powerful—an untold story that you simply must read."

—Natasha Lester, *New York Times*
bestselling author of *The Paris Secret*

"What an exciting new voice in historical fiction! I couldn't put down Alderson's novel of two young Black women testing their mettle and finding friendship and purpose during World War II. With fascinating historical detail and complex characters, *Sisters in Arms* casts a brilliant light on a group of women too long kept in the shadows."

—Kerri Maher, author of *The Girl in White Gloves*

"*Sisters in Arms* is a riveting tale of ordinary Black women doing extraordinary things against all odds in a critical moment in world history. Kaia Alderson does an amazing job bringing these courageous yet unheralded women out of the shadows and into our hearts."

—Jamie Wesley, author of *Slamdunked by Love*

"A riveting, character-driven tale about the all-Negro Women's Army Corps unit of World War II marks Kaia Alderson's debut historical fiction, a triumph of immersive storytelling about heroic Black women who served their country despite discrimination. An untold story finally getting its due."

—Denny S. Bryce, author of *Wild Women and the Blues*

"Eliza and Grace come alive in the pages of this gripping and inspiring novel of friendship, sisterhood, and the bravery of the women of the Six Triple Eight during World War II. Kaia Alderson's poignant story about the all-Black female battalion who faced discrimination head on in order to serve their country is an incredible debut not to be missed!"

—Eliza Knight, *USA Today* bestselling author

"Powerfully written, with emotional honesty and historical accuracy, *Sisters in Arms* explores the obstacles and triumphs of the unsung and only all-Black female battalion during World War II."

—Sharina Harris, author of *Judge's Girls*

"A beautifully rich story that dives deep into family expectations, sisterhood, and self."

—Carla Fredd, author of *The Perfect Man*

"*Sisters in Arms* is a much-needed history lesson about the role of Black women in the U.S. armed forces. Their battle wasn't just against the Nazis and the enemies of the state. Kaia Alderson's debut historical fiction novel is a tour de force of history, a unique story that has so much relevance to race relations in the twenty-first century. Alderson is about to be your new favorite author."

—Cheris Hodges, author of *Won't Go Home Without You*

"Beautifully written. Kaia Alderson has given us a historical gem that shines a spotlight on the lives of women who served in the only all-Black female U.S. battalion to be deployed overseas during World War II. In her fictional release *Sisters in Arms*, Alderson breathes life into a cast of dynamic characters and masterfully takes us on a journey of service and dedication to country, preservation of self, and strength in times of adversity. Grace and Eliza's story is a brilliant depiction of resilience, and highlights the untold history of Black women whose influence has previously been undervalued and ignored."

—Deborah Fletcher Mello, author of *Stalked by Secrets*

"Kaia Alderson's stunning historical fiction debut is the book we never knew we needed. A beautifully written love song to the brave, oft-forgotten Black women who courageously stepped up to serve their country."

—Farrah Rochon, *USA Today* bestselling author of *The Boyfriend Project*

"Readers will quickly be engrossed by Grace's and Eliza's courage and tenacity as they join the all-Black battalion of the Women's Army Corps. The story of the trials and victories of the women in the 6888th is one that deserves to be told, and Alderson does a masterful job of shining a light on these amazing women."

—Synithia Williams, author of *Careless Whispers*

"A smart and engaging look into a long-neglected area of American history. The ferocity and determination of the 6888th are an inspiration."

—Rebecca Roanhorse, *New York Times* bestselling author of *Trail of Lightning, Storm of Locusts*, and *Star Wars: Resistance Reborn*

"*Sisters in Arms: A Novel of the Daring Black Women Who Served During World War II* lives up to its bold title. The story of these brave female soldiers will have you rooting for them with the turn of every page—and brimming with pride. A triumph!"

—Kwana Jackson, *USA Today* bestselling author

"*Sisters in Arms* is a page-turner that cleverly follows two engaging, multidimensional fictional characters who bring to life the real story of a Black, female U.S. Army battalion during World War II. Grace and Eliza accurately embody the pioneering spirit and sparkling humanity of all the Black women soldiers who triumphed, despite the personal and professional double binds that came with being among the first women to serve in the military, while also being the first Black women to serve in the then-segregated Army."

—Emily Yellin, author of
Our Mothers' War

"With sparkling prose and inherent empathy, Alderson paints a realistic, compelling portrait of these amazing women who bravely forged a path for those who would come after them."

—Kianna Alexander, author of
After Hours Attraction

"A gripping portrayal of what it means to be a Black woman in the 1940s, and what it takes to overcome obstacles in the pursuit of respect, recognition, and independence. An inspiring and engrossing story that explores courage and the power of female friendships—a story that will stay with me for a long time. Alderson writes with a warmth that brings lightness and ease to otherwise heavy topics."

—Jane Igharo, author of
Ties That Tether

A Novel of the
Daring
Black Women
Who Served During
World War II

SISTERS *in* ARMS

KAIA ALDERSON

WILLIAM MORROW
An Imprint of HarperCollins*Publishers*

P.S.™ is a trademark of HarperCollins Publishers.

HarperCollins books may be purchased for educational, business, or sales promotional use. For information, please email the Special Markets Department at SPsales@harpercollins.com.

FIRST EDITION

Designed by Diahann Sturge
Stamp cancellation mark © Oleksii Arseniuk/Shutterstock, Inc.
Telegram and letter background © Paladin12/Shutterstock, Inc.

Library of Congress Cataloging-in-Publication Data has been applied for.

ISBN 978-0-06-296458-8

21 22 23 24 25   LSC   10 9 8 7 6 5 4 3 2 1

For Daddy,
thank you, for everything

And in loving memory of Carmen H. Washington,
whose Grace and Steele inspire me still

SISTERS *in* ARMS

TELEGRAM

WA WASHINGTON DC 5 23 PM JULY 9 1942

MR. & MRS. ERNEST STEELE

DEEPLY REGRET TO INFORM YOU THAT YOUR SON CPL
ANTHONY STEELE US ARMY IS PRESUMED DEAD IN
PHILIPPINES ISLANDS.

SMITH, THE ADJUTANT GENERAL

CHAPTER 1

New York City
July 1942

"YOU CAN BEGIN whenever you're ready."

Grace opened the folder that should have contained her sheet music. She would have cried had she been able to produce any more tears. She put the folder down and dug through her bag again. She found nothing else but her coin purse, her keys, and a letter she had grabbed from the mailbox on her way here.

"Is there a problem, Miss Steele?"

"I, uh . . ."

Grace Steele never left anything to chance. She always double-knotted her shoes. She always looked both ways before stepping off the curb to cross Lenox Avenue. She tuned in to her favorite radio show, *Our Gal Sunday*, five minutes early so she didn't miss the beginning. And she never, ever waited until the last minute to put her sheet music into her bag.

But today wasn't a normal day. And this wasn't any ordinary gig. This was her audition to get into the Juilliard School of Music.

Grace glanced at her watch, a gift from her brother, Tony, during the last Christmas they had all spent together as a family before he enlisted in the Army.

"Now you have no excuse to not make time for your music,"

Tony had said, snatching a nearby pillow and using it to protect his face against Grace's wrath. Unlucky for him, that position left his rib cage exposed. Grace landed an ineffective jab to his side. "Hey, is that any way to treat your favorite brother?"

She'd shaken her hand to dissipate the stinging pain in her knuckles. "You're my only brother, smart-ass."

He'd laughed, then wrapped his arm around her shoulders. "Merry Christmas, kiddo." He'd kissed the top of her head despite her squirming to get out of his embrace. Had Grace known what was to come, not only would she have cherished the feel of his arms around her, but she would have held on to her brother as tight as she could and never let him go.

"Is everything all right, Miss Steele?"

"I—" She gulped and immediately scolded herself for doing something so unladylike in front of the president of the Juilliard School of Music. The man was not only an esteemed pianist, composer, and conductor in the classical music world, but he was also her idol. "I seem to have left my sheet music at home."

"You left your sheet music at home. How disappointing."

Now the corners of Mr. Hutcheson's mouth fell. With that gesture, Grace knew all was lost. Forgetting to bring your sheet music to your audition at a highly respected music school was an unpardonable sin. Especially when it was for a competitive, all-expenses-paid fellowship to study with her idol at said music school. A fellowship she would never get now. It was an understatement to say Mama was going to hit the roof when she found out.

"However"—Hutcheson leaned back in his seat, bridging his long, elegant fingers—"improvisation is as necessary a skill for a pianist as is sight-reading the classics. Let's not make this a total waste of time. Surely there's something you can play from memory."

Grace blinked back tears. He was giving her another chance to prove herself. She swallowed. "Of course."

It was now or never. The problem was that her mind was drawing a blank. Without the sheet music as her guide, she knew only bits and pieces of her Handel audition piece. Mama had insisted upon it because of its complexity. Now that complexity was proving to be her downfall. Grace should have never let Mama have her way. Again.

The walls of the cavernous room began to feel like they were closing in on her.

Grace's lower lip trembled as she stared at the baby grand piano before her. It was magnificent. A Steinway with all the bells and whistles, no doubt. She hadn't seen anything like it since the one time she had performed at a holiday recital at the Apollo Theater.

She lifted her hands and let her fingers glide up the keys in a practice scale. Then her left thumb slipped on the last note. Her head whipped up, horrified.

"Sorry, I . . ." She quickly closed her mouth before she foolishly let it slip that uniformed visitors had come to her family's door the night before. And that a gold star now graced her home's window. Tossing out excuses was not in Grace's character. She wouldn't start now just because her brother was dead.

"It happens." Hutcheson didn't bother to hide his pity anymore. "It's natural to be nervous. How about you forget that I'm here? Pretend that this isn't an audition, that we're not at Juilliard. You're at home. Just relax and play. For yourself."

Her fingers froze at the suggestion. Home was the last place she wanted to be. And playing for herself would mean letting this man hear one of her compositions, opening up the most inner parts of her musical self to a stranger, sharing the jazz-inspired pieces that only Tony and his friends at the clubs had been allowed to hear. She could imagine her mother's face souring at the very idea of her daughter befouling the hallowed halls of Juilliard with that "trash music." Grace wouldn't dare. She would rather leave now, having played nothing at all.

"This is for you, Tony," she whispered. Grace closed her eyes, praying for the magic to return to her fingers. To just forget the words on that telegram that had shattered her world. Mama's grand plan for her aside, Grace was the one who chose to be here today. She came here to play. Mama's voice echoed in her head: *Steele women do not fail.*

She would not fail. "And for you, Mama."

Now, play something.

She took a deep breath, culling her mind for something appropriate that she knew well enough to play on the fly. Her fingers began to move at the first thing that came to mind: Beethoven's *Moonlight Sonata.*

She breezed through the opening notes of the piece. She smiled. The magic was back. But that magic took her only so far. She made it through the meditative first movement with no problem. After that, the piece sped up to a frenetic pace. Her out-of-practice fingers stumbled over the first refrain. And the next. Then her thumb slipped again. There was no hiding her clumsy playing now.

She looked up. Hutcheson was pursing his lips. Finally, he held up his hand.

"Maybe it would be better if we ended the audition here."

Grace's insides deflated, but she willed her spine to remain straight. She returned her hands to her lap. "Okay."

She gathered her things, including the useless folder, and stood to leave.

"When should I expect to receive your decision?"

Hutcheson smiled at her kindly. "I've heard too many people who I respect rave about your talent, Miss Steele. Your performance just now was . . . let's just say it was a disappointment. However, there is no denying that you do have talent. I would offer you a fellowship to study with me, but I don't think your heart is in it."

No! "Oh, but it is. Let me get my music and come back. I can do better," she pleaded. Tears overwhelmed her eyes. She no longer had the will to keep them at bay. "You must give me another chance. Otherwise, my mother will . . ."

The words stopped because Grace did not want to imagine what Mama would do. What she did know was that life with Loreli Steele was about to become even more unbearable once she came home without a Juilliard fellowship in hand.

"Miss Steele, I have been at this a very long time. I can see when a pupil has the fire in them to become a concert pianist . . . and when they do not. Success in this world does not boil down to talent alone. It comes down to the heart. And I can see that your heart lies elsewhere."

"I'm sorry to have wasted your time, sir."

"It was a pleasure meeting you, Miss Steele. Come back to me when you are ready to focus."

Grace forced a smile at him, then nodded. "I'll see myself out."

Grace hurried out of the building. A passing car splashed a puddle onto Grace's feet. Thankfully, Grace's dark blue rain slicker was a workhorse and her clothes stayed dry. But the insides of her galoshes were soaked. She was now humiliated and wet. She didn't think this day could get any worse.

Grace tightened her grip on her purse strap as a black Oldsmobile drove slowly past her. It was too late in the morning for a desperate Upper West Side housewife to still be on the prowl. But in Harlem, there was never a safe time of day for a Negro woman to let her guard down.

Grace had completed an education degree the year before, but the demand for teachers of any kind had been in short supply for a long time. For teachers who looked like her, even longer. Unlike the demand for Negro women in domestic work, which had never been higher. She couldn't stand on the corner of 125th Street and Lenox Avenue without at least one white woman pulling up to the curb and offering her a quarter an hour to clean her Central Park West apartment.

It was only when the Olds continued down Broadway without stopping that Grace relaxed. With her other hand, she pulled her head scarf tighter around her neck.

But she still had to go home and face Mama. First Tony and now this. To make matters worse, Daddy didn't know. He was out on another trip on Mr. Pullman's railcars. It would be up to Grace and Mama to deliver the blow when he returned home in a few days.

She looked across Broadway down 122nd Street, where, on the other side of Harlem, her mother waited. In that moment, she resolved to do two things. One, she would delay going home for as long as she could. And two, after the way she humiliated herself, she decided it was time to find another dream besides the piano.

The dream to become an international concert pianist had begun with Mama. Grace had gone along with it because, to her, it was a way to get out of New York, out of her mama's house specifically, and see the world. It had been Tony who had introduced her to the world of jazz and the freedom it represented. In time, it had become all that Grace wanted. Her dream for herself was to be free.

That was when she remembered the letter in her bag. The return address had read "The War Department." Why would it be sending anything directly to her? Grace's only connection to the military had been Tony. It had already sent its official notification of his passing to her parents. She fished the envelope out of her bag and ripped it open.

The contents had nothing to do with Tony or his death. Oddly enough, they mentioned only her. Inside was an application and a personal letter from Mary McLeod Bethune, inviting her to join the U.S. Women's Army Auxiliary Corps. Dr. Bethune's letter instructed her to go to the Army Building downtown for an intake interview and exam with WAAC officials.

A women's army?

Above, the approaching IRT subway rumbled. Grace was tempted to run up the stairs and escape to wherever the train took her. She tapped her bag. There was nothing in it except for her empty music portfolio. She had no change of clothes, no money, nowhere to go, and no plan.

But, according to this letter, she now had another option. Grace wondered what this women's army uniform would look like, what *she* might look like wearing it. She couldn't imagine that the military would send women into active combat. But surely when the war was over, they'd need to have support overseas from someone like her?

The rumble was getting louder as the 1 train came closer. If she hurried, she could make it up the stairs to the platform in time.

Or she could play it safe and take the crosstown bus home to face the "music" of Mama's wrath.

She stared at the steelwork that adorned the station. Next to the entrance, an Army recruitment poster challenged her with the question WILL YOU ANSWER AMERICA'S CALL?

She started jogging up the stairs. Grace had an answer all right: she was in no rush to go home anytime soon.

On the other side of Harlem

ELIZA JONES CONTINUED to type even though the phone on her desk had been ringing nonstop for the last three minutes. The only people who called her at work were her soft-spoken mother and some slightly less soft-spoken ladies—her friends giving her the scoop on the next "must attend" social event for Eliza's newspaper column.

She eyed the pair of white wrist-length dress gloves beside her that she would need shortly for one of those events. With rain clouds threatening, oppressive humidity was all but a guarantee today. She was not looking forward to subjecting her hands to that cotton prison. She could barely breathe as it was in the tailored lavender suit she was wearing for the occasion.

But all of that could wait. The article she was polishing was more important. She had received a tip through one of her high school classmates that four German spies had been captured on the beach on Long Island. If she could just concentrate on punching up the headline a little more, Daddy would have to put her down as a war correspondent candidate for the Associated Negro Press. Surely, now that the Army was forming a women's branch, he would see the value of her having military press credentials. He couldn't keep her on the society pages forever . . .

"Will somebody answer the damn phone?!" Daddy's voice bellowed from his office on the other side of the small newsroom. She jumped, hitting the wrong key in the process.

"Damn."

"And watch your mouth, young lady." He slammed the door to his office closed.

Everyone else quieted instantly. Eliza could feel all eyes on her back. She turned around and stuck her tongue out in the direction of Daddy's office.

The phone started ringing again.

"Eliza, will you *please* answer that phone before your father has a heart attack," said the reporter at the desk next to hers. Herb was their sports reporter. Eliza noticed that his desktop was empty, and it appeared that he wasn't in the middle of doing anything.

She yanked the handle out of the receiver. "*Harlem Voice.*"

"Is this Miss Eliza Jones?"

"Yes, that's me," she told the operator.

"Please hold for a call from Dr. Bethune." *Oh no*, she mouthed to herself as she waited for the operator to complete the connection. Daddy was going to have a fit for sure now. Why was *the* Mary McLeod Bethune calling *her*? If this was who had been ringing her phone off the hook for the last few minutes, she would never hear the end of it. Eliza riffled through the stack of notes on her desk, trying to recall if there was an upcoming social function in town where Dr. Bethune was expected to appear.

"Thank you for holding, Dr. Bethune. You are now connected."

"The WAAC needs you, Eliza Jones." No "hello" or "good morning" greeting had been given once the operator had made the connection. She was lucky that it had been a booming voice on the other end of the line. Otherwise, she never would have heard her caller over the loud background noise of the newsroom floor.

Eliza straightened in her chair as if the caller could see her. "Dr. Bethune?"

Dr. Mary McLeod Bethune was a legend in the Negro community. This powerhouse of a woman had not only founded her own school down in the Jim Crow South, but she had also served as an adviser to the last three presidents of the United States. If Dr. Bethune and the current president's wife, Eleanor Roosevelt, weren't the best of friends, they were darn near close to it. Eliza had heard that she was close to FDR's mother as well. While Dr. Bethune was friends with her parents, Eliza's own interactions with the woman had been limited to polite hellos whenever she came by the house for a quick visit when she was in town. She had no idea why *she* would be on the busy woman's radio antenna.

"Of course it's me, dear. Now, when should I expect to receive your completed WAAC application on my desk?"

The tone of the woman's voice made her feel like a schoolgirl who had been caught doing something naughty. That was ridiculous. She was twenty-three years old. She made herself slouch back into her chair before speaking.

Eliza racked her brain for a safe answer. The new women's auxiliary had caught her attention. But when she had mentioned the announcement of the new corps casually to her father, he had gone off on a tirade about how "those girls" were going to be used as nothing more than bed cushions for the "real soldiers," and she never brought it up again.

"I . . ." Her foot tapped the large handbag on the floor underneath her desk. Inside it was a folder containing all her application paperwork.

"Miss Jones, your mother informed me that you obtained an application from the downtown recruitment center two days ago." Dr. Bethune paused. "Is that information incorrect?"

How had Mother found out about that? Eliza thought she had been clever in going to the Army recruitment center in Lower Manhattan instead of the one a few blocks from the newspaper office near Strivers' Row. She should've known better. As publishers of the *Harlem Voice*, the largest Negro newspaper in the city, her parents knew *everybody* in Manhattan, both white and Negro. Mother had eyes and ears in every corner of this city. Eliza was still figuring out how to approach her father about her desire to join the WAAC. Now she had to deal with her mother blabbing about it to the internationally famous women in their lives.

If Dr. Bethune, who worked out of Washington, D.C., had known that Eliza had obtained an application the moment they became available after the newswire that announced the president had signed the new WAAC bill into law came into the newsroom, then her father definitely knew as well. Eliza tensed at that thought.

She toed her bag again. She was not in the habit of lying to people, and she wasn't going to start with *the* Mary McLeod Bethune.

"No, ma'am. Your information *is* correct." Eliza looked to the far end of the newsroom toward the office of the editor in chief. "But why would my application need to come across your desk?"

"Because I am working with officials here in Washington to ensure that Negro women are included in this new opportunity to serve their country. They are planning for the first WAAC Officer Candidate School to start in July. They're only allowing forty Negro women to be a part of that class. If you want one of those slots, Miss Jones, you must act quickly."

Eliza gulped. Yes, she wanted to do her part for the war effort. But she never thought that she'd have the opportunity to be a military officer while doing it. "I have completed the form and gathered copies of my birth certificate. I just need a recommendation—"

"Done." Dr. Bethune cut her off. Eliza gasped. She had been

thinking about asking her old high school principal when she interviewed him the next day about the upcoming senior formal dance. But to have someone like Dr. Bethune vouch for her instead? She was as good as in.

"Thank you." She paused. "But I still need a copy of my college degree. My father has it."

Eliza paused again. How would she explain to the indomitable Mary McLeod Bethune that the last time she had touched her actual degree was minutes after the commencement ceremony ended, when her father had snatched it from her grasp? It now hung on the wall in his office at home, just beneath his degree from Columbia University and her mother's degree from Jersey City State Teachers College. If she took it down, even just for a day, Daddy would definitely notice.

"I understand. You forget, I know your father. The man is a piece of work. You attended Howard University, if I recall correctly."

"I did." Eliza was stunned. This woman must have checked into her background already.

"Excellent, I'm having lunch with the dean and his wife this afternoon. I'll ask him about obtaining your records." Eliza could hear the smile in the older woman's voice. She winced as she remembered the C she had earned in a class on Chaucer during the spring semester of her senior year.

"And I'll take care of your recommendation. Personally. Now, how soon can you get down to an Army induction center for your psychological evaluation and physical examination?"

ONCE SHE FINISHED her call with Dr. Bethune, Eliza completed her article before going to her father. She held up her fist to the thick wooden door. Her heart had made its way into her throat.

She glanced at the article in her hand one last time. It was her best work yet. She knew the FBI was planning to announce its capture of the spies that evening. No newsman, no matter how he felt about "girl reporters," could pass up a scoop like this. There was no way he could keep her on the society beat now.

She knocked.

"What?!"

She pushed the door open. "Daddy, it's me."

"What are you still doing here? You are supposed to be covering that church ladies' luncheon at Abyssinian Baptist right now."

"I know. But I was working on this." She shoved the article in front of his face. Eliza bit her lip as she watched him scan the headline. He snatched the paper from her.

"German spies on Long Island?"

"If you hurry, there's still time to get it in the noon edition."

Her father didn't respond. His eyes were glued to what she had written. "This is good," he mumbled more to himself than to her. "Damn good."

"Thank you, Daddy." Eliza whispered the words, but on the inside, she was screaming, *Yes!* "Does this mean I have what it takes to take on meatier stories now? Or that you'll sign off on my war correspondent credentials?"

Her mention of becoming a war correspondent was what broke her father from his trance. "Are you still blabbering about that? Goodness, girl, you're like a dog to a bone, aren't you? How about we talk about that later. Okay, princess?"

Eliza bristled at his use of his old pet name for her. It had been cute back when she was still in petticoats. But she was twenty-three years old now. A grown woman. And here he was still calling her a little girl's nickname.

He brushed past her, her article still clutched in his meaty hand. "Daddy, wait . . ."

"I *said* we'll talk about it later. You're late for that luncheon. Go. Now."

"Yes, sir," she said to his back as she watched him hurry off down the stairs. He could be going to only one place. The typesetter in the basement. Yes! He was going to run her story.

She all but skipped off to the social luncheon that she was now forty-five minutes late for, her conversation with Dr. Bethune forgotten. Finally, she was going to have a story on the front page. She was on her way. As far as Eliza was concerned, this was the last society function she was ever going to have to cover.

LATER, WHEN SHE grabbed a copy of the afternoon edition, Eliza's article was indeed the lead story on the front page. But her byline was nowhere to be found. Instead, the story had been credited to Martin Jones—her father's name.

Eliza didn't have it in her to confront him. Nor did she go running to Mother as she normally did. Instead, Eliza Jones found her way to the downtown Army induction center with her WAAC paperwork in hand.

CHAPTER 2

ONCE SEATED ABOARD the subway, Grace chewed the inside of her lip as doubt overcame her. Joining the Army had nothing to do with Mama's plan for her. A college degree? Yes. Get a fellowship into the best music school New York had to offer? Definitely. Tour Europe and beyond as an accomplished concert pianist? Absolutely. Mama was always going on and on about how it was her dream for Grace to play a command performance somewhere where culture was appreciated, like France.

But to abandon it all for a stint in the military? No, no, no, no. Not even a consideration. Women weren't even *supposed to be* in the military. Were they going to make her shoot a gun at people? This was a mistake. She should go home.

Grace stood up to go back to the platform outside when the train car's doors closed. She sat back down as the subway began to rumble away from the 125th Street station. She was stuck.

I can always get off at 116th Street and backtrack home.

Grace was still on the train when it whisked out of the 116th Street station.

I can always get off at 110th Street and backtrack home.

AN HOUR LATER, Grace was in Lower Manhattan, standing before the Army Building on Whitehall Street. She looked at her watch.

It showed that it was a little before one o'clock. If she was lucky, she had arrived right before the after-lunch rush. It was now or never. Grace took a deep breath and entered the building.

Grace wasn't expecting to step into a whirlwind of people. There were young men everywhere both in civilian clothes and in uniform. Even though she was tall, she could not locate the reception desk in the chaos swirling around her at first. A patriotic fire had sparked across the country after Japan attacked Pearl Harbor. Since then, every physically fit young man was itching to sign up and do his part to retaliate. She envied them. They had the sense of purpose that she had been longing for. Attending Juilliard was supposed to give her that sense of fulfillment.

She tapped her fingers against her palm. Dammit, she was supposed to be back uptown filling out school enrollment forms right now, not here. She and Tony had had a plan. One that would take them on a faraway adventure. She as a musical sensation, with him as her manager. More important, Tony was supposed to come back. And now he wasn't. Grace had no other choice but to move forward.

Grace elbowed her way to the receptionist's desk.

"Hello, I'm looking for—"

"Are you lost?" the woman interrupted while smiling at her. "The service entrance is just around the corner."

"No, I—I'm here to—to . . ." Grace stuttered as she almost said "play."

A wrinkle formed between the woman's brows. "What?"

"I'm sorry. I meant to say 'sign up,'" Grace corrected herself. "I'm here to sign up for the new women's army."

"Oh. Them." The woman frowned, then gave her a quick up-and-down assessment. She pointed toward the row of elevator doors to her left. "They're on the third floor."

"Thank you."

The receptionist sniffed as she thrust a form at Grace. "You're the first Colored girl I've seen go up there. I guess they would be letting you all into the service too. I imagine someone has to be around to *service* the Colored boys."

Grace took the form and looked at it. It was an application. "Good day, ma'am" was all she could manage as a reply when she walked away.

Grace's hand trembled as she pressed the button to call down an elevator. The nerve of that woman. There was a huge WAAC poster in the lobby with the slogan FREE A MAN TO FIGHT on it, and she still had the nerve to insinuate that Grace was trying to become a woman of the night or something. She didn't need this. It was bad enough that she was supposed to have been home by twelve thirty at the latest. Or to have at least called Mama with the news by now. She was going to be in so much trouble when she finally got back.

One of the doors pinged right before opening.

"Well, if I'm going to be in trouble anyway, I might as well make it good trouble," she muttered to herself before stepping into the elevator car.

"What's that you say, ma'am?"

Grace gave the elevator operator a quick smile as she stepped into the car. She shook her head once in acknowledgment of his question but said nothing more. She leaned against the wall. She felt her back muscles sigh in relief. It was only when the elevator doors closed that she finally let her shoulders sag.

"Oh, you know, the usual."

"Which floor do you need?" He was a thin, dark-skinned man who reminded Grace of her grandfather, from the pictures that her mother once showed her.

"Third, please."

He hesitated a moment before pressing the "3" button on the panel. She watched him study her as the elevator creaked its ascent.

"Third floor? That's where those women army folks are. Young lady, it . . ."

Grace tensed. Not him too. "Please, don't say it."

The old man cleared his throat. "I was going to say 'it would be my honor.'"

Grace felt her face break into a smile. "I wasn't expecting you to say that. The receptionist just insinuated that I was a prostitute or something. Like I don't have an education or useful skills to offer . . ." Grace stopped. What skills did she have to offer outside of her musical talents and a teaching degree that she had yet to use? Her chin fell to her chest. "Never mind," she whispered.

"Pay her no mind. These folks around here aren't used to dealing with someone who looks like you whose job isn't to clean up after them."

The elevator stopped. The doors began to creak open.

The operator waved a nonchalant hand at her. "Folks like them are always going to underestimate folks like us. Now, go give 'em hell."

Grace smiled as she snaked her way around the line of men waiting to go into an office with PHYSICAL EXAMINATIONS printed on the door.

"Excuse me. I need to get through . . ."

A few of the guys in the line shifted so she could squeeze by. She noticed how very few of them even looked up to acknowledge her presence.

"I said *excuse* me," she repeated a little louder. She winced, hating how shrill she sounded to her own ears. Even so, two more of the men stepped to the side. But she didn't miss how they were frowning at her like they were trying to figure out what her problem was. "Thank you."

She made her way through the still-too-tight space that was opened up for her into the large gymnasium-like area. There were people in line everywhere in there too. One line for initial interviews. Another for physical examinations. And then a third for psychological evaluations.

This was the kind of place that made Grace feel claustrophobic. Her chest tightened and it became harder for her to breathe. Grace stopped. She closed her eyes, forcing herself to take a deep breath.

Look for the rhythm. Look for the rhythm. Whenever she found herself stuck in the midst of chaos, it took finding the music in the situation to calm her. *Look for the rhythm.* She took another breath and waited.

Then just like that she found it. It was an ebb and flow like the water crashing onto the shore, then pulling back out into the sea. It was almost musical, like a sonata. Her sonata.

Instantly, she heard the music. The low, melancholy notes embraced her, each slow and deliberate. Centered, she opened her eyes, then fell in step with the rhythm of the chaos of bodies around her.

She got turned around a few times with so many lines coming out of so many offices on the third floor. But Grace managed to navigate the flow of all those bodies like a composer wrangling the jumble of notes inside her head into something beautiful. Finally, she found a short line of about five other women near the far corner of the floor. None of these women looked anything like her.

Grace got in line behind the last woman. "Excuse me, have you been waiting here long?"

"Almost half an hour. They closed up shop for lunch. But someone should be back any minute."

Grace checked her watch again. One fifteen. She had promised Mama to be back by twelve thirty to help with a new shipment of fabric that was due to come in today. And then there was the new client fitting at two. How could she have been so irresponsible? Mama must be fuming by now.

Who do you think you are? Mama's words from over the years echoed in her mind. *These folks ain't never gonna let someone like you be better than them. You don't even have the backbone to stand up to me.*

Yes, she should just go. Go and face the music once and for all. Grace turned on her heel and stepped out of line. Right into a stack of folders being pushed into her midsection.

"Great, you're here. I need you to take this downstairs to the typing pool." An older woman who was wearing enough powder on her face to bake a cake gestured down the hall. The chain that was attached to her eyeglasses swung to and fro.

Grace was momentarily stunned. "What?"

The woman who had assaulted her with the folders frowned. "These induction files need to go down to typing. Snap to it."

She shoved the folders back into the woman's arms. "I'm not the errand girl."

Grace stopped herself short as soon as she heard the bitter tone of her voice. She took a deep breath, mentally willing herself back into good, compliant Grace. She pasted a smile on her face that made her cheeks hurt.

"I *don't* work here. I'm an applicant."

The woman bunched her brow while looking over the rims of her bifocals. "I was mistaken. You don't have to be rude about it."

"I wasn't . . ." Grace stopped herself. Going back and forth with this woman would only unnerve her further.

"Oh," the woman sniffed, as if realizing for the first time that Grace was standing there for a reason and not just for her health. "If you're looking to join the WAAC, you're in the wrong line. This one is for the applicants who meet the qualifications to become an officer."

Grace stepped back in line, now determined to do whatever it took to become a WAAC officer. Even if it meant standing up to Mama. Once in uniform, she would not be mistaken for someone who could be spoken to in any kind of way again. Everyone would know her qualifications no matter what they *thought* she looked like. She wasn't going anywhere.

"You're mistaken once again. According to this letter, I'm right where I belong." Grace fished the invitation letter out of her bag and showed it to the woman. She fought back a smile when the woman's eyes widened behind her glasses. And then she remembered the elevator operator's parting advice.

Grace Steele was more than ready to give these people hell.

CHAPTER 3

EXCUSE ME, MA'AM. Are you all right?"

Grace jumped as she blinked herself back into the here and now. There was a young brown-skinned woman approaching her. The first thing Grace noticed was how the woman walked with purpose. Each step she took was planted into the floor with such a sense of assurance that you would have thought she owned the place. Her shoulders were erect and thrown back as if she had not a care in the world. She held her chin up, so it appeared as if she looked down on everyone else in the hall despite her short stature.

She took her place in line behind Grace, then gave her a friendly nudge as she leaned in and whispered, "I didn't expect to see another one of us here. I'm so glad to see you."

The moment the newcomer smiled at her, Grace knew she didn't like this girl. Grace looked her over from head to toe, then frowned. If asked, she wouldn't have been able to name anything concrete that had tipped her off. She just knew.

It could have been the slanted angle at which she wore her flat-brimmed Sunday church hat with the netting pulled down. Or the white gloves that covered the hands clutching her portfolio tight to her chest. As the daughter of a seamstress, Grace was no stranger to a fine custom-made frock. It was clear as day to her that the clothes on Miss Young and Fancy's back *did not* come off the rack. Grace knew this young woman just thought she was so cute in her custom-fitted suit jacket and skirt—look at the way that suit hugged every one of her curves perfectly—in a bright lilac fabric that just screamed, *Look at me!* Grace sure as hell didn't earn enough of a living to afford the finely tailored suit the younger woman wore.

Even her perfume had caressed Grace's nose in a way that reeked of privilege. She wouldn't be surprised if the scent had been named "The Helped, Not the Help."

Who did this girl think she was, coming up in here looking like she had become a mother of the church a few decades early?

Grace spied a few stray strands of hair that stuck out from the sides of the woman's hat and sniffed. She would have *never* been seen outside her house looking a mess like this. Mama would have a total fit if she let herself be seen like this in public. She guessed when you had enough money in your pocket, you could leave the house looking any kind of way.

Must be nice.

Instantaneously, she felt bad for being so judgmental. That was her mama's voice taking up space in her head again. This wasn't the type of person Grace imagined herself to be. She fished out her application.

Grace extended her neck to give the illusion of looming over her. "Yes, I'm fine." She began filling out the form.

"Oh." What was left of this woman-child's smile evaporated. Her expression morphed into one that was haughty and shielded. "I apologize for interrupting you. You looked like you were a million miles away when I asked you if this was the line for WAAC applications."

"Yes, it is." Grace flicked her mouth into a quick smile, then returned to face the front of the line. The line had moved forward. Grace gladly took the few steps needed to close the gap.

Miss Sunday Best's frown deepened. "Thank goodness! It took me forever to find this place. More than one person just waved me off in this general direction with an 'it's over there'"—she pointed toward the gymnasium—"without specifying exactly where 'over there' I should go."

She exhaled loudly. The woman's eyes darted around as if she expected the boogeyman to jump out from around the corner at any second. The way she clutched her portfolio, you'd think she had her whole life within it. Grace loosened up her grip on the strap of her bag. Had she really looked like this just a few moments ago? Like she was scared of her own shadow with fear oozing out of every pore?

Grace lifted her chin, further extending her spine in the process. No, she was definitely better than that. She had to be better than *that*. But she also wouldn't throw one of her own to the wolves. In that respect, she was definitely *better* than the rest of the useless people who had given her direction so far.

Who are you to judge her when you were ready to hightail it out of here yourself a few minutes ago? The Christian thing to do is make small talk at least.

Grace made herself smile. She hoped it looked real enough. "Uh, nice weather we're having, huh?"

Her still-wet galoshes chose that moment to squeak against the floor. It would have been nice to have remembered getting splashed by that car earlier that morning before saying something as idiotic as that out loud. Grace spent so much of her energy lately erecting her mental defenses that employing the normal social graces with this stranger felt awkward.

"Oh, it's been dreadful!" The woman's demeanor transformed again. Her eyes widened along with her smile at Grace's engagement. "I had to catch a cab from the subway station."

Grace was about to take another step forward but stopped short. She cut a side glance at the girl.

"But the station is only a block away." She wiggled her toes against the wet socks that had molded to them. She wished she could have afforded such a wasted expense as cab fare for a two-minute walk.

"Girl, please, I'm not even supposed to be here." The girl smoothed a nonexistent crease down her side. "I can't have my parents asking me a million questions about what happened to my clothes and where I've been all afternoon."

"No, we can't have that," Grace agreed, just to be polite, while hoping to discourage further conversation. She looked down at her own rain-splashed coat. She would definitely have some explaining to do when she finally returned home. The state of her clothes would be the least of her worries when she got there. She gave the girl another awkward smile and then turned back to the line. They were almost to the office door.

Grace tapped her fingers on her side. She stared absentmindedly out a nearby window as she played around with a new melody in her head. *Tap, tap, tap. Tap, tap, tap.* The refrain would fit perfectly into a new composition she had started over the weekend. She opened her bag and looked for some scrap paper. She needed to write down the notes before she forgot them . . .

"Oh my, where are my manners? I've been blathering on about my parents and clothes and I don't even know your name. I'm Eliza. Eliza Jones. And you are?"

The notes Grace had hoped to preserve dissolved into the air as this Eliza Jones person formally introduced herself. Grace would have given anything for this girl to have forgotten her manners for at least another thirty seconds longer.

"I'm Grace."

Eliza Jones put out her white-gloved hand. "A pleasure to meet you, Grace . . . ?"

Grace dropped the recovered paper back into her bag. It was no use to her now. She shook Eliza's hand. "Just Grace is fine."

See, she could play nice, she thought as she faced forward again and continued to lead the way. She could be sociable. It felt like it had been ages since she'd spent any time with another woman—another *Negro* woman—around her own age.

"I almost lost my nerve to follow through with this until I saw you here. I hope we both make it into the WAAC. Girls like us have to stick together."

"I imagine this place can be intimidating if you've never been here before," Grace said as if she hadn't just walked down this hall for the very first time herself not even a few minutes ago. She continued to look straight ahead and could feel Eliza gazing at her. Grace braced herself to be called out as a fraud.

"Don't you think it's exciting that they're going to let women join the Army? And Negro ones, at that. Sorry if I seem so jumpy. When I hinted that I was thinking about joining up, Daddy all but locked me in my room."

Too many words were now being thrown at Grace for her to process, as they finally arrived at the WAAC office door. Small talk really wasn't Grace's thing.

"Yeah, it's great." Those were the only three words she could squeeze in while this Eliza person continued to pepper her with questions. Grace hoped that she never wore her emotions so openly on her sleeve as this poor creature following her.

"Next!" a voice called from inside the office. Grace gestured toward the door. "Here we are. It's been nice talking to you."

"Oh, thank you! And good luck!" Eliza grabbed Grace's outstretched hand and pumped it furiously. The motion caused Eliza to drop her portfolio. She immediately knelt to retrieve it. "Oh goodness. You must think I have butterfingers."

That, and more. Grace willed her face to remain in a neutral expression. On the inside she wanted to scream, *Shut up!* She really needed to muster up a little sympathy for this poor girl. Her nerves might be shot, but she had a lot more courage than Grace was feeling right now.

Grace sighed, tugged at the hem of her skirt, and knelt down to pick up some papers that had slid out of Eliza's portfolio. "It's understandable. Joining the military is a big deal. And then for them to now allow women, Negro women, at that . . . It's like they say, you have to be twice as good, right?"

Grace tried to scan the other girl's application. She felt pretty confident about her own chances of being accepted into the corps. But she had to know what kind of competition she was dealing with. Especially since Grace had no idea whom she would ask to write a recommendation for her. Her family pretty much kept to themselves. Maybe she could ask that elevator operator . . .

Eliza's eyes went wide. "You're right." They stood as she accepted the papers from Grace. She looked Grace up and down. "I can tell by the looks of you that you'd be perfect for something like this."

"Thanks." Grace looked away. Yup, she was officially a horrible person for being so judgmental toward this woman. "Yeah, well.

I doubt they take me. The only thing I know how to do well is play the piano."

"You shouldn't be so hard on yourself. You seem just as capable as anyone else in this line. You know what? I think we'll both go in there and wow those women's army people. And we'll both get in. They'll send us off to training together and we'll become the best of friends."

Grace stared at her in shock for a moment. Not because of how pure and naive Eliza's wish had been, but because of how *nice* it all had sounded to Grace.

"Well, aren't you quite the Pollyanna?" Grace winced as soon as the words came out. That was nasty even for her. She was always letting things fall out of her mouth without thinking about them first. This was why Grace didn't have any friends her own age. She had a bad habit of alienating anyone who tried.

Eliza's face fell. "I've been annoying this whole time, haven't I?"

"I—what I meant to say was—"

"Hello, are you going to stand there all day?" The woman in the office was now sticking her head out the door.

Grace looked back and forth between her and Eliza. "Wait, I just wanted to—"

"No. You go." Eliza urged her on with a graceful wave of her gloved hand. "All I wanted to do was wish you good luck. Or what is it they say before you go onstage? Break a leg."

"Thanks. You too." She opened her mouth to say more but hesitated. There was a question hovering on her lips that she had been meaning to ask. But no, it was stupid. What was the point in saying it?

Just ask! At this point, Grace had nothing to lose. She took a deep breath.

"Eliza, wait. Just wondering." Grace attempted a nonchalant shrug. "Who did you get to do your recommendation?"

Eliza lifted her chin, personifying all the arrogance that Grace had pinned on her from the start.

"Dr. Mary McLeod Bethune."

Grace's face fell. "Of course you did."

Yup, she was back to disliking this Eliza person. Intensely. Grace could tell that this girl had never achieved anything in her life that wasn't handed to her by her parents or through their connections. Hell, the girl couldn't even navigate an Army induction center without asking for help.

Then come to find out that she had been personally recommended by Dr. Bethune herself to join the Women's Army Auxiliary Corps? You couldn't get much better help than that unless it came from the commander in chief, Mr. Franklin Delano Roosevelt himself.

The weight of Dr. Bethune's name hung in the air between them as Eliza smiled up at her, chin raised. Grace willed her face into a neutral mask. She turned to the now irritated WAAC official. "I'm sorry to have kept you waiting . . ."

CHAPTER 4

"W HAT WAS HER problem?" Eliza muttered to herself as the office door slammed shut behind Grace.

Eliza squared up her shoulders and shook off the odd interaction. She returned all her focus to the office door in front of her. Whereas all the other doors she had seen in this building had the name of the office or department housed behind them stenciled neatly onto the glass, this one had a handwritten piece of paper that had been taped onto the door. It read "Women's Army Auxiliary Corps. Come in!"

When Eliza was finally called inside, she saw maybe ten chairs set out for waiting next to what appeared to be several check-in stations. One by one, a seated woman got up to follow a female clerk into the next room. Each time, the next person in line took her seat.

She looked for Grace despite herself. Part of her dreaded the awkwardness that would come if she did find her. But part of her also yearned for a familiar face. Finally, she did spot Grace. But she was already seated with who Eliza guessed was one of the recruiters.

It took about ten minutes for Eliza to be seated in front of a recruiter of her own. After a brief check-in confirming her name, identification, and age, she finally was escorted into the next section.

"You'll be getting your physical today," the clerk there explained. Eliza gulped. The woman had been pleasant enough when she had stepped into the curtained-off area, but that wasn't enough to make Eliza comfortable with the idea of taking her clothes off in front of a stranger.

Eliza looked around, unsure of what she should do. Whenever she had a physical with her family doctor, she had been escorted into a private examination room. One of the nurses would perform most of the checks, and then Dr. Anderson would come in at the end to proclaim another clean bill of health for the year.

"Take off your clothes except for your undergarments," the clerk continued. She pointed at another door. "Then take all of your belongings and go in there."

"Excuse me?" Eliza held a hand up to her chest.

The clerk, whose hair was dyed auburn and who spoke with a Queens accent, sighed. "There's too many girls coming in to apply for the corps to give each one of yous all of the physical examinations in one room. So, you gotta take off your clothes, go in there, and stand in line. They'll check your vitals, your teeth, make sure you don't have lice or anything. Y'know, give you a looking over."

The woman paused, her eyes darting up and down as she sized up Eliza from head to toe. "A very thorough looking over."

"Fine." Eliza felt her cheeks warm. She should probably find out who this woman's supervisor was and report her behavior. No. What purpose would that serve? Other than momentarily soothing her bruised ego, nothing. Like she had said, there were too many applicants coming through.

Besides, she was still the only Negro woman in this applicant line. The last thing she needed was to cause a scene.

Eliza waited for the clerk to leave before starting to unbutton her blouse. Well, the clerk might be off the hook from getting a complaint. But that Negro woman, Grace, she had met in the hallway . . . now, she had definitely been rude for no reason. What a shame. Eliza had been so surprised, but still pleased, to see someone like her at the Army induction center. She had not expected to find another Negro woman there at all. Eliza wondered again what "Just Grace's" problem was. Eliza had only been trying to be friendly.

Eliza stepped into the next room. Now she was in another line. But this one was a line of nervous-looking young women in a similar state of undress. There were various stations where the other applicants were getting their blood pressure taken, their ears and throats checked, and their fingers pricked and the resulting dot of blood collected in a small device and held up to the light. Then they disappeared behind a series of curtains. Eliza shivered. She had to assume back there was where the "very thorough" parts of the examination were occurring.

An hour later, a bewildered Eliza was putting her clothes back on. The last technician told her that all her physical examination results passed muster. Now all she had to do was ace the interview.

THREE HOURS LATER found Eliza striding out of her interview with a big smile across her face. She felt the session had gone well. Compared with the grillings she had experienced in college and around her father's dining room table, the softball questions the committee had thrown at her had been a piece of cake.

"Do you consider yourself a well-read person?"

"Do you think you could lead a group of women overseas and find them accommodations and other resources to get them settled?"

"What is the most stressful situation you've experienced and how did you handle it?"

At that last question, Eliza had almost laughed and blurted out that this whole WAAC application process was the most stressful thing she had ever been through. From being blindsided by the telephone call from Dr. Bethune, to rushing to that church ladies' luncheon, to that less-than-personal and definitely not private physical examination, it was a wonder that she hadn't crumpled into a pile of nerves by now. Instead, she said something about a college professor who had tried to give her a failing grade on an exam and how she had talked herself into a better passing grade.

If the steps down into the subway station weren't so steep, Eliza would have skipped. Instead, she danced all the way down while holding on to the railing. Oh yeah. She had totally knocked it out of the park.

AN HOUR LATER, Grace was putting on her shoes just outside the psychological exam area. Only a wooden door separated her from the four women who were about to grill her about her life, interests, and education. She was just about to pick up her bag to enter the interview area when she heard a burst of laughter come from within.

"I don't know what some of these girls were thinking when they decided to come down here and apply. Most of them can barely spell their names, but they want us to take them at their words that they are college graduates."

Grace hesitated. The recruiter who had first signed her in had said that these women had the final word on who got into the WAAC and whose application file got dropped into the trash bin.

Grace finished putting the strap of her bag over her shoulder as quietly as she could. But she made no move toward entering. Yet. Of course, she shouldn't be eavesdropping. She'd have no way to explain herself if she got caught.

Time was growing short if she wanted to set herself up to get into that first training class. It would start in a week, and they were going to let only forty Negro women train as officers. That Eliza girl she had met in line was most definitely a shoo-in. Who knew how many other Negro women there were around the country who were just like *her*. Grace *had* to get into that class.

"What did you think of that Colored one we just saw, that cocky one?"

Grace stood stock-still.

"Did you hear how she bragged about outwitting her professor? Said she'd welcome the challenge of leading a group of women overseas and making something out of nothing."

"Oh, that one," a slightly younger voice chimed in. She almost sounded like she was in awe. "I'd never have the nerve to say something like that in an interview."

"You know, it's the uppity ones who wind up causing the most trouble. But maybe a taste of military life is just what she needs to put her attitude in check."

"Her application *is* impressive. Her recommendation came up from Washington by courier. She got that Bethune woman to write it for her. You know, that Negro who always has her picture in the paper with Eleanor Roosevelt. Her school transcripts were in there too with a glowing note from the college president clipped to them. Hmm, it says here she had a 3.8 grade point average. But have you ever heard of Howard University before?"

Grace tensed. They had to be talking about Eliza.

Grace herself had graduated from a state college that had nowhere near the prestige of Howard. While the student enrollment there had been in the hundreds, her college president could not have picked her out of a lineup, much less written a note of glowing praises about her.

Well, you always knew it was a long shot. Grace frowned. She clutched her bag tighter to her chest. Maybe she was biting off more than she could chew with this particular ambition.

What had they called Eliza? Uppity? Grace shook her head. No. While that had been Grace's initial impression too, she now remembered Eliza more as confident. That was an emotion she had in short supply at this moment. There was a lull in the women's conversation. It was now or never.

It's time to face the music.

She knocked on the door, then pushed it open. "Good afternoon, ladies."

Grace smiled, then proceeded to give these women the performance of a lifetime.

CHAPTER 5

THE STREETLIGHTS WERE threatening to come on when Eliza returned to her family's Edgecombe Avenue brownstone. The dining room doors were open as she entered. She could see Mother setting down a plate of steak and potatoes in front of Daddy. Darn, she was *really* late.

"Look, Lil," her father boomed from his seat. "Our daughter has decided to join us. Have a seat. You're just in time for dinner."

So much for her plan to hide out in her room. Eliza pivoted back toward the dining room. "Daddy."

She set down her bag at the end of the table opposite her father. Eliza was not in the mood to be near him, much less talk to him. Her emotions were still raw from his stealing her article. Then Daddy tapped her usual seat. The one next to him on his left. The one where she normally hung on his every word while he expounded on the news of the day. The *real* news.

As soon as she sat down beside him, Daddy didn't waste any time laying into her. "Your mother tells me that you were extremely late showing up at that luncheon today."

He lifted his water glass to his lips and took a longer than usual sip. He stared her down the whole time. He took his time in returning the glass to the table.

Eliza almost fell out of her chair. Her mouth froze into an O. How had her mother even known? There must have been at least seventy-five other women in attendance, none of whom had been Mother.

She looked back and forth between her parents. Her eyes lingered on her mother, the gossip queen. She balled her fists on either side of her plate. She wanted to shake the woman sometimes. Eliza picked up her own water glass and took a sip.

"I find it interesting she would say something like that," she started, "considering she wasn't even there."

"A dear friend of mine had to pull strings to get you an invitation *and* to have you seated at her table." She looked directly at Eliza and raised her eyebrow.

Eliza attempted to engage her mother in a staring match. But the younger Jones woman had yet to achieve her mother's level of stare-down mastery. A second or two later, Eliza looked away, opting to study the design on the china plate before her instead.

"Well, you didn't have to tell *him*," she mumbled.

"I do when *your* actions make *me* look bad." A shrinking violet, Mother was not. "Instead of pouting like a toddler, why don't you tell us why you're so late for dinner instead?"

Damn, she's not cutting me any slack.

"I . . ." Eliza's mind raced for an acceptable excuse. *I took the wrong subway. I got off at the wrong stop. I got lost. I fell asleep on the train.* Any one of those would do, but she was reluctant to use any of them. Eliza was not in the habit of lying to her parents. She did not want to start now. It was her life. It was time she started taking charge of it, truthfully.

"I was at the Army induction center downtown."

It was Mother's turn to hesitate. Eliza watched her mother's spoon hover over the soup bowl. She thought she saw her mother's mouth curve into a flash of a smile, but it disappeared just as quickly.

"Were you?"

Emboldened, Eliza lifted her chin. "Yes. I was."

"What on earth were you doing down there?" her father's voice boomed, ending the intimate exchange between mother and daughter. "That has nothing to do with your society beat at the paper."

Eliza drew up all her courage, taking a deep breath. "I didn't go down there for the paper. I went down there for me."

"I don't understand."

"I went down there to enlist in the Women's Army Auxiliary Corps."

Her father stared at her for a moment. Then he shook with laughter. Spittle flew out of his mouth as he did so. "My daughter in the U.S. Army? Not while there is breath in my body. C'mon, tell the truth. You have a boyfriend we don't know about, is that it? Did you go down there with him?"

"There's no boyfriend, Martin." Mother was frowning now, her irritation evident in both her words and her face. She gave Eliza a pointed look. "I would know about him if there was one."

"Mother . . ." Eliza began.

"Girl, hush." Her father placed his hands flat on the table. "If there isn't any boyfriend, then somebody had better explain to me what my daughter was doing with that damned Army all afternoon."

Her father's freckled light tan face was beginning to bloom crimson splotches. It was never a good sign when Martin Jones's face turned red.

"Be mindful of your pressure, dear." Mother reached out for her husband's hand. He snatched it away.

"I'm not some damn baby, Lillian. I just want to know what the hell is going on."

"I already told you what's going on, Daddy. You're just not listening." And then Eliza added quietly, more to herself, "As usual."

"You got one thing right, young lady." Her father threw his linen napkin on his plate and pushed his chair back from the table. "I am not going to sit here and listen to no nonsense about my daughter going into the Army. I forbid it."

He stood up and began walking out of the formal dining room. He stopped under the threshold and turned. He held up a finger, pointing it at Eliza.

"You go back down there to that induction office and tell those people that you made a mistake, that you changed your mind."

"I will, just as soon as you print a retraction in the paper saying that I wrote that front-page copy and not you."

"Excuse me?"

"You heard me." Eliza stood up, almost knocking over her chair in the process. "You stole my article, Daddy. How could you?"

"Stole her article? What is she talking about, Martin?"

His head whipped back and forth between his daughter and his wife. He spared a big, toothy grin for his wife. "Nobody's stolen anything, baby. It's like I'm always telling you. Eliza here just doesn't understand the newspaper business."

"I don't understand the newspaper business," Eliza echoed. "How is that possible when I have lived and breathed it from the time I could walk until I went off to college?"

"Hold on, what I meant was—"

"No, Daddy. I will *not* 'hold on.' And I am not going anywhere to tell anybody that I've changed my mind. I'm in the Army now as of this afternoon."

"Not the white man's Army, you're not. I forbid it."

"You should've thought about that before you put *your* name on *my* byline. It's too late. You don't get to call the shots over what I want to do with *my* life this time, Daddy."

He put a hand to his chest and took a deep breath. "You *will* go down there and tell them people whatever you need to to get out of it. And after that, young lady, you are grounded."

"You can't ground me. I'm twenty-three years old."

"I don't care if you are *one hundred and three* years old. As long as you live under my roof you will do what I say." He turned to Mother. "Lil, you go down there with her and make sure she does it. I know some folks down in Washington. I'll call them in the morning. But for right now, I'm going upstairs to lie down. I have a headache."

Both mother and daughter silently watched as the head of the household lumbered out of the dining room. Eliza sat back down. Her eyes brimmed with tears. She bit the inside of her lip. She and Daddy had never screamed at each other like that before.

Once they heard the thump of her parents' bedroom door close, Lillian Jones turned to her daughter.

"So, what are you going to do?"

"I'll have to go back anyway to pick up my formal orders. If I get in, that is." Eliza picked up her fork and shrugged. She stabbed into her salad. "At least I don't have to lie about it now."

"Good." Her mother smiled. "I'll go with you."

"Just so we're clear, I wouldn't be going back there to get out of it."

Her mother silently sipped a spoonful of soup with all the grace of the socialite that she was. She put her spoon down, then dabbed the corners of her mouth with her napkin. "I know *that*. I'm just tagging along to make sure you follow through. Why did you think I called Dr. Bethune on your behalf in the first place?"

"Mother! You didn't!" Eliza grinned.

Her mother grinned right back at her. "Oh, you better believe I did."

Suddenly, Eliza didn't mind having a gossip queen for a mother. Well, not as much.

CHAPTER 6

I DON'T UNDERSTAND WHY you keep saying you enlisted in the Army, Grace." Mama, who had been lying on the sofa, pushed herself onto her elbow. "You were supposed to get into Juilliard, not the Army."

"No, Mama." Grace sighed. She had spent the last ten minutes—ten minutes that had felt like a lifetime—trying to make Mama understand how her Juilliard audition had become enlistment papers. By this point, she felt like she was beating a dead fish that had already been pulverized.

"Juilliard isn't going to give me the money I need to go to school there. But the Army will, if I stay in for two years." The requirement was actually at least two years, but really until the end of the war plus six months. But she was not in the mood to explain all that when Mama still couldn't wrap her mind around the basic fact that she was talking about a future that had nothing to do with music. "Look at it this way, I'll be entitled to more pay, opportunities, and benefits."

And, hopefully, more of a life.

Grace didn't dare say that last part out loud. Mama would throw a fit if she knew Grace had any dreams that excluded her or the plans she had made for them, much less one that took Grace away from the confines of their already cramped Harlem apartment on West 120th Street and left Mama behind.

"You can't join the Army. They don't let women into the Army. They definitely don't let women like *us* into the Army."

Grace sighed. "They do now, Mama."

"Who's going to take care of me when you wind up dead like your brother?"

The question, while not unexpected, made Grace wince. She had long since given up on trying to understand her mother or how her mind worked. She knew that there would be initial resistance to her announcement about her joining the WAAC. It always surprised her whenever Mama showed her just how selfish she could be. Grace recalled numerous times she had been left all alone in this apartment while Mama was off at some women's club rally, church mother board meeting, or a last-minute fitting for one of her clients.

But to bring up Tony like that? Leave it to Mama to pull no punches. Grace began to revisit her own doubts about what she had signed herself up for. Maybe it wasn't too late to back out.

No. The word came to her in Tony's voice. *You're going. If you don't leave now, you never will.*

"Mama, like I explained, I'll be making more money in the military than I ever would with you at the shop or by scraping by teaching private piano lessons and hoping for a teaching job to come through." Grace reached over to fluff the pillow behind her mother's back. "And Dad will be back soon."

Her father was a Pullman porter on the New York to Charleston line. His route had him away two or three weeks and home for one. He was due to come back home in a few days. Hopefully, before she was ordered to ship out to training camp.

"That's what your brother said when he left. You see how well all that extra money worked out for him," Mama mumbled as she leaned back into the pillow.

Go . . . her subconscious said in a ghostly voice.

Grace took Mama's hand and willed herself to have more courage. "I already talked to Mrs. Perez upstairs. She said she can check in on you in the morning and the evening when Dad is away on a trip. I was planning on sending her a dollar or two for her trouble."

"Trouble? Is that what I am now? You know, the only reason my hands are like this . . ." Mama was sitting fully upright now. She held up the fingers on her left hand that wouldn't straighten all the way anymore. ". . . is because of all that hand stitching I did so I could put food on the table for you. And this is how you treat me. You go off to God knows where and you—you pawn me off as 'trouble.'"

Grace looked up at the ceiling and sighed. She counted to three before she opened her mouth to respond, scared of what might fly out if she didn't keep herself in control. She lowered her chin, tapped out the opening strain of *Moonlight Sonata* on her right thigh, and smiled. "You know that's not what I meant. Of course you're not trouble. You're my mama."

Mama waved her off. "I don't know why I'm getting my nerves all worked up anyway." She cackled to herself. "You'll be back soon enough. Just wait until they make you do all that running."

Here she goes. Grace didn't respond out loud. There was no point in defending herself when Mama got like this.

Grace went into the apartment's kitchenette. She raided the icebox and cabinets to scrounge up some dinner. There wasn't much. Just some black beans and rice Mrs. Perez had brought over, a hunk of cornbread, and some dried beef strips. She threw it all into the pot on the stove and turned on the gas. Grace made a mental note to gather everybody's ration books and hit the market tomorrow.

Mama's eyes flicked up and down as she looked over Grace moving through the kitchen. She huffed. "Yeah, the only athletic thing you know how to do *is* run away. With your out-of-shape self."

Grace had been reaching back into the icebox for a packet of oleo, or whatever passed for butter ever since rationing had gone into effect. But she stilled at Mama's insult.

Don't do it. Don't say anything. Keep in control.

Grace pressed her thumb against the yellow capsule in the middle of the packaging. Hard. And then harder. The capsule broke. She slammed the softened mass onto the counter. She had not meant to do that as hard as she did. But Mama's words had hit their target. "Maybe you're right, Mama. We'll just have to see, won't we?"

Mama flinched at the unexpected noise. "What's wrong with you?"

Grace's hands gripped the edge of the counter. *A one. Two. Three.* She tapped out the first six notes of *Moonlight Sonata* with her fingers.

"Nothing, Mama." She looked up at the clock on the wall. She could do this. "Nothing at all."

"That's what I thought."

Grace picked up the package. She began kneading the yellow coloring that had released from the broken capsule into the rest of the margarine.

"Humph." Mama settled herself back onto the sofa. "Maybe this Army thing will do you some good. You could use some discipline again."

Grace flung a spoonful of the now yellow margarine into the

pot. She placed the utensil down on the counter carefully despite her shaking hands. "Yes, Mama."

"When you were performing . . . it gave you discipline. You used to practice every day. It was a sight to see. I used to brag to all my friends about how good you looked up there onstage, seated at a big old piano, and the lights focused on you . . ." Mama looked away as her words trailed off. "We used to be somebody around here. Everyone knew who the Steeles were, who you were . . . who *I* was. And now they don't."

"You're right, Mama. I don't have discipline." Grace didn't have the energy to remind Mama how it had been her unreasonable demands for endorsement fees that ended her access to the pianos at Mr. Lieberman's store. Come to think of it, all the goodwill that had been extended during Grace's brief period of stardom had ended when Mama had insisted that she could manage her daughter's burgeoning musical career herself.

"What a waste." Mama paused. Grace chose to say nothing, instead giving the simmering pot of food her full attention. She used a wooden spoon to give the contents a stir.

One. Two. Three. With her free hand, she tapped out the six notes again.

"Well, maybe they'll teach you how to cook. Put you in the mess hall. Then you'd be more useful around here when they send you back home."

Grace mimicked pressing the two heavy notes of the sonata into the countertop. Then she doled out a portion of the improvised dinner into a bowl, placed it on the table, and headed down the hallway to her room.

"Where are you going? Grace?"

"Out," she called over her shoulder.

"What about dinner?"

I lack the discipline to share a meal with you and not *wring your neck, you nag.* Grace took a deep breath and fixed her face before responding, "It's on the table."

"Those people killed my son! Why must you break my heart too?" Mama yelled out as the front door slammed closed behind Grace.

ONCE OUTSIDE, GRACE kicked the first garbage can she saw. In her mind, she had always justified Mama's controlling behavior by thinking of it as just what mothers who have daughters do. It was their job to make sure their babies grew up to be well-mannered, obedient "good girls." And as a Negro woman, it was just a given that Grace would not act in a way that embarrassed her family or the race.

She could live with that, Grace thought as she marched down the block. As a matter of fact, she liked the structure that living under that set of expectations put in her life. She was a "good girl," so she had clear boundaries of where to set her aspirations for a career, a husband, and a life. In that sense, Grace too would one day have complete control over her life and her own children. In a world where you didn't know if your loved ones would make it home over a police stop gone wrong, or a random person deciding that he didn't like how they looked or being jealous over something they had that he didn't, that was the most you could hope for.

It was when Tony had left to go into the Navy that Mama's demanding ways had become incorrigible. Prior to that, Mama sabotaging Grace's musical career had seemed like a one-off. An irrational one maybe, but still not the norm. However, when Tony left for boot camp, Mama's insistence on complete control over

Grace's comings and goings had dropped like an iron fist. Daddy would playfully get Mama to stand down.

For Grace, losing Tony meant losing everything. It had felt like her world had stopped. Yesterday had been one of those rare days she had made Mama smile. And then there was that knock on the door . . .

Several blocks later, Grace shook off Mama's fussing as she pulled open the back door to the jazz club. She recognized a number of the musicians who were taking a smoke break a few feet from the door. She had seen them at some of the other Harlem clubs she would sneak into with her brother from time to time when they were in the mood to see some "real piano playing."

The younger, hipper cats hung out here at Henry Minton's place. Grace had managed to talk them into letting her play around on the piano backstage. She hadn't had the nerve yet to ask to sit in on one of the late-night jam sessions she kept hearing them talk about, though. Heaven forbid word got back to Mama that she had been spotted playing that "devil's music" in some "lowlife" club.

Lately, she hadn't been able to get there as much as she would've liked. Mama had been keeping her busier than ever at the dress shop. Even if all she got to do tonight was soak up the energy of being around other musicians, it would be enough. It was a relief in itself to be out of the house, where she could let down her guard. But tonight was different.

She hesitated in the doorway. Every muscle in her body was tense. One thing the recruiters and examiners had hammered home to her that afternoon was that WAAC leadership was adamant that only the most upstanding women would be accepted into the corps. And, once in, they would be held up to the highest standards. Grace doubted that those standards would allow for one of its members sneaking through the back door of a Harlem jazz club at night.

Maybe she should have put a scarf on over her head before storming out of the house. Maybe she should leave. Or maybe she should not give a damn what other people thought about her for once.

The odds of anyone with any connections to the Army recognizing her here at Minton's Playhouse, of all places, were low. The lights were always dimmed, for one. And she always clung to the shadows anyway. Because despite Mama's hand maladies, she still had the best sewing skills on this end of Manhattan. Anyone who wanted to hit the town in the slickest threads came to Mrs. Steele's shop. At any given time, a good portion of the club patrons were wearing suits and dresses that Mama had hemmed herself.

However, what did it matter anymore if Mama did find out that she was here? She might as well go for broke. Grace stepped inside.

"Hey there, Miss Grace." The man she liked to call Father Earl waved her over. "Come over here. Word on the street is there's a gold star in your window."

Tony was the last thing she wanted to talk about right now. But she should have expected it. "Yes, it's true."

"Aw damn, baby girl." Earl wrapped his arms around her. "I am so sorry. He was one of the good ones."

"Yes."

Earl lifted her chin with his fingers. "I also heard you were down at that Juilliard school today."

"How do you know about my audition?"

A man in a tailored pin-striped suit, whom Earl had been talking to when she'd arrived, hovered nearby. It was the suit that threw her for a loop. He was in prime physical condition and too young to not be in a military uniform of some kind. It seemed like every day another boy in her neighborhood was receiving a draft notice.

This newcomer's ears had perked right up when Earl mentioned Juilliard. Grace frowned. She hadn't even been introduced to him yet. Why was he all in her business? She didn't want the first thing he knew about her to be that she blew an important audition.

He was leaning against the bar, nursing a drink that looked like it could have been water. Or gin. Probably a mixture of both. You never knew, given some of the riffraff that came through here. She noticed that he drummed the fingers of his free hand against his thigh, similar to her own habit whenever she was bored or nervous. He scanned the light early-evening crowd with an air of restlessness about him—a feeling that Grace herself battled with more often than not. He looked both out of place and right at home here at Minton's Playhouse. Exactly how she felt.

Now as for Father Earl, who was more popularly known as bandleader Earl Hines, she had grown to respect him once he had taken her under his wing. He took her seriously as a student both of classical piano and of this new sound the guys around here had dubbed "bebop." He had been the first one to call her amateur attempts at composition good.

She had never seen anyone play like Earl Hines could. They called his style "stride piano." Grace had been a solid classical pianist until she met this man. Ever since, Mama complained whenever she "tarnished her music with that swing rubbish."

Earl shrugged. "I keep my ear to the streets."

She leaned in closer to whisper, "Then you must know already that it didn't go well."

Earl patted her hand. "Chin up, baby girl. The world will soon learn to appreciate the magic in these fingers."

"Well, the magic wasn't there today." She pulled her hand away, studying her fingertips. "Anyway, none of that matters now. Right after, I went downtown and enlisted in that new women's army."

"Is that so?" Earl and his companion exchanged a look. "Then maybe I need to introduce you to my friend here. Grace Steele, meet Mr. Jonathan Philips."

She wasn't sure if she wanted to meet this man or not. He looked dangerous. The kind of dangerous that would have a girl like her making bad life decisions. And that had her intrigued. It didn't help that he was quite the looker too. But Grace wasn't "looking" for a man right now. Unfortunately, she couldn't look away despite her gut feeling that this man should not be trusted.

"Mr. Philips." She nodded in acknowledgment.

Mr. Philips held out his hand. She took it and gave it a firm shake. "Please, call me Jonathan."

Earl nudged Jonathan with his shoulder. "This girl here is one helluva player. Pardon my language, Miss Grace."

Grace felt her cheeks warm. After her audition fiasco, she was inclined to refute that statement, but she opted for a grateful smile instead. "You're too kind."

"Just speaking the truth. How about you play a little something for him."

"No, I'm just here to soak up the atmosphere." The last thing she wanted to do was embarrass herself again. Her "performance" at Juilliard was one thing. Mr. Hutcheson was a stranger. But here at Minton's? These men were like family—well, distant family— and the damage to her reputation with them would hurt far worse.

"Pshaw." Earl waved away her polite refusal. "Nobody who can play like you do comes here just to 'soak up the atmosphere.' You better go on somewhere with *that* noise."

Jonathan put his hand on Earl's shoulder. "No need to pressure the girl. There's nothing wrong with not wanting to jump into the jam sometimes. If she's scared, she's scared."

And then he shrugged.

He shrugged? Grace jerked her neck, taken aback. *He* shrugged!

They had barely exchanged hellos and this man, this playboy, this idiot, had the gall to question her nerve. As if Grace Steele didn't have a healthy-sized competitive streak running inside her. What a jerk.

"Sir." She balled her fists and put them squarely on her hips. "I'll have you know that I am not scared of anything."

Grace bit her tongue as soon as the words flew out of her mouth. The rest of the room quieted. Now the eyes of every other musician in the place were looking in her direction. Her impulsive streak really did have a way of getting her behind in trouble. She'd have to figure out how to get it under control. But unfortunately, today was not that day.

Earl gestured his hand toward the piano on the stage. "Then show him what ya got, sugar."

Grace took a deep breath. A lone spotlight shone over the piano. It beckoned to her. She sat down, shrugging out of her jacket. Mr. Philips—no, Jonathan—leaned forward to take it from her.

"You don't have to do this, you know," he whispered. His forehead was creased with what Grace assumed to be concern. It was a little too late for that. "I was just joshing you back there. You don't have anything to prove."

"Yes, I do." After the disaster of an audition she'd had that morning, she had to do this. She was less concerned about proving anything to Jonathan or to anyone else who was in that room. She had something to prove to herself.

But as she sat there, her fingers poised on top of the keys, her mind went blank. She felt her heart thud inside her chest.

From behind her, someone called out, "Take your time, baby girl."

She pressed a key. The wrong key. The few patrons sitting at the tables in the audience went silent.

Shoot.

She took another deep breath. And then she tried again.

It was an original composition that had been floating around in her head for years. It was a jaunty piece that suited the background noise of patrons resuming their conversations. To Grace's ears, the resulting buzz seemed to be speaking just to her. It was asking her a question. No . . . more like challenging her. A dare for her to step up to the moment. It said, *Are you gonna show them what you can do or not?*

That's when the link between her frazzled brain and the rest of her body disconnected. Her more confident fingers answered for her. *I've got rhythm. My name is Grace. I'm the queen of these keys. Get out my face . . .*

It was a fun little ditty she had created during the height of her public playing career. She used it to warm up her hands. Or, as in this case, to boost her confidence before tackling a difficult piece.

"That's my girl!" Earl laughed.

There was a slap of hands behind her, followed by a howl of laughter. It was the same kind of laughter that might erupt out of her father, proud and encouraging. She kept going, her fingers alternating between the fast-pasted theatrics of a virtuoso and the slower, melancholy phrasing of a blues vocalist.

Then she was really feeling the groove. She went with it, laying out everything she had onto the keys. She was having an out-of-body experience at this point, almost like her conscious self had floated up to the ceiling so she could watch from above. She clearly wasn't in her right mind. Because her right mind would have never told her hands to delve into her failed audition piece. But play it they did. And with nothing at stake here other than salvaging her wounded pride, she made it bop. Some of the older fellas in the room recognized the piece. They showed their appreciation for how she interpreted it into the rhythm of their world, of how they rolled on the streets of Harlem, by whooping and hollering.

"You better play that thing, girl."

And play she did. She kept on going until it felt like her fingers had said all that they had to say. Eventually, the bursts of a saxophone and trombone joined in as someone tapped out a beat with what sounded like drumsticks on the floor. She rode the vibe for a few minutes more. And then she was done. She tapped out the same notes with which she had started that jam session.

I've got rhythm. My name is Grace. I'm the queen of these keys. Get out my face . . .

She stood up. The room erupted into applause. She smiled, bowing with the same daintiness she had bestowed upon the audience at Carnegie Hall all those years ago.

All too quickly, reality crashed in. Her hands began to shake. Smiling faces came up to congratulate her, crowding around her. She became aware of how small that room really was. The walls felt too close together. She had to get out of there.

"Excuse me." She began pushing her way through the bodies

around her. How could a room feel so small while the back door seemed so far away? "I need air."

"C'mon now. Give the lady some space."

An arm draped across her shoulders while another began pushing everyone back. It was Jonathan. She sagged against him, succumbing to post-performance exhaustion. As soon as they were outside, she extracted herself from his embrace.

"I forgot why I never play in intimate spaces like this one . . ." Grace waved her hands in circles as she searched for the right word. "The crowd afterward is too much."

"That performance was incredible." He studied her for a moment, like he was trying to figure her out. "You were fearless onstage. But afterward . . . Are you scared of the people?"

"When they crowd around me like that, I can't breathe. I told you, I'm not scared of anything. But I don't like being in tight spaces. I hate feeling like I'm trapped."

Jonathan sighed. "Then what happened back there is my fault. I wouldn't have teased you like that if I had known."

"It's okay. I needed to redeem myself after I performed so poorly at my audition today. But I've decided I won't be playing in public anymore. I—I'm going to be trying something different."

"I heard you mention to Earl that you joined the military today."

"Yes, I ran out of that Juilliard audition and right into the Army."

"You don't say?" Jonathan looked at his watch. The lull in their conversation gave Grace the opportunity to consider him again. Yes, he was too polished for her liking. And he had a smart mouth. But he did have a streak of decency in him. She might have given him the time of day if there wasn't a war going on and she hadn't just signed her life away to the military.

"Look, I need to call it a night. My day starts early tomorrow."

Jonathan stuck his hand inside his suit jacket. He fished out a business card and placed it in Grace's hand. "Sounds like you'll be heading off to training camp soon. This is my contact information. If anything comes up while you're there or if you need anything, give me a call."

Grace looked at the card. Her heart sank as she read the words on it: ASSISTANT CIVILIAN AIDE TO THE U.S. SECRETARY OF WAR.

"Oh no. You work for the War Department." She backed away from him.

In the newsreel where the formation of the WAAC was announced, the director of the new corps talked about what an ideal WAAC soldier would be: ladylike and above reproach.

"It looks like I'm on my way out of the WAAC before I ever really got in. I don't see them tolerating someone who sneaks out of her parents' house to play music in the back room of a notorious jazz club. You won't tell on me, will you?"

She kicked a pebble down the ramp leading to the sidewalk. This was turning out to be the second worst day in Grace's life.

"Grace, why in the world would you think I'd rat you out for something so inconsequential as playing the piano in a bar?"

"Because I'm so used to having the rug pulled out from under me. It always happens."

She leaned on the railing with her forearms and looked out onto the street. Dusk was setting in. With the dimout in effect all over Manhattan, residents were beginning to pull down their blackout window shades. Most of the cars passing by were waiting until the last possible moment to turn on their dimmed headlights. The spirit of Harlem was still there, however, as a group of children played hopscotch in front of a brownstone across the street.

"Well, you have nothing to worry about from me." Jonathan

joined her at the railing, careful to keep a few inches of space between them. "It's not like I'm in the business of advertising to the brass down in Washington that I hang out in places like this either."

He gave her a crooked grin. She returned it. "Thank you."

He tipped his hat at her. "It has been real interesting meeting you, Grace Steele."

And then he was gone.

And Grace didn't have another chance to give him a moment's thought. A week later, the orders came, instructing her to board a train headed for Des Moines, Iowa.

CHAPTER 7

Harlem, New York
July 17, 1942

I N HER EXCITEMENT, Eliza had foolishly left her WAAC induction orders out on the dining room table for anyone to find. Unfortunately, the one who had found them was her father. Five hours before she was due to report to Army officials down at Grand Central Station, the silent showdown between Eliza and her father exploded into a yelling match.

"I have given you everything you have ever wanted, that you've ever needed. And still, you go behind my back and disobey me like this," her father thundered from the living room.

"No disrespect, Daddy . . ." Eliza curled her hand into a fist for courage, then took a deep breath. "But you've given me everything that *you* wanted me to have."

"So you're talking back to me now? From what I recall, you begged me to let you work at the paper." Daddy's nostrils flared like an angry bull's. Eliza took another step back. But she was not ready to yield. Not yet. She took another deep breath.

"Yes, you finally caved. But you won't let me work a real beat, like politics or sports, like I wanted. You keep insisting that I work the society pages."

Daddy held his hands up to his head like it was about to explode. "We've been over this before. A proper lady has no business in a baseball locker room."

"Female reporters do interviews on the field and in the dugout all the time. You know I can handle myself." Eliza put her hands on her hips. She was yelling now. Her heart felt like it was pounding through her chest. She had never yelled at her father before. Ever. She never would've dared. But what did she have to lose now? The worst thing he could do was kick her out of his house. That only meant she could skip his stupid dinner party this evening and get down to Grand Central Station a few hours ahead of her scheduled time.

She could feel the heat of his eyes boring into her. His chest puffed up and stayed as he held his breath. He had never hit her. But she imagined that it was taking everything in him not to smack her right then.

He yanked her by the arm and marched her down the short hallway to her room instead.

If he locks me in, I'm screwed.

He pointed a finger at the open suitcase on her bed. "You will unpack that bag," he ground out between clenched teeth. "And then you will put on something appropriate for dinner." He rocked back on his heels, his fists swinging at his sides. Oh yeah, Eliza noted. He was big-time mad.

"You *will* be dining with us at tonight's dinner party and you will be pleasant to my guests. Am I understood?"

Eliza jutted out her chin as they stared each other down in a battle of wills. Remembering Daddy's heart condition, she considered backing down. She had only committed to joining the WAAC at this point but was not officially in the military yet. Her formal induction would happen just prior to boarding the train.

Perhaps she had scared her father enough to let her start working some sports stories for a start.

Then again, if he wasn't going to take her seriously as a journalist going forward, she couldn't spend another night under his roof. He would get over it, heart condition or not. In time anyway.

She stepped forward, reclaiming her space. And then she smiled. "Yes, Daddy."

His face spread into a grin. "That's my girl."

Eliza didn't move an inch until he turned around and left her room. She closed the door behind him. Only then did she let herself relax.

She shut her suitcase and began snapping the latches. *It's a good thing I was finished packing. Now, time to come up with a plan B.*

Her biggest obstacle was how to get her suitcase out of the house without her father barring her exit. She sat down on the bed, holding her chin as she thought. The weight of the suitcase she could handle. But the bulk of it might make it unwieldy should she have to lift it. But that was what the porters on the train were there for, right?

However, navigating the suitcase out of her room *and* down the stairway on her own would cause too much of a commotion. Also, she had no reasonable explanation for putting it in one of the hall closets when she normally stored it under her bed.

And then there was the matter of getting her induction orders back. Her father had confiscated them into his bedroom when he found them.

"Martin!" Her mother's voice rang out from the kitchen. "Will you run out and grab some flowers for the table centerpiece?"

"What's wrong with the ones you bought yesterday?" Daddy

yelled back. From the sounds of it, he had retreated to his own bedroom after leaving Eliza's.

"All the heat coming from the kitchen has made them start to wilt." The pout in Mother's voice made Eliza roll her eyes. Mother had a knack for worrying about the wrong things. No one coming tonight would care about some drooping day-old flowers. Eliza wished she might worry more about how Daddy was suffocating her daughter's life.

"Fine," Daddy huffed. He stomped down the stairs and out the front door.

A minute or two later, there was a knock on her door.

"What?" Eliza whined as she opened it.

Mother barged past Eliza, making a beeline for the suitcase. She grabbed the handle, then yanked it off the bed.

"Mother! What are you doing?"

"He won't be gone long," Mother said, ignoring Eliza's question. "I assume you've finished packing?"

"Yes, ma'am."

"Good. Now, quick. Go make space for this thing in the storage closet. He never goes in there."

Eliza couldn't think of a time when her mother had so blatantly contradicted Daddy. Well, unless it had to do with buying a new pair of heels or letting her and Eliza spend an extra week out at Camp Minisink during the summer.

"Yes, ma'am!"

Eliza ran ahead to comply with her mother's request.

The two women made quick work of the task. Right after, her mother pulled Eliza's orders out of her apron pocket and handed them to her daughter.

"Now, I suggest you find a more appropriate place to put these than in plain view of your father. Your purse, maybe?"

"Of course. Thank you, Mother." Eliza threw her arms around her mother's shoulders. "But I don't understand. Why are you doing this? Why now?"

Mother sighed. "I love your father, but he is set in his ways. I let him dim my light years ago so he could shine. I won't sit by and let him do that to you too."

HOURS LATER, ELIZA drummed her fingers against her parents' big maple dining table for what must have been the hundredth time that night. She felt trapped within the long horizontal lines of her family's Harlem brownstone; the dining room's high ceiling hovered over her, threatening to fall in on itself and crush her. She was seated beside her mother, as dictated by the handwritten calligraphy on the place cards. Their next-door neighbors, an up-and-coming civil rights lawyer and his wife, occupied the remaining place settings around the table.

Mrs. Murphy, the woman who cooked for them on special occasions, pushed through the swinging door that led to the kitchen, holding identical platters containing steaming, fresh-out-of-the-oven pies.

"The dessert course, Mr. and Mrs. Jones."

Her father inhaled the aroma rising from the vent cut into the crust of one of the pies. "Mm. Blueberry, right? My favorite. Thank you so much."

He ever so carefully cut the pie and wiggled out a generous slice for himself. Then, with the same amount of care, he began divvying up the remainder for the rest of the table. Eliza sighed. Loudly. At this rate, the dinner party wouldn't be over until tomorrow.

"Eliza, sit up. Stop slouching." Mrs. Jones eyed her daughter for a second longer than necessary. Then she quickly pasted on a smile and joined in with everyone's laughter as Mr. Jones finished the punch line to another one of his stories.

Eliza stared at the grandfather clock that stood behind the head of the table. It was eight o'clock already. Her father had returned home with a new bouquet of flowers just as they had finished shoving her suitcase into the closet. She hadn't had a chance to ask her mother how she planned on helping Eliza leave on time without causing another blowout with her father.

Her parents' dinner parties normally went well past ten. Her orders had been to report to Grand Central Station by nine thirty that night. She straightened her spine with a sigh.

"Sorry, Mother." She sweetened her apology with a forced smile. She still had time. All she had to do was catch the D train at the 145th Street station across the street. She would arrive at Grand Central within an hour. It was time for drastic measures. Her father had left her no choice.

Eliza reached out for the plate of blueberry pie that had been offered to her. She dipped her chin in her father's direction. "Thank you, Daddy."

"My pleasure, princess."

She cringed again at the little-girl nickname. He really did think he had gotten the best of her so easily, didn't he?

When her dessert plate was empty aside from a few crumbs and smears of the dark purple filling, she wiped the corners of her mouth with her linen napkin, then placed it neatly beside her plate. It was time to put plan B into action.

Eliza pushed her seat back from the table. "I'm afraid I must excuse myself. Thank you all for dinner. It's been lovely."

Her father, who had been leaning back in his own chair with his hand on his belly, frowned at her. In a sickly-sweet voice that fooled no one, he said, "You have not been excused. Where do you think you're going?"

"Down to Grand Central, of course," Mother responded in the same tone she used to remind her father to take out the trash. Damn, Mother was good at this. Eliza stared at her with a cocked eyebrow.

"And why would Eliza be going down there now?" Her father smiled tightly, but he looked like he was ready to explode. "Our guests haven't finished their desserts yet."

"I do apologize for that, Mr. and Mrs. Marshall. But if I don't leave now, I'll miss my train." Eliza gave them, and her father, another smile. She knew she was laying it on thick, but she didn't care. She had to get out of there.

"What train?" Her father ground out each word between clenched teeth.

"The train I'm taking to Iowa."

Mr. Marshall, who was seated next to Daddy, chose this moment to jump into the conversation. "Dear child, what on earth would make you want to go to Iowa?"

"Training camp."

"Training camp? I'm sorry, I don't follow."

"I'm joining the military. The Women's Army Auxiliary Corps. I've been selected for its first class of Officer Candidate School."

"Why that's wonderful, Eliza!" Mrs. Marshall clasped her hands to her chest. The praise warmed Eliza's chest. Finally, someone was openly acting like they were proud of her.

Mother gently shook her head in Mrs. Marshall's direction. "Not now, Vivian."

Eliza glanced at Daddy. He had clenched his fork so tight that the skin covering his knuckles had turned pale. She could see the vein at his right temple pulsing. She quickly looked away. She pressed her hands against the tabletop and stood. He could get mad all he wanted to. She was still leaving his dinner table.

"Eliza. Sit. Down."

"Not this time, Daddy."

"We've already discussed this. I told you, you're not going anywhere. Especially if it has to do with that damned white man's Army."

"We didn't discuss anything. You yelled. And then you stormed out of my room like you always do."

"You want the sports beat that bad? Fine, we can *discuss* that later."

If he was finally caving on letting her cover sports for the newspaper, then she really did have his attention now. Eliza took another deep breath. It was now or never.

"It's too late for that. But you will hear me out now."

"I will—I will what?" he spluttered.

"It's been over a year since I finished college, Daddy. I spent four years on my own down in Washington. But you still treat me like a child."

"You *are* still a child—" Daddy began. But Mother cut him off.

"Let her finish, Martin." The tone of Mother's voice made Eliza pause and everyone else gasp. Mother reserved that tone of voice for insubordinate fund-raiser volunteers and out-of-line retail workers. "You were saying, baby?"

"Thank you, Mother. I, uh, I was saying that the only reason I haven't become more independent is because *you* browbeat me into taking the society column at the paper. You've been stringing me along with the hope that you might let me cover sports or maybe even politics. But you always have some change of heart or some other kind of excuse when it's time to deliver. And then you went and slapped *your* name on *my* byline."

"Slap my name on your byline?" Daddy began to laugh. He looked around the room as if checking for confirmation that no one else believed her accusation. He fluttered his fingers as if to wave her off. "You are being ridiculous, child. Now, sit down."

He picked his fork back up and began stabbing at his pie. You'd have thought he was a passenger on Agatha Christie's Orient Express.

"And you're ridiculous if you think I'll remain under your thumb any longer after you pulled that stunt, Daddy." Eliza started walking toward the French doors that separated the dining room from the front door. "Mr. and Mrs. Marshall, Mother, my apologies for disturbing your meals."

"Eliza Marie Jones. I'm warning you. If you walk out that door, you will not be welcomed back in." Daddy's words chilled the room.

Mother gasped. "Martin!"

Eliza stilled. Everyone there knew Daddy never issued idle threats. Maybe she was acting like a spoiled child. Maybe she should back down. There was still a chance they could talk it out, instead of her running away.

No. If she did stay, nothing would ever change.

"I'm sorry to hear that, Daddy. I would like to think that me coming home in uniform with officer's stripes would make you proud."

Eliza yanked open the storage closet, then grabbed her suitcase and handbag out of it. Her hand paused on the doorknob to the front door.

Now or never, she repeated to herself. "Mother, I'll miss you."

"Don't forget to write," Mother replied.

But it was what Daddy said as the door shut behind her that would haunt her.

"Those Army folks will chew you up, spit you out alive, and think nothing of it. And I won't be able to do a damn thing about it when they do."

CHAPTER 8

Grand Central Station, New York
July 17, 1942

B E CAREFUL OUT there in Des Moines. I need you to come back." Grace's father took her by the shoulders and studied her face carefully. "That is, your mother and I— *We* need you to come back. Back in one piece."

She saw his lip quiver right before he turned away. Grace blinked back tears. Daddy hadn't been the same since she'd had to tell him about Tony. Normally jovial and laid back, a more subdued Daddy now tried to turn what remained of their time together into a poignant father-daughter moment.

Once he had his emotions back in check, he squeezed her shoulder. "I know you think Iowa will be nothing but cornfields, cattle, and farmers. But us railroad porters talk. They say you can find everything you need there in town up on the hill on Center Street."

"Thank you, Daddy. I'll be fine."

Grace was thrilled that her father had come home in time to see her off. Though he was gone more than he was home, her heart ached knowing how much more distance would be between them when she left. Meanwhile, Mama had stopped speaking to her. The mounting tension between Grace and her mother had become intolerable.

Grace reached out to hug her father. He stayed her arm with his hand.

"I wasn't done, Grace. They also say that those same streets turn into the Sin City of the Plains when the sun goes down. You're a pretty girl and will be new in town. Watch yourself."

"I will, Daddy. But I expect the Army will be keeping us too busy to get into any kind of trouble."

"Mm-hmm. That's what they all say." He handed Grace her sweater as the loudspeaker announced that her train to Chicago, the first leg of her trip, was boarding.

"Just take care of yourself."

"I always do, Daddy. I always do."

"I know. But it's—it's different now. I need to know that you're safe."

He looked away to wave at one of the Pullman stewards pushing a cartful of dull green duffel bags and steamer trunks toward the luggage car. The man stopped and broke out into a wide grin.

"Ernest? Ernest Steele? I thought it looked like you." He took Daddy's extended hand and shook it profusely.

"Earl Robinson. It has been a while. They got you on the Chicago line now?"

"Yes, sir. I told the boss man I couldn't take riding down South on that Charleston route no more. Times was getting hard down there. I don't know how you do it. I moved the rest of my family up a few years ago. Ain't no reason for me to ever go back now."

Daddy's mouth flattened into a grim line. Grace didn't have to ask why. Back when she was three years old, a big riot had devastated the city of Charleston for several days. He had had to move their small family up north for the very same reason. But Daddy's brother and his wife had refused to leave, so Daddy remained on the New York to Charleston line to keep the connection with the rest of the family.

Earl nodded in my direction. "Who's this pretty gal you've got here?"

"This is my daughter, Grace. She's heading out to Chicago and then on to Iowa."

"Iowa?"

"For training, sir," she piped in. "I'm joining the Army."

Earl rocked back on his heels and gave Daddy a concerned look. "You're letting her be one of them gals they got to keep our boys company?"

"No, sir," she replied with finality. "I've joined to do my part so that our boys can be freed up to fight. The only company I'll be keeping is with myself."

Daddy coughed into his fist to hide his amusement. He cleared his throat to regain his composure. "Well, I was going to ask you, Earl, to keep an eye on my little girl. But it looks like she'll be able to handle herself just fine. Just fine."

"Ladies, this way." The Army officer with whom Grace had checked in upon her arrival beckoned her and a handful of other young women toward the platform entrance. He looked at his clipboard again, frowning. "Where is Jones? Is anyone here Eliza Jones?"

Grace quirked up an eyebrow when Eliza's name was called out. So Little Miss Thing had made it through after all. Grace hadn't had a doubt about it. She looked around. There were four other Negro women in the group besides her, and for that she was thankful. But none of them was the girl she had met at the induction center a week ago.

That's odd, Grace thought. Eliza had seemed so polished and put together. Definitely not the kind who would run late or, worse, flake out altogether on a commitment such as this. Grace wondered where she was.

The other women nodded at each other politely, but they were all busy saying final goodbyes to their families. Grace imagined there would be time enough to get to know one another on the train.

However, Grace noticed that of the white recruits in their grouping, none had yet to acknowledge them.

"I guess this is it." Grace smiled despite her own trembling lip. This time her father not only allowed Grace to wrap her arms around him, but he gave her a tight squeeze as well.

"I know I haven't been around as much as you would have liked lately . . . as much as I would have liked. Especially now that . . ." He looked off into the distance as he composed himself. "But I just want you to know that I'm proud of you. Proud of you for your talents with the music stuff and for having the guts to go off and do something like this."

Grace bit her lip to hold the tears forming in her eyes at bay. "I don't know what to say, Daddy."

"Ladies, I said let's move!" the officer hollered, causing Grace to jump. Her father frowned in the officer's direction. He grabbed her arm before she could step too far away.

"One last thing. The Army is full of people like that." He jerked his head at the now pink-faced officer. "People like that don't expect much out of people like us." He gestured his fingers back and forth in the space between their bodies. "They don't think we have sense enough to excel at anything they hold dear, much less know how to tie our shoes. Don't let any opportunity to prove them wrong pass you by."

Grace nodded in understanding. "I won't, Daddy."

"Remember, half the fun is the look on their faces when we show them how wrong they are."

Father and daughter shared a knowing smile and then hugged one last time. Daddy picked up Grace's suitcase and headed toward the platform. "No, Daddy, I have it. I need to get used to lugging it on my own."

"But your hands. Your piano fingers . . ."

"Will just have to adjust to a little abuse. I doubt I'll have the free time to practice much anyway." Grace bit the inside of her lip at the lie. She hadn't had the heart to tell him that she had decided to quit playing altogether. It would break his heart. Guilt tugged at her insides once again at all the extra shifts he had taken over the years to pay for her piano lessons.

They had now reached the train platform. Daddy handed over the suitcase to Grace.

Another officer with another clipboard asked for her name, checking her off when she provided it.

"I love you!" Daddy yelled out after her as she stepped away. Grace quickly hurried to her assigned Pullman sleeper car before she embarrassed herself with a display of emotions. She couldn't believe it. She was on her way. She was really doing this.

She set her things down on a bottom bed berth, then quickly lowered the window.

"I love you too!" she yelled out back at him. Then just as quickly raised the window. The exhaust accumulation left a smell in the tunnels beneath Grand Central Station. The last thing she needed was to start the trip with the stench befouling their already snug accommodations.

She returned to the berth where she had dropped her things and looked around. With a father who was a Pullman porter, Grace had been in and out of train cars all her life. But never before had she had the opportunity to ride in a sleeper car berth as a passenger.

Since it was evening, the beds were already set up. She pulled out her nightgown for later, then tucked her suitcase and bag in the compartment under the bed. She peeked out into the narrow passageway. From what she could tell, everyone else had been paired off in their individual rooms.

I guess I'm the lucky one who has a room all to herself. But having no bunkmate left her feeling rather lonely. The wall separating her from the room next door was thin. She could hear the excited yet muffled conversation of her neighbors as they introduced themselves and settled in for the long trip.

Grace sighed. She'd never had many friends, so she was used to the loneliness by now. Still, it would have been nice to have connected with someone right before she left New York.

She could hear the doors on either side of the car slam shut. That meant they would be rolling out any minute now. She closed the door to her room, locking it. Now all she could do was wait for the adventure to begin.

"Wait!" a voice called out from outside. "I'm here! I'm here! Don't leave!"

Grace looked out the window to see what the commotion was about. Out on the platform was a bedraggled, very *not* polished and *not* elegant Eliza Jones running up to the train. Neither the conductors nor the officers still on the platform looked happy to see her.

I guess she's not so perfect after all.

Grace felt tears welling in her eyes. She waved to her father one last time. The last thing she wanted was for these Army men to think she was the weepy type. She pulled down the window shade before any of her tears fell.

A few minutes later, there was a knock at her door. Well, pounding would be a better way to describe it.

"I'm not decent," she sniffed. "Who is it?"

"Hurry up," a male voice said from the other side of the door. "It's your new bunkmate and we can't get going until everyone is stowed away in their berth."

"My bunkmate?" Grace brightened at the idea. It looked like her wish for a new friend had been granted after all. Then just as quickly, she was filled with a sense of dread. *No, not her! Anyone but her.*

She got up slowly, abandoning the strand of hair that was half-way rolled onto her curler. Each step was heavier than the last. Maybe if she took too long to open the door, whoever it was would become impatient and move on to the next berth with open space. That only got her another round of banging on the door.

Shoot! Her own fantasyland this was not.

Grace wiped her face with a handkerchief, then unlocked the door.

She was almost knocked over by a body coming in. "What the . . . ? Hold on, I said I wasn't decent."

"I'm sorry. So sorry," an out-of-breath Eliza gasped. She turned around to the officer still in the hallway, who thankfully had averted his gaze down the passageway. "Thank you for accommodating me. I promise you I never run late. It'll never happen again."

"It had better not," he grumbled before marching down the hall and onto what Grace presumed was the sleeper car for the male recruits. To himself he added, "Another reason why they shouldn't have let girls into the Army."

Grace narrowed her eyes at his back. *And* that *is another reason why I intend to become the best soldier I can be. If only to prove* him *wrong.*

"Come in." Grace ushered Eliza inside. Once she closed the door again—and locked it—she added, "What a jerk."

Eliza dropped herself onto the bed with a thud. Grace gave her a good looking over from head to toe. Eliza was a sweaty mess. Gone was the polished woman she had met a week ago at the induction center.

"You look like you've just gone through literal hell."

Eliza smiled. "I feel like it." She paused a moment to take in her new accommodations. "I forgot how small these rooms could be. I never had to share one before. This should be fun, the two of us in here together."

"Yeah, fun," Grace echoed with a frown. It was obvious that Eliza was quickly making herself comfortable on what had been *her* bed up until thirty seconds ago. Her sympathy for the girl was quickly evaporating.

"Well, uh, the upper bunk is ready to go. I was just getting ready to go to sleep myself."

Grace watched as realization dawned on Eliza's face. The girl took in Grace's suitcase and toiletries that had been laid out on the bed. That is, the toothpaste and washcloths that were now being smooshed by Eliza's behind.

"Oh yes, of course." Eliza pulled Grace's hair maintenance tools out from under her. But the girl didn't get up from where she sat. "It's just that . . . well, it's just . . . Would you mind terribly if you moved to the top bed so I can be on the bottom?"

The car lurched forward as the train began to move out of the station. Grace grabbed on to the top bunk to brace herself. They were finally on their way. This should be a bittersweet moment for her. But instead, she was raging mad.

"You want me to move . . . to the top?" Grace asked. This girl barely made it onto the train in time, and now she was asking Grace to accommodate her further?

"I know it's a lot to ask. But I'm terrified of heights. I'll spend the whole night worried that I'll fall." Grace watched dumbfounded as Eliza widened her eyes and her mouth spread into a smile. Grace inclined her head. That angelic expression had no doubt been Eliza's bread and butter into getting her way in the past.

"What makes you think I'm not 'terrified' of heights too?" Grace held her fingers up in air quotes for emphasis.

Eliza's smile fell. This time, she looked Grace in the eye, woman to woman. "Because I can tell that you're not afraid of anything."

"Actually, everything scares the mess out of me." Grace folded her arms across her chest. "*Especially* heights."

This was a total lie, of course. But Grace was not about to let this obviously spoiled woman-child swoop in and totally disrupt *her* sense of order. If where she slept was that much of a concern, then Eliza should have made sure to get down to the station *on time*.

Eliza stood up—finally—and moved to the side. "Fine. I'll take the stupid one on top."

GRACE SPENT THE remainder of the night regretting that she didn't cave and take the top bunk.

As soon as Grace started drifting off to sleep, Eliza began her first of countless climbs up and down to get a glass of water, to go to the toilet, to come back and nudge Grace awake to help her find the toilet, to find her hair bonnet in her suitcase . . . it was yet one reason after another for the first half of the night. Through it all,

Grace knew she couldn't say one blessed word in protest because she had brought this upon herself.

At around half past midnight, Eliza finally went to sleep. That's when the snoring began.

"Unbelievable," Grace muttered to herself. She would've never thought someone so cute and dainty would be the one to call in the hogs so loudly. She covered her head with her pillow and said a silent prayer to not be placed in the same barracks or unit as Eliza once they arrived in Iowa.

Eliza's snores became louder.

"Dear God, make it stop. Please."

That particular prayer went unanswered for hours.

Eventually, Grace drifted off to sleep but was roused soon after, when she felt the train begin to slow down. She gave up on the idea that she might get any rest that night. She got up and pulled on a sweater over her nightgown. The temperature in the car had dropped noticeably. Grace sniffed. The air smelled like rain.

She exited the sleeper compartment, taking her blanket with her. There was a small lounge at the end of their car. Perhaps she could close her eyes in peace there.

She also brought some blank music sheets with her. The rhythms and sounds of the train ride had worked a new tune into her brain.

Once settled in one of the lounge's chairs, Grace gazed out the window. There were a few streetlights streaking past. This would have been an absolute no-no back in New York, where a mandatory dimout had been in effect since the middle of May. Too many merchant ships had been blown out of the water by German U-boats along the East Coast since the United States had entered the war. But this far inland, Grace imagined that enemy attacks from air or by sea would be less of a concern.

As the train's brakes screeched to a complete stop, Grace wondered where they were exactly. The station outside was dimly lit from what she could see out the window. Finally, she saw a sign that read COLUMBUS.

Thanks to her father's job as a porter on the railroad, she knew the name of every city on the Eastern Seaboard from New York City to Charleston, South Carolina. Her geographical knowledge was lacking once she started looking west. Aside from maybe Philadelphia and Detroit, her mind went blank on what cities lay between New York and Chicago.

A group of women walked past outside the window. From what Grace could tell, there had been a few stops so far where newly inducted WAAC officer candidates had gotten aboard. So this wasn't necessarily an unusual sight. What made this particular group unusual was that the first in this line appeared to be a brown-skinned woman, followed by too many white women for Grace to count. And the fact that they were escorted by a row of soldiers on either side of them.

Grace scoffed, "Now there's something you don't see every day. This group must be quite the handful."

A gust of cold air whooshed in when the outside door opened. Grace tightened her sweater around her. The women's footsteps sounded like clomps against the metal steps as they climbed aboard. A few minutes later, that same Negro woman who had led the line entered the lounge where Grace sat.

"Oh, hello," the woman said with a start.

"Good evening. Or should I say morning?"

"Sorry. It's a little after five o'clock in the morning. Wasn't expecting to see anybody at this hour."

Grace shrugged. "My new roommate snores."

The apples of the woman's cheeks blossomed into a full smile. "That'll do it."

"I'm Grace." She extended her hand.

The woman put down her bag and took Grace's hand. "Nice to meet you. My name is Charity Adams."

"Nice to meet you. I hear a Southern accent, but I doubt we've veered that far south on this train route. The station sign said Columbus. But Columbus where?"

"Ohio."

"What's a Southern girl doing all the way up in Ohio?"

Charity shrugged. "It's a long story."

"My roommate didn't sound like she'd stop snoring anytime soon."

As it turned out, Charity was actually a teacher from Columbia, South Carolina, who had been taking graduate summer classes at Ohio State University when she submitted her WAAC application.

"The last two days have been a wild ride. I had brought almost everything I owned with me to summer school, only to turn right around to haul it all back home to South Carolina. I had forty-eight hours to go home and drop it all off, then get back here to report for my induction in time."

Grace felt her jaw fall in astonishment. Her last week at home had felt like a whirlwind, with gathering the supplies on the recommended packing list. Then she'd had to repack her suitcase several times to squeeze everything into the suggested one to two pieces of luggage.

Charity stretched into a yawn. "Okay, now I'm tired."

"Well, now I feel bad for keeping you awake." The truth was Grace wanted to learn everything there was to know about this Charity Adams. Grace always considered herself tall. But she felt like a runt next to this woman. Not only was she tall, but she was intelligent and witty and had a confidence about herself that Grace could only wish for.

Charity excused herself and headed back to her sleeping compartment.

It had taken longer for her than most, but Grace's parents had been so proud when she had finally finished her degree from Hunter College. But to find out that Charity had gone on to start a graduate degree program as well? Grace felt another wave of shame wash over her for that disaster of an audition at Juilliard.

If you had gotten that Juilliard fellowship, then you wouldn't be here, she reminded herself. No, she would still be in New York under her mother's thumb, miserable. Grace scratched out a few more notes on her sheet paper. Truth be told, veering off course into the WAAC would actually open more doors for Grace. Her service would allow her to earn veterans' benefits once she finished her commitment. She could go to school wherever she wanted and study whatever she wanted. She would no longer be limited to the precious few fully funded fellowships in New York City that were available to girls who had ambitions like hers.

Logically, this all made sense. But she wondered whether she had given up too easily on the concert pianist dream, regardless of the fact that it had really been Mama's dream more than hers. She shoved the sheet music back into her portfolio.

All these shoulda, woulda, couldas were pointless now. Grace was in the Army. Going back was no longer an option. Only forward.

CHAPTER 9

"NEXT STOP, DES MOINES!"

The boom of the conductor's voice broke the silence in the train car, jolting Grace from her doze.

"Ladies, get your stuff together. We're getting off here."

With the time zone change and spending time stuck in train stations both planned and unplanned, Grace had had little sleep over the last thirty-six hours.

First the air-conditioning had conked out somewhere near Toledo. That had required them to get off the train and wait for the conductors to find another Pullman car to load them onto. Then, once they had arrived in Chicago—late—they had learned that they had missed the afternoon Rock Island Railroad train that would've taken them to Des Moines. That meant that they had been stuck in Union Station for the better part of the day, waiting for the evening one. None of the Army officials in Chicago were willing to let a trainload of young women loose in the city for a few hours. It was almost time to go to bed once they had finally boarded.

She peeked out the window for anything that would clue her in as to what time it was, but it was dark outside. A blue-black sky covered the landscape racing by, with only stray wisps of moonlight peeking out of the thick clouds to illuminate the houses, separated by large, hilly breaks that could only be farmland, and an occasional line of trees. Grace remembered hearing about a federal project where stands of trees were planted across the Midwest to act as windbreakers to stop the horrible dust storms that had crippled the region a few years ago. It was hard to make out in the dark, gloomy night, but some of those trees looked young enough to have been part of that effort.

She imagined that the landscape that was passing by her was beautiful in daylight. But at night, it looked so peaceful and innocent in comparison to the tall buildings and crowds she had grown up around. But then she remembered how looks could be deceiving.

While she couldn't see the city itself, she could see the gray skies surrounding the front of the train begin to lighten in a faint artificial orange glow. She could feel the train begin to decelerate. Eliza was snoring softly against her pillow, and Grace tapped her foot. "Wake up. We're here."

Eliza groaned as she sat up. She turned her neck to and fro, then stretched her arms. "I really hope the beds are soft when we get there. I never want to have to sleep on one of these trains again."

"Keep hoping, kid. The military isn't known for its luxurious accommodations." Grace shrugged into her suit jacket and then began to gather her things. The more the train slowed down, the more her hands shook. She had never been outside the New York City metropolitan area in her adult life. And now here she was in the middle of America's breadbasket. What the hell had she been thinking?

She repeated to herself silently, *For better or for worse, you're in the Army now.*

The brakes whined loudly as the train jerked to a stop. Grace reached into the storage compartment under the bed for her suitcase. Then she ran through her mental checklist:

Suitcase. Check.

Pocketbook. Check.

Portfolio with her sheet music. Check.

Sweater. Check.

Grace draped her sweater over the lower part of her arms to hide how much her hands were shaking. She couldn't believe it. She was really here. Out in the sleeper car lounge, they waited. She looked over her shoulder at Eliza and, behind her, their new friend Charity, who was already grinning with excitement. "Are you ladies as ready as I am?"

A still-half-asleep Eliza blew out a breath. "As ready as I'll ever be, I guess."

"Good." Charity grabbed Eliza by the arm. "Then let's get out of here and show these guys how to win this war."

There was a line of Army officers waiting for them when they stepped into the brick Rock Island train depot. All of them were white and male. And none of them looked happy to see this new group of arrivals.

"Go through these doors and to your left," barked the first one they encountered.

"Could you direct me to the ladies' room, please?" Eliza inquired.

The man propped his clipboard on his hip and glared at her. "You can pee when you get on base, girl," he drawled. "Until then, hold it while you go through these doors and go to your left."

Eliza's jaw fell in shock. "Excuse me?"

But Grace pulled her away by the arm before Eliza could say anything more. He had been wrong to call Eliza "girl," but it was also too early in their Army careers to get into trouble.

"C'mon, Eliza."

"Did you hear how he spoke to me?" Eliza continued to pull against her hold. That only prompted Grace to squeeze tighter.

"You'll have plenty of time to get yourself into trouble with these guys. Let's wait until it's for something that's actually worth it."

Behind them, Charity suppressed a laugh. "Are you two always like this?"

Grace looked over her shoulder and arched an eyebrow at Charity. "God, I hope not."

Once they passed through the doors and turned to the left as they had been instructed, they found themselves in an alley. Even though it was the middle of summer, Grace shivered from the cold. It had been raining, so the gusts of wind that whipped into the alley made it feel like early spring. They continued to step forward, following the line of women who preceded them. From what she could tell, the officers were checking off their names and then directing them toward a long line of drab green Army trucks. Their trio eventually made it to the front of the line and gave their names.

"Find a truck with space and hop on."

"Where are the porters to help us with our bags?" Eliza gritted the words out from between clenched teeth.

Grace turned around to see a breathless Eliza struggling to keep up with them. She rolled her eyes. *The girl must have packed like she was going on a vacation*, Grace assumed. As a habit, Grace always packed her bags no heavier than she could carry by herself if needed. But Eliza, still struggling with her own suitcase, obviously did not follow the same philosophy. And Grace was the daughter of a Pullman porter. She knew the expected service protocol, especially when there were as many women as there were here.

"Girl, you're in the Army now. It looks like we're going to have to make our own way." Charity shuffled her pocketbook and suitcase to the same hand. With her free hand, she lifted the other side of Eliza's suitcase.

There was a mad frenzy of women who had alighted from the now departing train. Grace, never the one to go out of her way to socialize, had pretty much limited herself to their train car during the journey. She was shocked by the number of women who stood ready to climb aboard the trucks with all of their worldly possessions in hand.

"Wow, and all of us here for officer training," she muttered to herself. She noticed one young woman off to the side who was struggling to keep hold of all her luggage. Tears were beginning to form in the corners of her hazel eyes, threatening to fall at any moment. Grace reached out to catch a bundle that was sliding out of the woman's grip. "You almost dropped this. Do you need some help?"

"Yes, I'd love . . ." But when the woman looked up, the smile on her face fell as she sized up Grace from head to toe. Then, to Grace's surprise, the woman frowned at her. She squared her shoulders and lifted her chin so she now appeared to look down upon Grace. She cleared her throat. "No, I do not."

The woman then snatched the bundle from Grace's hand, which caused her to drop everything else she was struggling to hold in the process. It all looked like a scene from one of the screwball comedy silent motion pictures Grace had seen as a child. Had she not been so shocked by the woman's rudeness, she might have laughed.

"Here, let me help you," Grace insisted. She put down her own belongings so she could kneel and pick up some of the woman's mess.

"You've *helped* quite enough . . . girl." Grace stilled at the way the woman's voice drawled around the word "girl" like it was venom.

"That's fine." Grace stood. There was no point in attempting to aid a person who obviously didn't want any help. She took a deep breath. That was the second time in a matter of minutes that she had heard someone who looked like her referred to as "girl." She really hoped that these were exceptions and not the rule in her new life here.

It did not surprise her in the least that most of the women here were white. Heck, she had been surprised when her father had told her there was a civilian Negro community here in Des Moines at all.

Eliza nudged her. "What was her problem?"

Grace sighed. "I have no idea."

"I suspect that we're too far above the Mason-Dixon Line for her liking," Charity quipped. She marched up to the steps that had been placed at the back of the nearest truck. "But that's something for her to get over. We have more important things to concern ourselves with. Like getting on this truck. C'mon."

This Charity Adams sure is a firecracker, Grace thought. *She is the type of person I would follow anywhere, even if she was leading me into battle.*

Grace smiled to herself as she followed Charity and Eliza up the steps and onto the truck.

Despite the gloominess of the morning, there was a soft golden glow that peeked from the gaps in between the canvas that covered the back of the truck. Curious, Grace took a look to see what it was.

"Oh!" The glow surrounded what could only be the state capitol.

It was on a hill just past the immediate vicinity of the train depot. She imagined that the lighting was a muted version of its intended glory because of the early-morning hour, but it entranced her just the same. One day, she'd have to come back with a camera to take a picture of it.

Grace's wonder at witnessing the sunrise was short-lived. When they arrived in front of Fort Des Moines, the luggage-laden new recruits were greeted by a never-ending burst of camera flashes as they descended from their trucks. Local and national press had come out in full force to catch a glimpse of the first class of WAAC officer candidates. They couldn't move an inch without some reporter shoving a camera or a notepad in their faces.

To make it worse, there were Army personnel left and right barking orders at the women to keep the lines coming off the trucks moving, to fill out luggage cards and attach them to their suitcases, and to make a beeline across a large open field.

It seemed that the first act of business on the Army's agenda was to usher them into a bright yellow building with a sign affixed to it that read CONSOLIDATED MESS HALL.

Eliza whispered to Grace, "What is a 'mess' hall?"

Grace shrugged in response. "Your guess is as good as mine."

They soon discovered the answer to that question when they found themselves in a line where cooks shoved plates of toast, bacon, and scrambled eggs at them.

They sat down at the nearest free seats. Eliza leaned in to sniff her plate. She giggled. "If this is the 'mess,' should I be scared to eat it?"

Grace shrugged again. "That's up to you. All I know is that I'm starving, and I haven't had bacon in over six months."

"Six months? I would die if I had to go without bacon for that long. I don't know how my daddy managed it, but we've had bacon every Sunday morning despite rationing."

Grace held a strip of bacon up to her nose and inhaled deeply. Despite Eliza's assumption, the reason it had been more than six months since she'd last eaten bacon had more to do with her family's limited earnings than war rationing.

"Mm. Maybe Army life won't be so bad after all." She took a bite and moaned some more.

Meanwhile, Eliza put down the fork she had been using to push around her scrambled eggs. She gave those eggs one last side-eye before setting her sights on her toast. She picked it up, sniffed it, then took a bite. Almost immediately, her free hand clapped itself over her mouth. "Oh my God!"

"What's wrong? Did you bite your tongue?"

"No. There's *real* butter on this toast!"

"No way!" Grace took a bite of her own toast. "You weren't kidding. Oh, it's been so long."

"That's nothing," another woman chimed in from a few seats down at their table. "They have *real* sugar for the coffee."

Eliza held the back of her hand up to her forehead in a dramatic fashion. "I think we've just arrived in heaven, ladies."

However, the meal quickly turned from heavenly into chaotic. The press spent most of the allotted time getting them to pose for "candid" shots rather than actually eating. When that was over, then came another shock for Grace and Eliza.

They exited the mess hall to a sergeant hollering, "Coloreds over there! Everyone else over here!"

Eliza leaned in and whispered to Grace, "What did he just say?"

"There has got to be some mistake," Grace murmured more to herself than in response to Eliza. The way she looked off into space in the direction of the officer barking orders at them, it was like she hadn't heard Eliza at all.

"Of course this is a mistake. I grilled my recruiter with every question under the sun. He assured me there would be no segregation. I told him I wouldn't sign up if there was." An image of her father smirking and saying "I told you so" floated in Eliza's head. No, this definitely *had* to be a mistake.

Harriet West, who had introduced herself to the trio on the truck ride from the train station, had a frown on her face. "Dr. Bethune told me Mrs. Roosevelt herself would make sure there'd be no separations. Not by race anyway. We should protest."

"Don't bother." Charity frowned as she grabbed her suitcase. "Good ol' Uncle Sam just pulled another fast one on us. C'mon. We'll address this another way."

It was Charity's command that broke Grace out of her daze. But Eliza looked like she wasn't ready to follow anyone yet. "The Negro papers said that there wouldn't be any segregation in the women's army," she grumbled.

Charity barked out a short, bitter laugh. "And you believed them?"

Eliza took offense to that and started to protest. "Hey, wait a minute! My family owns a Negro newspaper."

"She's right." Harriet put a hand on Eliza's shoulder. "Honey, the government would've sold you the Statue of Liberty to get you to sign those enlistment papers. I was Dr. Bethune's assistant before coming here. They had a hard time filling those slots they set aside for us. It would have made everybody look bad—Negro and white—if the recruiters had come up short. I know at least one of the girls they selected wasn't one hundred percent sure of her decision. I wouldn't be surprised if she doesn't show up at all."

Harriet's admission triggered Grace's old doubts about if she belonged here at officers' training, or the OCS, as they called it. It was beginning to sound like that invitation letter that had distracted her out of a Juilliard fellowship had been sent to her more out of desperation than any belief in her potential. Maybe she should ask whoever was in charge here about sending her home.

No. You're here now. You're not going anywhere.

"I thought I told you recruits to *move*." The sergeant was now in their faces. He wasn't quite close enough, though, for his spittle to reach them.

Eliza and Grace held their bags closer to them and scrambled out of his way, following after Charity and Harriet.

"What do you mean?" Grace demanded.

Eliza cleared her throat. "What she's saying is that both the Army and the Negro leaders were under pressure to make sure that all of the Negro slots were filled for this officer training class. Not enough women were signing up for this very reason."

"Basically." Charity shook her head calmly as she carried the rest of her belongings over to where the sergeant had instructed. But Grace wasn't fooled. She could tell by the way Charity yanked her bag in quick, deliberate tugs that the woman was irate.

"It's true," Eliza chimed in. "One of our reporters heard it from Dr. Bethune herself. She let it slip when he was covering the announcement that the corps was being formed."

Grace turned her head. "That doesn't mean she was telling the truth. What if she needed us sacrificial lambs to believe that for 'the cause'?"

"I refuse to believe that," Eliza whispered. She sounded like her resolve had begun to waver. "I had to throw a temper tantrum and walk out of my parents' dinner so I could report for duty on time.

I'm pretty sure my father has already changed the locks, if not written me out of his will entirely."

She looked at Grace.

"That's why I almost missed the train that night we left New York."

"Oh." Grace began to second-guess her initial assumptions about Eliza Jones. Maybe she wasn't a total spoiled airhead after all. Walking out like that in defiance of her father's wishes was something she'd never have the nerve to do, no matter what her age. "Eliza Jones, that took guts."

Charity stopped in her tracks and turned around. "Girl, you did what? My daddy would've had them stop the train."

Eliza quirked an eyebrow. "What makes you think mine didn't try?"

"Attention!" a red-faced officer screamed at both groups of women, shocking everyone into silence. "Since you all are new, I'm only going to explain this to you once. When I or any other officer calls you to 'attention,' you are to immediately stop whatever you are doing and stand upright with your chin up, chest out, shoulders back, and stomach in. Like this."

He took his hands off his hips and demonstrated the correct posture. "Now, let's try this again. Attention!"

Some of the women were slower to act than others. But it was easy to tell who there had grown up with a father in the military. It took a few moments for all of them to, more or less, assume the correct stance.

"That's better. Maybe there's hope for this little girl army after all." The officer went back to his clipboard. "Ladies, line up beside me as I call your names."

The grumpy officer eyeballed the white recruits as they scrambled to follow his instructions. As for Grace, Eliza, and all the other darker-skinned women whom he had ordered off to the side, he barely spared them a glance.

"Come on, ladies," he huffed. "I shouldn't have to tell you that I meant *straight* lines."

Grace could see him rolling his eyes. Why on earth had the Army picked this obviously unhappy individual to be in charge of a bunch of green lady recruits? She shifted her bundle from one arm to the other. They all just stood there awkwardly, watching the confused mass of women try to organize themselves.

Grace pressed her lips together. She nudged Eliza with her elbow. "C'mon."

"What?" Eliza was still eyeing the officer.

"Let's line ourselves up. We'll have to at some point."

"Why should we? They're ignoring us."

"Yeah, but there's no way that I'm gonna let *us* look like *that* mass of confusion over there." Grace nodded in the direction of the women still trying to line up to the officer's satisfaction. "That's the whole point of treating us any ol' kind of way. They don't *expect* anything better from us. I intend to prove them wrong."

"Well, when you put it that way . . ." Eliza huffed, but she stood up from the makeshift stairs she had been sitting upon. Grace was already working her way around the other women in their group, encouraging everyone to not only get themselves organized but also asking their names. Slowly, Grace went down the line. She pulled a few of the women out and directed them to different spots either toward the front of the makeshift line or toward the end. She had made it about halfway when she gestured toward Eliza.

"Jones! Your spot is here."

"What are you doing, Grace?"

"Putting us in alphabetical order. I might not have been in the Army long, but I've noticed enough to know that Uncle Sam does everything by the letter. In this case, that's alphabetically. Now, come on."

"Your friend there is a piece of work," one of their fellow recruits remarked.

Grace heard Eliza grumble behind her back, "Bossy is more like it."

Grace turned to correct her. "I am not bossy. I'm *organized*. Now get in line."

The officers were exasperated by the time they had sent the white recruits on their way. The one who appeared to be in charge squeezed the bridge of his nose and took a deep breath. While still looking down, he barked, "Fall in! That means I want you gals to line up. Do you think you can manage that without taking all day?"

"We are lined up," called out one of the ladies in the front.

"Alphabetically," chimed in another.

Grace, who was standing toward the end of the line, could've sworn the voice sounded like Charity's. Grace bit her lip to keep from snorting.

"Sounds like we have a jokester already. Now, I told you gals I'm not in the mood . . ." He looked up and abruptly stopped speaking. "Wait, who told y'all to line up like that?"

"We told ourselves, sir." Grace wanted to slap her hands over her mouth but didn't dare move. She hadn't meant to speak her thoughts out loud.

The man's jaw unhinged itself further. "Well, I'll be . . ."

He quickly regained his composure—his composure being frowning so hard that his face looked like a wrinkled pug's and harrumphing like a grumpy old man. "I bet you all think you're so smart. Well, nothing gets under my skin quicker than a bunch of know-it-alls. Let's get this right straight, you all know nothing. I don't care how much college these here forms say you have. You are nothing. And you will continue to be nothing until I say each and every one of you is worthy of wearing the officer stripes from this here United States Army. Is that clear?"

"Yes, sir," they all shouted in unison.

The grumpy officer harrumphed again. "It seems like now is a good time to introduce you all to the basics of military life." He held up his pointer finger. "One, do not do anything unless you are ordered to. I do not care who birthed you. I do not care who sired you. I'm your daddy now. That means from now on you do not move, you do not think, you do not eat, you do not shit, unless I tell you to."

Grace heard a few gasps at the officer's coarse language. One woman was even so bold as to breathe out an "Excuse me?"

"I did not give you permission to speak," he screamed, punctuating each word.

He waited a beat, then held up another finger. "Two, there is no place for girls in the United States military. You stopped being girls or young ladies or . . . whatever when you stepped off those trucks and onto the ground of this here military compound. You are now *soldiers*. That means I do not care if something is too heavy or you broke a nail or whatever female problem you might be having at the moment. Your job is to do what you are told and to do it well."

Up went his ring finger. "Three, do not embarrass me. Everything you do or say from now on is a reflection of me. I do not tolerate sloppiness and I do not tolerate excuses. The correct answer is not 'I don't know.' It is 'I don't know, sir, but I will find out.' Is that clear?"

They all nodded. A few added "Yes, sir" to their responses.

"Good. Now, fall in."

None of them moved. They looked at each other for clarification, but none of them dared speak.

Finally, Grace opened her mouth. "We do not know what 'fall in' means. Would you explain . . . sir?"

"It means I'm ordering you to line up."

Grace closed her eyes because she knew what was coming, but it had to be said. "We are lined up already, sir."

He marched over to where she stood. "Are you to be my smartass? There's always one in every class. Who are you?"

"Grace Steele, sir."

He stepped back and made sure he had the attention of every woman in the group. "No, you are not."

He approached her again, this time screaming in her face. "When I ask you who you are, you are to respond with your name, rank, and serial number. Now, I am going to ask you again: Who are you, soldier?"

"Grace Steele," she repeated without flinching. "I am a new recruit. I can't tell you my serial number because I haven't memorized it yet, sir."

"Then I suggest you learn it quickly." He leaned in closer and whispered, "I suggest you keep your mouth shut if you want to stay here more than a day. You and your kind don't belong here, and we don't want you here. Is that clear?"

"Yes, sir," she whispered back.

"Good." He addressed the entire group again. "Now, march

your fancy asses down to the barracks at the end of this row. Number fifty-four. It's time for you know-nothings to learn how to make up a bed."

Once his back was turned and their line began to move, Grace let her face break out into a full grin. Was that all he had to dish out—screaming in their faces and making up beds? She'd had piano teachers who were worse than that.

Boot camp was going to be a piece of cake.

SOON ENOUGH, GRACE would come to regret that thought. Who knew that in the military making up a bed required a good understanding of geometry and the use of a ruler? Grace had gotten the gist of it on her second attempt, although she had yet to nail placing the blanket at the requisite six inches below the head of the bed. She had been assigned the top bunk, which made precision difficult. But working together with her bottom bunkmate, a girl named Corrie Sherard from Atlanta, Georgia, both of their beds turned out better than most.

The other training staff who had been assigned to their company were slightly younger than the officer who had screamed in Grace's face. They had more patience with the women they were teaching. But none seemed particularly happy to be stuck with the "girl soldiers," or, in their specific case, the "Colored girl soldiers."

That evening, while everyone else was excitedly unpacking their luggage, Grace fell onto her bunk with a *thunk*. She was exhausted. So exhausted that the hard mattress felt like heaven. It felt like a week had passed since she stepped off that train this morning. The rest of their first day had consisted of finishing their on-site processing and receiving a battery of shots from the medical staff on top of the initial lessons on basic military commands and learning how to make up a bed the Army way.

Her feet ached. They were also cold. The rain had caused the grounds of the base to be muddy everywhere they went today. The dress shoes she had worn aboard the train were now caked in dark brown mud. That ticked her off. Only one day in and the WAAC already owed her a pair of shoes as far as she was concerned.

Grace hugged her pillow as she squeezed her eyes shut. Lieutenant Rogers, the drill instructor who had screamed in her face, had informed them that they would begin again at 6:30 A.M. the next day. However, their first task would be to report to the quartermaster after breakfast to be issued uniforms and other gear. She was looking forward to that, as it meant that she could stop ruining her personal clothes in all the mud around the base.

She smiled into her pillow as lights out went into effect in Barracks #54.

A voice on the other side of the barracks broke the silence. "I've never been away from home like this before."

Grace cracked an eye open and groaned. "I'm trying to get some sleep over here."

"I know. I'm sorry." Silence again. "Where is everybody from?"

Grace turned onto her stomach and put her pillow over her head. But her protest was in the minority; everyone else was eager to bond. Voices began to chime in out of the darkness.

"Columbia, South Carolina."

"Toledo, Ohio."

"Kansas City, Missouri."

"Chicago."

"Louisville."

"Texas."

"New York City."

"Boston."

"Washington, D.C."

"Los Angeles, California."

"Virginia."

"Connecticut."

"Florida."

"Nebraska."

"New Orleans."

"Atlanta."

"Indianapolis."

"Tuskegee, Alabama."

Grace felt no need to join in, since several voices had already called out New York. She was curious about what part of the city they were from. But in the end, what difference did it make? They were all here in Iowa now.

"Dang, we're from a little bit of everywhere, huh?" Grace recognized Eliza Jones's voice. "What were you all doing before you signed up? I graduated from college last year. I've been writing for my daddy's newspaper ever since."

The responses varied from dietician, to high school math teacher, to podiatrist, to law school student. A good number had been office clerks and secretaries.

And then a voice said, "I was a professional dancer. So whoever said they were a podiatrist, I'm coming to you about my feet."

That got a few chuckles, even from Grace. So someone else had a background in the arts? That reassured her some. She had begun to question whether she belonged here.

Grace felt her nerve begin to build. Then finally, she felt she couldn't hold back anymore.

"I was working toward becoming a concert pianist."

"Whoa. There's a lot of talent in here, ladies. The WAAC is lucky to have us."

"Yes, they are," came a grumpy voice from the middle of the room. "Now, will y'all shut up so I can get some sleep?"

Grace smiled. Whoever said that was now her favorite person in the whole world.

CHAPTER 10

Fort Des Moines, Iowa
July 20, 1942
(Day Two of OCS)

A TTENTION!"

Eliza had been in the process of introducing herself to Vera Campbell, who, to her surprise, had been a podiatrist prior to joining the corps, while they waited outside their barracks before breakfast. But their and everyone else's conversation ended immediately, with all thirty-nine women—since Harriet's prediction about the one no-show proved correct—standing straight and tall.

Lieutenant Rogers gestured toward another slightly older officer who was approaching them. "This is Colonel Donald Faith. He is the commandant of the training center here. He would like to share a few words with you."

He stepped back, giving Colonel Faith the floor.

"Forgive my interruption. I know that you all are eager to get to breakfast so you can start your first full day of training. I just wanted to formally welcome you all to the first WAAC Training Center here at Fort Des Moines. No doubt you realize that this is a historic moment for us all. With this being the first ever all-female training class, we thank you for your patience and flexibility as we work through making adjustments to our normal way of doing things around here.

"With that said, I know that some of you may have been, let's say, alarmed by the way our new arrivals were, uh, separated into companies yesterday. I apologize that our way of doing things may have made you uncomfortable. Had I been free to do so, I would have instructed my staff to handle it another way. At this time, the United States Army's policy is to separate our personnel by their color and, now, by gender. You will soon learn that in the Army, policy is policy and we must follow it to the letter if we are to achieve our mission."

He paused for a moment as if to allow for a response from the women. Eliza could feel the tension radiating from the entire company. She bit her lip to keep from screaming at Colonel Faith about what he could do with his apology. She dared not, for she knew that would only lead to her being on the first train out of there and back to New York, back to her father. Eliza wouldn't give Daddy the satisfaction.

By now, the silence that hung between the officers and soldiers had become awkward. Colonel Faith inserted his finger between his collar and his skin before clearing his throat. "I appreciate your understanding. Lieutenant, you may proceed with whatever you were about to do."

"Yes, sir. Soldiers, fall in!"

Colonel Faith executed a crisp turn and walked back toward the base headquarters.

Eliza was spitting mad as they marched toward the mess hall. She knew she wasn't the only one who was. She had caught the eyes of Vera and a few others while they were lining up. All of their eyes had been blazing.

The colonel's "apology" had felt like it had been more for re-assuring himself than to comfort anyone in their company. Eliza couldn't put her finger on why it did. But one thing she did know was that she had never heard of any white man in a position of power apologize like that, especially when it was to a bunch of Negro women. She wondered what had prompted it. The reason became clear when they marched into the mess hall for breakfast.

Someone had placed tented pieces of paper with the word "Col-oreds" on four of the tables in the farthest corner of the room, the ones closest to the door leading out to the latrines. The signage was completely unnecessary, since each soldier was required to sit with her own company anyway. Everybody already knew that all the Negro trainees had been assigned to Third Company. What couldn't be overlooked was that there weren't similar signs on any of the other tables, only theirs. Whoever had put the signs there did so for the cheap satisfaction of humiliating the entirety of Third Company while simultaneously putting them in their place.

All eyes were on them as they got into line to get their food. Not one of them said a word. They kept their chins up and looked straight ahead, with the exception of the occasional knowing glances at each other.

Once they were seated, Eliza was the first to speak.

"I'm calling my father about this as soon as I get the chance," she whispered just loud enough for the entire table to hear her. She was livid. Even though she was a New Yorker by birth, she had gone to school in Washington, D.C., a segregated city. She knew what to expect when she stepped off the campus of Howard University, which was why she rarely did so during her four years there. But this was Iowa, which was well north of the Mason-Dixon Line. There wasn't supposed to be any segregation here.

"What's he going to do?" came a flippant reply from the other end of the table. "Unless he has a direct line to FDR himself, tattling to Daddy isn't going to do anything except make us look like a bunch of whiny spoiled brats. We have to be smarter than that."

"He has a newspaper. He can write an editorial about it." The retort sounded weak to Eliza's own ears. Now that she had a moment to think, this was definitely not the kind of thing she wanted to complain about to her father on only her second day here. Just another reason for him to say "I told you so."

"It's not a half bad idea, though," Grace chimed in.

Now, there was a surprise. Eliza never imagined Grace Steele would cosign any ideas she had to share. It seemed like every time Eliza opened her mouth, whatever came out would get on Grace's nerves.

"Calling the newspapers part, that is. But we have to be strategic about it. Think about who each of us knows who is well connected enough to call the newspapers, the NAACP, and elected officials on our behalf. The people who can get the word out to get others to do the same. If it comes from us directly, then it does sound like a bunch of spoiled Negro girls whining about how boot camp is too hard. But if it is the community who's sounding the alarm . . ."

Nods went around the table. Eliza, starting to warm up to Grace's take on her idea, added in, "Let's not all rush to the post office at once to make our calls. That'll be too obvious. We've got to be cool so it looks and sounds like a routine call home. No getting on the line demanding to speak to so-and-so directly."

"Yeah, I like that," Grace agreed. Eliza nodded a grateful smile in her direction.

Eliza nudged the person sitting next to her. "Tell Harriet at the end to spread the word to the next table. Keep it on the hush-hush."

AFTER BREAKFAST, PICKING up their gear from the quartermaster had been more tedious than anyone anticipated. The process was supposed to be that you told the clerk your sizes and he issued you the correct-fitting garments. However, it appeared that no one had informed Uncle Sam that the Army was now enlisting women. They quickly had run out of the medium and small sizes. They had only five skirts in stock before the first two companies had been issued their gear. Eliza's jaw fell in horror when the supply officer thrust a stack of boxer shorts for underwear at her.

"Was anyone in our group issued a complete uniform?" Eliza asked when they were marched to their barracks next.

Her bunkmate, Alice, shrugged. "Doesn't look like it." She dangled a pair of standard-issue saddle shoes from her fingers. "I can't believe they expect us to march and do calisthenics in these." She gave a short laugh. "Thank goodness we have a foot doctor among us."

The women of Third Company quickly went through the process of storing their issued clothing and equipment into their lockers. Eliza, however, struggled with putting away her things. Back home, she would've just shoved it all in her footlocker and called it a day. But that wouldn't fly now that she was in the military. She chafed against the expectation that her personal items had to be folded and put away in the specific manner that some Army regulation book dictated.

"It's none of their business how I fold and store *my* underwear," she grumbled under her breath. "All that should matter is how clean they are when I put them on."

"Attention!" Lieutenant Rogers's voice broke into her thoughts. Eliza abandoned the precise fold she had been attempting and jumped to her feet. Rogers stood in the doorway of the barracks but did not enter.

"It was a shame we had such bad weather yesterday. Thankfully, the sun is shining now. It's a perfect day to take a jog around the base. Put on your PT gear and be outside in ten." He let the door slam behind him as he left.

Eliza groaned. "A jog? He can't be serious. I don't run. I'm from New York."

Grace, whose bunk was across from hers, turned around and looked at Eliza like she had grown a second head. "Girl, this is the military. All they do is run."

CHAPTER 11

T HE WOMEN OF Third Company were ordered to the base parade grounds two days after those infuriating COLORED signs had first appeared in the mess hall. A vehicle with American flags waving from the hood rolled up to where they stood. From what Grace could tell from the annoyed looks on their company commanders' faces, some bigwigs from D.C. were making an unannounced visit today.

A middle-aged white woman in a WAAC uniform emerged from the car first. Grace recognized the WAAC director, Colonel Oveta Hobby, from the pictures she had seen of her in the newspaper. Next came an older Negro woman who held out her white-gloved hand to be helped out of the car. The officer who had assisted Colonel Hobby out of the car stared at the woman's hand and paused. He looked unsure of what to do. It was only when Hobby commanded that he "help Dr. Bethune out of the car, Lieutenant," that he took her hand.

Grace blinked. She had not seen Mary McLeod Bethune in person before. Her first face-to-face impression of the woman left her in awe. Both her height and demeanor were imposing, even to one as tall as Grace. She didn't know which one of her fellow auxiliarists had made the call that led to the arrival of such an impressive entourage (although Dovey Roundtree, who had quickly earned the nickname "the Walking NAACP"; Harriet West, who had been Dr. Bethune's secretary prior to joining the corps; and maybe even Eliza Jones would be at the top of her list if she were to guess). But Grace felt the beginnings of reassurance that the slights her company in particular had endured in the last few days were about to come to an end.

Once Dr. Bethune had exited the car, Colonel Faith gave the command: "Parade, rest!"

Every woman lifted her left leg, stepping outward until her feet were about twelve inches apart. Grace was still getting used to standing for long periods of time. The transition to a more, although not much more, relaxed stance was a relief. The increasing heat of the relentless Iowa sun made Grace sway. She let her leg muscles slacken a bit as she mentally berated herself that she had to stop locking her knees lest she pass out.

There was yet another person making his way out of the car that had carried Hobby and Bethune. All thoughts of maintaining a straight spine and loose knees while looking straight ahead flew out of Grace's mind as the man she had met at Minton's Playhouse just weeks ago emerged from the vehicle. Every muscle in her body went rigid. Moments later, much to her horror, she found herself dizzy and falling to the ground.

When she came to, she opened her eyes to find that it was Mr. Jonathan Philips who was cradling her head.

Grace groaned as his too-handsome face hovered over hers. His features were drawn up in what looked like genuine concern.

"What the hell are you doing on my base?" she croaked.

"*Your* base, eh? I was going to ask you if you were all right. But

I think you've already answered my question." He looked up and yelled to someone off to the side, "She'll be fine. But she probably could use some water."

When he returned his attention to her, she frowned up at him. "It feels like you're stalking me."

"I'm not sure it's considered stalking when it was Colonel Hobby, your commanding officer, who insisted that I come along on this trip."

"My mistake." Grace pushed herself up onto her elbows. "Thanks for making sure that I was okay, but let's not make this a regular thing."

"What don't you want to be a regular thing?"

"This." She gestured her arm across her lap. "You coming to save little ol' me every time I feel woozy."

He laughed at her sarcasm. He held his hand against her back, supporting it, as she pushed herself all the way up into a sitting position.

"Miss Steele, are you saying that I make you feel woozy?"

"No," she snapped. "That's not what I meant at all."

"Are you all right, dear?" Dr. Bethune's face now hovered over Grace and Jonathan. "Mr. Philips, did you run track in school? I don't think I've ever seen anyone run that fast before."

"No, ma'am." Jonathan gave Dr. Bethune a wry smile. "Just didn't want her to hit her head, is all."

That's when Grace remembered where she was. She looked up to find all the Fort Des Moines top brass staring at her, in particular a red-faced Lieutenant Rogers throwing lightning bolts with his eyes.

Dread crept up her shoulders and neck. The whole world might as well have been watching what could be interpreted as an intimate moment between them. Grace closed her eyes.

"Get away from me," she whispered to Jonathan. "Please."

"As soon as I help you to your feet."

"No. This is the first time Negro women have been allowed anywhere near these people's Army. Jonathan, seriously, I don't need any more attention. Not when all eyes really are on us."

"You're right. I know better than anyone what this means to us, the race, to you." Jonathan nodded with a frown as he pushed himself back to his full height. Grace almost instantly regretted the warning. "I'll come back to talk to you later." He held up his hand when she opened her mouth to protest. "Because it's my *job*, Miss Steele."

Jonathan strode away back to his place among the WAAC and Fort Des Moines leadership, every one of them staring back and forth between the two of them curiously. There was none of the cool swagger in his step that Grace had admired back in Harlem. His now tight facial features said it all. Grace wanted nothing more than to run after him and apologize. But she couldn't. Unless one of these officers, who so far had held so much contempt for her and the rest of Third Company, ordered it.

She pushed herself back up onto her feet and resumed standing at attention. She took extra care to keep her knees unlocked this time.

"Colonels. Lieutenant. Dr. Bethune." Grace nodded at each one as she addressed them. "I apologize for the interruption."

They all nodded in one way or the other to accept her apology. But Lieutenant Rogers continued to throw daggers with his eyes in her direction.

I'll deal with you later, he mouthed at her. A new line of sweat broke out on her forehead, but she dared not move. She had no doubt that he would make good on that threat once the WAAC leadership had gone back to Washington.

Grace saw Jonathan hesitate a step before taking his place next to Rogers. There was no way that he could not have seen her commanding officer's threat. She watched as Jonathan leaned closer to Rogers. From this distance, it looked like his mouth had formed the words "But first you'll have to deal with me." Grace felt her blood go cold. This would not bode well for her.

From what she knew of Lieutenant Mitchell Rogers so far, Grace suspected that the man had never had the experience of a mother's love. He definitely couldn't have been married. It seemed like he hated being around women that much. But she couldn't quite put her finger on where he stood on having to turn civilian Negro women into soldiers. To his credit, she had never heard him sneer the term "negra gals" or the like. Well, not yet. But she had seen him bark at some of the white recruits who were in other companies in the regiment. So, who really knew what Rogers's deal was?

But he definitely hated women.

After the assembly, Grace walked ahead of the rest of her company as they headed to lunch. She heard a set of boots clomp up beside her. She looked over just as Eliza fell in step with her. "Good Lord, Grace, who was that? He's gorgeous."

"Nobody." Grace picked up her pace. She felt a mixture of jealousy and embarrassment swirl in her tummy at Eliza's assessment of Jonathan. She definitely did not want to discuss *him* with *her*. "Just a guy I know from . . . before."

"Just a guy, huh?" Eliza threw her a quick, skeptical look as they stepped to the side of the mess entrance. They had been instructed to enter the building as a unit today.

Eliza pressed on. "It looked to me like that beautiful 'just a guy' only had eyes for you. If I didn't know any better, I'd think he was interested in you."

"No, definitely not. Jonathan is just a friend. No . . . more like an acquaintance. I barely even know him, to tell you the truth. Just forget it. We can't . . ." Eliza's hand on her arm made her stop. Grace sighed. "Oh, just forget it. Okay?"

"Well, lookee here. Miss Cool, Calm, and Collected is babbling. Wait, do you like him?"

"Him? No! Ugh, absolutely not."

"You're babbling again."

Grace stopped and drew a deep, calming breath. "My nerves are all over the place, okay? I mean, I can't believe I passed out like that in front of everybody. In front of the WAAC director, Colonel Faith, and—oh my God—Dr. Bethune. I am so embarrassed."

"It happens to the best of us." Eliza looked her over, smiling when her eyes reached Grace's face. "You're blushing."

Grace rubbed her cheeks. "That's ridiculous. I'm too dark to blush. It's just the heat."

Eliza stared at her like she didn't believe one word that had come out of Grace's mouth. After a short laugh, Eliza resumed their march into the mess hall. "Just a guy. Girl, please. It's written all over your face. You've got it just as bad as he does."

"No, I don't."

In the past, Grace had always relished being the one who stood out. That is, when she was onstage. But today? She would rather be just another soldier. No one seemed to be giving Eliza or Harriet a hard time just because they happened to know Dr. Bethune prior to joining the corps. So why did it have to be such a big deal that she had met Jonathan Philips before today?

And now him showing up like this at Fort Des Moines? She still had his business card, the one he had given her in case she ever had any problems once she joined the corps. The irony was that she had not called him. Even though she had been the one to help iron out the plan for the Negro trainees' calling campaign, Grace had not actually called anybody when it was time for action. Unlike the other women, she didn't know anybody else with the connections or enough fame to make a difference.

Grace grabbed a tray and utensils as the lunch line moved forward. If they were lucky, they'd be having that tasty meat loaf again. And if they weren't so lucky, it was the sloppy joes. It was hard to tell, since the appearance of all these D.C. bigwigs had caught everyone by surprise. She frowned once she got to the serving counter. Hot dogs and potato salad. She eyed the plate suspiciously as she lowered it onto her tray. She hadn't eaten anyone else's potato salad besides the upstairs neighbor Mrs. Perez's since she was a small child. Though it was a simple recipe, potato salad required a practiced hand to come out right.

She gave the mess cook a pasted-on smile and said, "Thank you." He blinked at her blankly like she wasn't even there. Grace decided then that her portion of potato salad would be going right into the trash. Untouched. The two boiled hot dogs would have to sustain her.

She sat down at one of Third Company's usual tables. Thankfully, those damnable COLORED signs were absent. "I guess someone had the good sense to remove them before Dr. Bethune could see them for herself," Grace grumbled.

It was more likely that the signs had been removed so as to make the Negro WAACs' complaints look false or like they were overreacting to having been separated from the white WAACs.

"May I sit next to you?" Grace looked up and nearly fainted again. Dr. Bethune stood beside her with a pleasant smile on her face as she waited for Grace's response. Grace immediately stood up.

"Of course, of course. Please, sit." Grace held out the chair so Dr. Bethune could sit. So much for those hot dogs. There was no way Grace could eat them now. Her right hand began to shake. She slipped it under the table before Dr. Bethune could see it. She had admired this woman from afar for so long. She never imagined she would ever eat lunch with her!

"Aren't you the one who took that tumble earlier?"

Grace felt her cheeks warm. "Yes, ma'am. I'm so sorry for ruining the review."

"No apologies needed. It was so hot out there. I'm more concerned that you'll be all right."

"Yes, ma'am. I forgot to not lock my knees. There's so much to remember." Under the table, Grace began pressing Mozart's Fantasy no. 3 with her fingers into her thigh.

Dr. Bethune patted her shoulder like she imagined a grandmother would. Lovingly. Her soft hand warmed her. Grace's hands finally stopped shaking. "You'll be fine. I've heard good things about you."

"Me?" Grace squeaked. "You don't even know my name."

"Of course I do. You're Grace Steele. They used to call you the Mini-Mozart of Harlem."

Everything in Grace went still. She hadn't been called that name in years. *Dammit, Jonathan must have been running his mouth,* she thought. She didn't want anyone else associated with the WAAC to know that about her. "How—how did you know that?"

"I make it my business to know about all of the exceptional Negro youth in this country. That's why I made sure to have a WAAC invitation letter sent to your home."

Grace went still again. "That was you? You sent me that invitation?"

"Yes, I did. And I'm so glad you answered my call."

"Thank you for thinking of me. I . . . don't know what to say."

"You don't have to say anything. Just do your best. The race is counting on you. On all of you here."

"Yes, ma'am." Grace went silent. What else could you say after being told something like that? Dr. Bethune began to eat her lunch. Grace pretended to nibble on hers so as to not seem awkward.

"Dr. Bethune! It's so good to see you again." Eliza chose that moment to plop down on the empty seat across from them. "I don't think we've spoken since you called me out of the blue that day."

"Eliza Jones, my, how you have grown. I don't think I've seen you since you were—what—in high school?"

Grace couldn't help but feel like she was eavesdropping on a private conversation. She pushed back her chair and stood. "Excuse me. I'll let you two catch up."

"It was very nice to meet you, Auxiliarist Steele."

"It was an honor to have met you, ma'am."

Their afternoon training schedule was thrown off because of the unexpected officials' visit today. As a result, Third Company had a longer gap than usual between mealtime and the next activity. Grace planned on using her free time to go outside. And maybe just breathe.

ELIZA HATED TO see Grace go so abruptly. She knew that Grace had never met Dr. Bethune before today. She had hoped that by sitting down she could help them get to know each other better. Instead, Grace had sat there awkwardly pushing her food around with her fork. Honestly, Eliza didn't know Dr. Bethune that well herself. She was a friend of her parents', and they had always been around before to help facilitate the conversation.

At the thought of her parents, a wave of longing rushed over her. This was the first time Eliza had had a chance to think about them since she had arrived here.

"I imagine you heard from my father after I left."

Dr. Bethune chuckled. "Not from him directly. I imagine he's too mad at me for encouraging you to be here. Your mother said you ruined his dinner party with the Marshalls."

Eliza grinned. "Yes, I sure did."

"Normally, it isn't my place to encourage young ladies to defy their fathers. But in this case, I'm proud of you." Dr. Bethune beamed at her. "And so is your mother."

"Now you're just being kind." It's not that Eliza didn't believe the older woman. But when they had last spoken over the phone, Eliza had barely been able to get a word in. Mother had prattled on about her Housewives' League committees and war bond fundraisers, then rushed Eliza off the phone when Daddy came home. She hadn't spared a breath to tell Eliza that she was proud.

"She told me so herself. She's told me a lot about you over the years. She said you've become quite the cub reporter since you returned from school. Perhaps you should write her a letter. You know, 'report' on what your new life is like."

"That's a great idea, Dr. Bethune. Thank you."

A photographer from the local newspaper approached them

and asked Dr. Bethune if she would mind if he took their picture. "It'll most likely wind up on the ANP wire," he added.

"Not if my friend here doesn't," she responded.

"That would be swell. Daddy will have a fit when he sees me in an Associated Negro Press lead story when he could've had an exclusive scoop." Eliza chuckled.

"That's the spirit, dear."

COLONEL HOBBY AND Dr. Bethune left right after lunch, so it was back to work. A few hours later, Eliza practically collapsed onto her footlocker. It was such a relief to get off her feet, even if it was only for a moment. She leaned down to rub her calves. They'd just run at least five miles for the second day in a row. Her legs were screaming.

"Soldiers, attention!"

She, along with everyone else, quickly stood at attention next to their footlockers, as they had been instructed when they had first arrived. Her shins burned at the sudden movement. She did her best not to wince.

Lieutenant Rogers strolled into the bunk room. Jonathan Philips stood a few paces behind. Eliza could see him peripherally. She dared not look anywhere but straight ahead, though. Rogers's tone was all the indication she needed to know that he was not in the mood for even the smallest error right now.

"It has come to my attention that you ladies have been scheming behind my back since your arrival here. You've been organizing a telephone campaign, getting all of your mommies, daddies, and whoever else the hell you know to call up the top brass in Washington about what goes on here. That you don't appreciate being broken off into separate units like it's been done in the armies across the world for millennia." He paused. "Well, tough shit."

He used the last word to emphasize his disgust. A few of the women gasped their shock at his use of the expletive. Eliza could see Mr. Philips bristle at the word as well.

"This here is the United States Army. I don't care if they've classified you people as auxiliaries or whatever some busybody up in D.C. wants to call you. At the end of the day, you are under my command, and you'll do what I say. No. Questions. Asked. Is that clear?"

"Yes, sir," they all responded in one voice.

"Good. If you don't like what we do here, or how we do it, you are free to go down to base HQ and ask to go home. They'll be more than happy to type you up a dishonorable discharge and send you on your way."

Eliza heard Grace, who was standing right across the aisle from her, gulp. *Has Grace been thinking about quitting already?* Eliza shot her a worried glance. She didn't like where the lieutenant was going with this. Grace gave her an almost imperceptible shake of her head. Throughout the course of his reprimand, he had been pacing up and down the aisle at the center of the room. But now he stopped just in front of Grace. He turned his head to look directly at her.

"It also seems we need to have a little chat about fraternization with you ladies. Dating, flirting, and/or associating with persons above or below your rank will not be tolerated. That includes staff members from the War Department who may or may not be enlisted themselves. Do. I. Make. Myself. Clear?"

Eliza watched Grace as she said, "Yes, sir," right back in his face, loud and clear. That was the moment that Grace became her hero. Eliza smiled at her boldness. But only because the lieutenant's back was to her.

"Now, hold on a minute. These are ladies. That's taking it too far," Jonathan jumped in.

"I'm preparing these here soldiers for war. *These ladies* could wind up dead if I *don't* take it far enough," Rogers growled in return. "So if you do not like my training methods, again I say tough shit. You are free to go at any time. You are not my superior and I do not have to answer to you," he added in a lower voice, but still audible enough for all of them to hear. "Sir."

"Good day to you then." Jonathan left. There really wasn't much more he could say to what the lieutenant had said, no matter how dismissive it was.

"Now, back to you people's attempts at a mutiny."

More gasps went around the room. They might have been new to Army life, but they all knew that accusations of mutiny were not something to be taken lightly.

"I just want to know who the troublemakers are. Which one of you decided to ring up that meddlesome Bethune person, who then called up the goddamned *director* of the damn Women's Army Auxiliary Corps, and brought them to *my* doorstep? Tell me who that was, and I'll go easy on the rest of you."

Eliza could see Harriet West, who was standing a few bunks down from her, shift as if she were about to step forward. It was no secret that Harriet had worked for Dr. Bethune just prior to joining the corps. No one was going to fault her for calling her old boss. They were all in on the plan together. No, Eliza would not let Harriet take the fall for it all by herself.

Eliza stepped forward before Harriet could move, despite her tired legs, just as Grace did the same. They both said, "It was me," at the same time.

Harriet then got over her shock enough to move. "No, it was me."

One by one, everyone else in Third Company stepped forward. A chorus of "me too" followed suit.

"Oh, so I have a bunch of smart-asses on my hands?" Rogers came and stood between Grace and Eliza. He looked back and forth between the two of them.

"Then the two of you must have been the ringleaders. Follow me."

"Yes, sir," they said in unison.

Rogers began walking toward the exit. Both Grace and Eliza followed as ordered.

"The rest of y'all will have lights out an hour early. And no more telephone privileges until I goddamn say so."

CHAPTER 12

GRACE DUG HER shovel deep into the waist-high pile of horse manure. Doing so unleashed a fresh assault on her olfactory system.

"Jeez, who would've thought that it could smell any worse?"

Grace narrowed her eyes at Eliza's latest complaint. The two women had basically been joined at the hip for the last week. Not by choice either. Since even before they had gotten on the same train to Des Moines, this woman had been . . . well, *there*. A constant thorn in her side.

"Mmph," she grunted in response. Grace was not interested in engaging the other woman. Actually, she was loath to do anything that required opening her mouth. The last thing she wanted was to have the taste of this stuff on her palate too.

Eliza stared at her for a moment. When it became obvious that Grace had nothing to add to her grunt, Eliza shrugged and swiped lazily at her pile of dung. Grace frowned, then returned her attention to her own pile with renewed vigor. At this rate, they'd be spending the rest of their Sunday "off" mucking these stalls. This was not at all how she pictured her first week in the Women's Army Auxiliary Corps ending: already on her commanding officer's bad side and elbow-deep in crap.

"This really isn't fair," Eliza began again a few minutes later. "I'm getting Dr. Bethune back on the phone when we get out of here.

I don't see how these stalls are our responsibility when we're not even part of the cavalry. The Army guys here barely tolerate our presence. And that's just for the hint that we'll be taking over their administrative jobs when we're done with training. I doubt they'd ever let us ride any of these horses on 'official Army business.'" Eliza stopped and wrapped her arm around her shovel handle so she could make air quotes with her fingers.

With this latest round of Eliza's complaining, Grace stabbed the point of her shovel deep into her pile. She had had enough of this silly girl's antics. "The way I see it, it was calling up Dr. Bethune the first time that got us into"—Grace swept her arm around the stall like the most practiced of debutantes—"this—this . . . crap."

Grace was so annoyed that she forgot where she was and took a deep breath. That was a big mistake. All that got her was a giant mouthful of earthy, ancient dung smell. Grace doubled over in a coughing fit.

Eliza dropped her shovel, with the handle falling right into her pile, and came running over to Grace. "Oh my goodness, are you okay?"

Eliza patted Grace's back. Grace stiffened and gave Eliza a wide, horror-filled side-eye as she gasped for air. She sidestepped out of Eliza's reach. "I'm fine. Just fine."

She removed her gloves, shoving them into her back pocket, before reaching for her canteen. Grace took a long chug of water from the metal container. She coughed a few more times. Then, as unladylike as it was, Grace spit into the dirt near her foot.

Eliza's face wrinkled in disgust. She shook it off and moved toward her again, her hand raised and aiming for her back.

Grace held up her hand. "No. Please. Please don't touch me again. I'm fine. Really."

Eliza froze, her hand still up in the air. "But you—"

"I'm *fine*."

Eliza flinched at the way Grace ground out the word "fine." Grace had a momentary twinge of guilt. *What is wrong with you? She's just trying to help.*

Grace cleared her throat and tried again. "Thank you. But I just need a second."

Eliza turned back to her work with a pout on her face. "Well, you didn't have to be so mean about it."

This last comment made Grace see red. She straightened. "I'm sorry, what did you say?" Grace spied a pitchfork hanging on the far corner from them. It was probably a good thing it was so far away from them right now, for both of their sakes.

"I *said* you are being mean. And you have been acting mean to me ever since we met. For no reason, I might add." Eliza sucked her teeth as she studied her discarded shovel, its handle cushioned by the manure below it. She put her glove back onto her hand. Eliza reached and pinched the wooden pole between her thumb and forefinger. She looked up to the ceiling. "Lord, why does this have to be so disgusting?"

Grace looked up, mocking her. "Lord, why does she have to be so . . . *annoying?*"

Eliza marched toward Grace, her gloved fist now tight around the shovel handle. Her mouth was pulled into a taut line. Her nostrils flared hard with each exhale like an enraged bull's. When she was close enough, Eliza poked Grace in the chest with her finger. This time Grace's horror was justified. It was the gloved finger Eliza had used to pluck the shovel handle out of the manure pile.

"What is your problem with me?" Eliza punctuated each word

with additional finger jabs into Grace's chest. "I've been nothing but nice to you since we first met in New York. But you . . . you've done nothing but give me the cold shoulder and snide remarks in return. As a matter of fact, you've been giving the rest of us the ice-queen treatment. It makes no sense. These white Army boys don't want us here, and a good number of those white WAACs aren't happy to see us either. We should all be pulling together. We're all we've got here. What is wrong with you?"

Grace stretched her neck, taking advantage of their height difference to hover over Eliza. Grace took a step forward, purposely walking into Eliza's still outstretched finger. "Nothing is wrong with me."

Eliza gasped in shock, taking a step back. But to her credit, that was the only ground that the shorter woman yielded to Grace. Eliza narrowed her eyes, then pressed a second finger into Grace's chest, like she was pointing a gun at her. "Then you are delusional on top of being a bitch."

They both flinched at Eliza's use of the curse word. Grace gave her a half grin. "So Miss Moneybags knows how to use naughty words when she wants to?"

"I grew up in a newsroom." Eliza shrugged with a one-sided smile of her own. "When I was real little, sometimes the men forgot I was there. I've heard every bad word that's *not* in the book."

"I didn't think you had it in you."

"Well, it's not like I *want* to talk like that. But in this case?" Eliza frowned. She gave Grace a side-eyed once-over up and down. "I just call it like I see it."

Grace snatched up her shovel and got back to work. "Well, you're wrong."

"Ha!" Eliza sashayed back to her pile. Even though she stomped as she did it, it still looked like she was almost floating with—well, grace—as she did it. How did she manage to pull that off?

Maybe this girl isn't so bad after all, Grace mused. *She'd still be useless in a fistfight, though.*

"Okay, maybe I have been a bitch. But not without good reason to be." Grace sighed as she heaved another shovelful. "I wish I had the luxury to pick up the phone and ask Mary McLeod Bethune to get me into the corps. Or had extra money to buy the prettier dresses or to pay for me to go away to school. I didn't have it easy like you back home. The whole family had to scrape together to get the little something we had. And then I lost . . . I gave up everything to come here."

"And you think I didn't?"

"Maybe you did. I don't know. But whatever it is you gave up, I'm pretty sure you can get it back. I'll never get back what I lost." Grace felt tears threatening to spill. She blinked them back. "Damn. Have you ever felt like whenever we seem to get one foot forward, the world is determined to push us two feet back?"

"Yes, girl, every day," Eliza admitted. "Every single damn day."

Eliza drove her shovel deep into the pile this time. With a grunt, she heaved a giant haul into the wheelbarrow. "Now maybe if you'd stop lollygagging and actually put in some work, we can get this done before the sun goes down."

"So I'm the one who's lollygagging now?" Grace's eyes squinted with a newfound respect for the woman. Not that she would actually tell her about this newfound respect. She turned around and pulled up another shovelful of poop. The muscles in her shoulders burned, but Grace kept at it in a steady pace. She'd heard a rumor in the barracks that there would be a turkey and dressing dinner in the mess hall tonight. There was no way she'd be missing out on that.

CHAPTER 13

Fort Des Moines, Iowa
July 1942
(Week Two of OCS)

"PICK UP THE pace, Jones," Lieutenant Rogers hollered into his bullhorn as he rumbled past her in one of those open-top Army vehicles. "Whoever comes in last has to run an extra mile. Again."

His warning was clear. Eliza had been the last one to come in for the past week. She had had to limp out an extra mile every day while the others had been ordered to not help her. They could only watch.

Prior to training camp, Eliza had thought the hardest thing she had ever done in her life was stand up to her father. She was wrong. Now her shins were on fire. She estimated that she and the rest of the company had already covered the first two miles of this morning's three-mile run. The rest of the pack looked to be at least a quarter mile ahead of her.

"C'mon, girl." Mary, one of the other slower runners in the group, was a few paces ahead of her. "You got this."

Mary adjusted her stride to a pace that allowed Eliza to catch up to her.

"No, you go on. This is my struggle, not yours."

"No, E. It's all of ours. All for one, right?"

Eliza gnashed her teeth together and pressed on. So far, she had aced all of their other classes: basic commands, the Army and WAAC chains of command, map reading, and first aid. She imagined that she would've also aced firearms and munitions had the powers that be allowed them to carry firearms. But when it came to the physical part of the curriculum, Eliza was a complete failure.

While she had never been the most athletic type, she never considered herself to be the lazy sort either. She would swim at the Harlem Y whenever she could as a child. Granted, that occurred less and less as she grew older. She also had spent a lot of time running after stray balls when she watched the boys play stickball in the street. But those had always been short sprints, never these longer distances that the Army required.

Eliza slowed her stride as her chest started to burn. She thought the Midwest was supposed to be all wind and flat plains. She never gave a thought to the oppressive summer heat. Had she done so a few weeks ago, she most likely wouldn't have been so eager to be here now.

Finally, she stopped. Just for a minute.

"Are you all right?" Mary was looking back at her over her shoulder.

"I'm fine. Just need to catch my breath." Eliza leaned down and rubbed her leg. It started to cramp despite her efforts. "Oh no, not now. Not again."

"C'mon. I'll walk with you." A shadow loomed over her as someone tugged at her elbow. "The best way to stop a leg cramp is to keep moving."

Eliza stood up. To her surprise, the shadow belonged to Grace.

"Okay," she said warily as she gingerly took her first step. It had been a week since they had had their come-to-Jesus moment in the horse stalls. Since then, they hadn't spent much time with each other one-on-one. This wasn't intentional, more a result of the intense training days that were now their lives.

Eliza noticed that, while everyone else seemed to be naturally forming bonds with each other, Grace tended to hang back from socializing. She seemed to be more of a loner. On the surface, Grace came off as arrogant, stiff, and a know-it-all. Eliza wouldn't say that she was shy. More defensive, but that didn't feel like the right word.

To Eliza, she seemed more . . . melancholy.

"You know, Rogers is going to pop an artery when he sees you helping me." By now, they had increased their pace to a brisk walk.

"Yep, he probably will." Grace continued to look straight ahead. However, she had yet to let go of Eliza's arm. Eliza tried to pull away gracefully, but Grace's hand stayed where it was.

"He's going to stick you with another gig," Eliza warned.

"I imagine so. I hope it's kitchen prep this time. I prefer peeling potatoes to cleaning out the horse stalls."

"Yuck, both sound horrible to me."

Grace chuckled. "I imagine they would."

By now, the pain in Eliza's legs had begun to ease. "Well, I'll be doggone, you were right. Moving my legs does make them feel better."

Their conversation was cut short by the rumble of an approaching vehicle. When it stopped right beside them, Rogers jumped out.

"Steele, what the devil are you doing?" he screamed in Grace's face. She didn't flinch, but Eliza sure did. Come to think of it, Rogers spent a lot of time in Grace's face in particular. Eliza had yet to see Grace flinch.

"I was helping her."

"I didn't command you to do that."

"Yes, but—"

"See, that's what your problem is, Steele. There is no room here for 'yes, but' or 'I was just trying to help.' I bet you're one of them free spirit types. You always think you're the exception to the rule."

"No, sir, I—"

"There you go again with some exception, with some excuse. When are you going to get it through your thick skull, soldier? You are not exceptional. I don't care who you thought you were in the civilian world or who your little boyfriend down in Washington is. Here, you are nothing. Just like everyone else. Now, fall back in line."

Eliza watched Grace's jaw tighten. "Yes, sir." She saluted him and began to run on ahead. But Eliza could feel the anger radiating from her by her stiff posture.

Rogers returned his attention to Eliza. "As for you, when we get back, make it two extra miles for you."

"Yes, sir."

Eliza began a slow jog. Her legs were still on fire, but she was going to get through the rest of the run, plus those two extra miles Rogers just tacked on. She made a mental note to speak with Dr. Vera later on about what she could do to get her legs and feet with the program. She couldn't figure Grace out. One minute, she acted like she hated Eliza's guts. The next, she was shielding her from Rogers's wrath. But because Grace had stepped up for her once again, Eliza now felt fired up on the inside to push through the burn.

CHAPTER 14

Fort Des Moines, Iowa
August 1942

AS GRACE STEPPED off the bus that had brought them into town, the first thing she saw was the newspaper headline: "Army Will Send Our WAACs to England to Help Troops." She hurried over to the newsstand and dropped her nickel into the hawker's hand. She quickly began to scan the front page for the accompanying story. Her eyes widened.

Eliza peeked over her shoulder. "What is it? What does it say?"

A grin broke out across Grace's face. She rolled up the newspaper and swatted Eliza on the shoulder with it. "It says they're sending us to Europe."

"Us?" Eliza gestured her finger between the two of them.

"Us. WAACs. What's the difference? What matters is we are about to go places." Grace tucked the paper under her arm. As she turned the corner onto Center Street, there was a little extra swing in her step, despite being in uniform.

She loved coming into town whenever they were given leave to do so. The Negro community in Des Moines had embraced the thirty-nine women in the first WAAC officer training class with open arms. Whether it was to give a word of encouragement, a place to worship, or a much-needed press and curl, the local Negro community had been a breath of fresh air to the trainees. Today was no different. Dressed in their khaki off-duty Army uniforms, they stood out among the civilians passing them by on the street. Almost everyone nodded as they passed. More than a few smiled wider upon seeing them.

"How do you do?" Grace smiled back. But never too wide. While the appreciation of what she and her uniform represented had made her proud at first, she still didn't enjoy the extra attention. It only increased the pressure she put on herself to always be perfect, to never forget that everything she did didn't just represent herself or her family. She was representing her entire race.

Grace reached up to rub at the ever-increasing tension gripping her neck. She exhaled as the discomfort began to ease. Some days, she swore she carried the entire weight of Negro America on her shoulders.

"Are you all right?" Eliza's brow creased.

Grace waved her concern away. "I'll be fine once I get my head in Miss Hattie's shampoo bowl."

Eliza nodded in agreement. "I understand. I've been waiting for this all week. I swear that woman has magic in her fingertips."

"Hey there, soldier girls," a voice called out from the Billiken Ballroom's doorway. The Billiken was the nightlife hot spot on Center Street. Even though Des Moines wasn't as flashy as, say, Chicago or Kansas City, it still attracted all the top music acts that were on tour. And when those acts passed through Des Moines, they all booked a gig at the Billiken.

A man dressed in the slick threads of the hepcat style emerged. He had his hair pomaded down to a slick shine against his scalp. "I hope you all are coming back later on tonight. We've got some cats from New York playing."

Now Grace really wished she weren't in any uniform—off-duty dress or otherwise. If she weren't so noticeable, she would have picked up the pace and scooted on past like she had never heard the man. But there was another part of her that was curious. It wasn't like she knew *every* jazz musician in New York City. Just most of them.

She stopped. "Really? Who do you have in from New York?"

"Earl Hines and His Orchestra. As a matter of fact, here's Fatha Earl coming up behind you now. Wanna meet him?"

Eliza squealed. "Absolutely. I love his music."

"No. Definitely not him. We have to go." Grace flapped her arm to get moving again. Doing so caused her newspaper to drop to the ground. She felt her stomach fall with it as she bent down to retrieve it.

"Hey, Earl," the man called out. "Come over here and meet these lady soldiers. They say they're big fans of yours."

"Of course, of course. I love me some women in uniform." Earl came around to face them. His mouth spread into his trademark smile upon seeing Grace. "Well, well. If it isn't the Mini-Mozart of Harlem herself. I was wondering where you had disappeared off to. I know you said you had enlisted, but"—he reached out and fingered the lapel of Grace's uniform—"I never thought I would bump into you in the middle of Iowa."

"Earl." Grace nodded tersely. Her eyes darted back and forth between the musician she admired the most and Eliza, who was staring at Grace wide-eyed.

"Wait. Grace, you know him? You know Earl Hines?"

"Of course we know each other." Earl laughed. "She's the only piano player I know who's almost as good as me. She's one hell of a composer too."

"Piano player? Composer?" Eliza grabbed her by the arm. Grace immediately snatched it back. "How did I not know this? Wait. Did he just call you 'Mini-Mozart'?"

Grace would have given anything for the sidewalk to open up right now and swallow her whole. "The Mini-Mozart nickname is a bit of an exaggeration. And I wouldn't really call myself a composer. I just scribble down some ideas here and there."

"If you're as good as he says, then you must come back tonight," the club promoter chimed in.

"Sam, put her down on the list as my guest. Her friend too."

"Already done. What's your name again, little lady?"

Grace imagined this was what a deer stunned by oncoming headlights must feel like. It wasn't that she kept her musical past a secret from her new life here. It was just that she made a point to not play anymore. She darted her eyes from Sam to Earl and finally to Eliza. That girl liked to talk too much for Grace's liking. How could she not blab about meeting *the* Earl Hines when they got back to base and that Grace knew him from back home?

"Sorry, Mr. Sam," Eliza cut in, to Grace's amazement. "We have graduation tomorrow. Gotta get our beauty rest tonight."

"You sure? Earl and them put on a helluva show." Sam nodded at Grace. "You already know they do. And I'm not sure how much more beauty rest you could handle because I think you're both stunning already."

Eliza nudged Grace in the side with her elbow as she whispered, "This guy is a piece of work."

Eliza then gave Sam her most dazzling smile. "Aren't you the charmer." She laced her arm through the crook of Grace's elbow. "But I'm afraid we must get going or else we'll be late for our hair appointments. And we can't have that now, can we?"

Eliza winked at Sam as they continued on. Eliza nudged Grace again. "Say goodbye to your friend," she whispered.

Grace gave Earl a weak smile. "I'm so sorry. They have us under curfew. You know how the military is." She shrugged.

"I understand. Well, don't be a stranger the next time you're home. The word on the street is that cat up at Juilliard has been asking about you."

She laughed as they started to walk away. "That's a good one. You always were the joker."

"I'm not laughing, Grace," he called out as they turned into the hair salon a few doors down.

Once the door closed behind them, Eliza sat Grace down in one of the chairs in the waiting area. They nodded at Miss Hattie, who was finishing up the client who was already in her chair. "I'll be with y'all in just a minute."

"Take your time. We're in no rush." Eliza turned to Grace. "Here I was, thinking all this time that you were some boring goody-two-shoes stick-in-the-mud. It's bad enough you were holding out on that hottie in the War Department."

"What hottie in the War Department?"

"You know, that Jonathan guy."

"Why does everybody keep bringing him up? I've told you all time and again, we only met that one time right before I enlisted . . ."

"Okay, right. Whatever, Grace. You expect me to believe that after finding out you've got more secrets? We've been living and training together for the last six weeks and I'm only finding out now that you're some kind of musical genius. Girl, spill."

Grace leaned back in her chair and sighed. Eliza was right. She had to stop being so uptight all the time. The funny thing was that she thought, now that she had been in an all-Negro, all-female work environment, she *had* been loosening up some amid their ca-maraderie. But there were just some things she couldn't bring her-self to open up about, something that made her hold back still. Just thinking about her old musical life resurrected waves of anxiety. She could talk about the classical music stuff all day. But Eliza was sure to ask about how she was so friendly with jazz musicians. Any talk of jazz and the clubs would ultimately mean that Grace would have to talk about Tony. And she just wasn't ready to go there yet.

Despite that, she had felt herself starting to come around. It had been the little things. Eating her meals in a group of women who had become her friends instead of eating all alone as she had back in college. The comfort of looking over either of her shoul-ders at any given time and seeing her sisters in uniform working as hard at perfecting their drill commands or preparing to train the first group of regular enlisted women as she was. But when it came to "the rules" . . . she just couldn't seem to shake her prim and proper ways.

"I don't know if I would go so far as to call myself a musical ge-nius. Once upon a time, I was a cute little girl who was really good at playing the piano. Until I wasn't."

"Until you weren't what?"

Grace shrugged. "You know how it is. You grow up and things change."

"Okay, I'm ready for you Army girls now." Miss Hattie tapped her now empty styling chair. Grace got up before Eliza could ask her anything else.

THE NEXT DAY, the thirty-nine Black women in the first class of WAAC officers were commissioned as third officers. Only a few of their families came for the ceremony, mostly due to the distance and the cost. That was the case for Grace's parents. Her father couldn't get away from his Pullman porter responsibilities. Mama was entangled with making gowns for one social engagement after another. Her biggest client was the chairwoman of a war bond dinner that night back home in New York. Grace knew that Mama could've passed the reins off to one of the assistants she had hired. But that was the thing. Loreli Steele was too much of a busybody to do that. She would rather claim bragging rights over a dress she had made over witnessing her daughter's greatest accomplishment to date.

Because of her last name, Grace was one of the last in her training class to be pinned a third officer. She wanted nothing but to peek down the line to see how much longer until Colonel Hobby and General Faith would make it down to her. But she was trained better than that. She continued to stand at attention. Tall. Proud. Disciplined.

Grace pressed her fingers harder against the sides of her thighs. She had had her doubts at first. Especially during the early-morning runs they had been ordered to take those first few days. But she had soon grown used to the rigors and structure of a soldier's life. In fact, she liked it. Unlike in the civilian world, she could rely on her fellow officers in training to get the job done.

She smiled to herself. Correction, they had had to figure out how to work together to get the job done or there would have been hell to pay. Even if some of them did not like each other. Especially when any of them weren't getting along.

Eliza still got on her nerves more often than not. But they had seemed to come to an understanding. At least, enough of one to work with each other without ripping each other's hair out.

But most of all, being in the Women's Army Auxiliary Corps had restored a sense of structure and discipline that had been missing in her life. It replaced a deep craving in her when she had lost her desire to play the piano, when Tony had been taken from her life.

No one had ever told her how to get her heart to abandon a dream once the dreamer stops dreaming.

Somehow, having the expectation of being perfect coming from an external source was a lot less stressful than placing that same expectation on herself and then having to maintain it. Perhaps it was because the Army had stripped her of all her outside responsibilities. She didn't have to worry about getting Mama up out of bed and getting her ready for the day on top of doing the same for herself, and then cooking breakfast for them both. She only had to worry about herself.

The crunch of military boots grew louder as the head brass made their way farther down the row of newly commissioned WAAC officers. They were getting closer. Her turn was coming soon.

Grace only had to worry about the things she could control: making her bed, keeping her uniform clean and wrinkle-free, perfecting her execution of the drill exercises, issuing commands, and studying the Army's manuals. She'd had no control over the state of her physical conditioning at first. Her mama had been right about that. But she knew if she kept at it, she would be able to keep up with their instructor and the rest of her company on their daily runs. And she had.

Army life kept her busy. Too busy to think about any guilt her mama had laid on her when she was packing to leave for Iowa. Too busy to grieve for her brother. Too exhausted to miss her old routine of practicing her scales and perfecting the Mozart piece that had been giving her trouble for months.

Yes, Army life suited her fine. Just fine.

IT WAS HER father's ego that kept Eliza's parents from coming. They could have easily made it a newspaper business trip by accepting the invitation of the local Negro paper's publisher, Mr. Morris, to stay at his home. Eliza's mother had graciously accepted the offer at first, but then awkwardly rescinded it not twenty-four hours later.

Eliza gave Mr. Morris a wide smile as he snapped yet another picture of her. She was grateful that he had volunteered to attend the graduation ceremony in her parents' place. But she wasn't naive. He was a die-hard newspaperman at heart, after all. She knew good and well that that picture would be front and center on the first page of the next issue of the *Iowa Bystander*. She wouldn't be surprised if he had already sold it to the other members of the Associated Negro Press syndicate. Too bad she was more interested in having her byline featured on the front page than a picture of herself.

"OH, COME ON now, baby girl. I know you can smile better than that."

Grace watched Eliza whip around, her face brightening at the sight of an immaculately dressed older woman.

Eliza held her hands up high and ran into the nearby crowd, screaming, "Mommy! You made it."

Bands of jealousy gripped Grace's throat as she watched Eliza throw her arms around her mother. The two spun in a circle as they embraced. Mrs. Jones had moved a mountain—her husband, Mr. Jones—to be here today. There had been nothing to stand in Grace's mama's way to get here but a pile of dresses, yet she was still alone on her special day.

Grace waited a beat before heading over to the Jones women's enthusiastic reunion.

"Hello. You must be Mrs. Jones." Grace extended her hand to Eliza's mother.

Mrs. Jones squinted as she struggled to place her face. She took Grace's proffered hand by the fingers and gave them a gentle shake. "I've seen your face before. Where do I know you from?"

"From around Harlem most likely, Mrs. Jones. A pleasure to meet you, ma'am. I'm Third Officer Grace Steele." It was Grace's first time using her new rank while introducing herself. She liked the sound of it.

"Oh my goodness! Of course! Weren't you that little girl they used to call 'Mini-Mozart'?"

Grace ducked her head, her face warm, hoping no one else had heard what Mrs. Jones had blurted out. Meanwhile, Mrs. Jones looked around the crowd.

"Is your mother here? I'd love to meet her. She must be so proud of all your successes."

"No, ma'am. She's chairing a war bond fund-raiser tonight, so she couldn't come," Grace lied. "You know how it is."

Mrs. Jones's smile flattened into an understanding line. "Yes, well . . . I'll just have to be a proud mama for the both of you girls. Now, let me get a good look at you. You all look so sharp in your uniforms."

Grace let Mrs. Jones wrap her arms around her shoulders. She closed her eyes for a moment, pretending that this was her own mama, and not someone else's, holding her. But that fantasy lasted only a moment. Everything about it was wrong. Mrs. Jones's embrace had been too tight, too loving. Her delicate perfume had the wrong scent—jasmine, not Mama's signature rose.

Mrs. Jones stepped back, giving Grace's arm a final squeeze. "I know it's not the same as having your own mother here. But I'm sure she loves you in her own way. Your being here does mean a lot to the rest of us back home."

Grace was grateful for the hot breeze that blew a bit of dust in her eye. She blinked rapidly as her eye began to water. "Thank you for that, Mrs. Jones."

Grace did wish Mama was here for her. Just this once. To be a mother to her instead of always bragging about Grace as if she were a showpiece.

Mrs. Jones handed her a handkerchief and patted her on the back. "Mothers are funny like that, aren't they? What's important is that you're here, living your life for you. Now, chin up."

Grace complied with the older woman's command like the good soldier she was.

"That's better. Now, would you care to join Eliza and me for lunch?"

"I beg you ladies' pardon," a deep voice interrupted. "But I was hoping Miss Steele—pardon me, *Third Officer Steele*—would do me the honor of dining with me this afternoon."

"Mr. Philips." Grace inclined her head.

Mrs. Jones's hand flew up to her chest and gripped the strand of pearls she was wearing. "Oh my," the older woman said breathlessly. She reached out and gave Grace's shoulder a nudge.

"You don't turn down lunch invitations like this one, dear," she whispered into Grace's ear. "Especially when the man inviting you looks like him. Grr-roar."

"Mother! Try to behave," Eliza scolded.

Grace blinked. She couldn't believe it. Mrs. Jones had actually growled. And loud enough for anyone in the vicinity to hear her, including Jonathan himself. Grace felt her cheeks warm.

Mrs. Jones smiled innocently as she backed away. Grace's

mouth fell open in awe. The woman had absolutely no shame. She could see where Eliza got her fearlessness from. But in this case, it wasn't about the apple not falling far from the tree. Pfft, the apple and the tree were one and the same.

Grace could see that Jonathan was trying to pretend that he had not heard Mrs. Jones's feline antics. But she could see that his tan cheeks and the tops of his ears had a little bit more color to them. He was struggling not to laugh.

"Excuse me for a moment, ladies," he choked out before turning around to wipe the corner of his eye with a linen handkerchief.

This whole scenario was becoming more and more embarrassing by the second. There was only one way to end the craziness. Grace felt like she had been backed into a corner. She didn't like it, but she couldn't think of any other way. She took a deep breath.

"Fine, Mr. Philips. I accept your invitation. But under one condition: we must go to lunch in the mess hall. I won't have anyone thinking the wrong thing about me because they saw us alone together in town."

"Oh, you misunderstand. I wasn't asking you on a date, Miss Steele. I was inviting you—all of you, really—to the gathering St. Paul AME Church is hosting in honor of you ladies."

Grace felt her cheeks, along with the rest of her face, warm even more. She felt like she had been on the receiving end of a blow to the stomach. But she kept her chin up and shoulders erect through sheer will alone. "Oh. My apologies for assuming."

Jonathan inclined his head. "So, does that mean you don't have a problem being seen with me in public now?"

Grace narrowed her eyes at him. "Not when it's at a church function. That's altogether different, Mr. Philips." She stopped herself just short of adding, *And you know it.*

"Wonderful. Can I give you ladies a lift then?"

"I came with Mr. and Mrs. Morris of the *Iowa Bystander* news-paper," Mrs. Jones interjected. "I think it would be best if Eliza and I rode with them."

"Then I can go with you too . . ." Grace started.

Mrs. Jones waved Grace's plea away. "With all his photography equipment, there isn't room for anyone else. Sorry, dear."

The fake smile Mrs. Jones threw at her made Grace sick. "Oh. Then I guess I should . . ."

Jonathan proffered his arm to Grace. "Come along with me," he finished for her. "I promise I won't bite."

The church was only a few miles down the road. But to Grace, the ride alone in the car with Jonathan seemed to go on forever. She had been so mortified at the thought of riding with him that she had insisted on sitting in the back seat of the Ford Deluxe. As they pulled out, she felt even more self-conscious that everyone who saw them drive by would think she, as a newly pinned officer, was putting on airs.

She was busy looking out the window as the more industrial side of Des Moines passed them by when he posed a question.

"Have you given any thought to what you'd like your work as-signment to be?"

"No, I figure they'll put me wherever the higher-ups think I am most needed. But I was excited to see in the paper that there seems to be a need for us WAACs overseas."

Jonathan's mouth straightened into a firm line. She didn't like the looks of that.

"What?"

"This is off the record, but the odds of the Army sending any of you Negro WAACs overseas are low, at least for now."

Grace sighed and looked out the window. She tapped the seat with her fist. "Is there a reason why? Wait, don't answer that. I already know."

"For the same reason that there are almost no requests for Negro WAACs stateside. None of the base commanders want to deal with the additional 'headache' of having to house and manage a unit of soldiers who have to be segregated by race *and* gender."

"Then what was the point of all of that?" She jabbed her thumb back in the direction from which they had come. "Why have us go through the spectacle of training us for six weeks in the middle of nowhere and then making a big show of making us officers. Every day I read in the paper about small Allied victories here and there. Don't think I haven't noticed that there hasn't been any hint of an invasion of France or Japan in the works for the near future. All you see on the newsreels is 'Support Our Boys' and 'Buy More War Bonds.' The whole propaganda campaign around the WAAC is for every woman who joins, that frees up one more GI to go fight overseas."

"Now you know what my everyday life is like back home in D.C." Jonathan sighed. "Grace, I'm not asking you about your expectations to get you all riled up. I'm asking you privately—despite your protests back there—because I'm in a position to help you get assigned to *something* that won't have you waiting around and to *somewhere* that isn't more isolated for a New York City gal like you than here."

"What are you saying?"

"I'm saying that the only posts that are thinking about taking in you ladies are the ones that already have a huge Negro GI population. Right now that would be out in Fort Huachuca, down on the Arizona-Mexico border, or deep in the Deep South, like Camp Hood in central Texas."

"Well, I'll just go wherever I'm needed then."

Jonathan stopped at a red traffic light. He twisted himself so he could get a good look at her. "You're not *hearing* what I'm trying to tell you. I can make a recommendation to have *you* assigned to Washington. Working with me."

"Oh." Grace leaned back into the seat. On the surface, a Washington assignment would be ideal for someone like her who had no experience living in a nonurban environment. But technically, the District still adhered to Jim Crow segregation, even if the practices there weren't to the extreme found farther South. She hoped it would be more along the lines of what she had, unfortunately, become used to here at Fort Des Moines.

The decision to take Jonathan up on his offer to help her didn't require a Ph.D. But from Grace's vantage point, she was stuck between a rock and a hard place. There was no way she could accept his offer to "put in a word for her" to get a choice assignment. Her colleagues had been making innuendos about the nature of her relationship with Jonathan since his first visit to the base. If she let him do this, that would be turning a spark into an inferno. But if she didn't accept his help, she risked being sent to a location that would either bore her to death or put her at the risk of death.

Jonathan pulled the car onto the grassy lawn that served as the church's parking lot. Behind the building, she could see tables, benches, and streamers that were in the process of being set up.

"You know I can't accept your offer to pull strings for me to work by your side. And you know why. Thank you for looking out for me. Maybe it's best for me to go with the luck of the draw. Either I stay here in Des Moines or I don't. Whatever happens, it'll be on my own merit."

Jonathan frowned. "I understand. Forgive me for putting you in such an awkward position. But if you change your mind . . ."

Grace tapped her pocketbook with a smile. "I still have your contact information."

"Good. Now, let's go see about getting some pie."

IN THE END, the "luck of the draw" wound up leaving Grace in Des Moines as a company officer assigned to help train the first batch of WAAC regular enlistees. The now second officer Grace Steele then served as a convoy officer along with Charity Adams, escorting the first batch of WAAC privates down to Fort Huachuca in Arizona. And then it was back to Des Moines to wait for her next assignment.

Eliza was initially sent back to New York as a WAAC recruiter but wound up spending the rest of the year out in the field. In the meantime, hundreds more white WAACs had been deployed to meaningful assignments around the country. Grace loved shaping the women who volunteered into soldiers who could drill with razor precision. However, it was disheartening to watch class after class of talented young Negro women essentially pile up at Fort Des Moines, all waiting to be assigned somewhere, while their white counterparts went on to have a more exciting start to their military careers.

Morale on base among the Negro privates went south quickly. It was hard for Grace and the other officers too when they—whom Dr. Bethune still called her "best and brightest"—had become nothing more than glorified babysitters.

SIX MONTHS LATER, when the first contingent of white WAACs were on their way to Europe, Grace was still waiting for an assignment. She finally broke down and sent a telegram to Jonathan Philips. It read:

TELEGRAM

PULL YOUR STRINGS.
I'M READY TO GO TO WASHINGTON.

CHAPTER 15

Des Moines, Iowa
September 1943

CONGRATULATIONS, FIRST OFFICER STEELE."

Grace smiled at Charity's use of her new rank. She and a number of the women who had been her classmates in Officer Candidate School had been promoted and pinned that morning. Their promotions were a result of the Women's Army Auxiliary Corps disbanding to allow for the new Women's Army Corps, or WAC. The WAC was an official part of the U.S. Army, entitling them to all the benefits that the male GIs and officers enjoyed.

Charity, who herself had been made the commanding officer over the incoming Negro recruits, smiled at her. "It looks like you're headed to Washington, D.C."

"I'm what?" Grace couldn't help herself from breaking out into a grin. She hadn't been allowed to go anywhere outside Des Moines since she first arrived over a year ago, except for the one trip down to Fort Huachuca in Arizona to escort a batch of Negro WAAC privates to their assignment down there. It had been an uneventful trip, aside from the base full of Negro male soldiers who apparently hadn't seen a woman of color in a very long time. Since then, Grace had been doing nothing but shaping fresh meat off the streets into well-trained WAAC soldiers.

Charity handed Grace a telegram and an envelope. "Here are your orders."

Grace took the documents and looked them over. "I don't believe it." But the words on the telegram transcript confirmed it.

Whatever excitement had begun to bubble up inside her quickly burst when she opened the envelope and saw who she'd be reporting to. A frown quickly replaced any signs of excitement on her face.

"What's wrong?" Charity's brow wrinkled as she looked over her friend. "I thought you'd be happy to be back home on the East Coast and in a big city again."

"I thought I would be too. Until I saw this." She passed the orders back to Charity.

"I don't see anything wrong. Looks like you'll be compiling reports about and from Negro soldiers in the field. Sounds a heap better than standing out in the sun all day teaching the newbies how to march."

"That part sounds wonderful. It's who I'll be compiling those reports with."

Charity scanned the document again. "It says you'll be reporting to Jonathan Philips. I still don't see the problem."

"*He* is the problem. Every time we're in the same room, everyone else starts getting the idea that we're . . . a couple. I barely know the man."

"I remember him now. That man only has eyes for you every time he comes here. He's a problem, all right. One I wouldn't mind having at all."

"Yeah, well, now the problem is my boss."

Charity sniffed back her laughter. That only made Grace ball up her hands. Had there been a piano nearby, she would have thrown her palms against the keys.

"It's not funny."

"No, it's not." Charity wiped her eyes. She nodded at Grace's fists. "But it looks like you've figured out already how to keep your hands to yourself."

Grace sighed, then smiled at her friend's humor. "Keep it up and it'll be you catching these hands."

Charity hid behind her hands in mock fear.

Two days later, Grace, along with Eliza, was boarding a train headed east. Eliza had been assigned to the recruiting pool immediately after they had finished training and stationed in the Northeast, mostly handling New York City, Boston, and all points in between. She had volunteered to tour the larger bases to "sell" the Negro WAACs to commanding officers in hopes of getting them more, and better, field assignments around the country. On this trip, she was headed to Fort Knox in Kentucky.

In the time between receiving her orders and actually boarding the train, Grace had learned that the organizational shift from WAAC to WAC had created a loophole that allowed Jonathan to pull the strings necessary to get Grace an assignment in Washington, D.C., without looking like he was directly involved in doing so.

The trip started out uneventfully. But an hour after they left Chicago, Eliza began to notice that one of the white female passengers had been staring at them in a way that was beginning to make her uncomfortable.

Negro WACs had learned to get used to the stares when they were in uniform. It was very unusual to see a woman of color in uniform in certain parts of the country. The Army had implemented a recruitment quota system based on population percentages. Negroes made up 10 percent of the American population. Therefore,

Negro women could be no more than 10 percent of the WAC's ranks. It was the same with the number of officers, making women like Eliza and Grace even rarer. By now, there were fewer than one hundred Negro women who had earned officer stripes in the entire country.

So neither Grace nor Eliza was surprised by the woman's stares. But what happened next was something entirely new. When the conductor passed through the car, the Nosy Nellie grabbed him by the sleeve. She whispered something to him with her eyes narrowed and her finger pointed in their direction.

"Sorry, ma'am. I can't do that. That is a military matter."

"Then send in an MP!" The woman's whisper had grown louder and harsher with each word.

Eliza continued to leaf through this week's issue of the *Chicago Defender* newspaper unbothered. She was more concerned with looking for the write-ups on the upcoming Negro League World Series. Her hometown team, the New York Black Yankees, hadn't made it this year. But she was looking forward to the matchup between the Washington Homestead Grays and the Birmingham Black Barons nonetheless.

A few minutes later, the conductor escorted two military police officers into the car. Eliza and Grace shared a look when they saw the two men but went back to reading their respective periodicals.

"Officers, I demand that you arrest those two Negresses over there."

Eliza looked up again. This time, Nosy Nellie's finger was pointed right at her. Now everybody in the car, including the MPs, was looking at them.

"Is there a problem?" Eliza folded up her newspaper and put it back in her bag. She would've stood up, but Grace held her arm.

But Nosy Nellie was knee-deep in her own indignation now. "There is no way that those two . . . *people* are officers in the military. Who ever heard of such a thing? My son is in the military. A private first class." The woman's chest puffed with pride as if she had earned the title herself. "There is no way *my* son would ever stoop down to salute someone like her."

Eliza put her elbow on the aisle armrest and rubbed her palm across her mouth. The gesture was the only thing keeping her from blurting out that she wouldn't be surprised that someone who had her as a mother would be so disrespectful. But on the other side of her, Grace was pinching the life out of her arm.

"Ow," she whispered. "Stop."

"That's what I'm trying to do. Stop you from doing something stupid."

"Are you going to arrest them or not?" Nosy Nellie had now scrunched up her face like she had been sucking on sour lemons all day.

"No, ma'am. I will not." The taller MP was firm and loud enough that everyone in the train car could hear him clearly. The woman gasped.

"If I arrest them and it turns out that they are indeed legitimate officers in the Women's Army Corps, I'd be in a heap of a lot of trouble." The MP was now looking straight at Eliza. "I'm not risking a court-martial for myself because of your intolerance. Good day, ma'am."

The MPs then marched up and saluted them both.

"Ma'ams."

"As you were." She nodded at them, mouthing the words "thank you."

But old Nosy Nellie wasn't satisfied. She had clutched the con-ductor's sleeve into her fist again. "I demand that they be moved. Isn't there a separate Colored car on this train?"

"Ma'am, we're not in the South. There isn't any segregated car."

The woman's face bloomed into a purple fury. "Well, I refuse to sit here with those imposters another minute."

"I'm afraid there are no more empty coach seats, ma'am."

"Then I demand to speak to your supervisor . . ."

Grace squirmed in her seat uncomfortably as the eyes of the other passengers volleyed back and forth between them and the upset matron. The conductor shifted his weight from foot to foot. "I'll see what I can do."

He rushed back down the aisle, pausing long enough to mouth *I'm so sorry* at them before exiting the car.

"We're not moving," Eliza called after him. Grace swatted her arm. She swatted her back. "Don't hit me. We paid to sit here just like she has. I refuse to be inconvenienced because *she* has a prob-lem. Our money is just as good as hers."

"Will you hush? Behaving like that while in uniform is what *will* get you hauled out of here by those MPs."

Eliza knew Grace was right. But she was just so tired of the disrespect. That woman could have just as easily turned back in her seat, minded her business, and spent the rest of her trip never having to look at them. Instead, she not only chose to make a spec-tacle of herself, but she also took the extra step of attempting to get her and Grace in trouble. Luck was on their side that a military police officer with some sense had been called in and that he had assessed the situation with a rational mind. It could have turned into a confrontation that went sideways so easily.

The conductor returned with a Pullman porter behind him. They stopped beside Eliza's seat. He cleared his throat. "I'm afraid I'm going to have to ask you both to come with me."

"Why?" Eliza and Grace responded at the same time.

"It has been decided that it would be more comfortable for everyone involved if the two of you completed your trip seated elsewhere." The man pulled at his collar. He obviously wanted to be anywhere but here. Eliza might have had pity on him, if he wasn't kicking them out of their seats.

Grace looked at the porter. "Mr. Graham, what's going on?"

Grace's use of the man's name threw Eliza for a second. She forgot that Grace made a habit of introducing herself to every porter she encountered on the train. Invariably, almost all the older ones knew her father.

"It's gonna be all right, Miss Grace. I promise." They shared a look filled with silent meaning. Mr. Graham's mouth quirked. Eliza felt herself relax.

"Fine. We'll go."

They both quickly gathered their things. Eliza just wanted to get this over with. One day, when she was a civilian again, she vowed that she would become a reporter with her own opinion column, even if it wasn't with her father's paper. She would rail against these discriminatory practices as long as there was ink in her veins.

The conductor ushered them past a now smug Nosy Nellie on their way out of the car. The porter carried their bags behind them.

"Serves you right. You people will learn to know your place, no matter how many stripes are on those uniforms," the lady called after them, loud enough for all to hear.

Mr. Graham chimed in just as loudly. "I hope you two will be comfortable in the first-class sleeper cabin we made up for you. I hope you don't mind. It's all we have available on such short notice. Nothing's too good for our ladies in uniform."

Eliza turned to smirk at the woman and then followed the conductor and Grace out of the car.

The first-class sleeper turned out to be the top of the line in the Pullman fleet. Even Eliza gasped when Mr. Graham opened the door to the compartment. This was no mere cramped sleeping quarters. The room took up the entire train car.

"This can't be real." Eliza ran her hand along the arm of a padded chaise. The car was split into a sitting lounge in the front and a separate bedroom in the back.

"These furnishings look like they were selected with royalty in mind. My goodness, there's even a piano in here." Grace placed her bag on the floor beside the small upright piano. "I'm scared to touch anything."

"Not quite royalty," Mr. Graham said, and grinned. "It's the president's. They refurbished it up in Chicago and we're hauling it back to D.C. on this trip. Under the circumstances, I don't think he and Mrs. Roosevelt will mind if a few of our lady soldiers enjoy it for a few hours."

Mr. Graham returned with a slightly upgraded meat-and-potato dinner. A note from the conductor accompanied the meals, expressing his apologies for the earlier inconvenience.

AT 3:30 A.M. THERE was a knock on their door. A groggy Grace padded to the door and answered it. It was one of the porters.

"Sorry to wake you, Miss Grace. Just wanted to let you know that we'll be arriving at Miss Eliza's stop in about forty minutes."

"Mm, okay. Thanks." She started to close the door, but the porter stopped her.

"It'll still be dark when we get there. We have one more stop before then. A quick one. But it's enough time for me to call someone to meet her at the station."

"Thanks," she said sleepily.

"You just tell her to make sure she waits outside. There's no Colored seating in the station. And they don't take too kindly to when we break the rules."

"Okay." Grace closed the door.

She nudged Eliza, who was asleep on the other side of the bed. "Get up. Your stop's coming up in less than an hour."

"Okay, thanks."

Then Grace climbed back into her side of the bed. She was asleep before her head hit the pillow.

AFTER TRAVELING FOR the last eighteen hours, Eliza was glad to be able to step off the train. But it was so dark out there. The chill of the early-autumn morning made her pull her coat tighter around her. The porter followed her off with her bag, but only far enough to set it on the train platform. The train itself never actually stopped but continued to creep along the track at a snail's pace.

"I wish I could stay with you longer, but this is just a whistle stop."

Eliza nodded. "I understand."

She looked around, unsure of where to go next. She was the only one who had gotten off at this stop. Finally, she saw a light come on inside the station. Good, at least she had somewhere to go to get out of the cold.

"I wasn't able to get in contact with my cousin. But you should be fine. Just wait in the meeting place like Miss Grace told you. Nobody should mess with you there."

The train's whistle blew as it began to pick up speed. It didn't register until too late that she had no idea what the porter was talking about or where the designated meeting place was. Tension crept into Eliza's neck. She didn't like feeling uninformed. Especially when she was stranded in the dark at an unfamiliar train station in Kentucky.

It'll be okay, she assured herself. *Just go inside. Find a phone. Call for a ride. The base can't be too far from here.*

She picked up her bag and made her way inside the station.

Inside, the man who she assumed was the station manager didn't look too happy to see her.

"You're not from around here," he drawled.

"No, I'm not. But if you would direct me to the pay phone, I'll be out of your way."

"Ain't no Colored phone here."

Eliza's spine went stiff. "Okay, then I'll just wait over there." She nodded toward a bench in the corner.

"Ain't no Colored waiting area in here neither." He spat. The wad landed just shy of her toe.

"Okay." She stood still, not sure of what to do next. The man took that opportunity to size her up.

"Since when did they start giving officer's stripes to Colored gals? Surely you don't expect no white folks to salute you. Let you order 'em around." He started walking toward her.

"If you would show me where the exit is . . ."

"You ain't gonna order me around," he slurred. Now he was in her face. The sour tang of the whiskey on his breath assaulted her nose. She felt sick. That heavy dinner that she had been gifted earlier now felt like a very bad idea.

"I'm sorry to have bothered you. I'll go."

He grabbed her by the arm. "You ain't going nowhere."

She dropped her duffel bag and braced herself to run. Unfortunately, the alcohol hadn't dulled his reflexes. He tightened his grip on her arm, then jerked her to the ground.

"If you're man enough to wear that uniform, then you're man enough to face the consequences when you don't follow the rules."

Eliza froze in horror as his balled fist connected with her jaw. Pain shot through her skull. Then everything went black.

"KNOW YOUR PLACE, GAL."

The thud of the last kick to her stomach reverberated louder inside her long after her attacker had run away than his last words had. Eliza lay on her side, curled into a ball with her hands protecting her head. She was too scared to move for fear of subjecting herself to another explosion of pain. She had no idea how badly the man had hurt her or what her injuries were. She hurt everywhere.

Even now, her memory of the attack had begun to blur into a series of kicks, punches, spit, and pain, as the shrinking lights of the train moved farther away into the night.

As her body throbbed in agony, all of Eliza's thoughts converged into one irrational thought: Grace had let this happen to her. Hadn't the conductor said that Grace was supposed to have told her where to go? Grace, who was probably still sound asleep in her first-class cabin while Eliza lay here on the floor covered in her own blood and a stranger's spit. Every inch of her body screamed in pain. Grace had *known* Eliza would be in danger, yet she had done nothing to steer her away from it.

Eliza had always thought of herself as a forgiving person. But she would never forgive Grace for leaving her alone to die at the hands of that monster. Or possibly worse.

Thank God he had not done his worst to her.

As she lay there shuddering, her vision began to go dark, and on the inside, all Eliza knew was anger.

Oddly enough, it never occurred to her during the attack or as she lay there after, alone on the concrete floor, to be afraid that she would die. Death was the last thing on her mind as she slid into unconsciousness. No, the last thing she thought of was her father and his smiling face mouthing the words "I told you so."

In that moment, she knew she had to live and recover as soon as possible, if for nothing else but to spite the old man. And because she couldn't let Grace get off that easy. She would live so she could confront the woman who had proven once again that she was not Eliza's friend. She wanted to ask her why.

WHEN ELIZA WOKE up, she had to squint against a flood of bright lights above her. She blinked rapidly. Her eyes burned.

"I'm alive."

"Yes, you are," a woman's voice came from beside her.

"Grace," she slurred. Eliza tried to push herself up, but a hand on her shoulder stopped her. Pain shot down her arm. She groaned.

"You got that right. God's grace indeed."

"No . . ." That wasn't the Grace she had meant. "Need to talk to—"

"Shh." The smiling face of a brown-skinned nurse came into view. "Don't move. You need to rest."

"What's . . . broken?" Eliza was slowly learning that if she spoke slowly and took shallow breaths her chest didn't hurt as badly.

"Some of your ribs. A fractured right arm. And a lot of bruising. You're a lucky girl." The nurse leaned in closer. "Did he . . . ? Were you . . . ?"

"No."

"Oh, thank goodness."

Eliza closed her eyes. She didn't want to hear any more about how "lucky" she was. "Lucky" would've been not getting beat up at all. She changed the subject.

"Do they know who did this to me?"

"Officially? No." The nurse bit her lip. She looked over her shoulder. Satisfied that no one else was within earshot, she leaned in to whisper, "But I have my suspicions."

Eliza blurted out, "It was the station manager on duty."

"Shh. Shh." The nurse's eyes widened in alarm. She patted Eliza's hair, then her blanket. "Let's not get ourselves worked up." She got up and pulled the curtain around Eliza's bed, giving them some sense of privacy, then returned to her seat, leaning in close again. "Some things are best kept to ourselves. Like I said, you were lucky. Let's keep it that way."

GRACE WOKE WITH a gasp. "Eliza?"

Silence.

"Oh no. Please don't leave yet."

She ran into the sitting lounge.

"Eliza!"

The room was empty. Eliza and her bag were gone.

"No. No. No!"

Grace pulled on her robe and slippers before rushing out into the passageway. It didn't take long for her to find the porter who had knocked on their door earlier.

"You! Where did she go? Eliza?"

"Miss Eliza got off about an hour ago."

"I didn't—I didn't tell her not to go into the station."

His mouth fell into a grim line. "That's not good. Not good at all." He looked at his watch. "It's going on six o'clock now. Folks should be awake. Let me radio in to have somebody check up on her. You go back to your cabin. I'll come get you."

Grace went back to her cabin and sat on the bed. *How could I have been so stupid?*

She had grown to become protective of the younger woman. Eliza was smart and world-wise. But she wasn't necessarily street-wise. Reading the room wasn't always her strong suit. That station was a room that Eliza definitely needed to read correctly.

Grace started getting dressed while she waited for the porter to return. It didn't take long.

She jumped up when he knocked. "Anything?"

"No, not yet. But I'll keep trying. I told some of the other guys too. We'll all keep trying."

Despite the porters' efforts, they were unable to get any word of what happened to Eliza as the train continued on to Washington, D.C. It was only when she arrived at Union Station and saw an unusually serious Jonathan waiting for her on the platform that she knew.

Grace ran up to him. "Eliza. Please. Tell me you know something."

He shook his head. Before he could say anything, she blurted out, "She can't be dead."

"No, she is very much alive. But she's in bad shape."

Jonathan ushered Grace into a cab before giving her the details. Eliza had suffered a fractured arm and a few broken ribs. She would live. No one had been arrested for the crime yet. Jonathan doubted that anyone would be.

"What about the police? The MPs? Isn't anybody investigating?" Grace shouted, startling the cabdriver.

"Sorry," Jonathan apologized to the cabbie. He turned back to Grace. "We'll do our best to get local law enforcement to follow up, do a thorough job. But it's Kentucky. You know how these things go."

"Send me back out there and I'll make them do it."

"That I cannot do. Even if it were in my power to do so, I still wouldn't." He brushed a stray curl out of Grace's face. The simple yet intimate gesture surprised them both. He pulled away. "I . . . I probably shouldn't have done that."

Grace huddled into the opposite corner of the back seat. She averted her gaze to outside the window. "Where are we going?"

"I . . . We set you up at a boardinghouse where one of the other Negro WACs in the office is staying. You've had a long, emotional trip. You must be exhausted."

She sniffed. "Not too exhausted to do the right thing."

"You're not a civilian anymore. Right thing or not, you can't go back there without permission."

"Tell them I went AWOL then. I don't care."

"But I do care," Jonathan blurted out, again surprising them both. He cleared his throat before continuing. "D.C. is my town. I can keep you safe. But only if you stay here. My office already has people looking into who attacked your friend. Let them do their jobs. Let me do mine."

The cab stopped.

"We're here." Jonathan got out and came around to open her door. She wouldn't look at him, instead taking in the whole block made up of row houses. She wondered which one would be her new home.

"It's this way." Jonathan started walking toward the one to their left. "Mildred stays here. You two were in the same OCS class, so you won't be surrounded by total strangers. Mrs. Wilson runs the boardinghouse. She's good people. A friend of my family."

Grace let him ramble on. The warm timbre of his voice alone calmed her frayed nerves. She could feel the tension in her upper body begin to melt. Jonathan's earlier observation had been spot-on. Exhaustion and the emotions from the trip had taken their toll on her.

"This is a good neighborhood too," he continued, oblivious to the effect he was having on Grace. "I grew up a few doors down. Let's see, she said I could find the key under the mat. Mrs. Wilson will be back this afternoon. She teaches over at the high school. Did I mention she was my geometry teacher too?"

Grace watched him as he fumbled around for the key. Like he was anxious. Was this a crack in his usual smooth, confident veneer? Her breath caught. Wait, was he on edge because of *her*?

She studied him again with new eyes. It had been about a year since Grace had last seen Jonathan. There were no significant changes in his appearance; only the black-framed eyeglasses he wore were new. They made him look even more handsome than she remembered. This protective thing he was doing now—she kinda liked that too. He claimed that he wanted to keep her safe. She wondered if his safety net included her wrapped up in his arms.

She cut herself off from entertaining that line of thought any further. No matter how attractive he might be, he was off-limits. War Department men and WAC women did not mix.

He pushed the front door open. "Welcome home."

"Thanks." She stepped inside. The front hallway was neat. The rest of the house smelled inviting, like a warm sweet potato pie. "Nice."

"Mildred said you can share her room. It's the first one at the top of the stairs on the right. I'll just . . ." He stopped to stare at her. She stared back at him. He was the first one to look away. "I'll just take your bag up. Then I'll be out of your hair."

"Okay." Grace smiled. He was definitely nervous. She followed him up the stairs.

The bedroom was tiny. She had no idea how both she and Mildred would make it work without falling over each other. Jonathan was of a considerably larger size than Mildred. Right now, she could barely breathe with him in the room.

He turned around with a start. "Oh, I wasn't expecting you to be so close behind me."

"Sorry." But she wasn't sorry. Actually, she was enjoying being the cause of his jitters. Grace wondered how far she could take this. "You were right. I am tired. I think I'll take a nap while I have the house to myself."

"Good idea. Mildred can get you up to speed on where to go for your first day in the office tomorrow."

"Great."

"Good."

They stared at each other awkwardly with him looming over Grace. She was the one who made the first move, reaching out to him. He followed, cupping her face in his palms. The kiss that followed surprised them both. Grace knew she should pull away. But her normal sense of discipline seemed to have disappeared. She wanted to be irresponsible on purpose for once.

He pulled away first.

"I . . . shouldn't have done that either."

"Perhaps. But I'm not complaining." The truth was she was glad that they had done that.

"We probably shouldn't do that again. There are rules."

"Agreed." That was a lie. Grace wanted more. But she didn't have the nerve to push Jonathan any further.

"I should go."

"Probably." Whatever spell had made Grace forget her normal reserve was gone.

"Okay. Well, goodbye. I'll see you tomorrow."

"Okay."

He let himself out, locking the door behind him. Grace lay down on her "new" bed. She had no regrets about breaking the rules just now. The warmth from his lips on hers remained as she drifted off to sleep. It had been . . . delicious. Grace licked her bottom lip. Too bad what she and Jonathan shared could never happen again.

CHAPTER 16

Washington, D.C.
December 1944

T HAD BEEN over a year since Grace arrived in Washington, D.C. In that time, she had settled into a rhythm: go to work, come home, help Mrs. Wilson prepare dinner, and, on weekends, meet her father for lunch whenever he passed through town.

Mrs. Wilson's home had none of the stress she'd endured back home with Mama. Well, except for Mrs. Wilson's well-intentioned attempts to get her to go out more socially. Mildred would always block those attempts with a good-natured "She doesn't have time for another boyfriend, Mrs. Wilson. She has her hands full with the one she has at work."

"I *do not* have a boyfriend," Grace would protest every time. But that never stopped the teasing.

Despite the rumors and occasional comments, Grace and Jonathan worked well together. His job was to report on the morale of Negro military personnel to the secretary of war. He also followed up on, and did his best to resolve, any problems that they faced. It was Grace's job to collect the data he needed to compile those reports. She had already implemented several processes that eliminated a number of the headaches Jonathan faced in his stressful position.

Grace now considered him a friend. Most times, she was able to ignore the underlying hum of attraction whenever she was too close to him. Thankfully, he never broached the subject of that kiss.

Everyone who worked with her said she had been a godsend to the office. Grace was grateful to finally be making a contribution to the war effort. She just wished she could do something more. Something closer to the action.

It was like an answered prayer when Charity Adams called her out of the blue one afternoon.

Charity didn't waste a breath after she said hello. "If I were to ask if you wanted to go to Europe, what would you say?"

"I would say, 'Hell, yes!'" The old Grace would have never sworn out loud like that at work. But she hadn't been that old stickler for propriety since the train ride that had brought her here to Washington, D.C. She paused for a moment to absorb both what Charity had said and what she didn't say. "Why do you ask?"

Grace could hear the smile in Charity's voice as she hung up with a promise of "I'll see what I can do."

But when Grace excitedly mentioned the brief conversation to Jonathan later that day, he shared none of her enthusiasm.

"If you do make it onto the list for the European unit, I'll do everything in my power to get you off it."

"What?" Grace's face heated with anger. Not just at the admitted betrayal, but at the nonchalant way that he had said it. The words had come out of his mouth in the same casual tone he would use to comment about the weather. "You know better than anybody that I'm a top performer. Why would you snatch away the opportunity of a lifetime from me?"

"It'd be better than having the Germans snatch away your life. The Navy might have gotten the upper hand over the German

U-boats lurking in the Atlantic as of late, but that crossing is still too dangerous. You've seen the reports. We're still losing one or more ships with every convoy. You can still go to Europe *after* the war is over."

She griped about Jonathan's threat later on to her roommate.

Mildred shrugged. "If it were me, I'd go over his head."

"Over his head? The only person he answers to is War Secretary Stimson. That man barely knows I'm alive."

"Then go talk to *his* boss."

"Who, President Roosevelt? Please."

"If that's what it takes." Mildred shrugged again. "How bad do you want to go?"

A few days later, Charity called again from Iowa. "Off the record, I put you on the list. But nothing is guaranteed."

Then Grace's other WAC officer friends started receiving their orders to report to Fort Oglethorpe in Georgia for overseas training. No such orders came for Grace.

When Mildred received her orders for overseas training the next day, she asked, "Did you call the president yet?"

Grace picked up the phone and took a deep breath. She hadn't felt this apprehensive about doing anything like this since her failed Juilliard audition over two years prior. She still didn't have the nerve to dial up the White House. She imagined its operators received more calls than any one person could count. This was a request she had to be sure did not get lost in the shuffle.

Instead, she called her old Fort Des Moines classmate Major Harriet West. Major West, along with Charity Adams, was the highest-ranking Negro woman in the WAC. She had been sent to work in WAC director Hobby's office immediately upon their OCS graduation, which meant she interacted with the top officials who could override Jonathan's interference. Grace asked Harriet to meet her for dinner after work.

At dinner, Grace explained her situation to Harriet. "I thought you might be able to put in a good word for me. Or maybe get Colonel Hobby or even Dr. Bethune to—"

"Girl, I can't even get myself on that overseas list. Any time I have to travel on behalf of the corps, Colonel Hobby demands to know the exact date and time I'll be back."

Harriet's job at WAC headquarters was to track and report back on Negro issues within the Women's Army Corps. It was similar to the work Jonathan did on behalf of the War Department.

"It sounds like I'm in the same bind as you. Mildred said I'd be better off calling the president."

"That call would never get through."

"That's what I told her."

Harriet thought about it for a moment. "You know what? I know someone who is an even better option . . ."

"Better than the president?" Grace blurted out.

Harriet shushed her, then looked around their immediate area. "Girl, lower your voice. You know everybody in this town is nosy."

Harriet fished a piece of scrap paper and a pencil out of her pocketbook. She began scribbling down a phone number. "Call this number first thing tomorrow morning. But for the love of God, if they ask, you did *not* get it from me."

THE NEXT DAY, Grace picked up the phone again. Her hands were shaking by the time the operator answered.

"How may I direct your call?"

Grace took a deep breath. It was now or never.

"I'd like to speak with Mrs. Eleanor Roosevelt, please."

She didn't speak with Mrs. Roosevelt directly, of course. But she was put through to her assistant, Malvina Thompson. Miss Thompson listened to her request, then ended the call with "I can't promise anything, but I will let her know."

At the end of the day, Jonathan stormed out of the office after what sounded like a difficult call. He gave her a withering look on his way out. Almost begrudgingly, he said to her, "I have to admit I didn't see that one coming. You've got guts, kid. Enjoy the trip."

Grace didn't have time to ponder on the confusing comment. Her phone rang almost as soon as Jonathan had slammed the door behind him.

"Captain Grace Steele?"

"Yes, that's me."

The operator on the line said, "Please hold for Mrs. Roosevelt."

"Mrs. who?"

A crackle of static was the only reply. A moment later, the very distinct voice of Eleanor Roosevelt said her name. "Captain Steele. Are you there, dear?"

"Yes, Mrs. Roosevelt." Grace felt her heart leap into her throat.

"Do you still want to be a part of the unit of Negro WACs who are deploying out to Europe?"

"Yes, ma'am," she said breathlessly.

"Good. Then you are to report to Union Station tomorrow morning to take the train down to Georgia. Your orders will be waiting for you at your boardinghouse here in town."

Grace yelped.

"I'm sorry. What did you say, dear?"

"I can't believe it. Thank you, Mrs. Roosevelt. Thank you so much!"

"My pleasure, dear. You ladies go over there and do me proud."

"Yes, ma'am."

Unlike the many other times she had left town on official business, Jonathan did not come by Mrs. Wilson's that night to say goodbye. His slight stung more than it should have. They were just friends. No, friends who worked closely together. Grace should still be mad at him for trying to take away her opportunity to go overseas.

She would be better off forgetting she was ever attracted to him.

The next morning, Grace joined Mildred on the train down to Georgia. Jonathan did not come to see her off then either. And she was okay with that.

Six weeks later, she was headed to Last Stop, U.S.A., Camp Shanks.

CHAPTER 17

Camp Shanks, New York
Late January 1945

IT HAD BEEN a hell of a week by the time Captain Grace Steele was able to step out of the officer quarters that had been set aside for Negro WACs at Camp Shanks, which served as the New York Port of Embarkation.

It had started with boarding a train in Fort Oglethorpe with an unknown destination, then getting off a day or so later in Weehawken, New Jersey. They could see a line of troop ships and ocean liners waiting at piers across the Hudson River, the famous New York City skyline in the background. She had bent down to grab a handful of the dirty snow in her gloved hands, happy to be so close to home again. The brown dirt mixed into the white snow was a welcome sight. Her latest stint in the Deep South hadn't been a walk in the park. Jim Crow aside, the red clay mixed with the snow they had down there had been a nightmare to get out of her dirty clothes.

Since their arrival at Camp Shanks, it had been a whirlwind of equipment checks, filling out paperwork, and practicing last-minute drills. She had expected the paperwork to verify her emergency contacts and permanent address. But it was a grim shock to them all when they had been sat down in a room to complete their

last will and testaments and designate their life insurance beneficiaries.

Grace's pen hovered over the spot where she was to write her
next of kin. A sense of dread wrapped around her as she placed her
pen tip on the paper and wrote out her parents' names. When she
finished, she said a quick prayer—more of a plea really—that her
parents not be put through the anguish of another dreaded visit
from an officer in uniform because of her.

Grace shook off the grim thoughts as she handed in her forms
to the administrative WAC seated by the door on her way out.

"I'm glad to have all that paperwork done and over with." Mildred, her D.C. roommate, fell in step beside her.

"Yeah, I was looking for adventure when I first signed up. Never
thought it would lead to me having to worry about wills and insurance beneficiaries so soon in my life." Grace sighed. She was
over thinking about these kinds of morbid matters. She wished
they could just ship out already and let whatever would happen to
them happen.

GRACE GOT HER wish the next day. Her back ached under the
weight of her pack and all the other assorted gear she carried on
her person. Nonetheless, she continued marching forward. Her
heavy-soled boots stomped against the pavement in step with the
rest of her company as they made their way toward the trains. The
cold wind coming from the east off the Hudson River slapped her
in the face, causing her to squint. The brim of her military-issue
helmet offered no protection from the elements. That wasn't its
purpose. Shielding her from German bullets and bombs was.

What a sobering thought. It had been almost twelve hours since
word came down that her unit was officially on "alert." That meant

she, along with almost five hundred other Negro women, were on their way into an active war zone. Her heart began to thump a little bit faster. She couldn't wait.

Their pace began to slow gradually. Grace could see that the seemingly endless flow of soldiers was beginning to bottleneck up ahead. She had never seen so many bodies assembled at once. There had to be almost ten thousand soldiers marching toward the trains. Surely they weren't going to cram all of these people onto one ship. "Stay in formation, ladies."

She knew the command she had given was superfluous. The marching columns made up by the women under her command were perfect. This was even more impressive when she considered how much gear they all were carrying—the weight would've given even some men trouble.

But her girls were special. Their mere presence, at overseas training in Fort Oglethorpe down in Georgia and now here at Camp Shanks, was a first for the Army and for the race. Never before had a unit of Negro WACs been ordered overseas. Not during the Great War, and definitely not in the one they were currently engaged in. There wasn't anywhere on base or off at Camp Shanks where they hadn't been stared at since they had arrived. There wasn't a day when some newspaperman, from the Negro press or otherwise, wasn't following one of them around.

There was no way to deny it. Grace's girls were a very big whoop-de-doo.

"Halt!"

The other troops surrounding them began to break formation. Their complaints soon followed. What was taking so long? The packs on their backs and the gear that they carried were too heavy. Would they even set sail that day?

Grace remained at attention. She gave her girls a side-eyed glance, daring them to utter any kind of complaint. But again, that had been unnecessary. Each woman in the company she commanded stood straight, looked forward, and spoke not one word. But at any given moment, almost all of them cracked a smile. They were just as eager as she to go to Europe.

Grace remembered how eager to please she had been during her first review at Fort Des Moines in front of Colonel Hobby, Dr. Bethune, and . . . Jonathan. She leaned over to the woman closest to her and whispered, "Don't lock your knees. That's an order. Pass it on." The woman complied with her order, passing the message to the WAC beside her.

Her thoughts floated back to Jonathan and how she never said goodbye to him before leaving D.C. Why did she have to think about him now? She had been so mad at him for attempting to block her from being in this unit, from being a part of this historical moment. Anger flared in her belly. It was quickly replaced by another wave of regret.

About twenty minutes later, a groan erupted across all the assembled military personnel. The word had come down that no troop ships would be heading out today or the next. Only then did Grace's company let their displeasure be known. But Grace smiled because she knew something that they didn't know. She'd already had her orders in the event that this happened. When they got back to camp, she would be informing everyone that they all had been granted weekend passes.

"WHAT ARE YOU going to do with your forty-eight-hour pass this weekend?" Grace asked Mildred once they were back on base.

Mildred's face broke out into a wide grin. "With New York City a few train stops away? Any and everything. The base newspaper says a new servicemen's club just opened in Harlem."

"Really? Where? I grew up in Harlem." Grace couldn't imagine where a USO club could be located where a GI couldn't get into some "good" trouble nearby.

"Um, somewhere on Seventh Avenue. 124th Street, I think. Sorry, I'm still learning my way around that area. I'm from Boston, remember?" Mildred smiled.

"Seventh and 124th Street? That's where the Hotel Theresa is located." Grace raised her eyebrows. After Sugar Hill and Strivers' Row, the Theresa was one of the most desired residential spots in Harlem. "I'm impressed. Anyone who was anybody lived there. I might have to check it out. Let me know when you plan to go. You never know who you'll see in there."

"Okay, I'm getting a group of us together to go. I'll let you know what time we decide to head out."

"Great. I hope to see you there." She nodded as Mildred turned in the direction of the camp post office.

Even as the words came out of her mouth, Grace knew she said them just for show. Her plan for her forty-eight hours away from base had nothing to do with hanging out with anyone she knew from the WAC. The agenda she had already worked out on her own included grabbing a dirty-water hot dog and a slice of real New York–style pizza and seeing if any of her old friends were still hanging around the jazz club on the corner of West 118th Street and St. Nicholas Avenue.

As much as she missed her father, she was not too keen on visiting her parents' apartment a few blocks away. The odds were hit or miss that her father was in town anyway. He said in his last letter that he was going on another trip South. However, it was a 100 percent guarantee that her mother would be there.

That fact settled her dilemma. Grace and her father had exchanged letters since she left for training camp, which was how she'd been able to stay up on how Mama's dressmaking business had picked up since Grace had left home. And then there were the times they'd been able to have a quick bite together in D.C.'s Union Station when his route passed through town while she was there. As for her mother, Grace had not directly communicated with her in any way since she had first left for Iowa.

After facing the grim reality of completing her last will and testament earlier, she felt like she owed Mama the courtesy of one last visit before she left the country. It wasn't like she had any real excuse not to. She didn't know Orangeburg, New York, or the rest of Rockland County that well, but she'd heard the locals mention that the New Jersey line was just down the road. That meant that they weren't that far up the Hudson River from Manhattan. "Home" was so close, even if the apartment on West 120th Street hadn't felt like home in a very long time.

Grace grabbed her overcoat and ran out the door. One thing was for sure: she would definitely miss the bus if she stayed here another moment trying to decide whether she would actually go home. She would just play it by ear once she was back in Harlem.

CHAPTER 18

Harlem, New York
Later that day

T HE SUN WAS just starting to sink between the apartment buildings up the street when Grace arrived at Henry Minton's place in Harlem. It was much too early for anything to be jumping off in the main room of the club. She went in anyway. Pops the bartender was checking the liquor inventory when she came in.

"Grace Steele! Aren't you a sight for sore eyes." He put the whiskey bottle in his hand down into the well. "I haven't seen you in a month of Sundays."

He stepped out from behind the bar with his arms outstretched. Grace put down her overnight bag and hugged him. The apron that hung loosely around his neck reeked of whiskey and scotch. The old Grace would have recoiled from it. But the scent now took her back to nights gone by. She squeezed him tighter.

"The WAC has kept me pretty busy over the last, what, three years."

Pops stepped back to get a better look at her. "Well, look at you. I see you with your officer's stripes. Let me guess. A major?"

Grace laughed. "Don't I wish. No, I'm a captain."

"Well, ain't that something. Baby girl came home with some

rank. I hope that Army isn't working those magic fingers too hard. Nobody's here yet if you want to mess around on the piano."

"Oh gosh no. I haven't really had time to practice lately. I was hoping to say hi to the guys and maybe listen in on a jam session later tonight."

"Oh no, it's too early for anyone to show up yet. You know those guys won't get here until it's good and dark outside. I guarantee most of them haven't even made it out of bed yet."

"That's what I figured. I guess I'll just head upstairs to the hotel and check in, drop off my stuff. Maybe someone will show up by the time I come back later."

"You do that. Most of the old gang still work upstairs at the Cecil. Walter. Eugene. Wallace. All of those jokers are too old and broken down for Uncle Sam to draft. Make sure you find them and say hello."

She nodded her head at the familiar names. "Thanks, Pops. I will."

Neither Walter nor Eugene was in the lobby. Wallace was at the reception desk, but an irate woman with a fluffy fur cowl around her neck was demanding all his attention. Grace waited a few minutes. But the woman would not let up on her complaints about her cold room and the inferior thread count of her sheets.

Grace picked up her overnight bag with the intent of going back downstairs to wait it out with Pops. That's when Jonathan Philips came through the door. The sight of him filled her with both a sense of dread and a flicker of mischief. She had wanted to spend tonight not thinking about work or her responsibilities as a military officer, or having to worry about propriety when one's superiors were in the room. But she was also relieved that it was him and not some other member of the WAC or War Department brass. Jonathan seemed to understand the more impulsive part of her nature, the side of her that needed to cut loose in a jazz bar sometimes to maintain her sanity.

She walked up to him and offered her hand. "Mr. Philips, I'm surprised to find you here. I would have thought the Hotel Theresa would be more your speed."

"Ah, Captain Steele." He took her hand with a smile and shook it. "You're actually acknowledging my presence. In public."

"I couldn't find a place to hide fast enough without making a fuss. So I figured I might as well say hi."

"Has hell frozen over?"

"No, but it looks like Manhattan has," she quipped.

He chuckled. "Clever."

She inclined her head. "I prefer to think of my wit as more brilliant than clever. But thank you just the same."

"Touché. May I?" He reached out for her bag.

"If you must." She handed it over.

He pumped his arm to test the bag's weight. "This feels like nothing."

Her overnight bag wasn't as heavy as it was cumbersome to hold for more than a few minutes. Army life had quickly taught her the necessity of packing light and efficiently.

"I'm only staying in town for the night. I don't need much for that." She shrugged. "What are you doing here?"

"The same as you, I imagine. I was hoping to run into some of the guys at the club before they head south for the night. But it's obviously too early for that."

"What do you mean 'before they head south'?"

"It has been a while since you've been home, hasn't it?"

"Only because someone kept me so busy down in Washington

that I could never get a weekend away." She missed this, the easy banter they had shared. She was glad to see that he wasn't holding any grudges against her for what she had to do, what he *made* her do, by going over his head to be here right now.

Jonathan smiled at her, amused. "Yeah, most of the guys you're used to seeing around here at Minton's have moved down to Midtown. I'm afraid the more innovative cats are starting to spend less time in Harlem. The better-paying gigs are downtown."

"Where downtown?"

"Down on East Fifty-Second Street."

"Where all the songwriter offices are?"

"You mean where they used to be. Now it's becoming the new hotbed for the bebop sound."

"Wow. I guess it has been a while since I've been home. I had no idea."

"Well, if you haven't been down to East Fifty-Second Street before, now is the perfect time to remedy that."

"I appreciate the offer, but . . ."

"You have other plans. My apologies. I shouldn't have assumed."

"No, actually, I'm still waiting to check in." She nodded toward the front desk, where the lady was still giving Wallace an earful. "My bag is clunky enough. Dragging it through some high-end club seems like a bit much."

"I'm already checked in here at the Cecil. I can take your bag up to my room if you'd like."

"That sounds like quite the imposition."

Jonathan shrugged. "Not really. I was going to grab a bite to eat then head downtown anyway."

Grace still hesitated. "It almost sounds like a date."

"But it's not. I'm inviting you to tag along. We are still friends, aren't we?" He said the last part slowly. A crease formed between his brows.

The question left Grace at a loss for words. "Friends" felt like too small a word for whatever the relationship between them had become. Jonathan had been her annoying knight in shining armor at the beginning. They had become colleagues during their time in D.C. together. So maybe "former coworkers" would be more accurate. That is, if she could completely forget about the one kiss they had shared.

The problem was Grace hadn't. However, never at any point could she honestly say that Jonathan had been her boyfriend or even her beau.

"Friends," Grace said finally.

His eyes flashed with understanding. Then he broke out into a wide grin. "Good. I know a guy down on East Fifty-Second who said I'm welcome to bring 'friends' to tag along anytime." He held up his fingers in air quotes.

Grace felt trapped. But it was a trap of her own making. She scrunched her mouth into a scowl. She knew she still had the power to decline his invitation and wait for the furry lady to finish having her say. She could even tuck her tail and try her luck at home with Mama, though she was less than enthusiastic about the confrontation that was sure to await her.

"Fine. I'll tag along then, 'friend.'" She held up her own finger quotes, mocking him.

"That's the spirit. Let me take your bag up to my room. It won't take but a moment."

An hour later, Grace found herself enjoying coffee and a plate of macaroni and cheese at the Horn & Hardart on Fifty-Seventh Street and Sixth Avenue.

"Dinner at the automat is the least date-like meal I could think of around here," Jonathan told her with a smile. "That is, unless you let me splurge another nickel to buy you a slice of pie."

"Funny. But the last thing I need after all of this is pie." Grace gestured at her half-eaten meal.

"Let me guess, because you're watching your figure?"

"Heavens no. With all the marching, running, and crawling around on the ground we've been doing in training, my figure is fine. I probably need the extra calories. The truth is that I'm tired of pie. The new pie shop on base at Camp Shanks has been exquisite. But I've been eating my fill every day at every meal since we arrived last week."

Grace took a sip of her coffee. It was more bitter than she preferred, given that sugar was not as accessible to civilian establishments as it was within the Army mess, but still delicious. She had read once that the H&H automats served a type of coffee that was more common in New Orleans than in New York. She welcomed the strong taste after blurting out a mouthful about pie.

"Is that so? Looks like I'll have to try some myself the next time I'm up there." Jonathan checked his watch. "It's still a little early to hit the clubs. I was hoping to kill a little more time by tempting you with pie. Since that didn't work, might I interest you in a movie instead?"

Grace lifted an eyebrow. "A movie sounds like we're treading pretty close to 'on a date' territory. I insist on paying for my own ticket."

"Letting you do that would go against all of the good breeding my mother drilled into me as a boy." Grace began to protest but Jonathan held up his hand. "But in this case, I'll allow it."

Grace leaned back in her seat. "Why do I think you're toying with me?"

"Oh, I'm not. It's just that I plan on splurging for the cab that we'll be taking to the theater."

"Splurging for a cab is definitely 'on a date' behavior."

"Not when the theater is seven blocks away and there's three or four inches of snow on the ground, it isn't. In this case, taking a cab is just good sense."

Remembering the frigid tunnel breeze that had assaulted them as they had waited for the subway to go downtown, Grace pulled the edges of her jacket around her and mock shivered. "I can't argue with your logic. But I'll have you know that I have my eye on you, Mr. Philips. Don't think I forgot how slick you can be."

"Duly noted." Jonathan pushed his chair back from the table. "And on that note, I'm going to get *myself, and myself only,* a slice of pie."

"Just a movie" wound up being a picture show at Radio City Music Hall. *A Song to Remember* was the feature presentation of the night. She would have been justified in putting up a protest about this particular outing being too extravagant, but the storied theater soon had her enchanted with its luxurious lobby and plush seating. And all of her "not a date" concerns faded away once the motion picture started. It turned out that the story was about the famed pianist Frédéric Chopin's life as a child prodigy and his role in the Polish resistance. It might as well have been her life playing out up on the screen, aside from the European setting. The scene where Chopin played *Moonlight Sonata* at a concert hit her right in the gut. Her brother, Tony, had often asked her to play it for him.

Grace was in tears alongside the protagonist on the screen.

Jonathan took her hand and squeezed it. "Are you all right?"

"It's nothing. I'm fine." She was anything but fine. Without another word, Jonathan fished a cloth handkerchief out of his pocket and handed it to her. Embarrassed, she accepted it.

"We can get out of here if you like."

"No. I'd like to see the rest of the film."

After the film ended, Jonathan took Grace to a nearby coffee shop. Grace fiddled with her cup at first. She didn't have much to say because she was so embarrassed by her emotional display back in the theater.

"I apologize for suggesting the movies. You said you didn't want to go, but I made you go anyway. I thought a story about a famous pianist would be a safe bet."

"There was no way either one of us could have known that a story about Chopin would leave me in tears. I'm the one who should be apologizing. You were trying to show me a nice time on my last night in the city. And what do I do? Start blubbering all over the place. And then your handkerchief . . . I'm so embarrassed. Forgive me?"

"Only if you forgive me."

She smiled at him. "There's nothing to be forgiven for."

"Well, there you have it." He held out his hand to her. "Friends again?"

She took his hand into her own and shook it. "Friends. And I'll mail the handkerchief back to you after I wash it."

Jonathan waved his hand. "Keep it. Consider it as a memento of this night."

Grace swallowed a sip of her coffee. "Ha! I think tonight is the last thing I'd like to remember."

Jonathan leaned back, palming his chest. "You wound me, Grace."

"No, that's not what I meant, and you know it." Grace thought about it for a moment. "I did enjoy the movie. It was just . . . that song. It was my brother's favorite."

"Was?" Jonathan asked the question carefully. He looked up from his own coffee cup.

Grace bit her lip, then sighed. "He was killed early in the war. The Philippines."

"Oh, Grace, I'm so sorry." Jonathan's eyes softened with understanding. He opened his mouth as if to say more, then shut it just as quickly. Thankfully, he was one of the few people she didn't have to explain the horrors of the Philippines campaign to.

"Tony was my biggest fan. With him gone . . . it's why I don't play anymore."

"Damn. That was the last movie I should have taken you to."

She waved her hand at him. "It's all right. I've come to realize that the longer I'm in the military, the more that it fulfills my desire for the structure and order I used to enjoy while I was playing. But all without the pressures and heartbreak."

"That night I first met you, when you had the panic attack . . . is that the reason you stopped performing?"

"They had notified us about Tony the night before. My Juilliard audition was that morning. I blew it, obviously." She huffed a laugh to herself. "Mama had her heart set on my going to Juilliard. All so I could become a big-time concert pianist. But for me, that wasn't necessarily my dream. Tony was the one who introduced me to jazz. That night you met me, let's just say I realized that jazz was my musical heart, not classical. And the person who had given me jazz was gone."

"If you don't mind my asking, what was *your* dream?"

She held up her coffee cup as if about to sip from it. She smiled at him mysteriously from behind it. "It doesn't matter now. I've moved on to other things, more realistic things like the WAC."

"You forget that I've seen you play. That night at Minton's, I saw the look on your face once you dropped all your pretenses, when you really let go. Now that I think about it, you were making it up as you went along, weren't you? You looked like you were in another world. I've never seen you look so . . . ecstatic."

Grace smiled at Jonathan's description of her. She wished he didn't know her so well. "Fine, you win. I had no idea what I wanted to do with my life until Tony introduced me to the guys at Minton's. The music they were creating blew my mind. They were making up a new sound in those after-hours jam sessions. I wanted to be a part of it. I wanted to make music like that too. But Mama had a fit whenever I started to play in a style other than classical or hymns. That's when Tony started sneaking me out of the house after our parents were asleep to go down to the old Rhythm Club."

Grace finished the rest of her cup. By the time she put it back down on the table, she felt lighter. Finally sharing her story with Jonathan was liberating.

"Ready to go?"

"Yes."

Jonathan pushed back from the table and stood, walking around it to help Grace to her feet, then with her coat. When they emerged back outside, ol' Jack Frost was there to greet them. Grace shivered. She pulled her lapels closer around her neck.

"The Rhythm Club?" Jonathan started, returning to where their conversation had left off. "I've heard of it. That's over by the Lafayette Theatre."

Grace nodded. "That's the one. Down there, I soaked up anything they were willing to teach me. Henry Minton was the house manager there. When he opened up his own place back in '38, all the guys started hanging out down there instead."

"I heard the musicians union didn't hassle them as much at Minton's. That's why they all flocked there. With old Henry being a union rep and all."

"Yeah, the union . . ." Grace became quiet for a moment. She looked off into the distance up Seventh Avenue.

"What about the union?"

"I *could've* gotten a union card, but Mama wouldn't allow it. I was still too young then to join on my own. She didn't trust the unions after the Pullman porters organized. She had been a Pullman maid, but they fired her on the spot once they found out she had been passing union messages before they were recognized. That's why she took up sewing, to help pay the bills and for my music lessons. All that sewing is why her hands"—she held up her hands, her fingers rounded like claws—"are starting to look like this. They aren't as nimble as they used to be. And she continues to pretend that they are, despite the pain it causes her. Tony joined the Army to pick up the slack when money got tighter."

"I'm so sorry."

"He used to send me five dollars of his pay with a note that said 'For Juilliard.' Every month. My family believed in me, in my talent, to the point that they've all basically sacrificed themselves. All so that Mama could see me play onstage in some great music hall in France one day." Grace shrugged. "Nothing I can do about it now but move forward."

Her mother's refusal to let her get a union card effectively blocked her from the more lucrative gigs at the bigger venues that had started to knock on her door. It also kept her from performing publicly at the nightclubs in Harlem. The bandleaders who were coming through town were starting to offer her real good money. But those jobs would've required her to go on the road. *That* Mama specifically wouldn't allow. Not to play that "unholy" music, she had said. This happened during the worst of the Depression, which meant all the smaller, more acceptable venues and organizations that had been hiring her no longer had the funds to pay her.

No more paying gigs on top of Mama's arthritis progressing and the porters union's inability to finalize a contract with the Pullman company had devastated the family's main income sources. It had also caused an irreparable rift between mother and daughter.

Finally, Grace had said "no more" and enrolled in a teachers college. Once Grace had finished college and was old enough to obtain a union card on her own, anyone who had the funds was no longer interested in hiring her to perform. To make matters worse, no one had the spare change to hire a piano teacher for their children. And for all the advice she had received about education being a "safe" degree for a Negro woman, none of the schools were hiring.

Grace had wound up right back in Mama's seamstress shop, running the business side of the enterprise and helping out with the tasks that Mama was unable to perform physically or the assistants were too busy to do. The bookkeeping and managerial skills she had developed there had served her well in the military.

"What's keeping you from restarting your piano career now?"

"I don't know." Grace stopped walking and frowned. This was a question she hadn't pondered in a long while. True, part of her reluctance to rejuvenate her career had to do with taking away Mama's source of control over her life.

Grace thought back to the volumes of sheet music she had written since she had left home. The truth was she had become more interested in writing the music than performing it. But she wasn't going to share that desire with anybody. She was still coming to terms with it herself.

She shrugged, then started walking again. "Too many bridges burned in the more 'respectable' venues, I guess."

"I refuse to believe that. Talent is talent. And you've got it in spades. Surely enough time has passed where either those booking agents are no longer there or they can let bygones be bygones."

"Perhaps. Maybe when the war is over." Grace stared off into the urban canyon that was Sixth Avenue.

"I used to book musicians before the war. Maybe when the war is over, you might consider letting me—"

"No," she interrupted. "I appreciate the offer, but I was thinking about maybe making a career of it in the WAC. I think military life rather suits me."

She wrapped her scarf tighter around her neck, shimmying her shoulders in an almost faux shiver. "Now, about that cab?"

"Of course." Jonathan stepped off the curb, holding two fingers up. Several cabs raced past them. Only one of them already carried a passenger from what they could see. The rest had empty back seats. Finally, one pulled over a yard or so ahead of them. But once they were close enough for the driver to get a good look at them, he quickly flicked on his OFF DUTY light and pulled off.

She watched Jonathan's face harden in anger. Grace hadn't seen him lose his cool that often. But now? He looked like he was ready to break something.

"Not even for a lady in uniform?" Jonathan exploded at the retreating vehicle. "Seriously?"

Grace placed her palm on his forearm. "It's only a few blocks. We can stay warm if we walk fast enough. C'mon."

"What just happened wasn't okay."

"You're right. It wasn't." They looked into each other's eyes until an understanding passed between them. Another gust of wind blew past. She shivered, then smiled. "It's getting cold out here."

"Fine. Let's go."

Grace's long legs were the only reason she was able to keep up with Jonathan's anger-fueled stride. The honking car horns, sirens, and other background noises that Grace fondly associated with New York filled in the silence between them. She felt compelled to grab his hand, give it a squeeze. But that definitely was crossing into "date" behavior. She was at a loss on how to let him know that his attempts at chivalry tonight were appreciated, even if a racist cabbie made his gesture futile. She shoved her hands into her pockets instead.

"Thank you for offering to get us a cab. Maybe we'll get luckier later on, after we hit the clubs."

"Yeah. Maybe." Jonathan looked straight ahead as he continued to march down the slushy sidewalk. He kicked a small clump of half-melted snow out of his path. "I shouldn't have allowed myself to forget where I was. We're not in Harlem."

"No, we're not." This time, Grace did slide her hand into the crook of his arm. "But that doesn't mean we should let a few idiots interfere with the good time we were having."

"You're right."

They stopped once they reached the corner of Fifty-Second Street and Sixth Avenue. "Okay, Mr. Philips. This is your adventure. I'm following your lead. Which way do we go?"

"To the right. Let's hit Club Downbeat."

"Are you sure about this? The last thing I need is to be reported to WAC officials because I was spotted in a 'disreputable' place while in uniform."

"Not if you're with me. Don't worry. It'll be cool."

"It won't be your name printed in the newspapers if you're wrong."

"I know these guys. They won't snitch. But to be on the safe side, we'll go in the back door."

Jonathan clasped his hand over her wrist, then led her to a side door just a few feet before the main entrance. He gave the door three shorts raps with his fist.

"Philips!" The heavyset bouncer who opened the door held out his hand to Jonathan. Jonathan greeted him by slapping the proffered hand in return.

"My man Mack! Good to see you."

Grace stood back as the two men gave each other a quick hug.

"What brings you back to town?" That's when Mack noticed Grace standing there. He looked her up and down. Then he let out a long whistle. "Well, hello there. I think I just answered my own question."

"Calm down. I'm in town on government business. You know, the usual. And this is Miss Steele, a colleague and a friend. Nothing more. She told me she likes jazz but had never been down here."

Mack tapped Jonathan on the shoulder. "Yo, man, she got a sister?"

"No," Grace interrupted. "She does not have a sister. And she is capable of speaking for herself."

"My fault, my fault," Mack stammered as an apology. "You know how it is. Just making sure that I don't step on any toes. No disrespect intended."

Grace gave him a short nod in understanding. She didn't say anything else.

"Mack, you're making me look bad here." Jonathan redirected

the energy of the awkward exchange back toward him. "How about letting us in as a favor?"

Mack shook his head. "You know I can't do that, man. This entrance is for talent only. I've known you long enough to know that you shouldn't be allowed anywhere near an instrument."

Grace stepped forward again, this time with a cocky grin on her face. "Stop your yapping and let me in then. I'm the talent."

Mack held up his hands. "Whoa there, little lady. I don't see any instrument."

"I don't need an instrument. My talent is looking good." Grace put her hand on the door and pushed it open. "Jonathan, are you coming?"

"Yes, ma'am."

Mack held up his hands again. "Damn, bro. You've got a firecracker there. I don't envy you at all."

The doorway led them into a hallway backstage that was already filled with smoke. There was just enough light where Grace could see a few familiar faces.

Jonathan took her by the hand and led her into the audience. The trumpeter onstage had already started his performance. The main lights were dimmed, so they had to make do with sitting at a table in the back of the audience.

"Do you mind that we're not near the front?" Jonathan held one of the chairs for her to sit.

"No." Grace shook her head. "I don't need to be on top of the stage to enjoy the music."

Grace closed her eyes as the trumpet's clear, mournful notes enveloped her. She peeked through her lashes a few times to get a good look at the man playing onstage. He was a young guy. But she had yet to put a name to the handsome, dark-skinned man's face.

"Damn, he's good," she heard Jonathan mutter to himself.

"Ain't that the truth," Grace purred in response. "He must be new around here. I don't recognize him."

"Yes. I think he started coming around the clubs sometime last fall."

"Mm-hmm." Grace wasn't really in the mood for talking. It had been so long since she had been able to soak up this kind of music. She tapped her fingers on the tabletop, imagining the flourishes she would add if she were accompanying the horn player on the piano. She reached down into her purse for some scrap paper. When she found some along with a pen, she began scribbling down musical notes.

Jonathan nudged her shoulder. "What are you writing there?"

His voice's intrusion jolted her out of the creative haze she had been in.

"Nothing." She stuffed the paper back into her bag before he could get too good of a look. "Just an idea that came to me."

"You write music too?"

"No, of course not. Don't be silly." She forced a laugh to cut him off. Better to laugh at herself before he had the chance to laugh *at her*.

"There's nothing silly about it at all." He leaned in so that his eyes were level with hers. "As a matter of fact, I find it rather impressive."

She stared back at him, her lips parted. But nothing came out. She paused a beat. And then another, waiting for his laughter to come. But it didn't. The earnest expression on Jonathan's face held. And then understanding flashed in his eyes.

"That's why you stopped performing, isn't it?"

"Isn't what?" Grace looked away. She felt herself begin to flush. Even though both her skin and the room were too dark for him to have seen it, she cupped her hand around the back of her neck to hide the heat blooming there.

"At first I thought you must have come down with stage fright. Or something to do with your brother. But that isn't it at all. It's because you want to compose, isn't it? But when your mother discouraged you from exploring your ideas, you gave up on music altogether."

Grace really hated how Jonathan always found a way to see her in the moments that she most wanted to disappear. He was doing it again now.

"I think . . . I need some air." She stood so abruptly that her chair tipped backward. The person seated behind her in the tight, cramped space was the only reason it didn't fall all the way to the floor. She turned, further embarrassed. "Pardon me."

Grace turned back to Jonathan, who was now also on his feet, his expression unchanged. His attention solely on her. The intense look on his face made him even more—she swallowed—appealing than usual.

"This evening—all of it—has been lovely. But I think it's time to call it a night."

He placed his hand upon her back as he led her toward the exit. "Of course. Let's go."

This time, they were able to successfully hail a cab. To their surprise the cabbie was a Negro woman. She didn't balk when Jonathan gave her a Harlem address as their destination.

"My shift ends soon," she explained as she turned north onto Madison Avenue. "I was heading back uptown anyway."

Grace stared out the window as the cab headed north. She

marveled at how different this part of Manhattan was from the block that had been her whole world while growing up. The darkened city streets were also a sight to see. Vehicles passed each other with dim headlights, and almost every apartment window was shuttered by blackout curtains.

New York still operated under a dimout order after dark. A necessity to keep merchant and troop ships safe from lurking German submarines as they moved in and out of New York Harbor. Troop ships like the one Grace and her fellow WACs would be boarding in the very near future. Possibly within the next few days.

Then it dawned on her: she was about to enter a very active war zone where the threat of death was very real.

"Oh God," she gasped. She wrapped her arms around herself, hugging both sides of her coat. But that did little to sway the panic attack that had begun to envelope her.

"What's wrong?" Jonathan pulled her into his arms. His very sturdy, very safe arms. Grace turned to burrow her face into his chest. She felt like this was where she was meant to be all along. All the reasons she had cocooned herself with in the past as to why she should ignore the very real attraction between them evaporated. An attraction that had always been there, if Grace was being honest with herself for once. Ever since that night they first met.

"I pried too much back there, didn't I?" Jonathan murmured the words into her hair. "Your reasons for giving up music are none of my business. I apologize. I—"

"Shh, just hold me." Grace lifted her head. Her mouth was now against his neck. "Keep me safe. For as long as you can."

"Always."

WHEN THEY RETURNED to the hotel, the night clerk informed them that there weren't any rooms available.

"How can that be?"

"A large group of soldiers are in town on leave—"

Grace cut him off. "I know. I'm one of them!"

Jonathan placed his hand on her shoulder. The gesture was enough to keep her from going into a full-blown rage. But it didn't change the fact that she had no place to sleep tonight. She stepped to the side as Jonathan approached the clerk. All she knew was that it was too late to try to find another hotel or to attempt to go back up to base.

"No, it's fine. She can stay in my room."

"Sir, we are not that kind of establishment. This is a respectable hotel!"

Grace watched as Jonathan pulled out his wallet and slid a five-dollar bill toward the man.

"And I appreciate your *understanding* while we go upstairs and figure something out."

The clerk sniffed as he pocketed the money. He eyeballed Grace slowly, taking in her off-duty WAC uniform. "You better have her out of here by morning or I *will* call the MPs."

The threat caused a chill to snake up Grace's spine. Jonathan took her by the hand and led her toward the main staircase. "C'mon."

Once they reached the top of the stairs, Jonathan gave her hand a squeeze. "Don't worry about that stick-in-the-mud. Don't forget, I can call people too. Namely, the guy who owns this place."

"Even so, it's not your name that'll be ruined if it comes out that I spent the night in your room, with you in it. I don't like this. My parents' apartment is only a few blocks away. Maybe Mama will—"

"No." Jonathan stopped at room 204 and pulled out a key. He opened the door, gesturing for her to enter. "I'm the one who kept you out late. I'm the one who will make this right."

Of course he would. Making things right was what Jonathan was good at. He had always looked out for her so far. Even when Grace didn't want him to.

He followed her as she entered the hotel room. It turned out to be the tiniest room she had ever seen. The narrow bed took up the majority of the space. But there was an armchair crammed into the corner.

"How in the world are we both going to fit in here?"

"Easy. You take the bed. I take the chair."

Grace stared at the armchair again. It too, like the bed, was on the narrow side. "I don't see how you plan on fitting into it to sit in it, much less to sleep in it."

"I'll manage. If I can't make that work, then there's always the floor."

"Nonsense. I'll go to my parents' place. If you would get me my bag."

"No," he barked, surprising them both. "I'm not ready to say goodbye to you yet. That is, if you . . ."

Grace lowered herself onto the corner of the bed. If she was being honest with herself, she was reluctant to end the magic of this night too. Not that she had intended for it to end this way, sharing a hotel room with him. But the longer she was here, the more she was beginning to warm up to the idea. "It's okay. I can stay."

"Great." A boyish grin spread across his face that made Grace's insides flutter. She returned the smile. "Make yourself at home."

She nodded, then shifted her knees toward the small table beside the bed. She shrugged out of her coat first. Then she removed her watch—the one Tony had given her—carefully laying it out across the tabletop. That Christmas had been six years ago—a lifetime ago. Now here she was, on the verge of possibly making part of Mama's dream come true.

Grace wondered where this next leg of her WAC adventure would land her. Would it be England? Or maybe even Africa? She dared not imagine that she would finally get the chance to go to France. That part of Mama's dream had become her own. But to a different end. Instead of playing in the country's world-famous concert halls, she wanted to see if she could hold her own among other artists in the most culturally renowned city in the world.

Achieving that would require Grace to be bold, bolder than she had ever been in her life. She had to stop playing it safe. She had to go with her gut and trust that it would guide her on the right path. But right now, her gut was telling her that she should not let this night end without tasting Jonathan's lips against hers again.

She stood and went over to the armchair where Jonathan was attempting to make himself comfortable. He looked like a man trying to squeeze himself onto his kid brother's hobbyhorse.

"This is ridiculous." Grace held out her hand to him. "There's no way you'll ever get to sleep here. And . . . I think I would like it very much if you would sleep in the bed with me instead."

"I'm pretty sure you know that I'm attracted to you. Honestly, I've always been. But I won't take advantage of the position I've put you in tonight."

She arched an eyebrow. "Well then, what if it was me who was taking advantage of you instead? No strings attached."

"I don't understand."

"I'm saying that I would like it very much if you would spend the night holding me in your arms. And if you holding me leads to us doing something more? Well, I think I wouldn't mind that either."

Jonathan dropped his head into his hands and groaned. "You're killing me, Grace."

"Then say yes." She extended her hand to him again.

This time, he took it.

CHAPTER 19

New York City
Late January 1945

RIBBONS OF DAYLIGHT streamed into the hotel room through the thin gaps between the blackout curtain and the window frame. Grace opened one eye, then quickly covered it with her hand to block the sunlight. It had been so long since she had slept in a bed as soft as this one. She picked up her watch from the side table. It was almost seven o'clock in the morning.

She wriggled her limbs, which were twisted around the sheets of the rumpled bed. Her movements were unhurried. She had no incentive to rush, but then she remembered the night clerk's threat.

She swung her legs over the side and the bed groaned under her shifting weight. She winced as she stood. So much for her hopes for a silent escape. Even so, Jonathan's face remained buried in his pillow.

"The last thing I want is for things to become awkward between us." His words were muffled, but the meaning behind them was clear. "Last night—all of it—was about more than getting into your pants."

He turned and sat up. "I wasn't lying when I said I've had feelings for you for some time."

"And I meant it when I said no strings attached. Jonathan, last night was inevitable. Like a dream really." Grace scooped her wool stockings up from the floor. She sat down on the foot of the bed and began pulling the material up the length of her leg. "Let's not ruin it with empty promises."

He frowned. "There's nothing empty about what I'm trying to tell you."

"Then what are you trying to tell me?"

He paused, like he needed a moment to work up his nerve. Now, that made Grace go still. In all the time she'd known him, she had never seen him be unsure about anything.

"I would like to court you, Grace. Properly."

She shook her head. Those words were not supposed to be coming out of his mouth. While growing up, she had eavesdropped on her brother and his friends in the neighborhood talking about how they liked the girls who made it easy, the ones who gave it up without pressuring them into a relationship or any kind of a future together. Last night's "fling" with Jonathan was supposed to be like that. She had *wanted* him to see her as, well, an easy girl. One who would slip from his mind like they had never even known each other. Nothing more. He was supposed to be breathing a sigh of relief that she was making a beeline for the door, not giving her reasons to stay.

And his declaration shouldn't be making her heart flutter with longing for what could have been. Nor should it flood with regret.

Damn this war. Under different circumstances, she could easily see him as the kind of man she might want to spend the rest of her life with.

"That's . . . not what I want, though." She turned her back to him and finished zipping up her skirt. "We agreed to no strings attached, remember?"

"No, that's what *you* said."

"Please, I need you to make this goodbye an easy one. You know where I'm going, what I'm about to face." Grace paused. She threw her pillow at him. "More importantly, I need to get out of here in case that clerk makes good on his threat. Now get up!"

The rising sun broke through the gaps between the buildings as they rushed out the hotel's side door. With it being early Saturday morning, it wasn't unusual that they found themselves on a sidewalk without a lot of foot traffic.

A lone cab a block away sat at a red light. Jonathan waited for the light to turn green before lifting his hand up so the cabbie could see it. When it stopped in front of them, he opened the door for her.

He leaned forward to kiss her goodbye. She held her hand up to his mouth to stop him. One more of his kisses would be too much. Grace didn't think she could handle it. She shook her head. She held out her hand. "Goodbye, friend."

But Jonathan didn't take it. He stepped back as if she had physically pushed him with her rejection. Instead, he saluted her. "God be with you, Captain Steele."

CHAPTER 20

"GOOD MORNING, BABY. Rise and shine." Eliza's mother shook her awake.

Eliza stretched her arms, rolling onto her side. She wanted to stay there forever. She hadn't slept in a comfortable bed in a long time. Before she could recall what day it was, her mother was handing her a breakfast tray with a steaming mug on it. In the mug, to Eliza's surprise, was hot chocolate.

"Mother, how . . . ?" Chocolate was among those food items that had been rationed since before the United States had entered the war. Eliza felt her brow crease. Her mother had to have paid a pretty penny to get enough cocoa to make even this one mugful of the beverage.

Her mother winked at her. "I have my ways. It's probably best that you don't know. Now, drink up. Breakfast will be ready downstairs in a few minutes."

Eliza took a careful sip of the hot chocolate. The combination of the smell and the sweet, rich taste transported her back to more innocent days. Ones where the bubble of her parents' safe, privileged world would protect her from everything. For Eliza, it was a bubble that had popped when she had become too comfortable, too arrogant, and strayed too far away from the things that had kept her safe.

". . . and when we're finished, we have hair appointments with Miss Louise down at the salon. Everybody in the shop will be so excited to see you. They ask about you all the time."

Eliza set the mug back down on the tray. "Thank you, Mommy. But all this fuss isn't necessary. My hair will just get messed up again as soon as I put my helmet on it."

Her mother patted her arm, smiling at her. "Taking care of you could never be a fuss. You're my one and only baby girl. I love you."

Despite the emotions flowing from her mother's words, Eliza felt empty inside. No, she felt . . . helpless. Pitied even. No. Not ever again. She might have been foolish and broken once. But she had pulled herself out of that hole. She was better now. She was *stronger* now. She would not allow herself to be babied again.

She pushed her mother's hands away. "I'm fine now. Thank you for the hot chocolate. I'll see you downstairs."

Her mother began to pull back the covers on the bed. "Let me just help you before I go."

"No!" The word came out harsher than Eliza had intended. "I'm not helpless. I've got it."

That declaration made Lillian Jones go still. She picked at Eliza's comforter a few times with her fingertips before responding out loud.

"Well then. Since I'm not wanted here." Lillian stood, smoothing her skirt. "Breakfast will be ready soon."

Eliza held up her mug. "Please don't go through the trouble of fixing a big meal on my account. This hot chocolate is plenty."

Eliza watched her mother close her eyes, then hold them shut for a second longer than a normal blink. When they opened again,

Mother had a tight-lipped smile pasted onto her face. "I expect to see you in the dining room in twenty minutes."

"Will *he* be there?"

Her elegant mother let out a snort. It was clear she was done with Eliza's excuses. "We will be dining as a *family* this morning."

Eliza's shoulders fell, her mother's reprimand hitting its mark. "Yes, ma'am."

"Good." The corners of her mother's mouth relaxed into a more genuine version of her smile. "I'll leave you to it then."

Mother closed Eliza's bedroom door behind her. Eliza sighed as she placed the half-empty mug of hot chocolate onto the side table. She had forgotten how effective her mother's guilt trips could be.

She folded up the legs of the tray, then placed it on the floor propped against the side of the bed. She pulled back the rest of her covers and began getting ready for the day.

When her unit had been granted this unexpected forty-eight-hour leave, all Eliza had wanted to do was go to her parents' house and sleep in her own bed. It looked like her hopes for being able to sleep late for once were just folly now. She would have gotten more sleep back in the officers' housing near Camp Shanks where she shared a room with three other women.

She could only get so irritated by her mother's smothering behavior. After Eliza was attacked, something in her normally strong, confident mother had changed. The woman who had raised her to be independent and have a mind of her own now hovered and gave her barely enough room to breathe.

Eliza hadn't told either of her parents why she was in town or where she was going next. All she had said was that she had been given some leave and had decided to spend it at home. The reality was that she was scared to tell her mother about her pending deployment because she was afraid that the woman would lock her in her room, forcing her to go AWOL by default. As for her father, she couldn't have told him if she wanted to. He had refused to speak to her since she had entered the brownstone last night.

Now dressed, Eliza opened her bedroom door. She squared her shoulders as if getting ready to go into battle. Aside from the soft bed she had slept in, she was beginning to regret this visit home.

Her father entered the dining room about ten minutes after Eliza had seated herself at the table. He had a copy of their newspaper tucked under his arm as he sat down.

"Good morning, Daddy." Eliza held her breath, knowing that her father was capable of saying anything on a wide spectrum in response to her greeting.

Martin Jones took one look at his daughter, sniffed, then promptly opened the paper and held it up in front of his face. That was not the reaction she expected.

A moment later, her mother entered from the kitchen carrying a platter of food in each hand. Scrambled eggs were on one. A small pile of toast was on the other. From the corner of her eye, Eliza caught her mother frowning as she took in the scene between father and daughter. She put the platters down onto the dining room table with a little less grace than Eliza was used to seeing from her mother.

"Martin, how many times have I told you? No reading the newspaper during meals."

Her father made a big fuss of lowering one corner of the paper to make eye contact with his wife. "What do you expect me to do when this newspaper is the most interesting thing at this table?"

"I expect you to interact with your daughter. It's a rare treat to have her home these days."

"Well, if she had stayed home like I had told her to instead of running off to join that damned Army . . ." he began.

"Martin!"

"Daddy! Please don't start. What's done is done."

This time he lowered the newspaper all the way down onto the table. "I find what wasn't done to be inexcusable. I told you that damned Army was no place for you. That they wouldn't give a damn about you. That they wouldn't protect you. Do you know what it's like to have the worst of every nightmare you've ever had come true? To receive a phone call from a stranger out of nowhere telling you that your daughter, your only child, had been beaten and left for dead in a train station somewhere in the middle of Kentucky?"

"No, I—"

He cut her off with a wave of his hand. "No, you don't." He pushed his seat back from the table and stood. "And I pray that you never will. Excuse me, Lillian. I seem to have lost my appetite."

He began to walk around the head of the table and toward the French doors leading to the living room.

Her father's words had left Eliza feeling like she had been slapped in the gut with a ton of rocks. She had been so wrapped up in her own physical recovery, her own lost sense of control, that she had not stopped to consider how her assault had affected her parents. She heard her mother rush to her side. Lillian attempted to grab her hand, but Eliza flicked it out of her reach.

"Baby, he didn't mean any of that. He hasn't been the same since that day. He was just angry and scared. I was too. But you're here now, and we can see with our own eyes that you're fine."

Eliza pushed back from the table. "Sorry, Mommy. I'm not hungry anymore either. I think I should leave."

But before Eliza could get very far, her mother unleashed a rare display of fury.

"Stop." Mother held up her hand. "Both of you need to sit. Down."

Eliza stared as Lillian Jones lifted her chin and inclined her head at a forty-five-degree angle. Eliza felt like a naughty five-year-old who had been caught doing something she shouldn't have been doing under the weight of her mother's glare. She plopped back down into her seat. Her mother was not to be trifled with when she employed that tone of voice combined with *that* look. Daddy stepped back into the dining room with a sheepish look on his face.

Mother threw a heaping spoonful of scrambled eggs onto the plate in front of Eliza. "Eat your breakfast before it gets cold."

She moved on to drop another serving of eggs onto the plate at the end of the table where Daddy was returning to his seat. There was still another serving left on the platter.

"The two of you are getting on my last nerve." Mother put the platter onto the table and sat down. She leaned back in her chair. "I'm done."

When Eliza saw her mother's shoulders slump, defeated, shame overcame her. Mother took great care to maintain her posture. She never slouched.

"Here." She pushed the platter of toast toward Eliza. It slid across the table. The tower of bread toppled, leaving slices scattered across the space that separated mother and daughter. By this point, Eliza knew better than to say anything. She quietly picked up the one piece of toast that had managed to stay on the platter.

"Thank you." Eliza took a bite out of duty rather than hunger. The taste of real butter coated her tongue. Now she felt even worse. She wouldn't be surprised if her mother had had to barter a week's worth of sugar rations to procure the few tablespoons of real butter needed to prepare this simple meal. A sacrifice made in an attempt to make their first meal together as a family in a long time special.

Eliza collected the scattered toast back onto the serving platter. She handed it down to her father. "Here, Daddy." She held it out for a few seconds. When he still didn't take the platter from her, she didn't say anything. She just set it beside his plate. His continued silent treatment toward her was less scary than her mother's fury. She had been subjected to it before whenever they'd butted heads in the past. He was laying it on a bit thick now, but she knew he'd come around. Eventually.

Mother took a deep breath. She had never been a woman of many words. She let her more gregarious husband and daughter dominate conversations. Lillian Jones preferred to let her actions do her talking for her. Which was why she surprised them both with not what she said, but how much she chose to say now.

"Not that anybody ever asked my opinion on it, but it is important to me that my daughter have the opportunity to make her own choices for her life." She made a point to direct her glare at her husband then. "Unlike me when I was Eliza's age."

Daddy leaned back, affronted. "What's that supposed to mean?" he blustered.

"It means that by the time I was twenty-five years old, I had a one-year-old baby and was married to a man whom I had known all of my life, but who had returned from the Great War a stranger. That same war and my 'responsibility as a Colored woman of means' robbed me of my own dreams of one day living in Europe as a foreign correspondent for the local Colored newspaper. Instead, my husband lived out *my* dream, bearing witness to a war overseas, and I played the good little wife in a city where I knew no one, safe at home in the good old U.S. of A. knitting socks. Because it had been expected of me."

Eliza watched her mother as she paused to sip her tea. Eliza did not miss the shaking hand with which she lifted the china to her lips.

"On the day you were born"—Mother gave Eliza a fond look— "I vowed that I would do everything within my power to make sure that my daughter would not be trapped within the same gilded prison. Even if it meant butting heads with her father from time to time on what a 'proper young lady of means' should and should not be doing."

Daddy pressed his fingertips against the tabletop and leaned forward. "Lillian, you haven't seen as much of the world as I have. If you had been there in France and seen the way our own government treated us over there . . . you wouldn't be so eager to throw our only child into those bastards' hands."

"Don't use that tone of voice with me. Maybe there were times in the past when I would have cowered to that. But today is *not* that day."

Daddy sat back with his mouth hanging down against his chest. Eliza had never seen him like this. She pressed her hand against her mouth to keep from laughing.

Meanwhile, Mother had balled her cloth napkin in her fist and was squeezing it for dear life. "Maybe I would if you would just tell me about what happened to you during the war."

Eliza was amazed at how even Mother's voice was. How in control. But then Eliza saw her mother's knuckles whiten as she squeezed the napkin even tighter.

"How am I supposed to know if you don't tell me, dear?"

Daddy winced. Mother's arrow had hit its mark apparently. But then Daddy seemed to wither within himself. Daddy's head was down, refusing to look his wife in the eye. To Eliza's eyes, he suddenly looked very old and frail.

"I can't." He shook his head, his eyes closed tight. "No woman's ears should ever be subjected to that. They're too delicate."

"I'm offended by how much you underestimate me, Martin. I've given birth, for goodness' sake. I think I could handle *hearing* about a little carnage."

"Don't push me, Lillian."

"Have some faith in me, Martin."

Daddy shook his head, his shoulders slumping further. "Maybe if I had told you before about what happened to me, then you wouldn't have pushed our baby into the Army. And that monster wouldn't have put his hands on her. My precious baby . . ."

Eliza had been about to take another bite of the toast. But her hand stilled when her father choked back a sob. Mother stood and went to his side, putting her hand on Daddy's shoulder.

It was a private moment between husband and wife. One Eliza was sure that her father wouldn't have wanted her to witness.

"Yes, Daddy, the so-called worst did happen to me. But the most important thing is that I *survived* it. That should be proof enough that I'm made of tougher stuff than you've been giving me credit for."

"You don't understand." His eyelids closed tight. When they opened again, Eliza saw that they were filled with tears. "It's one thing to have lived it. You suck it up all while making promises to yourself that you will endure if only to ensure that those types of horrors never happen again. And then you become one of the lucky ones who gets to come home, only to be subjected to unimaginable indignities for having the *nerve* to hold your head a little bit higher because you did serve . . . all because of the color of your skin. But you persevere. You put your head down and work hard. Push against the obstacles put in your path because your skin is wrong, where you came from is wrong, how you speak is wrong. Despite all that you make it. You do everything humanly possible to erect as many barriers as you can to shield your wife and your baby from the horrors—the ones that still haunt you in your face and in your dreams. The next thing you know, a phone call confirms that a real-life nightmare has gotten its clutches on your baby . . ."

She watched her father's face as it transformed from that of the stern, gruff patriarch of their family into one of a frightened little boy. Eliza blinked back her own tears. She couldn't recall a time when her father had allowed himself to be seen in such a vulnerable state. It was as if he had transported himself back into another time, another place. The horror that shone in his eyes broke her heart.

"Every day since I stepped foot back onto American soil, I've wanted to tell you what happened to us. I've wanted to get that monkey off my back so many times." Now the tears were streaming down his cheeks. His voice lowered to a whisper. "Baby, I've wanted to so bad. But I just can't."

Then Martin Jones, the strongest man that Eliza knew, sank to his knees, covered his face with his hands, and wept.

"I owe you both an apology." Eliza's voice echoed in the silence of the grand room. "I should have paid more attention when my travel arrangements were made for that day."

She stood up and slipped into the embrace of her parents. "It was naive to not consider the safety of arriving alone at that time of night in a secluded place like that. I know that now. I promise you both that I won't take that for granted again. And I am sorry for putting you through that."

She pulled away to swipe at her nose, sniffing. "But if I did the safe thing by staying put at home, I would have exploded. I had to do something. Doing nothing more than writing puff pieces about society events wasn't it. I have to do what I can to make this world, this country, right. The fact that the two of you are arguing over me like I'm still two years old and not capable of speaking my own truth, making my own decisions . . . I'm not your delicate flower anymore."

Eliza watched her father press his lips together. "Maybe I could have listened to you more. Your mother doesn't know this, but I have been reading the letters you've been sending home. You have a good eye. A reporter's eye . . . Maybe I can find you a juicier beat to cover when you come home for good."

Eliza sighed. She was not looking forward to what she had to tell them next. But it had to be done. "I'm not supposed to tell you this, but given the circumstances, I think you both should know the reason why I'm back in town. I'm shipping out for Europe."

"You're what?" Her mother's eyes rounded. "I assumed that you would be stationed up at Camp Shanks, not just passing through. Wait, since when are they sending Colored WACs overseas?"

"They're starting with us, with me." She took a good look at both of her parents now, even when everything in her wanted to flinch and look away. "And there's a chance I might not make it back. We were supposed to ship out a few days ago. The rumor is that the delay is due to German subs lurking too close to the shoreline."

"Dammit. Of course you are a part of that secret group. The one the Negro press has been buzzing about off the record for the last month." Her father tapped his fist on the tabletop.

"Oh my God." Mother's eyes filled up with tears. "And here I was frippering on about hair appointments and tea parties and such. Now I just want to lock all the doors and hold you tight until it's time for you to go back."

"It's okay, Mother. You didn't know."

"That's it. I'm done." Daddy pushed himself back up onto his feet. He tucked his newspaper under his arm. "I pray to God that nothing happens to you all on your journey across the sea. But if anything does happen to you out there on the Atlantic, then this is me telling you I told you so."

He walked out of the room. Neither woman attempted to call him back. They knew how he was. But Eliza did run out into the living room and yelled after him. "You know better than most that there's a chance I might not make it back. Do you really want to leave things between us like this?"

"You already know the answer to that, baby," her mother said to her from behind. "He loves you too much. His heart won't bear it if anything else were to happen to you."

TELEGRAM

JANUARY 31, 1945

FROM: NEW YORK PORT OF EMBARKATION
RECEIVED: CAMP SHANKS

MESSAGE: HEADQUARTERS STAFF, SUPPORT STAFF, AND
COMPANIES A AND B OF THE ALL-NEGRO WAC UNIT ARE
HEREBY ORDERED TO BOARD THE ÎLE DE FRANCE AT
0600 HOURS.

CHAPTER 21

New York Harbor, Manhattan
February 1, 1945

THE DAY HAD started off full of anticipation and excitement. Grace's heartbeat quickened as their ferry approached the vessel that was waiting for them alongside the West Side piers. Not only was the ocean liner that would take them to Europe massive, but it was also famous. A few of the girls squealed when they saw ÎLE DE FRANCE etched on the stern of the ship. Grace almost squealed with them. She, along with most of the unit, had heard of the famous ocean liner from newsreel coverage at the Saturday two-for-one cinemas. She never imagined that she would get the chance to experience such luxury herself. Especially not while she was still in the military.

The loading of people, equipment, and munitions onto the ship seemed to have taken up the greater portion of the day. *What a madhouse!* It was two hours of waiting on the pier before Grace was able to order the women in Company B to "Forward march!"

Just as soon as Grace gave the command, Company B began marching up the gangplank with orderly military precision. Even while hauling all of their gear on their backs, her girls made her proud. Not a single misstep or stumble under their heavy loads. Not one of their Army-issued combat helmets fell to the ground.

Grace followed the last of her company up the gangplank. As soon as she set foot aboard the ship, the butterflies in her stomach began a-fluttering. The biggest boat she had been on before was a rowboat at summer camp, a mere blip in the water next to this ocean liner. She had never left the United States before. She had never marched straight into a war zone before. The ship swayed to and fro with the Hudson River's current as it flowed into New York Harbor and beyond it to the very wide and vast open sea. Grace felt her knees buckle.

The weight of the heavy pack on her back began to feel like it would crush her. Grace took the few steps over to the railing and gripped it tightly with both hands. She took a series of deep, controlled breaths until the tension gripping her lungs eased.

She looked over the side, hoping to glimpse something familiar to steady her. They were so high up above the pier. She might as well have been looking down from the Empire State Building's observation deck. There were so many people down on the pier below. So many faces. So much bundled cargo and material. It was just so much at once. Much too much.

And then, just when she thought she might pass out altogether, Grace saw a familiar face among all those people. *It can't be.* She blinked to clear her vision. But when she looked again, that face was still there. "Mama!"

Grace's knees buckled again. A hand shot out of nowhere to steady her elbow.

"Jeez Louise, Grace. Do you want me to get you a medic?"

It was Eliza. Now she knew for sure she was hallucinating. Eliza had barely said two words to her since they'd been assigned to this battalion. Each time they had shared the same airspace leading up to today, Eliza either ignored Grace's greetings or just looked through her like she wasn't there. There was even that one time she had pivoted a full ninety degrees to avoid her in the Camp Shanks canteen.

"No." Grace yanked her arm away. She was not in the mood for Eliza's sudden change of heart now. "I just need a minute."

"Are you sure? You look like you just saw a ghost."

"I'm scared of heights," Grace lied. Silently, she prayed that Eliza would get the hint and leave her alone. Leave her alone to process what she thought she had seen.

"Excuse me for having a decent bone in my body. Unlike some people, when I see someone in trouble, I go out of my way to help."

"What's that supposed to mean?"

"You tell me." Eliza took a step backward, thankfully giving her some room to breathe. "I swear, I don't know why I still give a damn where you're concerned. I, more than anyone, should know that you don't give a damn about anyone but yourself."

"That's not true." She stood to her full height. But Eliza had already disappeared back into the crowd. Grace would have followed her, but the ship's horn blared, indicating that it was getting ready to leave. Everybody on the deck surged toward the railing to wave and scream their final goodbyes. The press of bodies pushed her forward. She braced herself against the railing once more. She used the opportunity to find that face, to convince herself that it had been indeed Mama come to see her off.

But whoever it had been that Grace had seen down there was gone. What was supposed to have been the most exciting moment of her life had, instead, turned into one of her loneliest.

WHATEVER AWE SHE'D had over traveling aboard the *Île de France* was short-lived once they came aboard. Yes, the ship had been a high-class luxury liner in peacetime. But since France had fallen to the Germans, the United States had commandeered the *Île* and retrofitted it into a troop transport ship. That meant that while the exquisite chandeliers and trimmings were all still there, the plush staterooms now housed sixteen bunks instead of the previous standard of two guests per room.

The officers in their unit were housed together in the same stateroom. But this standard practice turned awkward, because Grace had been assigned the bunk right above Eliza's. Grace knew the tension between them stemmed from the night Eliza had been attacked at the Kentucky train station. Grace could only imagine what the woman thought of her now. She had tried to explain what had happened after the train pulled out of the station, but Eliza wasn't interested in her story. Her excuses didn't change the fact that her friend had been left alone and vulnerable when she needed Grace the most.

Grace finished stowing her belongings in the narrow storage locker that had been provided. Actually, everything in that stateroom was narrow. She felt the dreaded squeeze of panic begin to wrap around her chest.

I need to get some air.

Once out on the upper deck, Grace was relieved to have the space to move around unencumbered by her heavy gear. The cool February breeze coming off the water was a welcome treat. However, she was shocked by the number of other vessels that surrounded their ship. As far as she could see in either direction, there was an endless line of battleships, aircraft carriers, and what looked to be other troop ships. It was a jarring thing to see, especially with the New York City skyline in the distance getting smaller and smaller behind them. The reports of U-boat sightings in the paper now became more real. One could be lurking beneath them now, waiting for the right opportunity to strike.

She reached under her sleeve to finger her watch, the one Tony had given her. It had become her lucky charm of sorts since then. Although they had been instructed several times to ship home everything but the most essential supplies, keeping this watch with her, in addition to her Army-issued one, had been her one act of defiance. She knew of others who had their own contraband on board, including one private who had snuck a set of red satin pajamas by wearing them under her uniform.

But when Grace felt for the watch now, it wasn't there. She reached deeper into her sleeve. Nothing. And then it dawned on her: she had left it behind in her rush to leave Jonathan's hotel room after their night together.

Damn. Now she really did feel exposed out here in the middle of the ocean. The hairs stood up on the back of Grace's neck.

She pulled her fatigue jacket tighter around her. Suddenly, the cool ocean breeze didn't feel so good anymore.

GRACE MADE HER way down the serving line in the onboard dining area. At least the former French luxury ocean liner still had its advantages. Instead of the normal bland Army fare of sloppy joes, doughnuts, and coffee, the cooks aboard the *Île de France* were dishing out the best bread she'd ever tasted, along with something called a cassoulet. She recognized bits of chicken and sausage in the stew. The divine aroma hinted that wine was among the other ingredients.

They also had the option of sipping on French red wine with their meals. Evidently, the French were in the habit of issuing a daily ration of wine to their soldiers. Grace had never developed a taste for the dry, rich beverage. But then again, her opportunities to drink the stuff were limited to taking Communion at church.

She boldly placed a filled wineglass onto her tray. What was that saying? When in Rome, do as the Romans do. Well, aboard this ship, she was technically on French soil, even if it was a combination of the American and British navies in command of it. Grace smiled to herself at the thought that she was doing something "naughty."

"Please tell me that devilish grin was for me," a very handsome and very Canadian serviceman called out to her as she passed by him. Grace rolled her eyes at the unimaginative attempt to flirt with her. They were a few hours into their journey. Already, it was a rare moment when there wasn't a GI or an enlisted man of some other nationality who made a catcall or come-on to someone in her unit.

Most of the quips had been harmless. But the blatant leering she saw in some of the men's eyes made it apparent that Grace would have to institute a buddy system for using the facilities in the middle of the night. It seemed that too many of these male soldiers held the belief that these female soldiers' jobs were to "service" them rather than serve the United States in the war effort.

"Don't be like that." Dolores, one of the sergeants in her company, fell in step beside her. They had grown friendly during overseas training, since Dolores also hailed from New York. "That Canadian was kinda cute."

Grace rolled her eyes again. "And very white. Segregation might be a nasty business back home. But I'll be damned if I get court-martialed for giving them a hint of impropriety on my part. And you'd be wise to do the same, young lady."

"Young lady? You're only a few years older than me."

"Yes, I am. And I also outrank you." Grace swished past her

friend and settled at a table where a few of the privates in their unit sat. Several girls stiffened at their approach.

"As you were." Grace smiled.

Dolores slid into the seat beside Grace. She leaned in and whispered, "Does that mean you are ordering me not to make a move on that Canadian, Captain?"

"No," Grace replied with a disapproving frown, "but I should."

"Fine, then I'll just enjoy looking at him from afar. But if you don't mind me saying, Captain, I don't see why we couldn't go slack on the rules just a little while we're stuck on this boat."

Grace stared at her friend. These younger women had heads that were harder than granite. "No, we can't, because we still have a job to do."

"Yeah, I know." Dolores started picking at her plate. "What is this stuff? I've never seen anything like it before. Definitely not the usual Army fare."

Grace picked up her fork and stabbed at her food. She slid a forkful of the cassoulet stuff into her mouth. The rich stew overpowered her senses. "Oh my goodness, I think this is the best thing I've ever eaten."

"Girl, please, nothing could ever top my mama's cooking." Dolores sampled a bite, then moaned. "Except this. Ooh wee, Frenchie back there put his whole entire foot in this."

Grace playfully swatted her friend's shoulder. "Can you at least try to pretend you have some home training? We're in public for goodness' sake."

Grace turned and caught the handsome Canadian soldier smiling their way. She quickly turned back to her plate. "See what you did, Dolores?"

"What?"

"The cute Canadian. He's staring!"

"Is he really now?" Dolores fluffed the imaginary hair on her shoulder. She boldly turned, caught the soldier's eye, and smiled her killer smile. "Good. Let him look."

"Dee, turn your sassy self around this second. If you keep looking at him like that, he's going to think you're interested and come over here."

"Well, that was the plan."

"If you keep it up, I will pull rank on you—" A shadow darkened their table, abruptly ending their banter.

"You gals look like you're hot for some action. Is this seat taken?"

Both Grace and Dolores looked up, expecting to see their new Canadian friend. Instead, they found themselves smiling like two fools up at the beet-red face of a red-haired American private. Grace's smile instantly fell. But before she could shoo him away, Eliza appeared out of nowhere, elbowing him to the side.

"Actually, it is." Eliza glanced at his uniform. "Private."

"Is that a fact?"

Grace couldn't quite place his drawl. It was definitely Southern, though. She tensed. Whatever was happening here, it could easily go sideways.

"I believe you meant to say, 'Is that a fact, *Captain?*' Didn't you?"

Grace held her breath when Eliza stepped closer to the private, who towered over her by at least a foot. His build suggested that he might have done physical labor in his civilian life. Eliza held her chin high nonetheless, challenging him.

The spoiled little rich girl Grace had met back in that induction office was nowhere to be found.

All the chatter and clinking utensils at their table stopped.

Everyone stared at the private. His face turned even redder. He stepped back.

"My apologies, *ma'am*." He turned on his heel and walked away. Around him, his buddies snickered into their knuckles. His shoulders hunched, and his hands curled into fists. His back might have been turned to them, but they all heard him mumble, "Little bitch," clear as day. Everyone around them went silent.

Eliza started toward him. Grace grabbed her wrist just in time.

"Let it go."

Eliza tugged her arm, but Grace's grip held firm. "And let him get away with that?"

"You won that battle, but you won't win the war. Now, sit down."

"Grace, I am not in the mood for your goody-two-shoes bullshit—"

"I said sit down!" Grace tugged harder. This time, she got Eliza's attention. "So I can thank you for handling that jerk."

"Fine." Eliza sat. Her eyes continued to blaze with fury. Grace wouldn't have been surprised if smoke started coming out of her ears.

"Here. Eat this." Grace shoved her tray in front of Eliza. "It's delicious."

"I'm not hungry." Eliza folded her arms across her chest and pouted.

"There's the bratty little girl I knew at boot camp. But right now you need to cool down. What were you thinking? You looked like you wanted to fight that guy."

"It's a good thing they refuse to arm us women. Otherwise, that would've turned out a lot differently."

"I hope you're joking." Grace waited a beat. Eliza's expression was still serious. "Please tell me you were joking."

Finally, Eliza crossed her eyes and stuck out her tongue. "Okay, okay. I wasn't *that* serious. But when we get to wherever we're going, I'm going to see about all of us getting some training in hand-to-hand combat, so we have a way to defend ourselves."

Grace instinctively held her hands to her chest. It was a protective reflex. The fear of injuring her hands had been a daily concern in her life prior to joining the military. The idea of using them to harm someone else horrified Grace. "Don't you think that's a bit much?"

"What else can we do?" Eliza grumbled. "The Army top brass is adamant in its refusal to arm female personnel. They promised America that its daughters would only be subjected to the battles of administrative work to win the war, never actual combat. Heaven forbid if the Germans attacked and boarded this ship."

She pointed her spoon at Grace to emphasize that last point. Grace rubbed the spot where her watch should have been. Of all the times to leave her lucky charm behind, why did it have to be now?

Eliza scooped the stew onto her spoon and tasted it. "Oh wow, this *is* good."

CHAPTER 22

A WEEK AGO, GRACE had been so eager to get on this boat. Now she wanted nothing more than to get off it.

Their days at sea consisted of going to the mess hall three times a day, drilling on the ship's top deck with the winter ocean winds whipping around them, and looking to see who didn't show up for drill practice because they were seasick that day. On any given day, about a third of their unit was out of commission.

Grace had been ill herself for a day or two initially. Luckily, she adjusted to the constant rolling waves better than most. That had been her only excitement on the trip, outside the confrontation between Eliza and that insubordinate Army private that first night on board. She and Eliza were still playing the awkward dance of not speaking to each other. Well, outside of what was necessary when you lived in cramped quarters together.

Now it was the end of another day. Grace was getting ready for bed. Her rolled blanket had fallen off the foot of her bed and down to the floor a few feet below.

"Again?" Grace sighed and climbed down the rope ladder in her socks. She would be so glad when they were on dry land again and things would stay put because the floor wasn't rolling back and forth.

"C'mon, Eliza!" Grace had once again stumbled over the handles of Eliza's duffel bag, which had been stuffed haphazardly under the bottom bunk where Eliza slept. "How hard is it to keep your things tidy? You've been living like this long enough to know better."

Grace couldn't believe that they both had been in the WAC for so long. Some days, she had a hard time remembering what civilian life had been like for her.

"Sorry." Eliza picked up the offending bag and threw it on her bed. "Had you told me you were coming down from your bunk before you climbed down, I would have moved it out of your way."

Grace did her best not to roll her eyes. Eliza must have caught a glimpse of that struggle because she pursed her lips and asked, "Is there something you'd like to say?"

"Nothing that wouldn't cause an unnecessary argument."

Eliza crossed her arms over her chest. "Try me."

"Fine. I will." Grace took a deep breath. *Here we go.* "I didn't give you a heads-up that I was coming down because the response would've been another round of heavy sighs and sucked teeth. I'm damned if I do and damned if I don't."

"That's not true."

"It is true. I've been getting an attitude from you whenever I open my mouth. Honestly, I'm getting tired of it. I really wish you would just let me have it. Say what's on your mind."

Eliza opened her mouth but never had a chance to respond. The ship's siren blared, making everybody jump. Before they could get over the shock, the ship lunged to the right. Everything that wasn't bolted down when flying.

Everything, including Grace. Her shoulder hit the wall hard. She yelped. But she was just one voice in a chorus of screams and yells. Not just in their stateroom, but from all the quarters along the hallway.

The lights flickered, then went out altogether. Then the ship lunged again, this time to the left.

"What the hell is going on?" The ongoing siren drowned out Grace's question. She pushed herself to her feet and grabbed on to the nearest bedpost. As the lights flickered back on, she saw that Eliza had done the same.

The ship jerked violently once more. It was zigzagging back and forth at regular intervals now. Had the captain, or whoever was at the helm, gotten drunk?

Something—maybe an engine—roared outside over the ship.

"That sounded like an airplane," someone yelled in the darkness.

"Is it one of ours? Are we under attack?"

Someone else sobbed.

There had to have been an explosion somewhere nearby, because the ship pitched violently and then creaked. Thankfully, it remained upright. But the zigzagging continued.

"Oh God, are we being bombed?" Grace wondered out loud.

"Oh no," Eliza whimpered. "Bombs can only mean the Germans are here."

Grace's heart went still. Because she knew—somehow, she just knew—that there was no way Eliza was wrong. A German submarine was lurking out there, and it was looking to blow them out of the water.

Suddenly, it became clear why Mama cut Grace off completely once she left for boot camp. Mama's gut reactions were seldom wrong. She had known somehow that the Army was going to get her last surviving child killed.

"Oh, Mama, I'm so sorry I never gave a thought about how this would affect you." Grace closed her eyes. A chill settled deep in her bones. She began to shiver.

Grace had no idea how long the Germans chased them. The lights blinked on and off. A lump had formed in Grace's throat. Despite the crash of items being thrown around her and the whimpering of other women nearby, all Grace could hear was her heartbeat and the rush of blood against her eardrums. Was this how it had been for Tony in the end? Did he know the moment death had come for him? Or had it made him suffer, alone in the dark, before it stole his life? Every muscle in Grace's body froze, waiting for the inevitable explosion of fire, water, and metal to snatch her away. Only heaven knew if her final moment would be engulfed in a ball of heat or pressed down by the weight of the ocean as she sunk to her watery grave.

As officers, it was Grace and Eliza's responsibility to keep the troops under their command calm. However, they were barely keeping it together themselves. Grace could feel her anxiety flaring as the sirens blared on and on with no indication from the crew of letting up or even giving some kind of update. Normally, tapping her fingers in a soothing rhythm, no matter how tense the situation, would calm her some if not all the way down. But there had been no opportunity to do so with the boat jerking back and forth.

The sirens stopped finally. Grace let herself enjoy one full second of relief before she forced her head back into the game.

"C'mon." She grabbed Eliza by the arm. "We have to check on the others."

Eliza didn't move. Grace didn't have time to waste, so she left her friend behind. When she reached the enlisted women's quarters, Grace's eyes darted around to assess everyone's condition.

One girl was grabbing up a handful of hair rollers that had fallen to the floor. Beside her, another private, Mary Bankston, if Grace recalled correctly, appeared to have stumbled to her knees but was in the process of pushing herself back onto her feet. Grace reached out her hand to help Mary up.

"Are you all right?"

"I will be." Mary held her arm and made circles with her wrist. Satisfied that it was still in working order, she nodded. "Luckily, I don't have to type anything in the near future."

Another private, Lydia Thornton, had her arm around a woman, whispering what sounded like a prayer in Spanish. "*No temeré mal alguno; porque tú estarás conmigo . . .*"

Grace remembered when Lydia had first arrived at Fort Des Moines as a newly enlisted recruit. The young woman barely spoke English. She had come from way down in southern Arizona, right on the Mexican border, the product of a union between a Negro soldier stationed at nearby Fort Huachuca and a local woman of Mexican American origins. Lydia could understand the English spoken to her for the most part, but speaking it herself to others had been a challenge. Both officers and trainees alike had rallied around her to help get her language skills up to speed.

Grace sighed with relief that the enlisted women seemed to have survived the ordeal in one piece. But once she made it back to her quarters, she realized that Eliza, on the other hand, was in bad shape.

Whether or not they were still friends anymore, Grace had been around Eliza enough in the last two and a half years to know that the woman's armor had cracked. Grace could not recall a time when she had ever seen Eliza not smiling or rallying back with her determined chin leading the way and her eyes with a "don't mess with me" squint to them. But now, Grace was at a loss. The change had happened in what seemed to be the blink of an eye.

Grace found Eliza curled on the floor in the fetal position, with her hands covering her head. Her eyes were shut tight to the point of straining. She was shaking. But what really struck the fear of God in Grace was that Eliza's mouth hung open like she was screaming, but there was no sound. Grace rushed over to her. Now standing over her, Grace could hear that Eliza was making a sound: a low, screeching moan, similar to the dying dog she had come across with her cousins the one summer she had gone to visit her mother's relatives down in South Carolina.

The boat cut hard to the right. Eliza yelped from the jolt. They weren't out of danger yet it appeared.

Grace, who had stumbled but had managed to catch herself before falling on her face, got on her hands and knees and crawled toward her fellow officer. Eliza was moaning again, the same word over and over. "No!"

Grace reached out hesitantly, gently pressing her fingertips into Eliza's shoulder. "Hey, are you hurt?"

Eliza responded with the windmill-like fury of her arms. "No! No! No! No! No! No! No!"

All Grace could do was cover her face with her forearms as she slid herself just out of Eliza's reach. "Hey! I'm a friendly. It's okay. We're okay."

Well, they were okay *for now*. But Grace wasn't going to be the one to remind anyone that they were still in very real danger of being blown out of existence.

"No!" Eliza moaned again. By this time, the woman's arms had gone back to protecting herself, cradling her sides and the rib cage Grace knew to have been broken when Eliza had been attacked in that train station. The attack Grace had been helpless to stop from happening. No, the attack that had been *her* fault.

Dammit. That was why Eliza had been such a bitch to her in recent weeks, wasn't it? Guilt ate at her insides. Just as it had when Grace had arrived in Washington, D.C., and found out the extent of Eliza's injuries. Just as it had when she had reached out to Eliza by letter and telephone and received no response.

Grace took a deep breath. Back then, she had been unable to help this woman who, despite everything, she would call her friend. But dammit, she was in a position to do so now. She reached out again, wrapping her arm around Eliza's shoulders.

"Shh," Grace soothed. "It's okay. We're going to be okay."

For all she knew, they might die tonight. If that was what fate had in store for them, then they would spend their last moments together.

As friends. Whether Eliza liked it or not.

"No, it's not okay," Eliza whimpered. "He beat me. I couldn't do anything about it then. And I . . . can't do anything about it now."

"Yes, we can," Grace countered. "As long as we have breath, we can pray. And if those Germans board this ship, we'll be ready."

"How? They wouldn't give us guns. Wouldn't even train us on them." Eliza snorted. Grace noted that the tension in Eliza's arms had slackened and that she had begun to let herself lean against Grace.

"We will fight with whatever we can get our hands on then. This ship is loaded to the brim with munitions. They might not have taught us how to use those guns, but we'll figure it out if need be."

Eliza leaned back and stared at Grace. "Why are you here anyway, helping me?"

"Because you need it."

"What's your angle? You don't help anybody unless something's in it for you."

"Like I said, because you need it."

"You've never gone out of your way to help me before. You let him . . . you let me walk right into an ambush."

Grace stilled. "That's not true. I mean, I . . . It was late. I didn't mean to fall back asleep. As soon as I realized that you were in danger, I tried to get you help. We all tried . . ."

The ship jerked again. Eliza yelped. Grace tightened her grip around the woman's shoulders. The hold she had on her, in turn, comforted Grace.

"What matters is that I'm here for you now. I won't leave you now. I know you think I abandoned you in Kentucky. Yes, I messed up. But I did try to make it right. I got the porters to go on the radio for help. We did our best. I screwed up. I am so sorry. So, so sorry."

"In my head, I know that there was nothing you could have done that night. But I've seen how you can be persistent and clever when you want to. So I can't make those two facts jibe in my head to make it okay."

"I understand."

The ship jerked again before Grace could say more. Both of the women tensed. Grace held her breath, bracing herself for whatever happened next. But neither made a sound this time. It was funny how the two of them kept finding themselves thrown together—in this case, literally—when Army life as a Colored woman got tough.

Another moment passed. And then another. But the ship seemed to be staying its course. What in the world could be happening out there?

"I know I come off as a bitch. But I'd like to think that when the moment requires it, I'll always do the right thing. At least, I try to anyway." Grace paused a beat. "When I'm not too busy being a coward," she finished.

"Being a coward might have its place." Eliza pushed herself into a sitting position. She sniffed, then wiped her nose on the back of her sleeve. Grace raised an eyebrow.

"That wasn't very ladylike."

"Whoever said my aim was to be a lady?"

"All those fancy clothes you like to wear."

"Most of which I had to ship back home while I was packing up for this deployment. They said we could only bring one civilian outfit with us. Besides, my mother bought most of that stuff. The fancy stuff I mean. If I had my way, I'd live in Chuck Taylors and dungarees."

"I can't see them letting you cover society events for your family's newspaper like that."

"I never wanted the society beat. That was my father's doing. I've always wanted to cover sports. Baseball, that's my dream."

So now Eliza was telling Grace her deepest dream that she feared would never come true? Grace knew then that hell must have frozen over. Or, more accurately, that hell was literally chasing them down to the ends of the earth.

"Whoa. I never would have thought baseball."

"Yeah. I've loved the game all my life."

"Really?"

"Yeah, even played a little. I was recruited to play for an all-girls traveling softball league once. My father threw a fit."

"You didn't stage a walkout like you did to join the WAC?"

Eliza chuckled. "No. But only because he locked me in my room."

"He what? I'm surprised he didn't try that again when you told him you got in the WAC."

"Only because I planned ahead. I had my bag stashed in the front hall closet. I left in the middle of a formal dinner with our neighbors. Right in the middle of the dessert course."

"Let me guess, he was too much of a good host to run out after you?"

"Something like that."

"Wow, that's some story." Grace paused. "So what are you going to do when the war's over and you go back to the States?"

"I'm not sure. But I have thought of going for something more dramatic, like showing up to the newspaper's office unannounced and banging out some baseball coverage on a typewriter."

"Yeah, I can see you doing that." Grace's gut reaction when she had first laid eyes on Eliza at the induction center had been right. The woman was fearless. She had more gumption than Grace had in her little toe. Grace remembered having some of that fearlessness about herself when she was younger, back when she was still performing recitals and practicing piano under Mama's strict tutelage. Grace had been terrified right before each and every time she had to go onstage to perform. But once she was seated at the piano bench, she felt like she owned the world. Until the one day when sitting there instead made her feel like the world owned her. And it had crushed her without a second thought. "I wish I could be that brave."

"You are. When you want to be."

"No, I mean, the thing I wanted most . . . I had it at my fingertips once. But when I got it right in my grasp . . . I froze and messed it up."

"What's that?"

"Juilliard. I used to play piano. I was really good. Good enough to be invited to audition. But I messed it up. The plan was to study at the best music school in Manhattan and then become a world-famous concert pianist. That was Mama's dream for me. For me to grace some French stage someday. I went along with it because I figured it was the only way to get me out of my mama's house. But I never told her the truth. But my brother knew. He was my biggest cheerleader. Tony sensed that I had no desire to play only the classical stuff, so he turned me on to the hipper stuff. But he's dead now. The Philippines."

"I'm so sorry, Grace."

Grace shrugged it off, not wanting to discuss Tony any further. "What I really want to do is compose."

There, she had finally shared with another person her dream of composing. This was the first time Grace had admitted that aloud. Of course it would be when her own fate was uncertain.

"So that's why I always find you scribbling on sheet music when you think no one is looking."

"Guilty as charged. But I still wouldn't mind going to Paris."

"Well, if the Germans don't blow us out of the water, you just might get your chance." Eliza smiled. It was the first time that Grace could recall Eliza genuinely smiling at her since they had come aboard.

Grace exhaled. The release of air caused her shoulders to drop, like they had just released the weight of a load she had been carrying for far too long. It felt good to have finally shared her actual dream with someone. Jonathan had tried to pry it out of her. But she hadn't been ready to accept it for herself yet. But now, under her own terms? It felt right. It was *her* dream. Not Mama's. Not Jonathan's. Not Eliza's. Something that *she* wanted for herself.

Why the hell did she need someone else to believe on her behalf for her to see it through to fruition? Why did she need someone else's approval to walk into a Juilliard audition with the confidence to knock it out of the park? She had performed on the Carnegie Hall stage by herself when she was thirteen years old.

Grace's arm dropped from around Eliza's shoulders. She had a sudden urge to run away, far away from this ship, the Germans lurking outside, her life in the WAC. Run back to the fool she had been at that audition, when Mr. Hutcheson asked her if performing was what she really wanted to do. He must have sensed her true desire to compose when she stumbled over the musical selections as written, preferring to improvise her way through the pieces instead. She decided that whenever she returned to New York, she would go back and request—no, demand—one more opportunity to show him what she could do on a piano. To have the confidence to declare her true aspiration: becoming a composer. To show him who she really was inside.

Now that her life was on the line, she was ready to take all the risks her former self had been too scared to breach.

"Thanks. I haven't had anyone believe in me in a long while."

"And thank you. For . . . looking after me tonight. My body healed from the attack long ago. But my mind . . . well, let's just say I'm still working on that. And thanks for not laughing at *my* dream. Girls like me aren't supposed to want to be sports reporters."

The truth was Grace had never actually hated Eliza. She had hated herself.

Grace wiped her eyes with the back of her sleeve and sniffed.

No more. The ridiculous war with Eliza that she had concocted in her head was over.

"Does this mean we might finally become friends now?"

"I think so."

"Good. Then I hope we get off this boat and through the rest of the war in one piece so you can make that happen, Eliza."

Eliza leaned back to get a better look at Grace. "Make what happen?"

"To see you become a sports reporter . . . *and* spite your daddy."

Eliza laughed a little, but it soon trailed off. "Yeah, that would be something."

The ship had kept a steady course for a while now. The beat of boot steps and yelling in the hallway had gone silent.

Eliza pushed herself to her feet, wiping off her bottom. She reached out her hand to Grace. When Grace took it, she helped her to her feet.

"But most of all, I wish you peace."

Eliza studied her for a moment. "Thank you. I wish the same for you."

Grace had no idea how much time passed before they heard the all clear. She flexed her fingers. A whoosh of relief escaped her lungs when she felt them wriggle at her sides. She was still here. She was still . . . *whole.*

CHAPTER 23

GRACE AND ELIZA continued to work together overseeing their troops in the days that had passed since the U-boat chase. Despite the terrifying event, there were still drills to practice, outgoing letters to censor, and flirty GIs to chase off. Eliza was more than happy to keep herself occupied with busywork. She hadn't slept much in the aftermath of the U-boat attack. The few times she had managed to fall asleep, visions of the man attacking her in the train station again and again snatched her back into consciousness.

However, the tension that had chafed between her and Grace had significantly decreased, if not disappeared altogether. Eliza was mature enough to admit that most of that tension had originated with her. Since there was no hope of ever bringing the true culprit to justice, she had directed all her anger at the easiest target, Grace. Now that they were working together, they were quickly becoming a well-oiled unit with a reputation for efficiency and a one-two punch when needed.

When the *Île de France* finally arrived at its destination, they had no way of knowing exactly where the ship had docked. No word had come down through the officers' grapevine yet. All that anyone could say with any certainty was that they were "somewhere in Europe."

Finally, their group received the order to line up on the deck with all of their gear for inspection. This was unusual because inspections usually happened once the troops got off the ship, and they were still on board. Whispers buzzed down the line, the women wondering why they were being singled out.

One private groaned, "I'm not getting on one of these troop ships ever again. The only way I'm going home is if they build a bridge over the Atlantic Ocean."

Poor Millie Veasey had been confined to her bunk the entire trip, sick. Unfortunately, she hadn't been the only one who suffered from a horrible bout of seasickness. The others responded to her with a chorus of "mm-hmms."

"Calm down, ladies," Eliza ordered. "The sooner you line up, the sooner we can get this inspection over with, and then the sooner we get off this thing."

Finally, Grace gave the order for everyone to fall in line. Like everyone else, Eliza was curious herself about this break in protocol. But wondering about it wasn't going to change anything. She took her place in line in front with the rest of the officers in their group.

Her questions were answered the moment she spotted two familiar faces in WAC uniforms, who were accompanied by an older Negro man, also in uniform. The woman leading the way was none other than her old friend Major Charity Adams, followed by her right-hand woman, Noel Campbell. She remembered them both very well from Officer Candidate School. The gentleman with them, the one sporting the general's stars . . .

"Straighten up, ladies. We have visitors. And one of them is a general."

Then she followed her own order, willing her spine to stretch straighter despite the weight of the pack on her back. The party of senior officers was just about to step off the gangplank and onto the deck of the ship. Grace likewise quickly composed herself, yelling, "Attention!"

"Thank you, Captain Steele. Captain Jones." Charity—or Major Adams, Eliza mentally corrected herself—gave them the briefest nod hello. Major Adams turned her head slightly to address the rest of the WAC soldiers. "Ladies, welcome to Scotland."

Scotland, huh? That would explain the thick accents she had trouble understanding coming from down below on the docks. What in the world would they be doing in Scotland?

"I'm happy to see you all have arrived here safe. It is my pleasure to introduce you to Brigadier General Benjamin O. Davis Sr. of the United States Army." The major gestured toward the brown-skinned man in uniform beside her.

Eliza blinked a few times because she didn't believe her eyes. Benjamin O. Davis Sr. was a legend back home in Harlem. As much as he was on the pages of the Negro newspapers, the man's name and face were familiar to everyone in their group, and even more so to Negro soldiers in the U.S. military. Davis was one of the very few men of the race to have attained the rank of general in the U.S. Army. Charity gave them all a moment to get over their awe before she continued.

"Well, the good news is you won't be in Scotland long. We're getting on a train headed for England as soon as we get off this ship," Charity started off. "The bad news is ETO Command—also known as the top brass over the European Theater of Operations—has ordered us to be ready for a review parade three days from now. And I gave him my word that you all would be ready."

THEY DISEMBARKED FROM the ship and made it onto the train without incident. Grace was exhausted by the time she had a chance to sit down on her assigned berth in the sleeper car. However, she did not fall asleep immediately upon lying down. She tossed and turned, but no matter how she positioned herself, she couldn't get comfortable. She was used to thin pillows and scratchy blankets by now. It took a few more minutes for her to figure it out.

It was her berth. It was too short for her long body. She pushed herself up onto her elbows and looked around the sleeping car that had been reserved for officers. *All* the berths looked like they were a good foot shorter than what she remembered them being back home in the United States.

Grace groaned. Every muscle in her body burned with exhaustion. She *had* to get some sleep.

She shifted again, this time into a contorted position that had her at as much of an angle that she could manage with her leg dangling off the side. She balled her pillow up into a lump. There, not perfect but better.

As she drifted off—finally—to sleep, Grace wondered how much more this new experience would force her to contort herself to make it work.

GRACE JOLTED AWAKE when Eliza shook her shoulder. "Get up. We're almost there."

She blinked, but even with the haze of sleep gone from her eyes, still all she saw was darkness. The only light was that of the moon streaming in from the window. Grace attempted to push herself up into a sitting position. She groaned. Her arms and legs all felt as heavy as lead.

She tried again. This time she succeeded in sitting up. Her reward for her efforts was bumping her head against the bunk frame above her. She groaned again. Were all British people unusually short? Grace herself stood at five feet ten inches. She was beginning to suspect that she would not just "blend in" with the local folk here for a variety of reasons, the least of which being the color of her skin.

Now that she was upright, she had a better view out the window. The moonlight revealed a dark countryside and what looked like ancient stone walls parceling the land. She assumed the buildings off in the distance were homes.

None of them had any lights on, though. *That's right, the blackout.* Grace had been under only partial blackout conditions back home in the United States. But here in Great Britain, they were under full blackout orders. She had never seen anything that dark, not even when she had been stationed in the Midwest.

However, she had seen the newsreel images of a smoldering London after long nights of German bombings. Her heart had ached for all the people over there who had been senselessly killed and displaced. Oh wait, Great Britain was no longer "over there." It was now "right here." Grace shivered. She was now right in the middle of it herself. They all were, wherever they were.

"Do we know where they're sending us yet or what we'll be doing?"

"No."

"Great, the mystery continues." Grace yawned. There was a sour taste in her mouth. She ran her tongue against her teeth. She needed to brush them before she went anywhere. "Any word on the ETA?"

"A half hour, give or take."

"Then scoot over. I'm getting up." Grace pushed herself to her feet. She just about stumbled to the floor. The steady rumble of the train moving over the tracks wasn't the problem. She had been on enough trains within the last two and a half years to be used to that. When she stood, she swayed back and forth like the sea as it crashed upon the shore. Her sense of balance had been off ever since she had gotten back on dry land. It was like her body thought it was still on board the *Île de France*. An arm reached out in the darkness to steady Grace's shoulder.

"They call it 'sea legs.'"

Grace grabbed the post attached to the berth. "So, we're doomed to stumble around like drunkards now?"

Eliza laughed as she let Grace's shoulder go. "No, they say it should last a few days—a week at most—to get your sense of balance back to normal."

"But we only have two days until we have an inspection parade for that general."

"Yup."

"So basically, he's setting us up to fail."

It was Eliza's turn to sigh. "Yup."

Grace shook her head gently in the darkness. "Some things never change. Not even on a completely different continent."

Grace began shoving the few personal items she had taken out back into her pack. It had been so cold when they had first settled down for the night that she had opted for sleeping in a clean uniform, so she'd be ready to go when she woke up, aside from her teeth and hair.

"It's not the Europeans. They tend to be more curious about us American Negroes than prejudiced. Only an American would set us up for this type of impossible task."

"And how would you know that?"

· "Mother and I came over on holiday to the UK and France the summer before I started college."

"Of course you did."

"Don't you go starting all of that 'rich girl' business again. I thought we had come to an understanding. We had a truce."

"Okay, fine. I'll direct my ire at the one who deserves it—this general who couldn't wait a few days. It's going to be so much fun when we disappoint him by showing him just how flawless our group of ladies can be."

They laughed. After all the differences they'd had between them since they first met, it felt good to bond with each other.

"I know that's right," Eliza affirmed between giggles.

Soon enough, they all were filing off the train and into Birmingham station. They had been told that Birmingham, the second-largest city in England, had mostly been spared from the wrath of the German bombers. But they soon learned that the locals had a stoic stiff upper lip about the reality of their blitz experience. The inside of their transport became eerily quiet as the convoy passed by the remains of a bombed-out building. It was the first of many they saw as they went through the city. It was one thing to see a sight like that in fuzzy black and white on the newsreels back home. It was an entirely different thing to have it right in front of you a few footsteps away, charred and crumbling in real life.

Finally, they found themselves on the grounds of the King Edward boarding school.

"A boarding school?" Grace exclaimed when she saw the sign on the building. "I wasn't expecting that."

Classes had been suspended, as many British parents had whisked their children off to the safety of the English countryside or even as far away as Canada. The now empty campus would be their home and workplace until . . . well, until whenever they were ordered to move on to somewhere else.

But for now, this was their new home.

The school itself dated back to the 1500s. There was quite a lot of stonework and hardwood floors in the buildings that would serve as the enlisted women's barracks and the officers' quarters and the classrooms that would serve as their workspaces. Not much in materials that would provide natural insulation. Grace wrapped her winter overcoat tighter around herself as they were given a tour of the place.

But the biggest shock was yet to come. Ever since they left Scotland, most everyone had been pretty vocal about their desire to bathe in some form or fashion as soon as they were settled.

"I just need five minutes to wash this travel stink off me," one private said wistfully once the enlisted women had been allowed to select their bunks. "And if there's a bathtub somewhere, I might just die and go to heaven."

"There's no bathtub. There's barely even what I'd call a proper shower," another woman said. "I can't even describe it. You have to see it for yourselves."

The shower "room" turned out to be an open courtyard with water spigots along the wall.

"You've got to be kidding." Grace's breath came out of her mouth in visible white bursts as they stood in the open-air cold. "I expected that we wouldn't have any privacy stalls. But no roof? It's the middle of February!"

Another girl turned on one of the spigots, then pulled her fingers out of her gloves. "The water's cold too. And there's only one knob."

Grace shivered at this unexpected reality for her troops. Charity, however, gave the girls a reassuring smile. "I know it's in no way ideal. But we'll learn to make the best of it somehow."

Later, when the officers finally had a chance to get settled in their own quarters, Grace was relieved to find that their shower was located indoors. But they too had only cold water in which to bathe.

"How much longer until it gets warmer here?"

Eliza shrugged. "I don't know. I guess we're about to find out."

There was no time to spare on complaining over the less-than-modern accommodations. They now had only two days to get ready to impress an unimpressible general.

CHAPTER 24

Birmingham, England
February 1945

MAJOR ADAMS INFORMED them that their mission here in England was to get the mail moving to and from the troops in the European theater again. Every able-bodied man had been yanked into combat duty to support the Normandy invasion the past summer. In the six months that had passed since then, the incoming mail had been piling up at the nearby U.S. Army airfield. Grace almost fainted when they were escorted there to inspect the six airplane hangars filled with the accumulated mail. And she wasn't the only one.

"Filled" didn't begin to describe the mess that stood before them. All six of the hangars were stuffed from floor to domed ceiling, wall to wall, front and back. Even in the cold weather, the stagnant air reeked of wet, rotting paper and decomposing baked goods sent in what must have been Christmas packages from over two months ago.

One of the mailbags began squirming. Out of the corner of her eye, Grace saw some of her girls' eyes bulging as a rat gnawed through the fabric sack and scampered away, its jaw still chewing on some goody. It skittered too close to one girl as it ran past, and she actually fainted.

"At ease. Somebody help her." Grace had had her company standing at attention. But after what they had been shown, everyone needed a break.

When the girl had been revived and was able to stand on her own power, Major Adams continued. "As I was saying, *this* is our assignment. We have six months to get these hangars cleared out. But in the meantime, General Lee will be here in two days. We will be marching in a review parade for his inspection. Anything less than perfection is unacceptable. Are we clear?"

"Yes, Major," they all replied in unison.

"It is my understanding that most of you are still dealing with sea legs. With that in mind, we will be splitting you all up into three eight-hour shifts. Starting tomorrow. You ladies need to get settled and get some sleep. Off to the barracks you go."

GRACE WOKE THAT next morning at five in pitch-blackness, disoriented. Normally, she was pretty good about waking up on her own on time. However, with the time zone and latitudinal changes, her body was not cooperating with her now. She attempted to stand. But she still wasn't used to being back on land and nearly tripped over her own feet.

"Dammit."

"Are you okay?" Eliza's groggy voice called out.

"Yeah. I could just use a whole day in bed."

"Couldn't we all?" Grace heard Eliza's sheets rustle and then it was quiet again. That girl had the nerve to roll over and go back to sleep. Grace padded her way to the footlocker where she had stored her toiletries. She wound up stubbing her toe on . . . something in the process.

The rest of the morning didn't go any better. Thankfully, everyone in her company reported to drill practice on time. But the sharp precision they'd had back when they were boarding the ship in New York was gone. The women were tired, unbalanced on their feet, and freezing cold despite their winter clothes.

After lunch, everyone was a little bit more awake for their crash course in sorting and processing the mail. There were information cards kept in filing boxes for each of the several million U.S. servicemen who had been deployed to fight in Europe. That was in addition to the U.S. government employees and Red Cross workers who were also on the Continent. It would be one team's job to organize and maintain these cards as daily reports of personnel movement came in. It would be another team's job to match each piece of mail with its intended addressee's information card to find out where that letter should go.

One girl lost her cool during her practice sort. "This letter is addressed to 'Johnny in the Army.' There's, like, ten of them like that in this bin. What are we supposed to do with these?"

Grace pinched the bridge of her nose. "How many more impossible tasks can they throw our way?" Grace didn't miss the private's frown. She quickly clarified. "My irritation isn't with you. Put those letters in their own bin. We'll just have to form another squad to handle the ones that require a little more digging to match up with the right information card."

It was turning out to be a very long day.

By the time they showed up at the mess hall at eight o'clock for a late dinner, Grace and everyone else in her company were nodding off into their plates. They had literally worked themselves, as the old folks would say, from "can't see to can't see." That night, Grace was asleep before her head hit her pillow.

All too soon, it was the morning of General John Lee's review.

A trumpet blaring reveille yanked Grace and everyone else from their well-earned slumber. It was pitch-black in her room. Now more acclimated to her new surroundings, she fumbled to pull the cord on her tableside lamp.

She found Eliza's watch beside the lamp. It was 4:00 A.M. Damn.

Grace fumbled out of her sheets. Momentarily forgetting where she was, she pulled her legs out of the bed and dropped them down onto the ice-cold ancient wooden floor. She hissed a curse, then slapped a hand over her mouth. But then she remembered one of the perks of being an officer was that she shared a room with only three other women, unlike the enlisted members of the unit who had to sleep twelve to a room. They had arranged their quarters so that each room had a member of each of the three different work shifts, so that they could have some semblance of privacy, peace, and quiet at some point in the day.

Grace had become less of the stiff, strictly by the books type she had been in her early days as a WAC. However, the new, more relaxed Grace was going to have to step down to her old stiff, no-nonsense, über-orderly self for the day. The reversion back to the old Grace started before she arrived at the mess hall. When she dressed in her uniform, she made sure every crease was straight, every stray thread was tucked away, and everything pinned was on securely. She examined every woman under her command with the same eagle-eyed precision.

"Browne, stop slouching. Sit up!"

"Young, your hair looks a mess. Fix it."

"Lewis, you look like you're about to drop dead asleep into your eggs. I need you awake!"

The word must have spread with a quickness that Captain Steele was not the one to be messed with that morning, because the majority of her company made a beeline in the opposite direction whenever she came near for the rest of chow time.

"Report down to the parade grounds by oh eight hundred hours sharp, private. Spread the word. That's an order."

"What is, ma'am—the oh-eight-hundred part or the spreading-the-word part?"

"Both." Grace didn't yell at the private, but her firm reply came out in a way that let her know that no further questions would be tolerated. Grace wasn't especially interested in making or maintaining any friendships on this particular morning. She didn't have time for that.

She got up and carried her tray toward the front to discard her mostly untouched breakfast. In the few days since their arrival, the cooks in the battalion had proved themselves to be more than competent in the kitchen. Quite honestly, their food tasted like a gourmet feast in comparison to the typical Army chow back in the States.

Her stomach growled as she fastened the buttons on her heavy double-breasted winter coat. But she only trusted herself to keep down some buttered toast—mm, real butter—this morning. Charity had confided in her officers the day before that she had bragged to the general that her girls were perfection in motion when they drilled. Grace's shoulders had been a mass of tight muscles ever since. She slipped on her gloves and tucked her scarf into her coat.

She tapped out the opening phrases of *Moonlight Sonata* on her thigh. First, the traditional way, followed by a little bit jazzier rearrangement of her own design. Grace felt her nerves melt away. Now she was ready to head out to her company's designated staging area.

The wind blew right through her the second she cleared the school's main building. She tugged her scarf tighter around her neck as she approached the staging area. The "parade grounds" were actually an open sports field adjacent to the school buildings. Had it been in the United States, there would have been football goal posts at either end or a baseball diamond carved into the grass with one corner framed by dugouts on either side. But this one was just a huge empty field encircled by a wooden fence. Grace could see brick residential homes on the other side of the fence. As more enlisted women came outside, faces peered out the windows.

Ever since they had arrived two days prior, the locals had been eyeing them with curiosity. Charity had told her officers that she and Noel had been receiving stares everywhere they went since their own arrival in England almost three weeks ago. Grace had yet to see a person of color in the city who wasn't a part of their battalion. But some of the guys at the airfield had mentioned that they had seen a handful of men from the Caribbean the last time they were on leave in London. Hearing this gave Grace a touch of homesickness, as she remembered the strong West Indian presence back in Harlem. And the American drivers of the trucks that had brought them into town from the train station had been Negroes. But she hadn't seen any of them since that first day.

"Good morning, Captain." Major Charity Adams strode toward Grace with a confident smile. There was a sparkle in her eye, but Grace didn't miss the way she clenched her fist at her side. It looked like the major was a bag of nerves too. "Are we ready?"

Grace stopped to stand at attention and salute her. "Ready to get out there and show 'em what we got, ma'am."

"That's what I like to hear. At ease."

Grace relaxed. She started walking again, stepping into pace alongside the major.

"Now tell me the truth: Do you think our girls are ready? I

know you all have only been here two days . . . a hectic two days, at that. The last thing I want is to lose face in front of the general. Of all the people, he's the one we need to look out for. As you can see, he's the type to stick us in a bind just so he can see us fail."

"Mm-hmm. Yes, I know the type."

"In this case, I think you already know that failure is not an option." Her mouth curved into a slick half smile.

"No, ma'am. It's not. That's why I've instructed the girls in my company to march like their lives depended on it."

"That's what I like to hear, Captain." Major Adams then excused herself as her second-in-command, Captain Noel Campbell, alerted her that General Lee's staff had arrived.

Soon the rest of Grace's company had assembled at the parade staging area. They quickly lined up in review formation as word came down the line: "Heads-up! Major Adams is coming back!"

"Attention!" Grace barked the order. All her soldiers stiffened, their arms at their sides, and looked straight ahead. "Remember, ladies, soft knees! You will not embarrass me today by passing out. Is that clear?"

"Yes, Captain," her company spoke as one.

"Good." Grace took her place in the front.

A moment later, Major Adams approached with Captain Campbell following a step behind her. "Nice. Exactly what I like to see. Looking good, soldier!" Major Adams all but hollered in one private's face. Grace clenched her fists tighter. But, thankfully, the private did not flinch.

Major Adams's face broke out into a wicked grin. "Yes! That's what I'm talking about! You all are not just *the* battalion. You are *my* battalion. And *my* battalion has *got* to look good."

Major Adams stopped when she got to where Grace stood. She

was still grinning. With a nod, she said, "This is it, Captain Steele. What we've been preparing for since we first met on that train to Des Moines. Let's go show the Army brass over here how it's done."

Grace grinned right back at her commanding officer and friend. "Yes, Major. It would be my pleasure."

The battalion spent the next hour marching through Birmingham. The parade route took them along the city streets. Now Grace and the other soldiers were able to get a sense of their new home for the time being. Since the purpose of this particular parade was for the general's review, the city residents had not been formally invited to come watch. But the locals lined the roads on both sides, nonetheless. They cheered and waved at the women as they marched by. For Grace, it was a little disconcerting at first to receive such a rousing welcome from so many people who looked so different from her and to hear her native language spoken in a way that was different from what she was used to. But their friendliness was infectious, and quite frankly, she had to catch herself several times to keep from breaking rank and waving back.

But on the inside, she was beside herself. She had finally made it to Europe against the odds. Who knew? Maybe she'd even get the chance to see Paris one day in the near future.

Soon enough, their procession was filing back onto the parade grounds adjacent to the King Edward School. The ceremony ended. General John C. H. Lee was pleased.

Now it was time for the women of the newly designated 6888th Central Postal Directory Battalion to get to work.

CHAPTER 25

Birmingham, England
March 1945

B Y THE TIME the second half of the battalion arrived in Birmingham a few weeks later, the now formally commissioned 6888th Central Postal Directory Battalion had organized itself into a fully operational twenty-four-hour machine. With three eight-hour shifts working continuously one after the other, the backlog that had filled six airplane hangars when they had arrived had been cut in half.

On the tail end of the morning shift, Grace retrieved another bundle of letters from one of the mail bins. There was an hour left in her company's mail-sorting shift. Her fingers danced through the stack as she muttered each of the names to herself. "Bobby. Robbie. Bob. Rob-O. Ro-Ro . . ."

Not one had a last name attached to it. Grace had been astounded by the number of mailed items that came through like these when her company had first been assigned to sort all the letters addressed to "Robert," or what they jokingly called the "Bob Job." Now, a month later, matching each letter to one of the several thousand Roberts currently deployed in Europe was just another day at the office.

"How many do you think we can knock out before quitting time, Captain?"

Grace looked up as Private Mary Barlow grabbed a bundle of her own from the bin. She returned the greeting with a nod. "Your guess is as good as mine." Grace watched Mary walk back to her workstation.

Grace held up a parcel that had burst open on one end. It looked like something inside it had melted.

Mary pointed at the honey-colored goo that had leaked onto Grace's hand. "What a mess. What do you think it was?"

Grace sniffed her hand. A mix of menthol, peach, and petroleum jelly assaulted her now wrinkled nose. "I'm going with hair pomade and chewing gum."

She grabbed the rag that she kept on her desk for instances like this. When she finished wiping off her hand, the rag looked like it was on its last leg. Grace sighed as she dropped it into the trash basket beside her desk. It had been her last one, and her fingers still had a thin layer of residue on them.

"I'll get you some more." Mary got up from her workstation again. She went out into the hall where the laundry unit set out a stack of rags for them each day.

Meanwhile, Grace studied the outer packaging for clues that would help her figure out who the intended recipient was. It had been addressed to "Robert G., U.S. Army, Somewhere in Europe."

"Great," she muttered to herself. Grace carefully pulled out the contents of the package. She smiled when a small, now empty jar of Dixie Peach Pomade fell onto her desk. However, the letter inside was not so easy to remove. It turned out that the chewing gum that Grace had also correctly guessed was in there had melted, causing the paper to adhere to the packaging.

Mary returned with a fresh set of rags. She placed them on the corner of Grace's desk. Then she handed Grace one that had been dampened with cool water.

"Thanks." Grace wiped the last of the residue from her hand. She held up the Dixie Peach jar with her clean hand and grinned. "Looks like I was right on both accounts. Let's hope the gum and the grease didn't make the letter completely illegible."

Mary laughed. As she returned to her station, she added, "Good luck with that."

"I'm going to need it." Grace returned her attention to the letter. Destroying a good portion of the outer packaging was inevitable. She jotted down all the information she could glean from it before she went for her scissors. The return address simply said "Mom." No help there. Thankfully, it had been stamped by the sender's post office back in April of the previous year.

"An almost year-old letter from Dublin, Georgia, huh? Something is better than nothing." Grace wrote this information down on her notepad. There wasn't anything else on the outside that looked useful. She took her scissors and began to carefully cut the packaging and the gum away from the letter. When it was freed, she unfolded the letter.

My dear baby boy . . .

This was the part that Grace hated most about her job—reading someone else's letter. In most cases, the letters contained run-of-the-mill greetings, best wishes, and innocent gossip about family and friends. That did little to lessen the feeling each time that Grace was intruding on a stranger's privacy. However, a letter's contents provided the clues that ultimately led her to the rightful owner.

Some men came by the house today with some sad news.
Germans shot down Anthony's airplane over in Africa last
week. I'm sorry to say your brother is gone, son. I need you
to take good care of yourself over there. You're the only one I
have left . . .

Grace gasped as her eyes darted back to the name "Anthony."
The letter fluttered to the floor. Her hands shook as an invisible
vise took hold of her lungs, stealing her air. Her body may have
been there in that cramped office in a drafty school in the middle of
England. But her mind snatched her back to that sticky summer
evening when a knock at her family's door had changed everything.
A knock that she wished had never been answered.

Mary rushed over to her side. "Grace, are you okay?"

"I'm fine. I . . ."

This was not the first time she had read a letter informing a soldier of a loved one's death. She handled letters like these at least
once a week. But this was the first one where . . .

"This letter says that his brother has been killed. His name was
Anthony. Tony . . ."

The letter had been written lovingly by hand. But all Grace
could see was the typewritten telegram that her own family had
received. How reading the words "regret to inform you" snatched
all the warmth from her body. How she had sobbed when the uniformed visitors had given them the news. Grace put her fist in her
mouth. She bit her knuckle to keep herself from sobbing aloud.
Her whole body vibrated from the restraint.

"Maybe you should go lie down." Mary placed her hand on
Grace's back. "You look like you've seen a ghost."

"No." Grace shook Mary away. "I have to find this Robert. He needs to hear this from his mama and not from some strangers or a damn telegram."

She picked up the pages of the letter from the floor. It took several tries to collect them all since her fingers were still unsteady.

Mary took a reluctant step back. "Are you sure? I can get the chaplain. You look like you should get looked at by a medic at the very least."

"I'm fine. It's just a shock. It's . . ." Grace paused, grasping to find the right words.

"Too close to home," Mary finished for her. "Too much like your brother, right?"

Grace stared at Mary, not expecting the younger woman to have known about Tony.

"His name was Anthony too. You talked about him that night when the Germans attacked our ship. I overheard you when Captain Jones lost her cool."

"That's right. I did. That was an intense night. I'm surprised you remembered anything."

"Your composure is what got me through that night. And every day that we've worked together since we've been here. You always keep it together when everything else is falling apart. I was terrified that I was going to die on that boat. It was my lowest moment since joining the WAC."

The vise grip on Grace's chest loosened. She had perceived her lack of emotion during stressful moments as proof that she was a heartless bitch. It was a shock to hear that the young woman before her instead found it admirable. "I'm glad to hear that I was helpful."

The response sounded empty to her own ears. Ironically devoid of emotion. She smiled at Mary, hoping that her mouth could convey the warmth that her words could not.

Mary returned the smile. "You made me want to be brave. I'm just humbled that I'm able to be here now to return the favor."

Now there was a lump in Grace's throat. "Thank you."

Grace looked up at the clock. Only a few minutes left in their shift. She nodded her head in the clock's direction. "It's almost quitting time. How about you run on ahead a little early. I'll cover for you."

Mary chewed half of her bottom lip. "Are you sure?"

"Yes. I'm sure a few minutes to yourself in the barracks ahead of everyone would be a treat. And I . . . I'll be fine."

A smile broke out across Mary's face. "Well, when you put it that way. I guess I'll see you tomorrow, Captain!"

It was only when the door closed behind Mary that Grace put her head down on her forearms and cried.

Once she had cried herself out, Grace wiped away her tears and got back to work. So far she knew that this Robert G. and his brother, Anthony, were from somewhere in Georgia. Grace jotted this information down on her notepad. She began to scan the letter for more clues.

> Once word got out about Anthony, the neighbors started coming by with food. So much food. I'm afraid most of it will wind up in the trash. But Randy Johnson's mother from down the street did drop off one of those 7UP pound cakes you boys like so much. She visited for about an hour. She said she thinks he's somewhere in Belgium. Maybe you two will bump into each other. How swell would that be? I hate to think of you over there with a bunch of strangers when you receive this letter . . .

Grace wrote down a few more notes. A few of her Bob Job girls had made a list of all the Roberts in their files. They kept it next to the cubbies where they filed their index cards for each soldier stationed in Europe. Grace got up and grabbed it along with a fresh notepad. She made a list of everyone on it who had a last name starting with G and a home address in Dublin, Georgia—a total of about twenty names in all.

Then she went over to the next room where they kept all the soldier cards for last names beginning with J. There she was able to find the card for a Randy Johnson whose hometown was Dublin, Georgia. With his home address in hand, Grace was able to find her Robert G.—also known as Robert Gordon of the Fourth Infantry Division—who thankfully lived on the same street.

"Yes!" Grace pumped her fist in the air.

"What are you still doing here, Captain?" Sergeant Dolores Browne popped her head into the workroom. Dolores worked the evening shift but liked to get herself settled in early.

"Oh, sorry. I thought I was alone. I just made another impossible match."

"Woohoo!" Dolores joined Grace in pumping her fist in the air. The Bob Job crew had created a tradition of celebrating every time one of them matched a letter with incomplete addressee information to a soldier's card.

"Thanks." Grace grinned. "I'll just finish repackaging this and I'll be out of your way."

Dolores reached out her hand to take what was left of Robert Gordon's package from her. "You've been here long enough. I'll take care of it."

"Okay. Thanks."

A few minutes later, an emotionally exhausted Grace fell face-first onto her bunk in the officers' quarters located across the street from the main building of the King Edward School.

"I am so tired," she moaned into the pillow. Each word was punctuated by a pause for emphasis. "I'd give anything for a warm shower and some leave so I wouldn't have to move for forty-eight hours."

Eliza leaned over the side of her bunk, located above Grace's. "I can't grant you a weekend pass, but I can score you an invitation for a home-cooked meal."

Grace rolled over and propped herself up onto her elbows. "Tell me more."

Eliza grinned at her, then jumped down from her bunk. Without blinking an eye, Eliza then plopped herself down onto Grace's bunk. This was one of Grace's pet peeves. Eliza had a bad habit of taking up space—one she was totally oblivious to—and Grace had a thing about other people's behinds on her bed. However, Eliza's mention of a home-cooked meal overrode Grace's annoyance. She bit her tongue.

"As you know, my duties as Special Services officer require me to go off-site around town to procure various supplies, equipment, and services. A side perk of that is it puts me in contact with the local population. And a lot of the local population have been curious about us, so naturally they like to come up and talk to me . . ."

Grace rolled her eyes. Eliza always took forever to get to the point. It got on her nerves. "Girl, stay focused. Skip to the 'home-cooked meal' part."

"I *am* getting to it. Hold on to your knickers."

"My what?"

"Knickers. It's what they call underwear over here. Anyway, most of the locals just want to say hello and extend thanks for us

Yanks coming to the British people's aid. So I was on my way back from a public relations visit with the lord mayor's staff. I bumped into this older lady—a Mrs. Louise Brown—while she was picking up her ration coupons at city hall. As it turns out, her only son is 'somewhere in France'—well, that's what she thinks, she doesn't know for sure. She tells me that she wants to extend a kindness to the Americans that she hopes some French family might be bestowing on her son. She said that I look like a nice girl and why don't I bring a friend along over to her flat."

"So you want me to tag along with you to a total stranger's house in a city we don't know in a foreign country."

"Yeah."

Grace frowned. Her gut told her this was not a good idea. However, she had been working on not being such a stick-in-the-mud since they'd come to town. *And* after her meltdown over that Bob Job letter this afternoon, she had an urge to do something a little out of character.

Grace bit her lip. "Did the old lady look like she could cook?"

Eliza's mouth spread into her trademark smile. "She sure did."

"Fine. Count me in." Grace kicked her feet into Eliza's side. "Now get your butt off my bed."

This was how Grace and Eliza wound up in the company of one Mrs. Louise Brown and her spinster flatmate, Miss Agnes Moore, for Sunday evening dinner. Grace and Eliza had even gifted the widow and spinster with a bar of chocolate that had survived their Atlantic crossing, much to their hosts' delight. It was not lost on the visitors that hosting them for a meal had taken up a portion of their meat rations for the week. They hoped the rare treat for civilians this side of the Atlantic would help to make up for their sacrifice in the name of hospitality.

Before Grace and Eliza knew it, the midnight hour was creeping upon them. More than once, they had glanced discreetly at their watches and exchanged knowing glances as Mrs. Louise and Miss Agnes—as they insisted on being called—continued to chatter on about what their homeland had been like before the war. The Americans had attempted to excuse themselves politely, noting the late hour. But that didn't deter Mrs. Louise from pulling out a cardboard box of pictures depicting her son as a youth.

"He was such a cheeky chap back then." Mrs. Louise chuckled nostalgically at a picture of her son, Edwin, as an infant in his "nappies." She looked over to Miss Agnes affectionately and squeezed the woman's hand. "We were so fortunate that Agnes here came into our lives in those years after my Edmund was killed in the Great War. He died at the Battle of the Somme, you know. I should have a picture of him in here . . ."

Mrs. Louise stretched her fingers toward the back of the box.

"Is it normal for dinner to go this late?" Grace whispered to Eliza. They had been there since five o'clock in the afternoon. It was now going on half past eleven.

"How should I know?" Eliza whispered back, shrugging. "Maybe late-night meals are just how they do things over here."

Eliza settled back into her hard, threadbare chair. She stifled a yawn behind her palm. She didn't want to alarm Grace, who had given her a suspicious look when she told her what time dinner was supposed to start. Back home, social calls such as this one would have been set for a little earlier in the afternoon. It was a necessary precaution owing to the air raids the city had suffered under the last few years.

Mrs. Louise looked up from the box of photographs on her lap. "Oh no, I'm boring you with these pictures, aren't I?"

Eliza quickly pasted a smile on her face. "It's just getting a little late is all."

Mrs. Louise glanced at the ancient clock on the corner table. "Oh dear, it is late." She and Miss Agnes shared a look. It was obvious that Mrs. Louise felt bad. It looked like the woman was finally going to bid them farewell.

Eliza nearly jumped out of that uncomfortable chair.

But then their host looked at her flatmate again. Miss Agnes raised an eyebrow. Mrs. Louise's shoulders dropped in defeat. "I'm almost done with this box of pictures. It won't be but a few minutes more. You don't mind, do you?"

What had that look from Miss Agnes been about? Eliza hadn't been able to get a bead on her all night. The woman had a nervous air about her, almost domineering actually, that sent Eliza's reporter instincts abuzz.

"If you're sure it'll only be a few minutes more. We really do have to get back to our post. We'll be in big trouble if we arrive after curfew. Or, worse, we could get caught in an air raid or something."

Eliza hated to play her guilt card on the old woman. It had been almost a year since the last German night raid had fallen upon Birmingham. But the urban landscape still bore the scars of bombed-out buildings in the city center and rows of recently dug graves in the nearby cemeteries. With active hostilities with the Axis still going on across the English Channel on the Continent, the threat of another German attack was a very real and constant concern.

"We haven't had an attack since you Colored WACs arrived in the city," Mrs. Louise assured her.

"Yes, only that one night of air-raid warnings. But no bombs,"

Miss Agnes chimed in with a sickly-sweet smile. "You Yank ladies seem to be the stroke of luck we've needed around here."

Mrs. Louise chewed her bottom lip. "Oh, Agnes, they're right. It is getting late. How about I fix you up a bag of leftovers for your lunch tomorrow?"

Grace gave Eliza a look that screamed she had better keep her mouth shut. Eliza almost blurted out that that wouldn't be necessary, but she didn't want to insult her hosts' hospitality. The meal itself had been nothing fancy: a meat pie—the British women called them pasties—that was more vegetable scraps than meat. The tea was weak but still tasted better than the plain brackish well water that the American women were slowly but surely becoming used to.

British civilians had been subjected to rationing and making the most of what they had for far longer than the American public had back on the home front. But the conversation and start of new friendships made the time spent together seem like a four-star outing.

Eliza took a sip from her teacup. She smiled politely as she forced herself to swallow it. She considered herself a coffee girl. She had never much cared for tea before the war. She had grown to loathe it now that she was living in England. But she dared not insult her hosts over something so insignificant in the greater scheme of things.

"Mrs. Louise. Ma'am . . ." Eliza gently placed a hand on Mrs. Louise's wrist when she returned from packing up the leftovers. "I really do want to see the rest of your pictures. But it is getting quite late and we really need to get back to our quarters."

"Oh, but you mustn't!" Miss Agnes's protest came out a bit more forceful than she apparently intended, causing them all to jump in their seats. The woman had been quiet for most of the evening, sharing very little of herself. "Oh, I am sorry. We just wanted to see if the rumors are true."

Grace and Eliza gave each other quizzical looks. Grace shrugged, then stifled a yawn behind her fist.

"What rumors?" Eliza asked the older woman gently.

Now Mrs. Louise had the grace to look sheepish. "I apologize. I know it was rude of us to keep you two out so late. Especially since we've had such a lovely evening together. But we just had to know . . . I just had to see it for myself."

Grace leaned forward. "See what?"

"Why your tails, of course. That's what them American fellas told us about you all before you came."

"Tails?" Grace and Eliza asked the question at the same time.

"They said that back where they come from, all the . . . the . . . the . . ." Mrs. Louise paused. Her cheeks turned pink with embarrassment. She looked to her friend for assistance.

"I believe the word you are looking for, my dear, is the *Negroes*." Miss Agnes paused after whispering the word. Then she cleared her throat to continue. "Those American boys were quite insistent that your people grew tails down to their ankles once the clock struck midnight."

An uncomfortable silence followed. Eliza's mouth opened, but she quickly closed it. What did one say in response to such a preposterous admission? She watched as their hostesses hung their heads in shame. As much as she wanted to chastise these women for believing this story for even a second, what was the point? She was more annoyed with the mean-hearted American soldiers who had fed them these lies.

"I told Agnes that it couldn't possibly be true," Mrs. Louise chimed in as an attempt in her defense, her cheeks now rose-colored. "I told her I would prove it to her, I would. And now here we are, the both of you exhausted, and it's all my fault."

Just then, the grandfather clock in the entrance hall of the flat rang out its announcement of the midnight hour. Both Eliza and Grace stood. Eliza smoothed down the back of her skirt with her hand. "As you can see, no tails. We're still human beings. Two arms. Two legs. That's it. Just like you."

Miss Agnes pushed herself to her feet and extended her hand to Eliza. "Please accept our sincerest apologies."

"I accept." Eliza took the proffered hand and shook it. "A mean trick was played on you at our expense."

"We insist that we make it up to you. We have enjoyed your company so. Please say you'll come back for afternoon tea. We'll have you back home before dusk. You have our word."

Mrs. Louise eagerly nodded her head in agreement. "And you must take our torches with you to get safely back home."

The older woman handed them each a flashlight with brown paper over the illuminated end to dim it in accord with local blackout regulations.

Grace smiled. "How could we say no to an offer like that?"

ONCE OUTSIDE, GRACE shared a good laugh with Eliza over the unexpected turn that their evening had taken. She grabbed Eliza's arm as she attempted to stifle a giggle with her other hand. "Girl, what on earth . . . ?"

"I was starting to feel bad since I all but dragged you to come with me tonight." Eliza sniffed as she attempted to get herself together. "All I know is, if I ever figure out which one of these white boy GIs told those two sweet ladies that lie, someone is going to get a piece of my mind."

"And to think I mistook you for a prissy miss the first time I met you."

"Ouch. My feelings." Eliza playfully clutched her chest to be dramatic. Grace wasn't the first person to make that assumption about her. The prissy rich-girl veneer was something she had been molded into her entire life. She was just glad that her friend had finally been able to see through it. She rolled her eyes at her former nemesis.

Grace knocked her in the shoulder. "Girl, please. We both know that you're made of tougher stuff than that."

"You're damn right I am."

They turned the corner onto the main road that would lead them back to their quarters at the King Edward School. The back of Eliza's neck prickled. Even with the blackout in effect, the difference between the residential street and the main drag was drastic, going from little blips of light peeking from behind blackout shades to total darkness.

Much darker than that train platform in Kentucky had been. The flashlights they had been given provided them only so much visibility. They could see maybe two feet in front of them. Anything could be lurking in the darkness. Watching them. Waiting for the right moment to attack. Eliza picked up her pace, leaving Grace in the dust.

"Hey, wait up!"

"No, *you* hurry up," Eliza called back over her shoulder. Behind her, she heard the pounding of footsteps coming closer. Common sense told her that it was only Grace catching up. But common sense had not been her default line of thinking since she had been attacked.

"If anything were to happen out here," Grace huffed between breaths once she caught up, "we stand a better chance if we're *not* separated."

"True, but the faster we walk, the sooner we get to safety." Eliza did not let up on her pace, now grateful for all those hated miles she had been forced to run during her early days in the corps.

"I've got your back, you know. You're not alone. Not like . . ." Grace's voice drifted off. For that, Eliza was grateful.

"The only thing that would've changed had you been there with me that night is that we would've been in the hospital together, instead of me being there alone."

They continued to trudge along in silence for a beat. Eliza mulled over what she had said, realizing for the first time that she was relieved no one else had been hurt that night in Kentucky.

"I know you're tired of hearing me say it, but I am so sorry—"

"I know." Eliza cut her off. As annoying as Grace's never-ending apologies had become, the anger she'd had toward her had begun to ease. But the energy behind it was still there, itching beneath her skin. It was time to do something more productive with it. Tonight's adventure had given her an idea as to what that something could be.

"What were Mrs. Louise and Miss Agnes saying about jujitsu back there?"

"That was Mrs. Louise. Something about it being popular among the young people here and that her son had been into it. Why?"

"The corps' policy about refusing to give us guns or any weapons training doesn't sit right with me. If I had been armed that night, then maybe . . ." Eliza paused. "Or even if we were armed now, I wouldn't be as freaked out. What if I arrange for the battalion to have self-defense classes? Then maybe we'd have a fighting chance if any one of us got cornered again."

"I think that's a great idea, Eliza."

"Great. I'll get started on setting it up tomorrow."

A WEEK LATER, Eliza stood at attention with tears threatening to stream down her face. The cool morning breeze burned her eyes, but that was not the cause of her tears. She had made good on her plans to set up self-defense training for the unit. Last night had been the first class. She was paying for it now. Every muscle in her body was on fire.

It had been torture dragging herself out of bed earlier. The cup of watered-down coffee she had been able to snag hadn't helped any. A nice warm bath would have been better. She hadn't had the opportunity to enjoy that type of luxury in over a year. The wind cracked its whip against her face again. This time, she was too tired to blink the tears away.

By the time her section was ordered forward to be presented, she was marching blind.

Eliza, along with the 6888th Battalion's afternoon work shift, had been ordered out to the parade grounds because some high-ranking general from London was coming to inspect them.

The problem with being the only all-Negro WAC unit in Europe was that every general stationed in England felt it was his duty to come to Birmingham to see "what them Colored girls were about." Eliza's friend Charity, now the battalion's commanding officer, had been working magic to make sure that these visits, which in truth were really intentional disruptions to their assigned mission, were spaced out and had the least impact on the daily operations. Which was why the remainder of the battalion was either working the morning shift or sleeping off the overnight shift.

Luckily, the women of the Six Triple Eight had become adept at accommodating these requests so that the military brass came and went as quickly as possible. Today's inspection by Lieutenant General Eugene Butler seemed to be no different from the rest.

Eliza's part of the procession stopped before the grandstand. As the officer over Special Services, she stood behind the unit's executive leadership team. The wind was now behind them, giving her an opportunity to clear her eyes enough to get a good look at their latest visitor. Lieutenant General Butler resembled a bulldog. He looked like the type of Army brass who strolled through the mess hall at the busiest times just for the kick of having the most soldiers saluting him all at once.

Butler puffed his chest out then grunted his approval. Eliza followed her battalion leadership onto the dais.

"Yep, he's definitely that type," she muttered under her breath.

Charity glanced back just long enough to shush her, then returned her attention to the next row of WAC soldiers approaching the dais to be reviewed. Eliza swallowed back the yawn that threatened to crawl out of her throat.

Oh yeah, once this guy was gone, she was definitely going to find an excuse to slip away for a ten-minute nap. Despite her exhaustion, Eliza felt good about the fact that she had taken the first step toward reclaiming her sense of well-being. She had learned only a few basic holds last night. But more important, she also had learned how to get out of those holds. Having to put on a show for ego-filled windbags like Butler here previously would have left Eliza feeling helpless, forced to do what the stars on his shoulder demanded. But now? She studied him from behind, pinpointing his potential weaknesses.

He might have authority over me to a certain extent. But he does not control me. A few minutes more until all formalities would be over and Butler would be gone. Eliza smiled and began to count down the seconds until he left.

That's when the boom of General Butler's voice invaded her revelry.

"I said I wanted to inspect your *entire* unit during my visit, Major Adams."

Eliza redirected her gaze back in front of her. The man's bulldog features had gone into attack mode. His jowls appeared to sway with irritation. His underbite had become more pronounced.

Eliza watched as Charity's back straightened. Instinctively, Eliza and the other Six Triple Eight officers surrounding her did the same.

"Sir, ordering the entire battalion out here would bring our operation to a halt." Charity's voice was deferential but firm. "The women that were presented to you are the only ones available who are not working toward our assigned mission or who have just finished their work shift and are now asleep."

"I demand to see them all before me. Now. That is an order, young lady."

"Respectfully, General, what you are asking of me is impossible." Eliza watched Charity flex her hand, which was out of Butler's line of vision, into a fist.

Butler lifted his chin. He puffed out his chest again. "Then maybe I should bring in another officer—a *white* officer—to relieve you of your command. One who will teach you how to follow orders properly, soldier."

An officer near Eliza—she dared not turn her head to see who—gasped. Eliza herself could've spit nails. The nerve of this man. There was no denying it. Charity was in the right—it didn't make any sense to halt operations for a parade. But sometimes being right could cost you everything.

She didn't care how many stars the Army had slapped onto his shoulder. Eliza would have gladly slapped off each one of them.

Charity lifted her own chin, then took a deep breath. Eliza held her own. The muscle in Charity's jaw twitched once and then twice. Anyone who knew the woman could tell that she was fighting mad.

Amazingly, she kept it together. With her shoulders back and her chin high, Major Charity Adams then uttered the five words that would sear themselves into Eliza's memory forever: "Over my dead body, sir."

This time, no one made a sound. Shock did not begin to adequately describe what Eliza felt in that moment, what everyone else up on the parade dais must have felt. Charity had stood up to and dared to defy one of the top-ranking American generals in Europe. Only President Roosevelt and General Eisenhower held a higher authority than him.

Eliza bit the inside of her cheek as she watched General Butler shove his scowling face right into Charity's. "That can be arranged, Major."

Charity didn't cower. Hell, she didn't even blink. Eliza was impressed with how she remained still as a block of granite. Butler continued to stare her down.

In the end it was he who took the first step back, Charity failing to give him the groveling act he so obviously craved.

"I'll see to it that you are court-martialed. If I'm feeling generous, maybe I won't have you shot for insubordination," he grumbled before storming away.

They all saluted his back. After Butler and his entourage had finally driven away, Charity gave the "at ease" command.

Eliza went over to comfort her friend. "What an ass—" She froze as soon as her hand palmed Charity's shoulder. The woman's entire body trembled with rage.

"Don't," Charity growled through clenched teeth.

Eliza had not realized how much tension she had pent up in her own body until she took a step back. The tense moment on top of the sore muscles from the self-defense class had her ready to collapse.

Eliza checked her watch. Only a few minutes until the mess opened again for lunch. She made the decision then that she would rather skip the meal to get in a much-needed nap. She was just about to make her exit when Charity called everyone back to attention.

"All battalion officers are to report to my office within the hour. Even the ones who are asleep."

"Yes, ma'am," they all responded in unison.

Eliza groaned on the inside. She already knew she was going to have a long night ahead of her. She and Noel, who was beside her, shared a worried look.

SIX HOURS LATER, Eliza found herself in Charity's office, still awake, with every muscle in her body throbbing. She was surrounded by her fellow officers and every policy manual and memo that had been issued to them by the Women's Army Corps and the European Theater of Operations high command. She had been listening to everyone's ideas with her eyes closed, if only to give them a break.

"I still say this article of war here is the way to go," Grace shouted over the hum of voices. She held up a book, jabbing her finger at a specific passage. "It says it right here. You can't completely stop an operation for immoral reasons."

"But ordering a troop review isn't 'immoral,' though," Eliza jumped in, her words slurring from exhaustion.

"It is when the motivation behind it is to satisfy one man's ego," Grace argued.

"True. But how are you going to prove it?" Eliza leaned her head back against the wall behind her. She held her wrist up to her mouth to muffle a yawn. Then she closed her eyes.

"Sorry we're not entertaining you enough, soldier," Grace snapped.

"Don't start. Please."

"Ladies, let's focus." Charity had chosen well in selecting Noel Campbell as her second-in-command. She too had been in their officer training class back in '42. Noel had always been their voice of reason who could yank them back on track during times like these.

"You're both making good points. Whatever our strategy is, we've got to keep it by the books. That's where policy comes in." Noel nodded toward Grace. "And we've got to have crystal clear proof that Butler violated policy." Noel gestured at Eliza, who dipped her head in acknowledgment. "Those of us who were there can tell you. That man was not only a bigot but a bully as well. It oozes from his pores. But saying so isn't going to help Charity get off the hook for backtalking to a general."

This time, everyone in the room nodded. They all had been in the corps long enough to know what was at stake here. They couldn't afford anyone making the battalion look bad, which in turn would make every one of their sisters in the corps look bad. Any perceived "bad" behavior from the Six Triple Eight ultimately would reflect back onto every Negro woman back home—whether she was in uniform or not.

The thought reverberated in Eliza's head: *any perceived "bad" behavior* . . . Eliza got an unexpected jolt of energy. "That's it! You nailed it on the head."

Eliza was on her feet so fast that Noel had to jump back. "I did?"

"Yes. Wasn't there a memo not too long ago that said something about not mentioning race?"

"Girl, please." Noel rubbed the bridge of her nose between two fingers. "You have no idea how many memos cross my desk on a daily basis. Can you be more specific?"

"I think I remember that one," Grace chimed in. "It instructed everyone in the field not to make any decisions or opinions based on race. We got it about a week ago."

"Of course you would remember something like that. You damn near have a photographic memory," quipped an officer in the back.

Grace tossed a balled-up piece of paper her way. "No, I don't. I'm just super organized."

"Super organized or not, I think you two just saved my behind." Charity stepped forward into the middle of their make-shift circle. "I remember seeing that memo too. If it didn't come from Eisenhower himself, then it came from someone directly under him."

Eliza grinned. "Someone like that would definitely outrank ol' bulldog Butler."

Charity returned her smile. "Exactly."

"It sounds good." Grace spoke slowly, like she was mulling it all over in her head. "But I'm not following how that would help us here."

"Eliza, maybe you should explain for the officers who weren't there." A smiling Noel, once again, steered them back on track.

"Butler messed up when he threatened to replace Charity specifically with a white officer. He darn near yelled the word 'white' in her face." Eliza looked at Charity. "I remember that part clearly because I watched her ball up her fist when he said it."

"Girl . . ." Charity blew out a heavy breath. "I wanted to smack him so bad. He had just had breakfast too."

Charity shook her head while waving her hand in front of her nose. They all laughed at that. Eliza noted that it was like a collective sigh of relief. The tension in the room had finally lifted.

When the laughter died down, Eliza asked, "So, do we have a case?"

Charity nodded. "Yes, I think we just might have a shot."

"Good. Now can we go get some sleep?" She added a yawn for dramatic effect.

"No, we can't just drop it," Grace retorted. "Charity is in some deep shit. You'd want her to pull out all the stops if it was your ass in hot water."

The room quieted. Even Eliza went still. She couldn't recall a previous time when she had heard Grace use such language. A twinge of shame washed over Eliza. But she was sooo tired. Not just physically from last night's class, but also mentally from clashing with the bigotry of Army brass at almost every turn it seemed.

"Maybe. But I just don't see how we'll be able to worm Charity out of this one. Before we were able to outsmart these fools because we were stateside with our connections and families close enough to back us up. You couldn't have better connections than the ones

I had through my daddy and you saw what still happened to me. And now we are going toe-to-toe with a high-ranking general? All we've got is us over here. Nobody has got our backs, I tell you. We can't even get a Negro GI to look our way. They're too busy fawning over every white girl who crosses their paths."

"Enough." The exasperation in Charity's voice silenced both Eliza and Grace. "Do you two ever stop?"

"No," the rest of the group said in unison.

"You would think they were real sisters," Noel added.

"We are all sisters," Charity said. "Sisters in arms. Ones who could use some sleep. Let's come back tomorrow refreshed and ready to be productive."

"Thank goodness." Eliza pushed herself to her feet. She hated how the movement was filled with all the caution that a woman twice her age would take. That made her wince even more. Eliza was about to turn twenty-six. Yet the energetic, spirit-filled young woman she had been just three years ago seemed from a lifetime ago. When had she become such an old-timer not just in body but also in mind?

CHAPTER 26

ELIZA PUSHED HER hip against the self-defense instructor's side and slid her arm around his back. Guy Hughes, at six feet two inches, had to be a solid two hundred or more pounds. Her fingertips only just made it to his waist.

"There's no way," she grunted as she attempted to reach farther.

"There is and you can," Guy assured her. "You've seen women in this class smaller than you pick me up and throw me onto the ground. If you can't reach, then you'll have to figure out how to adjust to make the move work for you."

Eliza stretched out her fingers again. She still came up short. Out of the corner of her eye, she saw Charity enter the gymnasium. Her mouth quirked a smile as she watched Eliza struggle.

"Just great," Eliza grumbled.

"Here." Guy guided her hand to the waistband of his pants. "Grab on to me here. Hold on tight."

She gripped his pants like it was a lifeline.

"That's it. Now, let me have it."

Eliza grabbed on to his arm that was closest to her and pulled. She pulled again. The burly Midlander barely moved.

"What's the holdup, Jones?" Charity called out to her. "Hug him like you mean it."

"Damn." She let go and stepped away. The last thing she needed was to be heckled by her fellow officers right now. She balled her hand into a fist, then let go. Her fingers shook from the exertion of today's class. "I can't do it. You're too big."

"You were fine until the point where you needed to transfer your weight."

"I keep worrying that I'll mess up somehow and hurt you."

"As long as I hit the mat, I'll be fine. Your problem is that you're in your head too much. You're worrying too much about the wrong thing. The point *is* to hurt your assailant. I'm not asking you to bloody kill anybody. Your only concern should be to incapacitate him enough so you can get away."

The word "assailant" triggered memories of the drunk man who had attacked her. And of another who had challenged her rank aboard the *Île de France.* "That's the problem. Should another man try to hurt me, I'm afraid I'll be out for blood."

Guy gave her a crooked grin. "Attagirl. I knew you had some fight in you."

"You got a minute?" Charity had taken their break in practice to approach them.

"Sure." Eliza wiped her face with a hand towel, hoping she looked warm from the exertion of pulling on Guy and not from embarrassment. "I was just getting a few extra throws in after class."

Guy gathered his things. "See you again in class tomorrow?"

"You bet." Eliza nodded and he walked off.

"I'm impressed with the self-defense program you started here," Charity said. "You've come a long way from the girl I met on the way to training camp. She would've been too worried about breaking a nail to grab on to a big guy like that."

"Yeah, well, that girl you met on the train has been through some things in the last three years."

"Yes, you have." Charity paused. "Which is why I am concerned about you. Especially now that I've seen how physically intense this self-defense class is. You haven't been yourself since you were . . ."

Eliza watched Charity's mouth open and close while she looked for the right words. She hated how everyone wanted to pussyfoot around what happened to her. But Charity was her friend, so she helped her out. "You mean, since Kentucky?"

"Yes, since Kentucky," Charity echoed. She looked relieved. "Despite my rank, I'm still your friend. I'm worried about you."

"I'm fine," Eliza said quickly. The medical staff back at the hospital, then her mother, and now her commanding officer had all hinted at without spitting it out that she might need to talk to someone about what had happened to her. She didn't.

"Right." Charity tugged at the hem of her uniform. "Well, I just came by to thank you for your input with the memo. You saved my behind—despite your complaining."

Charity's eyes shone with humor now. Eliza let out a sigh of relief, glad that the awkward moment had passed. She made like she was going to swat Charity with her damp towel. "Well dang, you could've said so in front of the rest of the girls."

"Perhaps. But I didn't know for sure until today that that memo would work as a defense."

"Wait, today was the day you were supposed to go face the music at HQ in London, right?"

Charity nodded. Eliza dropped her arm.

"What happened?"

"Luckily for me, Butler's superiors had no interest in generating the bad press that would come with court-martialing me. Once they heard the specifics of the conversation from the both of us and I reminded them of their own words in that memo . . . well, let's just say that Butler got his behind handed to him."

"No way!"

"Yes, while I was in the room too. Afterward, Butler even chased me down and apologized."

"No way!" Eliza repeated.

"He said, 'It's not often that anybody gets the best of me, soldier. But you did, and I deserved it. Please accept my apology. I was out of line. If you have need of anything in the future, do not hesitate to call me.'"

"What?" Eliza would have given anything to see that. "You, my friend, are a miracle worker . . ."

Just then, Noel came rushing in. "Charity, come with me. Something's happened."

Eliza and Charity shared a look. The words "something's happened" never meant anything good. Eliza picked up her pace and followed her commanding officers back to Charity's office.

"PRESIDENT ROOSEVELT IS dead," Charity announced to the hastily assembled full battalion before her. Unlike General Butler's whims, Charity had decided that this tragic event warranted a full stop to their work.

A number of the women gasped. Some wept openly, while others attempted to wipe away their tears discreetly. Charity's words made Eliza's blood run cold despite first learning the news over an hour ago when Noel had called her and Charity into her office. On a certain level, she wanted to cry. But the tears wouldn't come.

Another part of her wanted to scream. But the sound continued to stick stubbornly in her throat. Eliza swallowed to get it moving.

Grace, who was beside Eliza, nudged her shoulder with her arm. "Are you okay?"

"Fine." Eliza continued to look straight ahead, not budging from her attention posture one hair. It seemed like all the constant things she could rely upon in her life were being snatched away. She could barely remember a time when Franklin Delano Roosevelt hadn't been the U.S. president or, before that, governor of her home state. His fireside chats had been a comforting presence on her father's radio during the bleak economic times of her childhood through now with the shifting uncertainties of war. And when FDR's words had failed to comfort her, her father's arms had been there to embrace her and soothe away her fears.

All of that was gone now.

Her hands buzzed with an energy that felt like ants marching across her palms. She wanted to push something. Or punch it. Or even claw it with her fingers until the anger dissipated.

She balled her hands into fists instead.

"There will be no more work today. We'll be spending the rest of the day in mourning to honor our commander in chief's passing. You are dismissed," Charity commanded. The battalion remained in formation for a few seconds longer before individuals began walking away.

"I hate when my hands get that way." Grace extended her own fingers into a series of stretches.

"Like what?" Eliza wasn't really interested in whatever oddball hand-care thing Grace obviously wanted to show her. The woman treated her hands like they were her prized possessions.

"When they get all antsy feeling. They usually get that way when I'm feeling some kind of way and I can't shake it off. I find the best thing is to do something with them."

Now, that got Eliza's attention. "Something like what?"

Grace shrugged. "I don't know. Back home, I'd play the piano—"

"I don't want to play the damned piano."

Grace took a deep breath and shook off Eliza's interruption. She reached up to rub the back of her neck. A range of emotions played across her face. Eliza momentarily forgot about her itchy hands. "But that's not the point, is it? Try writing a letter. Or maybe throw balled-up socks at the wall."

"Or pick up a full-grown man and throw him onto the ground."

"Wait, what?"

Eliza waved her away. "Never mind. I'll see you back at our quarters later. I just remembered that I need to swing by the gym."

"Oh, okay." Grace, oddly enough, looked relieved.

WHEN ELIZA GOT to the gym, thankfully Guy was still there. "I'd like to give that move I've been struggling with another go."

Guy held up his arms. "I'm all yours."

She spent the next hour successfully throwing him onto the mat.

Afterward, an exhausted Eliza staggered toward the officers' quarters. Her body ached but her mind was racing. She had done it. She had picked up and thrown down a full-grown man.

She felt like a part of herself had been coaxed out of a dark, fear-filled place that had been buried deep inside her. Eliza felt like she could take on the world.

Eliza pushed open the front door to the sound of whoops and cheers. The noise disoriented her for a moment, yanking her from her own internal celebration. She grabbed a younger officer—a second lieutenant—by the arm. Eliza didn't know her as well as some of the others. She thought her name was Julia.

"What in the world is going on?"

"Get ready to start packing up your things." Julia grinned. "We're going to France."

"You don't say. Well, that is good news." Eliza returned Julia's grin. "When do we leave?"

"I'm not sure. Probably within the next few weeks."

Eliza let go of the other woman's arm and continued on to the room she shared with Grace. When she got there, Grace was in an unusually bright mood.

"Did you hear?"

Eliza dropped her bag onto her trunk. "About France? Yeah."

"I can't believe it. This is a dream come true. I've waited all my life to go to France." Grace dropped herself onto her bunk with a sigh. "Do you think we'll get to go to Paris?"

Eliza sat down and began pulling off her shoes. "Not if there's a chance that the Germans might bomb us, we're not."

"Don't be such a spoilsport." Grace threw a balled-up sock at her. Eliza ducked in time for the sock to fly over her head.

"I'm not, just being realistic. Trust me, I'm as happy as the next person to be shipped off to France next. That means my chances of getting a decent cup of coffee are about to increase tenfold. But most importantly, it means no more tea!"

CHAPTER 27

Somewhere on the English Channel
May 8, 1945

THE EARLY-MORNING FOG over the water was thick as stew. No matter how many times Eliza tried swallowing, the lump lodged in her throat, unbothered. Her body remained tense, on edge. It was too quiet out here. It was too peaceful. She didn't like being unable to see out over the horizon. Hell, she couldn't even *see* the horizon.

It was her first time out on the open sea since they had arrived in Scotland on the *Île de France*. The German U-boat chase they had experienced stayed at the forefront of her mind. And how she had broken down afterward. The confidence that had started to reemerge during her last weeks in England began to waver.

A passing British seaman stopped short when he saw her. "It's all right, love. No German sub would dare come this far into the Channel now."

Eliza responded with an unladylike grunt. She didn't care how much the onboard crew assured her that the English Channel had been safe for passage since the Allied invasion of Normandy almost a year ago, or that the English Channel was not actually the "open sea," paling in comparison to the vast Atlantic Ocean. Being out here on the water meant that she was under the control of others—of the ferry crew, of whatever or *whoever* might be lurking behind or under their vessel. More succinctly, she had no control, and she didn't like it.

"A smile wouldn't hurt, you know. There's already enough drudgery in the world."

Eliza turned her back to the seaman. She stopped herself just short of telling him what he could do with his early-morning cheer. Grace's no-nonsense demeanor would've been more welcome right now.

Dammit. She clenched her hand into a fist. This wasn't who she was. Grace was the bitchy one, not her. The darkness within had blindsided her just when Eliza thought she was beginning to feel like herself again.

An hour later, the fog that enveloped the ship broke to reveal the crumbling remains of a ruined city. Most of them let out gasps at the sight, including Eliza. She was one of the few on board who had visited Le Havre prior to the war. She was shocked at the dissonance. Gone were the medieval towers and spires reaching up into the air; they now only existed within her memories. She remembered the city as a thriving, bustling seaport town when she had passed through with her mother on their way to Paris. Children running through the market stalls just off from the docks where their mothers and grandmothers sold their wares and foodstuffs. There had been so many people then.

"What happened to all those people?" she whispered to herself.

And then the most astonishing thing happened.

As the ferry started to pull in alongside a makeshift dock on the otherwise bombed-out wharf, Eliza heard singing. When they got close enough, she was able to recognize the song as "La Marseillaise," the French national anthem. That's when she saw the people.

The streets were filled with people dancing and hugging in addition to the singing. It was quite the contrast to see women and children celebrating in the streets with tears streaming from their eyes amid the rubble of the port city. The pops of champagne bottles being opened could be heard everywhere.

Major Charity Adams emerged from an Army jeep waiting near the end of the plank walk. She had a huge smile on her face. "Welcome to France, ladies."

Eliza saluted her commanding officer. "Dancing in the streets to celebrate our arrival, eh? How did you manage to pull that one off, boss?"

"Don't I wish. No, I have the most wonderful news. The Germans have surrendered. The war in Europe is over."

Not one of them waited for the order to be dismissed before they whooped and hollered along with the French citizens around them.

NOT EVEN THE discomfort of the windowpane-less train with holes in its roof that they boarded next could dim their jubilation. And when they marched out in Rouen, it was to the cheers of a never-ending wall of soldiers awaiting them. Evidently, word had spread like wildfire that a WAC battalion was going to be stationed in Rouen. It looked like all GIs within a day's drive had poured into the city where Joan of Arc had burned at the stake five hundred years ago. Word must have also gotten out that they were a Negro WAC battalion, because Negro soldiers made up most of the crowd.

"Where's Susie?"

"Hey! Hey! Dolores, I see you. It's me, Ronnie from Hartford."

The officers did their best to keep everyone in formation as they marched on. Marching alongside a column of enlisted women,

Eliza felt exposed. Each time the excited crowd lining the streets pushed forward, it was she who was jostled, and pushed, and clawed at. She envied those women who were lucky enough to be positioned in the middle of each row, shielded by their sister soldiers on each side.

"Coming through. Come on, guys, step back."

Eliza tried to keep the men at bay by pushing them back with her arm when she could. But even doing that became more and more difficult as the enlisted men's excitement grew. Eliza felt beads of sweat roll down the sides of her face. Each breath was becoming more difficult to exhale. The energy along the route had changed. The back of her neck tingled. She felt like she was being watched. Like a predator was on the verge of making his move. And she was the prey.

This wasn't good. She had to get out of there.

Another surge of men pushed forward, then pandemonium broke out. A pair of hands gripped her arms and yanked her away.

"Put me down!" Eliza's yell was drowned out by the roar of the crowd. She tried to fight, to flail her arms outward. But whoever had grabbed her had her arms pinned to her sides.

"No use fighting, bitch. I gotcha good. And I know you girls don't have any weapons."

She recognized her captor's voice. The twang of his accent plucked at her memory. A wave of terror paralyzed her. It was that private from the *Île de France*, the one she had put in his place when he had refused to acknowledge her rank over him. The one who had called her a "little bitch."

He hauled her into a deserted alleyway, too far away from the crowd of Negro soldiers for anyone to notice them. *Shit.*

Time and distance faded away. Eliza was alone again in that deserted Kentucky train station. But this time, she wasn't defenseless.

"What are you doing here?" Her teeth gnashed together as she continued to fight his grip on her.

"Me and my buddies heard some Colored gals were coming through here today. Haven't seen any more of y'all over here since I got off that boat. Figured it had to be you. Thought I'd come say hi to an old friend."

Her shock now gone, Eliza tried to jab her elbow into his side. Unsuccessfully. "We have never been friends."

"That's right. We aren't friends," he slurred. "You're the bitch who embarrassed me in front of my whole company. And none of them will let me forget it."

The private manhandled Eliza as he put her down. He pushed her against the brick wall, the one hidden in the darkness of shadow. He let her go but pressed his hand to her chest, taking liberty to wiggle his fingertips against her breasts. With his other hand, he tugged at his pants.

"Damn zipper. These cheap things always get stuck at the wrong time," he mumbled to himself.

Eliza took advantage of the private's distraction to widen her feet into a fighting stance. "Here, let me help you with that."

She reached out for his lower hand, getting a firm grip around his wrist.

"Huh?" The private looked up, his jaw slack with confusion. His sour breath reeked of cognac.

Good, he's drunk. She smiled at him. She reached around his waist with her free hand as if to hug him, then stretched as far as she could until she had a good hold of his waistband. "Been drinking the good stuff, eh?"

"Gimme a sec and I'll be feeling the good stuff too." He laughed. His foul breath assaulted her nose again. Eliza didn't share his amusement. It was taking everything in her not to vomit onto his face. Instead, she focused on the new skills she had acquired since they had last met.

Eliza flexed her legs to stabilize herself, then used her core strength to flip the man sideways onto his back as hard as she could. He was out cold the moment his head hit the ground.

"You idiot, my body *is* my weapon."

Eliza stumbled out of the alleyway back onto the street. She mouthed the word "help," but no sound came out of her mouth. The stars must have aligned in her favor anyway, because at that moment, a Negro officer came around the corner. He rushed over to her.

"Ma'am, are you okay? I can help. I'm a doctor."

Eliza attempted another step. She stumbled. The officer reached out just in time to catch her. Only then did she pass out.

ELIZA WOKE UP in semidarkness. What looked like late-afternoon sunlight streamed in through a small four-paned rectangular window. The floor was covered in straw. And the smell . . .

She held a hand to her nose and mouth. It smelled like she was in a barn. She pushed herself up onto her elbows and looked around for clues to confirm her suspicion.

The first thing she could discern was that she had been laid across an old wooden table. She gripped its sides and leaned from side to side slightly to test its stability. The table proved to be solid. That was good at least. And she wasn't in a barn. She spotted a cupboard against the wall. There was a fireplace behind her. No, calling it a hearth would be more accurate, for the space it occupied was wide enough to accommodate several cauldrons in addition to just a fire. Suddenly, she felt like she was in the medieval dwarves' house from that animated *Snow White* motion picture she had seen with her father a few years ago.

Her father . . . She gulped. His parting words to her before she had shipped out came back to her. *I told you so.* Dammit. Wherever she was, she was more determined than ever to survive this ordeal so she could shove his words right back into his face.

"You might've told me so, Daddy," she muttered to herself, "and I survived anyway."

She pushed herself into a full upright sitting position. Her legs dangled over the side of the table. She felt her head sway in a circular motion. That couldn't be good. But she was too stubborn to lie back down.

Footsteps echoed nearby. They were heavy. Soldier's boots heavy. She tensed. She looked around frantically for anything that she might be able to use as a weapon. She spied a poker next to the hearth. Her stomach growled as another wave of dizziness overcame her. The footsteps got closer and closer.

Damn. She was in no condition to put up a fight just yet. She would need to figure out how to bide her time until she regained her strength.

I told you so. I told you so . . .

"You're up. Good. How do you feel?" The male voice came from behind Eliza, causing her to jump. The Negro officer from the street stood in the doorway. Her tension eased. Instinctively, she knew he intended her no harm. She was safe. This man was nothing like the one who had attempted to abduct her and do even worse things to her.

I told you so.

Her "savior" didn't wait for her response before looking down at the clipboard cradled in his arm. She reached for her opposite shoulder.

"I'm fine. But I am a little . . ."

"Good, good, good. I gave you a quick look over once I brought you here. A few bruises on your arm. I imagine the unconscious man we found in the alley you came out of had something to do with that. Other than the scare I imagine you experienced, everything else checked out fine."

It dawned on her that she had slammed her captor on cobblestone. If he died, she was done for. Who would believe that she hadn't intended to kill him? A chill fell upon her. The truth was that she had. "That man. Is he . . . ?"

"He'll have quite the headache when he comes to, but he'll live."

"I didn't kill him?" Eliza said, dazed.

"Disappointed?"

"No!" she blurted out. That wasn't exactly the truth, but to have this man hint at what she had been thinking . . . Hearing it out loud left her stunned. "No, I just . . ."

"You don't have to explain anything. His buddies looked none too happy when they came to collect him. I wouldn't be surprised if he ended up with a black eye or two to go with the concussion you gave him.

"Do you want to try to walk around?" He came over and offered Eliza his hand. "I won't let you fall."

It wasn't his words that made Eliza pause. It was the way that he had said them. And how they had drowned out the sound of her father's taunting in her head. The silence was a relief after all these months.

"Wait, who are you?"

"Dr. Noah Roberts. I'm the medical officer assigned to your unit."

Eliza ignored his hand. A Negro doctor? He was a doctor *and* an officer too? It was rare to encounter male officers of her own race since she had entered the military. She tried to recall the last time she had been around another one. Too long.

It was going to be a madhouse in their officers' quarters once word got out about him.

Well, she wasn't going to be one of the ones falling over herself to get his attention. After her scare with that drunk private today, flirting was the last thing on her mind.

Eliza, feeling a little bit more clearheaded, pushed herself off the table without Dr. Roberts's assistance. With one hand still on the table, she took a few tentative steps. Then she bent her knees a few times to test her balance. No stumbling. That was an improvement.

"I think I'm going to be fine, Dr. Roberts. Now, can you tell me where I am?"

He grinned at her, making him even more handsome than before. She'd be damned if her knees didn't wobble a little. "Welcome to Caserne Tallandier."

Eliza had not heard of Caserne Tallandier during her previous travels through the region. As Noah led her to a primitive-looking building, he explained that the post had been constructed in the previous century to house Napoléon's troops.

"I must warn you that the buildings hold heat about as well as a sieve holds water."

"I think we can handle that." Eliza smiled. "We've been living in a drafty British school since February."

"You don't understand. These buildings were built before central heating was invented. And they've never been updated."

Noah led her into a room that must have been a barn in a previous life. The women from her battalion were lined up to receive what looked like burlap sacks from fair-skinned men with POW marked on their sleeves.

"What is going on here?"

"They're being issued mattress covers." Noah nodded toward a corner that had bales of hay stacked sky-high. Women were stuffing their mattress covers with fistfuls of hay. "And that is where you'll be filling them."

"With hay?"

Noah nodded. "Welcome to France, Captain Jones."

There were more than a few grumbles by the time Eliza made it over to the hay pile. Eliza would have added to them herself were she not an officer. But thinking back to her stall-mucking punishment during her early days at Fort Des Moines, she smiled to herself and gave thanks that the bales of straw smelled way better than that manure had.

She was not still smiling, however, when it came time to sleep on her hay-filled mattress. Sleep did not come easy that evening as blades of straw poked through the cover.

"Hey, can you be still down there?" Grace called down from the upper bunk. "All your moving around is keeping me up."

"It's not my fault that this bunk bed frame is as old as France." Charity and Noel had briefed the officers after everyone had settled in. German POWs had constructed new bunk beds for the enlisted women's barracks. They had run out of time on the ones intended for the officers' quarters.

"Ow!" Another blade stuck through her bedsheet and her nightgown and into her back. She would have given up already and made a pallet on the floor if not for the cold draft. Noah's warning about the lack of heat had been an understatement. "Seriously, Grace. How are you not tossing and turning on these things?"

"I laid out my duffel bag in between the mattress and the sheet."

"Good idea." Eliza pushed herself out of bed. Just as she had emptied out the remaining contents from her own duffel bag, the lights flickered out. "Great."

"It looks like you'll just have to suck it up for the night, rich girl. Look on the bright side. It'll help you build some character."

"Not funny."

So far, this trip was a far cry from the visions of elegance and grandeur that had filled the imaginations of the Six Triple Eight.

CHAPTER 28

Rouen, France
July 1945

THE ONE IMPROVEMENT that Caserne Tallandier had over the King Edward School was that the workspace was big enough so that all the women assigned to the mail operations could work their eight-hour shifts at the same time during the day.

Grace was making her rounds when she spied another large canvas bin of corrected mail ready to go out to the field. She started pushing it down the hallway to the loading docks. Or attempting to anyway. The bin's contents were heavier than she anticipated.

As a company officer, Grace didn't have to pitch in with matching letters and parcels to individual soldiers anymore. The work was being completed at a pace now that allowed her to assume more of a supervisory role. But she liked to help with some of the more mundane tasks when possible.

"Let me help you with that," said an accented male voice, causing Grace to jump. Hans, a German prisoner of war who had been brought in to assist with the heavier manual labor duties, came from behind her. He easily maneuvered the bin over the doorjamb.

"Thank you. But I could have handled it." The words came out hesitantly. Grace was still getting used to working alongside men who would have shot her on sight only a few weeks ago. With honey-blond hair and startling blue eyes, it also didn't help that Hans was helpful and attractive. Day by day, it was becoming harder for Grace to reconcile that this man was supposed to be her "enemy."

There had been approximately three hundred German POWs who had constructed the women's bunk beds in the barracks and performed the rest of the work needed to ready the place for their arrival. A good number of them remained after the Six Triple Eight's arrival in Rouen to serve as the maintenance crew and to do any of the menial tasks that they needed on a daily basis.

"What kind of gentleman would I be if I let you ruin your beautiful hands with this thing? How would you play your music?" Hans smiled at her. Grace looked away.

Why does he have to be so damned charming? Hans always seemed eager to help her or share a pleasant word. And when he had mentioned that he had been an aspiring musician before the war, Grace had shared stories of her own musical adventures. It turned out that he was as much of a closeted jazz fan as she was.

"I wish you would stop bringing that up. I told you I don't play anymore."

"I don't understand why you keep saying that. Your eyes light up whenever you talk about music."

"Which is why I *don't* want to talk about it." Grace sighed. She added almost as an afterthought, "I never should have told you."

Hans stopped. He gently tugged her arm until she was forced to look at him.

"You can tell me anything. You shouldn't feel ashamed to love the things that make you happy." His eyes searched hers. It was almost like he was pleading with her to give in to something that had nothing to do with music. She pulled away. Hans was cute. But he wasn't *that* cute.

"I did love music. Very much. But that was before . . ." Her voice drifted off. Despite this unexpected bond that they shared, Grace wasn't ready to talk about Tony with Hans. That would border on betrayal to her brother's memory. It had been Japanese soldiers who were responsible for his death. But the Germans and Japanese had been allied with each other in the war.

No, in that regard, she couldn't afford to see Hans as anything but the enemy.

"*Bâtard!*" Sylvia, one of the Frenchwomen that the battalion employed, spat on Hans's shoe. Grace was shocked at the venom in her voice.

"Sylvia!"

The young woman barely said a word on most days. Grace could see she must have been a stunning beauty at one time. Now her face was etched with premature lines and her ear-length hair grew in patches. The war had not been kind to her.

"You should not be so friendly with this German trash, Capitaine."

Hans held up a hand. "It is all right. I should get this post to the trucks before they leave."

They watched him walk away, pushing the heavy bin along. Grace didn't miss how tightly he held his jaw before he left. Sylvia spat again, this time on the spot where Hans had stood.

"Sylvia, I've never seen you be so unkind."

"I have no reason to be kind to them. You don't know how bad it was here before you came. Those men are monsters." Sylvia pointed at Hans's retreating back. "*He* is a monster."

Grace looked back in the direction that Hans had gone. She

had heard rumors about what the Germans had done: forcing the Jewish population to wear yellow stars on their clothes, the starvation rations while the German officers feasted like kings, and then stealing people in the middle of the night. Grace had a hard time reconciling those accusations with the prisoner she knew, a man who had an artist's soul.

"People do bad things in the heat of battle . . ."

"What battle?" Sylvia shrieked. "France had already surrendered when he came. When he seduced me with his charm and promises of food and sweets. He shot my sister when she accused him of stealing my virtue. He shot her then laughed at her after he made her beg for help. And still he let her bleed to death. She was sixteen. Tell me, what battle was raging when that happened?"

"I . . ."

Grace had also heard rumors from American troops who were returning to the coast from places like Germany and Poland. The stories they told about what had happened to the people who had been taken prisoner made her shudder in horror. She hadn't believed them then. Those guys were always lying about something in hopes of impressing a gullible WAC.

What if they had been telling the truth?

Grace suddenly felt cold despite the heat of the July sun. She took the younger woman's hand and squeezed it.

"I apologize. I shouldn't have commented on things I know nothing about."

Still holding on to Sylvia's hand, she led them back to the mail-sorting workroom.

NORMALLY, GRACE SPENT her free time alone on her bunk scribbling on some sheet music. The sights and sounds of the unfamiliar surroundings had a new melody floating around in her head. This weekend, however, she was the ranking officer on duty. That meant she had to make herself available to the enlisted women in the post's recreational facilities. Sylvia's story was still heavy on Grace's mind as she walked over to the rec room. The image of Hans laughing over a girl's corpse had chased the music from her mind. She was glad for the excuse to be around people.

The rec room was housed in a long building near the front gates that led into town. Normally, officers shied away from the spots where the enlisted women liked to hang out. Grace and the others knew it was hard for them to enjoy themselves with their superiors lurking in the corner. Luckily, the rec room was mostly empty. It looked like Grace would be presiding over a quiet Friday night on post.

This was Grace's first time going in there. What she found was surprisingly nice. One half of the building had been transformed into a makeshift beauty parlor. Thankfully, they had been able to transport all of their hairstyling supplies and equipment over from England. The other half of the building had been transformed into a lounge with a few chairs and tables. There was even a Ping-Pong table at the center of the room. Grace wasn't sure if she wanted to know how Eliza and her team had managed to procure that.

"However they did it," Grace muttered to herself, "they did a damn good job in here."

But what Grace had not expected to see was the beautiful piano tucked in the corner. She knew that it had not come over from England with the battalion. She would have noticed it before. How on earth had such a magnificent thing survived the ruin caused by the German occupation and Allied bombings on this side of the English Channel?

Grace stood before it reverently. It took her a few moments before she dared stroke its keys.

"Beautiful," she whispered. She ran her fingers across the keys. Some of them had seen better days but all of them worked. Intrigued, she sat down on the bench. But when she placed her hands on the keys to play, her mind went blank.

Grace hadn't played or practiced a note since she had joined the Women's Army Corps. Looking back, she realized that military life, and the uncertainty of war hanging over her head, hadn't afforded her the time nor the opportunity to play in the last three years.

Grace stroked the keys again. Then she went through her scales. *When in doubt, go back to the basics.*

She tickled out a quick rendition of "Mary Had a Little Lamb." It was the first song she had ever learned how to play. She played it again, this time with a little more flair to it. And again, leaning into each note to evoke a gospel feel into the song. The extra drama that this added to such a simple children's song made her giggle.

Grace fooled around some more with a few go-to refrains. Those refrains morphed into her old standby.

I've got rhythm. My name is Grace. I'm the queen of these keys. Get out my face . . .

A slow clap interrupted her fooling around. Grace turned. She frowned. There stood Hans with a broom tucked into the crook of his arm. "I knew it. I knew when I saw your hands that you were a master. That was magnificent."

"Thank you." Grace clasped her hands together and placed them in her lap. Hans's smile was as bright as ever. But Grace no longer found it alluring. Now it looked . . . feral. His charming demeanor made her skin crawl. The gleam in his eyes had turned into a predatory shine. How had she found anything about this man appealing?

"We must play a duet together." Hans sat down next to her on the bench. His broom fell to the floor. Their shoulders brushed. His face was so close to hers that they could've kissed if she wanted to. But Grace most definitely did not want to kiss him. She scooted over and almost fell off.

Grace stood. "The bench is only big enough for one person. I'll go."

Hans stood too. He reached for her hand with a pout. "Not so soon. I was hoping to spend some time with you. Maybe hear more of your music."

She pulled her hand out of his and looked around. The room was still empty. "I'm not comfortable with that."

His smile fell, causing the planes of his face to harden. "That *schlampe* told you her stories about me."

"*Sylvia* told me you did horrible things to her and her sister. But not just her stories. I've heard about the detention camps too."

"I see." Hans tented his fingers under his chin. "All those things they say we did, all the immorality . . . We were just following orders, you know."

"You were just following orders?" Grace closed her eyes so she didn't scream. This guy couldn't be serious. She couldn't believe she had almost fallen under his spell. The charm, the good looks, the attention—it was all a scam. Hans was nothing but a con in a pretty package.

If he thought that "just following orders" nonsense would fly with her, he had marked the wrong person. Grace took a deep breath. Her side ached with a phantom pain. She palmed her rib cage, remembering how a bigot's boot had broken Eliza's bones in

that same spot. Grace thought of all the times when it would have been so easy for her, Eliza, and the rest of them to just go along with the status quo, to turn the other cheek and not put up a fight.

"You forget who you're talking to. I am a female Negro officer in an all-female Negro unit in the segregated United States Army. I, along with every single woman in this battalion, have had to deal with immoral orders given by bigots and bullies. All of us have had to deal with that bullshit since day one."

Hans shook his head. "We fought for the honor of the fatherland, not that madman and his ludicrous ideas. I am a proud German. I am not the only one who thinks as I do. If I hadn't shot all of those people—that girl . . ." He paused to reflect on that last thought. Grace watched as the anger in his eyes turned into horror. "You don't understand. If I hadn't obeyed, they would've shot me!"

Grace sighed at his pitiful excuses. She was not impressed. "You speak of your honor and your pride as if this is some new rodeo for us. We know that there is strength in numbers. Our army refused to give us weapons, but we know that we don't need guns to fight for what's right. So, if you're looking for my sympathy for what you have done—the abductions, the torture, the destruction of families, the intentional starvation of the local population, stealing a young girl's innocence, the killing of innocent noncombatants in cold blood—with the excuse that you were 'just following orders,' you need to take that thinking somewhere else. I am not the fool you think I am. Is that clear, *prisoner?*"

Hans looked down. His head hung in shame. "Yes, ma'am." His words, thick with emotion, came out more heavily accented than usual.

"I think you should leave now." Eliza stood in the entrance, holding the door open for Hans. He shuffled through without another word. They both watched him until he was out of sight.

"Girl, are you okay?" Eliza rushed over to Grace. She tried to put her arm around Grace's back, but Grace turned away.

"I'm fine." That was a lie, of course. But Grace wasn't about to admit that she had briefly fallen under the spell of a German prisoner.

"Are you sure? Because for a second there, it looked like you two were kissing."

"No, we did not kiss." Grace shuddered at the thought. "He forgot his place."

And I had almost forgotten mine.

"Okay. If you're sure."

Grace knew Eliza well enough to know that she wasn't buying it. Grace didn't care. Hans was gone. And she hadn't done anything stupid. She sat back down at the piano. "Let's talk about something else. Where did this piano come from? It's in too good condition to have come from anywhere around here."

"I have no idea. It just showed up a few days ago with a note attached that said someone in the War Department raised hell about the 'Colored girl unit' needing a piano."

Grace frowned. "Someone in the War Department, huh?" She had an idea who that "someone" was. And knowing Jonathan, he was bound to do something stupid like have Dutch tulips delivered to her once a week. That, or worse.

Eliza continued to prattle on. "Yeah, you wouldn't believe some of the strange deliveries that have arrived for us since active hostilities ended. Just the other day, a local showed up with a donkey cart full of cheese. The guy who brought it insisted that we keep the donkey."

That got Grace's attention. She looked up. "Did you?"

"Hell, no. I already have enough pains in the ass around here. The last thing I need is a real live ass to look after too."

As they shared a laugh over that, Grace had to admit that their relationship had come a long way since Eliza had first asked her for directions to the WAAC enlistment office back in New York. She wouldn't say that they had become the best of friends over the last few years. But things had become easier between them since the U-boat scare and after that wild night at dinner with those older ladies in Birmingham.

"CAPTAIN STEELE! THERE you are." Three of the enlisted women who worked under Grace rushed into the rec room and made a beeline for her. Mary Bankston and Mary Barlow were privates first class. Dolores Browne was one of her sergeants.

"Evening, ladies. What can I do for you?"

The two Marys looked to Dolores. Evidently, she was the spokesperson of the trio.

"We wanted to know if you would grant us forty-eight-hour leave effective immediately. We just met some guys who said they would give us a lift to Paris."

Now that there weren't any second or third shifts, the women in the battalion had more time and opportunity for recreational pursuits. One of the most desired destinations was the French capital.

Paris was located about eighty miles east of Rouen. Close enough to make a day trip under normal circumstances. But with the current condition of the roads, mere months after active war combat had ceased, traveling the short distance might as well have been driving across the width of the United States. The main road still bore the scars of bomb craters, debris, and the burned-out shells of combatant vehicles. If that wasn't bad enough, the traffic generated from the constant flow of the Red Ball Express—the Allied truck convoy carrying supplies from the coast to Paris and back—was enough to clog the road on a twenty-four-hour basis.

Grace frowned. "I don't know, ladies. You know that we've been reluctant to grant leave passes for Paris. With the roads still a mess, the ones who have attempted the trip wind up coming back late and not reporting for duty on time."

"C'mon, Cap," Mary Barlow pleaded. "This might be my only chance to ever go to Paris. Shoot, I'm willing to walk there if I have to. There's nothing to do around here with everything in Rouen bombed out."

"Tell me more about your plans." Grace found it difficult to maintain a stern-faced expression to the request made by the three women who stood before her. She knew they had worked through the Fourth of July holiday. They all were hard workers.

By the time they finished stating their case, Grace had already made up her mind. She had a soft spot where Paris was concerned. She understood their desperation to visit the city.

"All right, fine. You all can go." She started signing their leave passes. "But I'm concerned about your new friends' plan to take a 'shortcut' to get around the traffic. Please, be careful."

The three women sighed at the same time. "Yes, ma'am. We will," Sergeant Browne promised.

Grace smiled as she watched the three friends walk out the door. She wondered if she and Eliza would remain friends like that once they all returned home to the United States. A wave of sadness washed over her to think that they might not. They could barely stay away from each other's throats for more than a few weeks at a time.

"Eliza?"

"Hmm?" Eliza looked up. She had begun to inventory the equipment for the battalion's softball team. She dropped a catcher's mask into the team's traveling trunk.

"I know we briefly talked about this before, but have you given any thought to what you're going to do when we go back home, now that the war is over?"

"I'm not really sure. My father actually spoke to me the last time I went home." Eliza hesitated, then closed the lid on the trunk. "But only because my mother forced us all to be in the same room together. He shared some things that were . . . Let's just say that particular conversation was hard. I still want to write for my family's newspaper. But I don't know if working for my father is a good idea. He's so set in his ways."

Grace nodded her head in understanding. "I can relate. Things haven't been right between my mom and me since I enlisted. Not since my brother was killed really. After our U-boat scare, I've been thinking more and more about going home and making things right."

Eliza was quiet for a moment. "That's tough."

"Yeah, Tony was the one who kept Mama and me from biting each other's heads off." Grace rubbed her arms where goose bumps had sprouted.

"Do you have any place to go when you go back to the States?"

Grace's mouth fell into a somber expression. "No, not really. I was such a—a bitch before I joined up that I didn't really have any friends. No one I'm close enough with to let me sleep on their couch while I figure out what's next."

"It sounds like we're just a pair of homeless messes, huh?" The smile on Eliza's face was good-natured enough. But Grace caught a sense of melancholy behind it as well. She could relate.

"Yeah, I guess we are." Grace returned the smile. "Maybe we should just reenlist."

"Oh no!" Eliza shook her head. "I've had enough of these people's rules and regulations, thank you very much. I might as well have never left my father's house. I can do better for myself out on the street than to put up with another unnecessary order around here if I don't have to."

"Maybe I could try to get into school again." Grace thought back to her disastrous audition at Juilliard. She bit her lip. "Never mind. It's reenlistment for me."

Grace's fingers absently stroked the piano keys. Her fingers flurried over the first few notes of *Moonlight Sonata*. Each keystroke reminded her of the night she spent with Jonathan. She stopped abruptly.

"Why'd you stop?"

"That particular piece has too many memories tied to it."

"Too bad." Eliza shrugged. "You sounded pretty good."

Grace decided she wasn't in the mood to play any of the music that she used to play. It was time to move on. She would not spend another moment wallowing in the what-ifs where men were concerned. Whatever she'd had with Jonathan could never be. And Tony? He would want her to start living her life. More important, she was beginning to want that for herself. She was tired of grieving over what could have been.

Eliza had emptied out the travel trunks again. She had gloves, bats, and other softball gear laid out on the floor around her.

"Do you need any help?"

"No, I'll be fine."

"What is all this stuff for anyway?"

"Our softball team heads out for the WAC championship tournament tonight. But get this, the only reason they'll be able to get there in time is because of that general who tried to have Charity court-martialed. Remember that guy?"

"Yeah. General Butler, right?"

"Yeah, him. Anyway, now he acts like he and Charity are the best of friends. When she told him that we were having trouble coordinating the team's travel, Butler let us have his personal train car to get there."

"No way!"

"Girl, yes. I never would've believed it had I not seen the orders authorizing it with my own eyes. He should be here in an hour or so to welcome the team aboard personally. I tell you, anything is possible."

Grace laughed along with Eliza. But on the inside, her thoughts returned to Tony and wished that platitude were true. "Can you cover me for a few minutes? I want to go grab some sheet music out of my trunk. I might as well tinker with some song ideas since we have a piano now."

"No problem." Eliza looked up from the softball equipment. "Are you sure you want to run over there alone? In case that POW is lurking around."

Grace shook her head. "I'll be fine. But if anything happens, I'll scream for you to save me."

She stepped out into the humidity of the early evening. Her thoughts wandered back to the question: What was she going to do when it was time to go back to civilian life?

You make your dreams come true, that's what. Her brother's voice echoed in her mind. *Her* dreams. Studying composition at Juilliard. Playing her own music in Paris one day. Money, nerve, and distance had been her obstacles in the past. But here she was now within driving distance of Paris, yet she had not made plans to go. The only thing that was standing in her way was herself, and the fact that she lacked the nerve to take the first step toward everything that had been laid out at her feet.

The real question she should be asking herself was: Why was she still standing in her own way?

When Grace turned the corner, she wished she had taken Eliza up on her offer to walk her to their quarters. She spotted a man waiting in the shadows of the entrance. Her steps slowed to a halt.

When the man stepped out into the lamplight so Grace could see his face, she screamed.

CHAPTER 29

"J ONATHAN!"

"Hello, Grace." He stepped back and leaned against the doorjamb. That's when she noticed how much thinner he was now than when she last saw him.

Grace rushed to his side, grabbing his arm. She was shocked to find that she could grip his forearm and almost have her fingertips touch. She looked him over again, noting how much sharper his cheekbones were under his skin. "What the hell happened to you?"

He grimaced as if his first instinct was to shake off her assistance, but he didn't actually try to fight her off. "Italy happened to me."

"You're supposed to be back in D.C. pushing papers. What in the world were you doing there?" Grace unlocked the door. She guided Jonathan into the small lounge just off the entrance and onto a worn love seat. She sat down beside him.

They had received reports of the fierce fighting the Negro troops had encountered in Italy. Some of the men who had been injured there had been shipped to hospitals in England where they had been stabilized. The stories that they told had been bleak.

"It's my job to check on our Negro troops no matter where they are in the world."

"Yes, but I didn't know that meant you would go into an active combat zone."

"Well, it wasn't when I got there. We were ambushed. I spent three days curled up in a foxhole."

"I'm so glad you made it out alive." Grace winced as she remembered her manners. "Would you like some tea?"

"Tea? No. Something stronger? Yes."

Grace smiled. "You know we're not allowed to have any alcohol on post. I'm probably not even supposed to have you in here."

"We'll just say I stopped by on official business."

She frowned. "Is that why you're here—just for official business?"

"Is this your way of saying that you missed me?"

"No, I—"

He waved his hand, cutting her off. "It's okay. You don't have to explain. We said all that needed to be said in New York. You and I are an impossible situation." The creases around his eyes softened as if to tell her that all was forgiven. He leaned back. "Did my surprise arrive?"

"The piano. You shouldn't have . . ."

Jonathan shrugged. "I figured you might have more practice time now, with the war in Europe being over and all. Don't worry. I sent the piano with no strings attached. Just being a friend."

Grace stared at him again. She couldn't believe how handsome he still was, despite his physical changes and the twinkle in his eyes that now looked more haunted than mischievous. She also noted how she felt less stressed about him being here. Alone with her. But a lot had happened to them both since they last saw each other. Each had experienced the devastation caused by the war with their own eyes.

Or maybe it was because the war was now over. In a few months' time, she wouldn't have the eyes of the Women's Army Corps on her neck. That is, if she decided not to reenlist. Would he still be employed by the War Department? If so, then maybe . . .

Then maybe nothing. That chapter between them was closed. Like they both kept saying, they were just friends now.

Her lips trembled. "Thank you."

Grace looked at the clock on the wall and cursed softly. "I really must be on my way. I'm the officer on duty this weekend. Eliza's covering for me. And I've been away for too long as it is."

"Good old Grace Steele. Every time I see you, you're racing off to somewhere."

She shrugged, leaning into him gently. "What can I say? Where 'we' are concerned, there seems to be a curse of bad timing."

"Yes, well . . . I can't argue with that." In the course of laughing, Jonathan wavered a little bit. She feared for a moment that he was going to slide off the love seat.

"What are you doing here, Jonathan? You need to be in a hospital."

"You're probably right. But I had to see you."

Grace looked away. "That wasn't a good idea."

"Probably. But I didn't want to leave Europe without giving this back to you." Jonathan fumbled in his pocket. When he pulled out his hand, he produced an envelope that had clearly seen better days. "Here. Take it."

Grace took the envelope with her free hand. It fell open—the glue looked as if it had dried up ages ago. Inside was the watch that her brother had given her on that last Christmas he had been home. A lump of emotion formed at the base of her throat. She blinked back tears.

"You found it. Thank you so much. You have no idea what this means to me." Grace threw her arms around Jonathan's neck.

Impulsively, she leaned in to plant a kiss on his cheek. But her sudden embrace threw off Jonathan's balance. He turned his cheek in the process of regaining his equilibrium. Which meant that Grace's lips landed right atop his instead.

Now it was Grace's turn to fumble. Jonathan wrapped his arms around her waist. She was on her back, and he above her. Neither seemed eager to pull away. Finally, Jonathan drew them both into a semi-upright position.

Grace put her hand to Jonathan's chest. He covered her hand with his own. His eyes connected with hers. His brow wrinkled as the question hanging in the air between them remained unspoken.

"I'll miss you, Grace." He pressed his forehead against hers. She leaned forward, causing the tip of her nose to rub against his.

"I know." Their lips brushed as she spoke. She felt the tension in his body, his struggle to restrain himself. The contact had been brief, lasting only the length of time it took her to breathe the two syllables. There was no way that it could have been considered a kiss, right?

"I wish I could kiss you." He removed her hand from his chest and returned it to her side. Then he pressed his hand, now free, on the arm of the love seat just behind her.

He wasn't leaning in any farther, but he wasn't pulling away either. He hovered in a state of limbo. The energy between them was charged. Her breath hitched as she realized what he was doing. He was letting her know that the next move was hers.

"But I won't," he said, their lips touching again as he spoke. He closed his eyes and groaned.

"I know." Touch. Touch.

"Stop . . ." He paused. He exhaled. The burst of air caressed her bottom lip. But most important, he didn't move away. ". . . doing that."

"I can't." She flicked her tongue against his mouth. "I don't want to. Not really. But I don't want to let you go either."

This was the moment that she should have turned her head, stopping this madness, and sent Jonathan on his way. Back to America. But that most likely would mean sending him out of her life for good. It was the right thing to do. No, it was the *safe* thing to do.

If Grace was being honest with herself, she was tired of playing it safe. For once, she wanted to be reckless. And she didn't want to feel guilty for doing so afterward.

Yet, she also didn't want to throw her military career in the toilet. Even if part of her was more than ready to return to civilian life.

She reached up and cradled his head between her hands. And then before she could think too much of it any further, she kissed Jonathan on his forehead.

"Take care of yourself, Jonathan."

Finally, he backed away. He studied her face for a moment. "I understand," he said quietly.

He stood, shoved his hands in his pockets, and turned to leave. With his back to her, he said, "Take care of yourself too, Grace. But if you ever need anything . . ."

"I know."

"Good."

"Until . . ."

He stopped, looked over his shoulder, and grinned at her.

"Until."

GRACE WAITED THERE in the shadows for a few minutes. She swiped away the lone tear that escaped the corner of her eye. Saying goodbye to Jonathan like that had hurt. There was still a part of her that wanted to run after him and explain herself. To beg him to wait for her, to not give up on her while she followed through with her commitments here in Europe and to the corps.

But she knew doing that wouldn't change anything in the long run. It wouldn't be fair to either one of them to prolong the inevitable—the timing would never be right for them as long as she was in the corps and he was an adviser in the War Department. Every moment she spent alone with him jeopardized her reputation and her future. And she would make a fool of herself if she were to suggest that he quit his job for her. He was a man, after all. He had his pride.

Love didn't put food on the table, nor did it pay the rent. They both knew better than most that a musician's pay was sporadic at best. It was even more unreliable when that musician was a woman. And then there was the chance that he might stay in the War Department, while her life was still in New York.

Grace sniffed back the rest of her tears as she wiped that errant one with the back of her hand and onto the side of her skirt. Great, she'd been away from her post too long. She ran up to her room and grabbed some blank music sheets and a pencil.

Grace emerged from the shadows with her shoulders thrown back and a renewed sense of purpose in her step.

She hadn't made a reckless decision this time. But she hadn't made a safe one either. Instead, she had chosen what was right for her.

CHAPTER 30

WHERE THE HELL have you been?"

Grace returned to the rec room to find it in a state of panic. A few girls were huddled in a corner comforting another private who appeared to be inconsolable. All of them had tears streaming down their faces.

"Sorry, I got sidetracked on my way back here. What happened?"

"There's been an accident. We received reports of casualties. Some of our girls are . . ."

"What?! Who? Are they okay?"

The clerk turned away to stifle a sob. "Last we heard they were on their way to the hospital. It . . . it didn't sound good."

"Who? Who is on their way to the hospital?"

"Captain Jones didn't say. She took the call since you weren't here. And then she ran out to meet them there since she was the most senior officer we could find."

Grace sank down into the nearest seat. Her buoyant spirits from just a moment before completely deflated. Crap.

"I should've been here. I should've been here to take that call." She stared off into the distance as shock settled in. She felt numb as her eyes darted around, following the activity in the room. It took a moment for it to dawn on her that she was the only officer.

This was no time for her to be sitting there dumbfounded. She needed to do something.

Grace shook herself out of her fog. She grabbed the shoulder of the soldier closest to her, the one who had updated her when she first came in.

"You, find Jonathan Philips. He's a civilian aide to the War Department. He's in town. He may even still be on post. I left him no more than ten minutes ago."

WE CAN'T FIND Captain Steele anywhere. You have to go to the hospital in her place.

The words echoed in Eliza's mind as one of the Six Triple Eight's MPs wormed their Army jeep around the pockmarked, muddy road. Part of Eliza's mind had shut down at the thought of having to enter another hospital. She had not set foot in one since she had been attacked.

Her hands gripped her seat as the jeep lurched over a rock in the road.

"Slow down," she snapped at the MP. "The goal is to get there in one piece."

She continued to maintain a tight, white-knuckled grip on the edges of her seat with each bump, jump, and squeal the jeep made. It was too easy for Eliza to imagine herself being thrown headfirst over the hood and wracked with the pain that would surely follow. The jeeps that the U.S. Army personnel used had nothing to keep their passengers inside the vehicle or strapped down to their seats.

It was bad enough that she had to go to the hospital in an official capacity. The last thing she needed was to be admitted to one as a patient again. At this thought, an imaginary vise began to squeeze its grip around her lungs. Great. She hadn't had a panic attack since the U-boat chase on the ship that had brought them to Europe.

"Where the hell is Grace?" Eliza muttered to herself. What a time for the most reliable person she knew to disappear. Grace had better have a good reason for being away so long.

Eliza struggled to stay present when they arrived at the field hospital. The sight of all the medical supplies, the blood smeared across a doctor's jacket, the weariness in the nurses' eyes . . . it all threatened to yank her back into the memories of her own ordeal. The vise around her lungs came back with a vengeance.

She put her hand on the arm of the nurse who had been briefing her.

"Excuse me. I haven't heard a word you've said. I—I think I need to sit down."

The nurse gave her a terse nod, but her eyes shone with understanding. "Of course. I understand. Shall I get you some coffee?"

"Yes, that would be great. Black please." Eliza was grateful that she was in France for a situation like this. She loved the English dearly, but she had consumed enough tea there to last her a lifetime. She would always be a coffee girl at heart.

The nurse came back with a steaming mug of coffee. Eliza inhaled its scent first to center herself before taking her first sip. It wasn't the best-tasting stuff, but it was the jolt she needed for the situation at hand.

"Thank you for this." Eliza gestured at the mug in her hand. "Now, you were saying that three of my girls were in a jeep accident?"

The nurse confirmed that there had indeed been a jeep accident. Then she went on to confirm the worst. Privates First Class Mary Barlow and Mary Bankston had been killed in the accident.

Sergeant Dolores Browne had been seriously injured. She was still alive, but barely. The prognosis for her was not good.

"I'm so sorry. Did you know any of these women?" The nurse gave her a sad smile.

Eliza's heart sank. "Yes, I did know all three of them. Well, I didn't know them well, but I knew them by name."

The two Marys had been regulars in the unit beauty salon. Eliza remembered signing up Dolores herself during a quick recruiting trip back home right before her attack. A lump formed in her throat. The only reason that Dolores had even joined the WAC was because of her. And now she might die too . . . because of her.

"I hate to do this to you, but the two deceased women . . . their dog tags flew off and . . . we need someone to identify the bodies."

Eliza forced herself to focus back on the woman in front of her. The one who was wringing her hands. Who had probably been here in this hospital for way longer than her shift required. The one who looked like she would rather be doing something, anything, other than asking this of Eliza. Eliza could empathize with her, because she felt the same way.

"Okay." It was jarring to hear her own voice sound so small, so distant. So weak.

"Thank you. Come right this way." The nurse gestured for Eliza to follow her into the stairwell. The building itself didn't look like it had been built to be a hospital. It looked more residential. Maybe a grand mansion at some point in time. Sometime before the war. Had Eliza not been focused on the ornate fixtures on the walls, it might have dawned on her that whether or not this building had once been someone's home, they were going down the stairs and not up. Down to the cellar. But it wasn't some family's cellar anymore.

Because if the upstairs had been turned into a makeshift hospital, then that meant the cellar was now functioning as a . . .

MORGUE.

The handwritten sign on the door was a shock. What was she doing here? She couldn't do this. She wasn't ready to face death. She hadn't been two years ago when it had been her lying in a hospital bed, broken mentally and fractured physically.

"They're in here. You don't have to stay long. Just enough to confidently say which Mary is which."

Eliza took one step toward the door then stopped. The nurse placed a hand on her back. Eliza stiffened.

"It's okay. I know this is difficult."

"You have no idea."

"Honey, I've been working in a war zone for the last three years."

Eliza gave her a weak smile. "You've got me there."

"Take all the time you need. I'll be right beside you."

Eliza looked at the nurse, really getting a good look at her for the first time. Her dark brown hair was pulled back into a severe bun that was tucked neatly under her nurse's cap. Her eyes were kind, but they shone with a weariness that must have come from seeing too many young people killed, maimed, or permanently changed too soon over the course of the war. A war that had finally ended only a few months ago. Eliza had never met this woman before, but there was something about her that made her at ease. That made her feel like she understood or sympathized with this horrible tragedy more than she would with someone else.

Her skin looked like it had a slight tan to it. That wasn't so unusual now that it was summer. But Eliza wondered when she would have had time to lie out under the July sun. She was a nurse. The war might be over, but she imagined that the work of the hospital staff was never over even in peacetime. There was a question that Eliza was tempted to ask—if only to delay the inevitability of having to go into the morgue and look at those young women's remains—but now was not the time or place to ask something so rude. So instead, she opted for something that was safe.

"I'm so sorry, but what is your name?"

The nurse studied her for a moment before answering. "Jane."

"Hi, Jane." Eliza took a deep breath. "Okay, I'm ready. I think."

The nurse gave her a reassuring smile. "C'mon, then. Let's get this over with."

AS JANE HAD promised, the process of identifying Mary Barlow and Mary Bankston had been quick. Eliza had prepared herself for the worst visually, but, thankfully, both women had sustained very little damage that she could see. They both looked like they were sleeping peacefully. Before she turned to leave, she had to fight off the urge to reach out and attempt to rouse them, if only to prove to herself that they were indeed gone.

Next, Jane led Eliza back upstairs and down a long hallway to check on Dolores Browne. As they reached the end of the hallway, she stopped short. To her surprise, Noah, the doctor who had helped her, was coming out of Sergeant Browne's room. He had emerged with his mouth flattened into a grim line. But when he saw the two women approaching him, his face brightened visibly.

"Nurse Jane." He smiled. "Captain Jones."

He had paused before he said her name. The sound came out of his mouth almost reverently, like one would say a prayer. Eliza was in too much of a daze over the current tragedy to think on it beyond surface observation.

"Noah." She nodded before clearing her throat. "How is she?"

"Not good. She's proving to be a fighter. But I'm afraid that the extent of Sergeant Browne's injuries are too vast for any hopes of recovery."

Eliza's heart sank. But that last shred of hope in her gut held on fiercely. Surely if she had been able to recover from her own injuries, that meant that Sergeant Browne could too. Besides, the bodies of the two Marys barely had any signs of damage. How much worse could the lone survivor be?

Sadly, her opinion of the good Doctor Noah here dimmed a little bit. She vowed then and there to keep the light of hope lit until her soldier proved him wrong. She pasted on a grim smile, but her eyes beamed at him, *You're wrong.*

"I understand," she responded. "I'm ready to go in to see her, if that's okay."

"Of course."

Eliza must have lulled herself into a cocoon of denial after seeing the two Marys, because she was not prepared when she saw Sergeant Browne's condition.

The woman Eliza found lying on the makeshift hospital bed barely looked like a person, much less the vibrant young woman who had made a point of saying hello to her every afternoon during lunch. Her foot slanted at an odd angle. Her chest was bound in bandages, an indication of broken ribs. The rise and fall of her breathing was so slight that it took a few moments for Eliza to detect the movement. Dolores's left arm was in a cast that was suspended in the air. Eliza could empathize with those obvious injuries, having been in a similar situation herself. She winced in sympathy as she reflected on the aches and pains that she had experienced.

But none of that prepared Eliza for when she finally built up the nerve to look at the sedated woman's face. Nothing about it was recognizable. From the swollen blackened eyes, to the misshapen, puffy nose, to the split lips that parted just enough for an oxygen tube to enter. That opening was also big enough to see a space where her front tooth should have been. Eliza gasped in horror despite herself.

"Oh my God," she whispered into the hand she had clasped over her mouth. "That poor, poor girl."

But the most horrible thing about that moment was that, in Eliza's mind, she no longer associated the broken body before her with a colleague or one of the soldiers who had been entrusted into her care. Instead, she saw herself as she had been in the immediate aftermath of her attack back in Kentucky. This had been her. This was what had flashed through her parents' minds when they had received *that* phone call about their daughter. This was what her father had so stubbornly tried to shield her from when he had basically disowned her to keep her out of "that damned Army."

And now Dolores's family would be receiving the same call. Eliza felt herself tumble back into a hole that she had fought so hard to climb out of. A hole she had vowed she would never allow herself to fall into again.

She ran out of the room. Noah followed her. "Captain Jones? Eliza, are you all right?"

"Oh my God," she repeated. "Oh my God."

Then she fainted, crumpling into Noah's arms.

GRACE ARRIVED AT the hospital to find a Negro doctor cradling an unconscious Eliza in his arms in the hallway. She rushed up to him, her arms reaching out to Eliza. But she pulled back just short of reaching her.

"What happened? Did she get hurt too?"

It would be just her luck for Eliza to get injured too while rushing to cover Grace the one time she wasn't where she was supposed to be. That was what she got for indulging herself "just this one time." She would never forgive herself if Eliza's injuries were permanent. Or worse.

"No," the doctor responded. "She fainted as soon as she saw Sergeant Browne's condition. Excuse me."

He walked past Grace and set Eliza down on a nearby empty gurney. A nurse, whom Grace was only just noticing, picked up Eliza's hand and began tapping it.

"Are you all right, honey? This is Nurse Jane. Remember me? It's going to be okay."

Grace held her breath as they waited for a response. The nurse began tapping Eliza's hand again.

"C'mon, honey. Wake up."

Eliza's eyelids fluttered. She looked over to her side at the nurse. "Jane," she slurred. "Good to see you. You said you wouldn't leave my side."

"You gave us quite the scare," the doctor chimed in.

Eliza looked up and then smiled upon laying eyes on him. "It's you. Aren't you getting tired of this knight-in-shining-armor routine?"

He chuckled. "I'm just glad I was in the right place at the right time to catch you. Again."

Grace raised an eyebrow. She wondered what that was all about. But that could be dealt with later. "You mentioned Sergeant Browne. As in Dolores Browne?"

The doctor nodded his head in affirmation.

"She's under my command. She's in my company. How is she?"

"Not good."

"Oh no." It was more the way he said it than what he said that filled Grace with dread. It was she who signed off on their leave, Grace thought. So that meant that Grace was responsible for whatever happened to them. That's when she remembered the others. "Wait. What about the Marys? Bankston and Barlow. They left with Dolores. Are they in bad shape too?"

The nurse, the one who had said her name was Jane, reached for Grace's hand. Grace did not like the look of pity Jane was giving her. "Come with me, honey. Let's talk."

It was a talk that Grace would have paid good money to never have heard. Mary Bankston and Mary Barlow were dead. If she had denied their last-minute leave requests, they would still be alive, and Dolores wouldn't be hanging on to life by a thread. Grace hated how, upon hearing the devastating news, she had reverted back to that numb place inside her. The one in which she had existed for so long after receiving notification of her brother Tony's death.

She had worked so hard to climb out of that hole. It hurt, even now, to think about how it had been for her back then. Grace had been an entirely different person. It hadn't been healthy to hold all that grief and despair inside like that. She knew that now. She had promised herself that she would never allow herself to go back to that emotional void again.

Yet, here she was.

She wanted to be anywhere but here in this hospital, with these people who were all looking for her to do something, take charge, come up with a plan. Those were the last things she wanted to be thinking about, when all she wanted to do was curl up in a hole and just not think.

No, she had grown too much for that. People depended on her now. It was time for Grace to face the music.

"Eliza, I'm so sorry."

"Where were you?" Eliza's eyes had a vacant cast to them. A pallor had fallen over her skin. Grace looked away. It was hard to see her like that.

Grace never had a chance to answer the question. It was at that moment that Jonathan came rushing in.

"Grace? I came back as fast as I could. The girls said you needed me." He cradled her face in his hands. "Oh, thank God, you're okay."

They all stared at Jonathan's intimate gesture.

"You were with *him?*" Eliza's mouth twisted in disgust.

"I can explain." Grace pushed away his hands. "Jonathan popped up out of nowhere. He had to give me something . . ." Grace stopped. Her explanation sounded like just a list of excuses to her own ears. She had dropped the ball, and at Eliza's expense. Again. "I lost track of time."

"You lost track of time?" Eliza sat up from the gurney. Her mouth was twisted in disgust. "Isn't that convenient? Miss High and Mighty, with all her rules and lectures about how fraternization is the quickest way for a young, naive private to get sent home. It turns out that ol' Captain Steele here had been doing it with this War Department stooge all along, weren't you? It's bad enough that I caught you damn near kissing a POW."

"What?" An astonished Jonathan looked to Grace for an explanation. Her cheeks burned with embarrassment.

Before she could get a word out, their battalion executive officer, Noel Campbell, turned the corner. At her side, of all people, was General Butler. They both looked astonished.

Grace gasped before whispering, "Butler's here too? Great."

"Fraternizing with POWs?" General Butler boomed. "Is what

I just heard true, Captain? And then you left your post to have an intimate encounter with an official from the War Department?"

Grace had never been more embarrassed in her life, not even when she had messed up her audition. Her vision blurred as her eyes filled with tears. There was no way she could deny what everyone else had known, or suspected, to be true. Not after Eliza had blurted out her assumptions in front of their chain of command.

Grace's chin dropped to her chest. "Not entirely. I never kissed any of the prisoners."

"Oh, Grace." Noel sighed. "I never thought in a million years that you would be the one to do something so stupid. Come with me." Noel shot Eliza a glance, then whispered to Grace, "Especially since this accusation has been made so publicly. I'm not sure we'll be able to sweep this under the rug."

General Butler pointed at Eliza. "Nurse, is that soldier fit to resume her duties?"

Jane nodded slowly. "Yes, sir."

Noel jumped in before Butler could say anything else. "Good. You can finish up here while I take Captain Steele back to our headquarters. Report to me as soon as you get back."

Noel turned to General Butler. "I'm sorry you had to witness any of this. I'll investigate Captain Steele's behavior personally and report back to you, sir. We'll not take up any more of your time today."

"I'm beginning to think I was wrong in letting you all continue to lead yourselves. This girl deserves nothing short of a court-martial. I'll be waiting for your report, Captain Campbell. Philips, come with me."

"Yes, sir."

Everyone saluted Butler as he marched out. Jonathan followed. Both men looked like they couldn't get out of there fast enough.

Eliza mouthed the word "sorry" to Grace. Grace did not respond. Yes, part of her was angry at Eliza for blurting out her secret like that. But she could only be so mad at her. In the end, the only person she could truly be angry with was herself. She was the one who had broken the rules. She knew the consequences of getting involved with Jonathan from the moment she had first laid eyes on him so long ago.

You forgot that you can't afford to not be more perfect than anyone else, Grace Steele.

"As for you, Grace." Noel looked her in the eye. "Come with me. We need to talk."

CHAPTER 31

ELIZA SOUGHT OUT Grace as soon as she returned to Caserne Tallandier. Grace was in their shared quarters with a pile of laundry on her bed. But she wasn't putting the clothes back into the closet. She was packing them into her duffel bag.

Grace announced, "They're moving me downstairs for the time being. And then they're sending me home," before Eliza could get a word out. "And I am to have no further contact with Jonathan Philips."

She made no other move to acknowledge Eliza and went back to shoving work fatigues into her bag.

"I am so sorry. I didn't mean to blurt any of that out. I was just so shocked to see you with Jonathan." The sound of her useless apology made her cringe. "If I had any idea that a general, much less a senior officer, was within earshot—"

Grace cut her off. "Noel said they will most likely be forced to court-martial me."

"But they don't have to, right? We can talk it over with Charity. I mean, if Charity could maneuver her way out of backtalking Butler, then surely we can cook up a way to get you out of this."

"Whether or not they can pull that miracle out of their sleeves, one thing is for sure: I'm going home."

"But—"

Grace held up a hand and shook her head. "It was my own fault that I wasn't there when I was supposed to be. I was foolish. And I hate that my carelessness is why you had to see Dolores and the two Marys like that."

"Don't give up yet . . ."

"Honestly, Eliza. I'm not in the mood to talk about it anymore. For what it's worth, I am truly sorry I put you in that position."

"You might not be in the mood, but I . . ."

Grace laid her with the coldest stare that had ever been thrown Eliza's way. She shivered despite the July heat trapped inside the room.

"I *said* drop it."

"Fine." Eliza stood, smoothed her skirt, and left their room. Her big fat mouth was no doubt about to be the reason Grace was going to be court-martialed and tossed out of the Women's Army Corps. Fine. But she wasn't going to let this go without a fight. Eliza made herself scarce by making herself busy instead.

She waited until she was back in the privacy of her office before she let the tears fall. But she had little time to indulge herself with crying. As part of her duties, it was her responsibility to organize the funeral service arrangements for their deceased soldiers. Luckily, Charity had taken it upon herself to break the sad news of the deaths to the rest of the unit. What Eliza hadn't expected, however, was how many of the women would come to see her to volunteer to help.

In fact, this turned out to be a godsend, as the Army's burial protocol during wartime was to place the remains as is in a plain wooden box and then ship it off to the cemetery that had been established on the Normandy coast after D-Day. Even though active hostilities in Europe had ended two months ago, there were still too many bodies coming in from the battlefields to justify an exception for the two Marys.

When three privates who had previous mortuary experience

came in to volunteer their services, Eliza burst out into tears of relief. Within a day, she had been able to procure everything that was needed to funeralize Mary Bankston and Mary Barlow according to their Protestant and Catholic faiths, respectively, as well as bury their remains with the same care that they would have received had they passed away back home in the States.

Later that afternoon, Hans knocked on Eliza's door. "Captain Jones, may I have a moment of your time?"

"Make it quick." She was surprised to see him seeking her out. It had been several days since that night in the rec room. Since then, he went out of his way to avoid her. She imagined he did the same with Grace. He carried himself with a lot less bravado than he had in the past. He now stood before her with his chin lowered and his shoulders slumped.

"The other men and I are making caskets for the girls—I mean, women—who died. They were kind to us when many of us don't deserve it. We hope you find our craftsmanship a worthy alternative to those plain boxes your Army uses."

He had her attention. The cheap pinewood boxes that had arrived looked like they would fall apart if the wind blew. Eliza eyed Hans warily. "Where are you making these caskets?"

"In the old stables. I'll take you."

Hans led her to a pair of sturdy hardwood caskets in the making that would have been the pride of any undertaker back home. Crosses had been expertly carved on the lids. They had even found a bit of parachute silk to line the insides.

"I'm impressed." Eliza ran her hand over the woodwork. "Thank you."

She walked back to battalion headquarters shaking her head.

"It's amazing that the same hands that could create such beauty chose to commit such horrors against another human being."

"GOOD JOB, JONES." Charity slapped Eliza on the back. "It looks like our girls are going to have a decent burial. Is there anything else you need?"

"Just a favor on your part. That is, if Grace agrees to it."

Charity sat on the corner of Eliza's desk. "I'll do my best."

"We need music for the funeral service. Using records is out of the question because there aren't any available. A few privates claimed they knew how to play the piano. I've heard them play. None of them will do."

Charity nodded with understanding. "Grace is the best musician we've got. And you want my permission to let her perform."

Since the night of the accident, Grace had been spending all of her free time at that piano in the rec room. It soon became clear to everyone in the battalion that not only could Grace play, but she was a virtuosa. She proved herself to be versatile enough to play any style of music. Also, she played with a depth of emotion that could touch the bottom of your soul.

"Yes, ma'am." Eliza grinned. "She claims she hasn't touched the piano since she was a civilian. I heard her play something the other day from memory. She was phenomenal!"

"Phenomenal, huh? Fine, I'll allow it. Now you have the honor of trying to convince Grace to play."

Eliza ducked her head. "I was kind of hoping that you could just order her to do it."

Charity held her hands up. "Oh no! This is your mess to clean up."

ASKING GRACE WOULD be no easy task. First of all, Grace had already moved out of their shared room in the officers' quarters, having been assigned to an empty, less spacious room in the basement as part of her "punishment." It was the first time in three years that Eliza had had a room to herself. She should be relishing the privacy she now had. But instead, she felt lonelier than ever. Even though she had grown up as an only child and should be used to it, Eliza felt like she had lost a sister.

Eliza still saw Grace on a regular basis, however. The Special Services team worked out of an office next to the rec room. Eliza found her in the rec room when she sought her out.

"Grace, can I talk to you for a minute?"

Grace's fingers went still on top of the keys. Eliza wasn't all that knowledgeable about classical music, but she thought she recognized the piece that Grace had been tinkering with. She took a deep breath and went out on a limb.

"Was that Bach?"

"Yes, it was. What of it?" Grace had yet to turn away from the instrument. Had yet to look Eliza in the face. Eliza swallowed again.

"I know that what you were playing isn't the easiest piece to master. But here you are, playing it from memory. Wow."

Grace sighed with her entire body. There was no way that Eliza could've missed her irritation. "You interrupted my 'genius' level of play to tell me something that I already know?"

Eliza wanted to both laugh and wince. There was that old spark of arrogance that Eliza had come to love over the years and that she was now beginning to miss.

"Yes, well . . . what I really want to know is why none of us have ever seen you play before now? I mean, you could have been on a USO show all this time. Instead, you've been here with us. You have so much talent. I don't understand."

At that, Grace pushed back her seat from the piano. "You could ask the same of Vera. She was a foot doctor before the war. But the Army saw fit to use her as an administrative officer. All those boys out there marching for days with boils and God knows what else on their feet. But here she is, along with the rest of us, not using our talents and specialized knowledge."

This time, Eliza did wince. Her attempts at buttering up Grace were obviously not working. It was time to woman up and just ask.

"Grace, look, the funerals are set for tomorrow. I thought it would be nice to have music played at them. Would you—"

Grace cut her off before she could finish. "Of course. I'm not a monster. I knew both of the Marys. I liked them."

She returned her fingers to the keys. Grace held them there, tense. Everything in her posture said, *Are we done now?*

"Thank you. And for what it's worth, I really am sorry."

"They're going to send me home any day now. I still don't know if I'm getting kicked out or not. The worst part is that I never got a chance to see Paris. Since I was a little girl, it's been a dream of mine to visit Paris." Grace then closed her eyes and began playing the most somber piece of music that Eliza had ever heard.

Eliza opened her mouth to respond. But what could be said in response to something like that? Instead, she just nodded in Grace's direction and left. Eliza had wanted to say that her next project would be to figure out a way out of this mess for Grace. But words were pretty much useless at this point. All that mattered now was action and results.

AS PROMISED, GRACE performed the music at the funerals the next day. Thankfully, Noel and Charity had been sympathetic in giving her permission to do so. But their hands were still tied in getting her out of a court-martial. To their credit, however, they were still poring over their Army procedural manuals and working every connection they had to figure out a way around it.

In the end, she was ready when the time came for the musical selection. Grace had played the most haunting rendition of Beethoven's *Moonlight Sonata* she had ever heard herself play.

Her fingers glided over the opening notes of the piece effortlessly. By this point in her life, she had played it so many times that the song felt like an old friend. An old friend who had crafted and boosted her confidence as a child, but who later had abandoned her on the worst day of her life, only to return to comfort her on the days when her spirits had sunk even lower. Then came the time when Grace herself had turned her back on it, finding solace in a new, snazzier combination of notes in the bebop sound she had discovered.

As Grace continued to play, her thoughts shifted to the moment at hand, to the women who had been lost in the tragic accident, and to the one woman who continued to fight for her life. The last update on Dolores's condition had been grim. There was little chance that she would survive her injuries, but that didn't kill the hope among the women of the Six Triple Eight.

Grace glanced over at the caskets at the front of the altar of the hospital's chapel. Both of the women who lay inside them had been in their early twenties. Grace felt old at that thought, even though she herself was only a few years older. *No, you're turning thirty next year*, she reminded herself.

She'd had a full life once. She continued to have one now. She'd just been too absorbed in her self-pity to see it.

Grace finished the last bars of the piece with a flourish. The audience's hushed silence followed. She stood up and dipped slightly into a bow. *That was for you, Mama.*

She stared at the caskets again, shaking her head. Such a waste. She vowed to herself to never waste her life living in the past ever again.

After the funeral service had been dismissed, they all learned that Sergeant Dolores Browne had succumbed to her injuries. Then Major Adams pulled Grace to the side to tell her two things. One, that her musical performance had moved the major to tears. And two, that Grace's orders had arrived with the travel arrangements for her journey back home to the States.

TWO DAYS LATER, Eliza stayed in her seat in the front row of the chapel long after Dolores's casket had been removed and loaded onto the truck that would carry it to the American cemetery in Normandy. It had hurt to see the young woman's remains when she had put up such a fight to live. It had hurt that much more because Eliza had been that girl hooked up to tubes and bound in casts not too long ago.

Eliza had survived her ordeal. Dolores should have survived hers too.

"Would you like some company?" Noah stood just far enough away to give Eliza space if she wanted it.

She tapped the seat beside her on the pew. "Company would be nice."

After Noah sat down, he asked, "How are you doing?"

"I'm okay. It's just senseless. The three of them survived the war. Yet they're all gone."

Noah squeezed her hand. "I know. The sad thing is how many

of these jeep accidents I see every week. So many lives gone for no reason. I love it here in France. But I'm starting to wish they would just send us all home."

She squeezed his hand back. She liked how warm and soft it was. How it made her feel safe. How *he* made her feel safe. Eliza sighed, then leaned against him. It was good to have a friend by her side again. One who she knew had her back.

"Why do I sense that there's more behind that sigh than Sergeant Browne's passing?"

"Just thinking about Grace. I feel so bad. My big mouth got her in a heap of trouble."

Noah slipped his fingers beneath her chin, lifting it off her chest. "I don't know all the details, but it sounded to me that she broke the rules. She knew it. He knew it. They knew the risk they were taking by getting involved."

"True. But she doesn't deserve to get kicked out of the corps for it. Grace Steele is a damn good soldier. I don't know of anyone else who follows the rules as closely as she does. She doesn't even report to Jonathan directly anymore. And the war's over. What does it matter?"

Noah leaned back. "Hmm, maybe that's the problem."

Eliza turned and stared at him. "What is?"

"I haven't known you long, but I have seen you knock a grown man out cold. You're not the type to tackle an illogical rule by following it."

Eliza felt the beginnings of a plan forming in her mind. "You're right. I should be figuring out how to break it."

She smiled for the first time in days. The time had come to get creative.

July 5, 1945

Dear Mr. Secretary Stimson:

I hereby resign as the civilian aide to the secretary of war
effective immediately.

Sincerely,
Jonathan Philips

Postmarked July 6, 1945, Rouen, France
Received July 10, 1945, Washington, D.C.

CHAPTER 32

Rouen, France
July 1945

IT IS AS much your fault as it is mine that Grace is in trouble. And *we* are going to fix it."

Eliza had tracked down Jonathan Philips right after Sergeant Dolores Browne's funeral. He was staying at a private residence turned soldier rest home on the outskirts of the city. She'd had to bribe a member of the 6888th motor pool to drive her out there.

He offered her one of the chairs in the home's parlor. Eliza placed the typewriter case she had brought with her down beside it. She noted that he made pains to sit on the small couch across from her.

"There's not much I can do, I'm afraid, considering that the complaint against her involves improper conduct with me. What did you have in mind?"

"I want you to quit your job."

Jonathan looked like he had to stop himself from falling out of his seat. "I'm sorry. You want me to what?"

Eliza scooted her chair closer to where he sat and leaned in. "We still have a shot at getting her off the hook. The main charge against Grace is for fraternization. With you. She might have a defense if we show that you no longer work for the War Department."

Jonathan leaned back on the couch, chuckling. "I'm afraid that's not how it works, sweetheart. That defense might work had I submitted my resignation before she got in trouble. It won't stick if I quit today and made it effective retroactively."

"I know. That's why your resignation letter was lost in the mail."

"Come again?" Jonathan gave her a look that made her feel like she had been drinking too much of the local brandy.

"We run the mail going to and from the United States. If we say a letter got lost or delayed, then it was lost or delayed."

He steepled his fingers beneath his chin and thought about it for a moment. "You seriously want me to quit my job so you can tamper with the mail in the hopes of getting the charges against Grace dropped?"

Eliza picked up the typewriter case and set it onto the coffee table. Once she finished opening it and setting it up, she folded her arms across her chest and leaned back. "Yes, that's exactly what we're going to do."

TEN MINUTES LATER, Eliza finished typing up the letter. She handed it to him along with a pen. "Now, all you have to do is sign."

"This will never work."

"Why? The war is over. Unless you were planning on making a career out of the civilian aide thing."

"No, actually, I was planning on doing this very thing after I got back home." Jonathan took the cap off the pen. He hesitated. "Quitting while I'm still here in Europe is going to make this a logistical nightmare."

"If Grace loses her right to her veterans' benefits, it's going to make her *life* a nightmare."

"You're right." Jonathan signed his name. "She earned every last one of them. No thanks to me." He handed the pen and letter back to Eliza. "I hope this works."

Eliza pulled out an ink pad, a date stamp, and an envelope. She twirled the numbers back to a date before the accident occurred and stamped the envelope. She tucked the letter into the envelope and sealed it. "Thank you."

"You might as well give that back to me. I'm flying back to D.C. tonight. If we're lucky, I'll have Grace in the clear before she returns to New York."

"At this point, whatever works."

WHEN ELIZA RETURNED to Caserne Tallandier, one of the mail-sorting clerks gave her a letter. "Can you pass this to Grace? It just arrived. I can't find her anywhere."

"Yeah, sure." The envelope was marked URGENT. Eliza recognized the return address. It was in Harlem. "It looks like it's a letter from home. I'll run this over to her right now."

But when Eliza got to Grace's room in the basement, she wasn't there. The room was emptied of all personal effects. The only thing that remained was a note on the bed that said "Received permission to leave for the coast early. Going home."

"Damn." Eliza looked at the letter again. There was something about it that niggled at her to open it. Then she noticed the script on the envelope. It had been written by a woman. Eliza knew for a fact that Grace's mom had never written her since she left home. "That means whatever's in here has got to be important."

Eliza ripped it open and scanned the note inside. "Oh my god! She has to read this note."

Somewhere on the Atlantic Ocean
Two weeks later

DESPITE THE COLD, Grace spent a few minutes each morning on the deck of the Liberty ship that was taking her home. She told herself, and anyone else who asked, that she did it for the fresh air and to clear her head. In reality, she knew that it had to do with maintaining her sanity and reassuring herself that, unlike during her last transatlantic trip, there were no Germans lurking under the seas, trying to blast them all out of the water.

On this morning, she leaned on the railing and studied the waters surrounding the ship. Or at least, what she could see through the fog that had rolled in. Satisfied, Grace closed her eyes and listened to the water lapping against the hull. She took a deep breath of the sea air. Having been crammed in a ship with about three thousand other returning soldiers for two weeks, she relished these precious moments of solitude.

This trip across the sea had been way more uneventful than her first one. The battle-hardened infantrymen were much more interested in joking with their buddies than flirting with her. None of the officers bothered with leading drill exercises on the deck. What would've been the point? The war for everyone aboard this Liberty ship was essentially over.

She had been among approximately five hundred of her sister soldiers from the Six Triple Eight going over to England. While there were a few WAC companies aboard this ship coming home, there were only a handful of other female soldiers who looked like her aboard. She no longer had anyone to order about. Aside from meals, Grace kept to herself.

She spent most of her time trying not to think about how close she had been to Paris. Ironically, a rumor had started circulating as she was leaving Rouen that her battalion would soon receive orders to move on to the French capital. If that came to fruition, it would be a dream come true for the women of the Six Triple Eight. But not for Grace. Her adventure of a lifetime was coming to an end.

The fog rolled across the deck as Grace resumed her walk. But there was one particular difference on this day. Seagulls circled overhead. More than usual. Grace felt her heartbeat speed up. More birds meant that they were close to land. Land meant that she would have to face the music soon. She would finally learn what her fate in the military would be.

Soon enough, a few buildings began to peek through breaks in the fog. Then the fog retreated altogether to reveal the Lower Manhattan skyline. Grace smiled despite her dread. *We're home.*

A FEW HOURS later, Grace found herself back at Camp Shanks. "Last Stop, U.S.A." had become her first stop back on American soil. Grace had been escorted to a windowless room. She knew that a debrief would be part of the demobilization process, but she hadn't expected to be in a room by herself.

The WAC official who went over her files with her was nice enough. But after listening to the woman drone on about what could and couldn't be shared about her experience once she was a civilian again, Grace had had enough.

"Am I getting an honorable discharge or not?"

The woman wrinkled her brow, confused. "Of course you are, sugar. Why would you ask such a thing?"

Grace, surprised, refused to allow herself to relax. "I got into a spot of trouble over there."

The woman took her hand and giggled. "Didn't we all? Let me take another look."

The WAC official scanned the papers laid out in front of her again. "Oh, I see it now." She pointed to an entry on Grace's record. "It says right here. The investigation and review of possible misconduct has been dismissed. The Army's bureaucratic nightmare can be our blessing sometimes. Whatever you did, sugar, you're free and clear now."

Only then did Grace allow her shoulders to slump in relief. She took the papers the lady handed her and got out of there as fast as possible.

NOW GRACE STOOD on the landing outside her parents' apartment. She had spent the last ten minutes mustering the courage to knock. What should have been the most familiar place in the world to her now felt foreign. She debated whether coming back here was a good idea at all. She had no idea if Mama still held a grudge against her for leaving.

In a different time and place, she would have gotten Tony on the telephone. He would have told her what the temperature was with her mother. He would have already smoothed over the differences between mother and daughter. He would have made home feel like home again. But in the here and now, she no longer had him to act as her crutch. Tony was dead. She wasn't sure if she felt brave enough to handle a face-off with her mother. Not yet anyway.

I should just leave. Grace slung her canvas duffel bag back over her shoulder. She was about to go when the door opened.

"Grace?"

Grace dropped her bag. It tumbled down the stairs behind her. Before her stood what could only be a ghost.

"Tony?"

Tears filled Grace's eyes. She blinked them back for fear that they would dissolve the image of her brother forever.

"Yeah, kiddo." He grinned. "It's me."

CHAPTER 33

Paris, France
October 1945

ELIZA SAT ALONE at an outdoor café table, staring off into the distance. The steam from her coffee had stopped rising from the cup almost an hour ago. Everything that had made her fall in love with the city of Paris as a child was present—the lights that were beginning to twinkle, the Eiffel Tower peeking between the buildings at the end of the block, the scent of that morning's fresh bread from the bakery next door still perfuming the air—yet none of it triggered any kind of reaction from her.

It had been little over a month since the Six Triple Eight had been reassigned from Rouen to Paris. Ironically, the magic that had seemed to bond the 855 women together from the start had dissipated once they had been immersed in the magic of the iconic city. Previously, they all had been crammed together working and living in the same confined spaces. But now, they were housed in hotels all over the city and saw each other only at work. The mail distribution workload was a fraction of what it had been when they had first arrived in Europe.

With fewer pressing deadlines chasing them, there was more time and opportunity to explore the delights of Paris either on one's own or in small groups. Enjoying Paris was what Eliza thought she would be doing now that she was finally here. Instead, all she wanted was to go home.

Her fingers toyed with the edges of the letter in her hand, which had arrived that morning. It was proof that she had done one thing right.

Operation Hail Mary a success.

Jonathan Philips

Eliza was relieved. It was bad enough that she hadn't been able to get that last-minute letter to Grace before she sailed off for home. The one Grace's mother had sent with the news that her brother, Tony, somehow survived that Japanese assault in the Philippines, had spent the last three years fighting as a guerrilla in the jungle, and had now come home. Eliza would have liked to have seen that happy reunion.

"Bonjour, Mademoiselle Capitaine."

It was Noah. She greeted him with a half-hearted smile. She reached absently for her coffee, then choked it down when the cold liquid hit her palate.

Noah bit his lip to keep from laughing at what must have been a horrified expression on her face. "Is the Parisian version of coffee not to your liking?"

"No, it's cold," she said between coughs. "And even if it was still hot, this isn't anywhere near the quality of the stuff I tasted when I was here before the war. The old girl might be going on five months since her liberation from the Germans, but she's not all the way back to herself yet."

"I'll take your word for it. This has been my first opportunity to visit Paris. I find myself taking a liking to their chicory café. It reminds me of a family trip we all took down to New Orleans when I was in college." Noah gestured toward the empty chair on the opposite side of the table from her. "May I?"

"Of course. New Orleans, huh? I've never been but have always wanted to go. My parents, being the son and daughter of Southerners who escaped from the South, always had an excuse for why they'd never go back down there whenever I asked."

"That's a shame. I'm from Alabama myself. Don't believe everything you hear about us down there. Our people down South are some of the most salt-of-the-earth people you'll ever meet. As for them white folks . . ." He shrugged. "Not all of them are bad. But as for the ones who are, they make the devil himself look kind. We all just make a point of not going where they are."

Eliza laughed at that. "Okay, I'll take your word for it."

"I can do you one better. Have dinner with me this week. I heard about a spot in Montmartre that serves food from back home with a French twist. You can't get any closer to New Orleans cooking than that."

Eliza had begun spending more time with Noah since the battalion had been reassigned to Paris. With Grace gone, Eliza had taken to moping in her opulent hotel room. Noah put an end to that with invitations to explore the city with him. Unlike her, it was his first time visiting. But, through Noah, she enjoyed seeing the city with new eyes.

"I'll go. But we better make it soon. They told me this morning that I finally had enough points accumulated to go back home if I wanted to."

"That is good news! But it looks like you weren't happy to hear that for some reason."

"No, it's just that . . ." Eliza frowned, unable to find adequate words to describe how she felt. She was more than ready to get out of the WAC and go back to civilian life. But she wasn't looking forward to resuming the life that she had left behind three years ago. "The last thing I want to do is go back to the expectation of being my daddy's little princess. I can't pretend to be that girl anymore. Too much has happened."

"Who says you have to go back to that?"

Eliza went still. She stared at him. "Well, first off, I have nowhere else to go."

"Forgive me if this is too personal, but what have you been doing with your pay all this time?"

"I tried to be frugal with my day-to-day expenses. I put some in savings, but not nearly enough to live on my own. The rest I sent back home to my mother."

Noah clapped his hands. "Perfect. Do you think she'll give that money back to you when you go home?"

"I . . . Honestly, I have no idea. Maybe. That is, if she hasn't told my father about it all this time. I could see him now, puffing out his chest and declaring that he's keeping it as reimbursement for raising me and sending me to college."

"Of course he wouldn't. I'm sure he loves you and wants what's best for you."

"Oh, he does. He's also a know-it-all, self-righteous bastard," she said with a grin.

Noah laughed at that. "He sounds like a real piece of work. I can't wait to meet him."

Eliza raised an eyebrow at that. "What makes you think I'll let you stick around long enough for you to have the chance?"

"Touché." He leaned back in his chair. "I'll leave that on the back burner for now. So, have you heard anything from your friend since she left?"

She handed Noah Jonathan's letter. "Only this. But nothing yet from Grace herself. I don't blame her. She barely spoke to me after that day at the hospital in Rouen." She sighed. "I like to think that if she did bother sending me a letter it got lost in the mail."

They both chuckled at that. Noah reached out and placed his hand over hers. Once again, it felt like a warm blanket on her skin. But she tried to keep her feelings in check. Eliza was sure that this feeling was nothing more than part of the high, now that the war was over and they found themselves in the world's most romantic city.

"Give her time. You two have been through a lot together. Even if you spent the majority of it butting heads with each other. She's probably adjusting to being back stateside and finding her way. Just like you are now."

"Yes, maybe she is. Just the same, I wish everybody would stop asking me about her. Everywhere I go, all I hear is 'Where is your friend? Where is that girl? I heard she can play her some piano.' But get this. Charity even received a request from someone higher up asking if Grace was available to play at some fancy reception here in the city. That one came in yesterday. It hit me right in the gut. She told me once that it was her dream to become a concert pianist and to play here one day. She came so close to living that dream."

"Maybe she can come back once everything settles down enough for civilian travel."

Eliza scoffed at that. "I don't plan on mentioning it to her to find out. She hates me enough as it is."

"Then it sounds to me like you have nothing else to lose."

Eliza quieted after his comment. The thought of that didn't sit right with her. She had lost so much already it seemed. Her relationship with her father. Her innocence. Her freedom to come and go as she pleased. She hated to think that she would also have to live with losing the one woman in the WAC who had most become like a sister to her. The sister she had always longed for, even if Grace was an annoying Goody Two-shoes.

"That right there is where you are wrong. I don't want to *lose* her."

Noah studied her for a moment. "Not that I consider myself a consolation prize in any way, but you still have me. That is, if you want me."

"Noah, I . . . We barely know each other." Eliza knew that was a lie even as the words came out of her mouth. She just didn't want to face the inevitable drifting apart once the two of them returned home and their lives returned to "normal."

"I know. It's not something I'm looking for you to give me a definitive answer on at this moment. I'm just letting you know that my interest is there for you to pursue if you should so choose. And on that note, I'm due back at the hospital soon. I'll leave you to what's left of your coffee."

"Thank you. As for what you said, all I can promise you right now is that I'll think about it."

Somewhere on the Atlantic Ocean
December 1945

THANKFULLY, THE ONLY major drama Eliza experienced on this final leg home had occurred right before they had shipped out of Le Havre. Charity Adams was a part of the Six Triple Eight contingent that was coming home with Eliza. With her rank of major, she was the highest-ranking woman on the ship. A group of white nurses protested when they had been informed that a Negro woman would be their commanding officer for the duration of the trip. It had turned into a standoff between them and Charity and the ship's captain. The ship's captain finally gave them an ultimatum: "You can stay and live with it. Otherwise, get off my ship while there's still a gangplank."

The reluctant nurses chose to stay. They had not caused any problems since.

What Eliza and the other women of the 6888th had not expected on this trip was to see the direct result of their efforts right before their eyes. There had been a mail call their first day out at sea. They all looked at each other wordlessly with glassy eyes as all around them battle-hardened combat soldiers broke down into tears as they opened packets of mail sent by friends and family back home. In some cases, it was the first words they had received from home all year.

Eliza felt herself grinning from ear to ear as she looked back on that moment. It had been a fitting end to the life-changing adventure that had been her time in the Women's Army Corps. And now, she was on her way back home. She had no idea what waited for her there or what new battles she would have to fight with her father.

She had seen Noah only a few more times, but they never did go on that date. Soon after their talk at the outdoor café in Paris, he had received his own orders to ship out. He had been too busy getting ready for them to meet. All Eliza knew was that the ball was still in her court. At least, she hoped it was, although she didn't see how they could build on what they had started in France a thousand miles apart. He understood that they may not see each other again, with him returning home to his family in Alabama and her not certain if she would settle back in Harlem or wind up someplace else. That last talk had left Eliza both hopeful and rudderless.

She was so deep in her thoughts that she almost missed the foghorn's blare. The foghorn had not come from the ship itself but from somewhere out in the mist. Eliza turned her head, straining to hear. But there was nothing more. She had obviously been on this ship too long, because now she was starting to hear things.

The foghorn blared again. And then like magic, the mist parted, revealing behind it the unmistakable jagged outline of the New York City skyline.

Eliza smiled so hard that her cheeks hurt. *We're home.*

ELIZA HAD PLANNED to kiss the ground as soon as she was back on American soil. But they had arrived back at Camp Shanks, where there was at least a foot of snow on the ground. She settled for the feel of a good old-fashioned snowball between her mittens instead.

"Duck!" she yelled at the closest fellow Six Triple Eight member to her. That woman turned out to be none other than Major Charity Adams. Eliza threw the snowball and hit her friend square in the shoulder.

Charity sputtered, "I'm still your commanding officer, soldier!" And then they both broke out into laughter. Next thing she knew, Charity had returned the favor by hurling a handful of snow into her face.

The entire group continued on, throwing the occasional snowball as they went. None of the crowds that they had seen in the papers overseas were there to greet them. A local officer pointed in the direction of a nearby bunker. "Go thataway for debriefing, ladies."

"That's it?" Eliza grumbled. "No official greetings? No fanfare?

No nothing? You'd have thought we were over there on a pleasure trip instead of serving our country."

A few others nodded in agreement as they headed toward the bunker. Most of them had spent two or three years of their lives in the Army. They all had seen the welcome-home fanfare previous soldiers had received in the papers and newsreels while overseas. But for the WACs returning home today, no one had thought to organize anything. Not even a Red Cross welcome wagon. The few people who were there paid little mind to the newly returned batch of female soldiers. It was a slap in the face to their service. "I guess not much has changed in the good ol' U.S. of A. while we were away."

The pride that had swelled inside Eliza left her in a whoosh.

"Forget them. C'mon, girl." Charity pulled Eliza along.

An hour later, Eliza emerged from her final discharge meeting. There were a few taxis parked along the curb and a smattering of families searching among the small milling groups of soldiers, both male and female, for a familiar face. Eliza shaded her eyes as she scanned the crowd. She had hoped to have one last goodbye with Charity before she headed back down South. But she knew Charity had had a tight window to get to the train station. Still, Eliza had hoped to see her friend off properly. They had had quite the adventures together on and off through the years. She hated that, like with Grace, another friend was gone without a proper goodbye.

CHAPTER 34

Harlem, New York
December 1945

WHILE THE SHOCK of finding out that Tony was still alive had begun to wear off, not a day went by when she wasn't thankful to see his face at the breakfast table.

With Tony back, the tension between Grace and her mother was gone. Time and space and miracles made both women appreciate the opportunity they had to repair their relationship. But that didn't stop Mama from nagging Grace about her future.

"I think you should give Juilliard another go," Mama started as she passed Grace the bowl of grits.

Grace sighed. "You won't let up, will you, Mama?"

"What? All I'm saying is that you shouldn't let all that talent go to waste."

"I've already told you, I don't want to just study the classics anymore. I want to play jazz." Grace braced herself. They'd had the same conversation over breakfast for the last five months. It always ended with Mama telling her that playing the classics was the only way to pay the bills *and* stay right with the Lord.

But this time, Tony surprised them both by chiming in. "You know, Mama, you should hear her play the other stuff sometime. She's really good."

Mama stared at him like he was a small child who had jumped into grown folks' business. Then she sat back in her chair, like she was chewing over what he had said. "You know what? As of today, I'm washing my hands of it. I've been blessed to have both of my children survive the war. Who am I to steal your joy? You want to spend your life listening to that noise? I say go for it. Just don't waste that talent."

GRACE FOUND HERSELF outside Juilliard again that same day. But this time, instead of staring wistfully at the nameplate on the building, there was no hesitation as she walked through the door. She would either make a fool of herself or not. But she refused to live another day of her life with this *thing*, this fear, hanging over her head. She had just survived the U.S. Women's Army Corps as a woman of color, for God's sake. She had, for reasons still unknown, escaped the humiliation of a court-martial and managed to keep her veterans' benefits. Surely she could stomach a piddly piano audition. She had nothing left to lose.

"Excuse me, ma'am," she said to the receptionist. It was a different woman from the last time she was here, thank goodness. "I'm here to play."

Later, Grace emerged from the building wearing a big smile on her face. She clutched the folder filled with enrollment paperwork to her chest. She had done it. Starting in January, she was going to be a graduate piano composition student.

She couldn't wait to tell her brother. But she wanted to play it cool. The cool thing to do would be to take the next crosstown bus home. But there was someone else she needed to tell first.

Grace crossed the street and picked up the receiver on the pay phone there. She put in some coins and waited for the operator to answer.

"Yes, operator. I'm calling Washington, D.C. The number is DuPont-7521. Yes, I'll hold."

In France last summer, Grace hadn't had a chance to ask Jonathan about what his plans were when he returned to the States. She had no idea if he had gone back to D.C. or if he even had the same home telephone number. Grace chewed her lip. She had gone with her gut with every other decision she had made today. She would just have to continue to trust her instincts now as well.

And the rich timbre of his voice came over the crackling line. "Hello?"

"Jonathan, it's Grace." She paused. "I got into Juilliard. And they're going to give me a fellowship to cover anything my veterans' benefits don't."

Silence. Grace's heart began to race. Dammit, she really had screwed it up with him back in France. *Why isn't he saying anything?*

"Well, I'm sorry to have called you out of the blue like this. It's just that . . . I wanted to thank you for your support and for encouraging me. You saw something in me even when I had stopped believing in myself. I had settled for what was 'safe' when I met you. You pushed me out of my comfort zone. I'll always be thankful to you for that."

"Well, that was quite a mouthful," he started when Grace finally paused to take a breath. "First off, Juilliard . . . that's wonderful! I knew you had it in you. I always did."

"Thank you. I still can't believe it."

"Your parents must be so proud. Your brother too."

Now it was Grace's turn to pause. She shouldn't have been surprised that Jonathan knew about Tony. It had been his job to know about such things, after all. "I haven't told them yet. It all just happened a few minutes ago. You were the first person I wanted to tell."

"I'm flattered."

"Listen to me. I just blurt out my good news without asking about you. How are you? Are you feeling better since I last saw you? Are you still with the government?"

"I'm fine. I just needed rest and some good food, both of which I got on my return trip back to the States. And as for the government . . . no, I turned in my resignation as soon as I got back in town. Now I'm in the process of resuming the business I had before the war."

"Before the war," she echoed. "Gosh, that seems like a whole other lifetime ago."

"Yes, it was. A lot has happened since then."

There was another awkward pause. There was so much left unspoken between them. Grace could feel her euphoria begin to wane. She no longer had the courage to make the first move.

Jonathan saved her from having to do so. "One of us had better say something, or the operator is going to cut this call short before either one of us wants it to end."

"I'm sorry. For the last time we saw each other. My job . . ."

"Yeah, I know all about that. But you have nothing to apologize for. I'm the one who came and sought you out. And you wound up bearing the brunt of the fallout. If you'd let me, I'd like to make it up to you."

"Whatever do you mean, Jonathan?"

"I mean, I believe I owe you Paris."

"I'm sorry, I'm not following."

"I'm saying that in addition to rebuilding my law practice here in D.C., I'm also looking to get back into the music business as well. I wasn't just a lawyer. I was also a talent agent. What I'm offering you, if you have nothing else planned next summer, is that

I think I can get you some gigs over in France." He went on to explain that one of his jazz artists was planning a summer European tour and his usual backup pianist wouldn't be able to go because of a scheduling conflict.

He added, "I don't think I'll have any trouble convincing Fatha Earl Hines to let you tag along. The word on the street is that you made an impression over there with your piano playing. There were some requests sent to WAC ETO headquarters, but you had already left for the States."

"What?"

"Wait, Eliza didn't tell you?"

"Tell me what? Jonathan, I haven't spoken to Eliza at all since I left France. What did you do over there to get me out of that court-martial and save me from a dishonorable discharge?"

Jonathan paused again. "That wasn't me. That was your friend Eliza."

Harlem, New York
March 1946

IT WAS THREE months before Grace was able to confront Eliza about Jonathan's revelation. Part of the delay was because Grace wasn't ready to let go of her bitterness over how everything went down in France. While she had been more forgiving in the immediate aftermath, resentment hit Grace once her ship back to the United States had set out to sea. And now that she knew Eliza had interceded on her behalf? Well, Grace wasn't quite ready to not be mad all over again.

Grace showed up unannounced at the Strivers' Row office of the newspaper that Eliza's family owned.

"I'd like to see Eliza Jones, please."

The office receptionist stared at Grace like she had walked in off the street and demanded to see President Truman. The old Grace would have never shown up without having an appointment set up. But she wasn't that person anymore. And since her afternoon music composition class had been canceled, she had had the time.

"I'm afraid I can't help you without an appointment. Perhaps I can set you up for a later time?" From the way the woman was frowning at her, Grace doubted the sincerity of her expressed helpfulness.

"I'll wait." Grace backed herself into one of the wooden chairs in the waiting area. If there was one thing that she had learned during her time in the WAC, it was how to remain focused no matter the discomforts at hand.

The receptionist's mouth flattened into an annoyed line. "Suit yourself." She then picked up the phone receiver and covered her mouth. From what Grace could make out from the woman's whispers, it sounded like she had called someone high up in management for guidance on how to handle Grace's request. Eliza's father was Grace's guess. From the bits and pieces Eliza had shared about him over the years, the man had sounded like a real piece of work. She imagined she was about to get a face-to-face confirmation of that assessment.

Shortly after, an immaculately dressed woman emerged from what she imagined was the executive office suite. She walked up to Grace with her hand extended and a smile on her face. Grace, while surprised, returned the smile. It was Eliza's mother.

"Grace Steele, I thought your name sounded familiar. How are you, honey?"

Grace took her hand. "Mrs. Jones! It's good to see you."

Lillian yanked her into a hug. "Where have you been? You shouldn't have taken so long to come see me."

Grace stepped back. "I got the impression that you weren't a part of the newspaper's daily operations. I was actually looking for Eliza."

"Yes, Veronica"—Lillian gestured toward the receptionist—"told me. I'm sorry, hon, but Eliza isn't here. She's home packing."

"Packing?"

"I'm sending her down South on assignment."

"*You're* sending her? But I thought your husband ran the editorial side of things here."

"He did. But he put his back out playing golf over the weekend. He's at the house too, resting. That means I'm in charge for now."

"Wow, a woman editor in chief. My how times are a-changing."

"Yes, they are. Although it will probably take hell freezing over for my hardheaded husband to finally retire and let me take over full-time." Lillian grinned. "Now, why don't you come on back to my office and tell me how I can help you?"

Grace was reluctant to talk to Mrs. Jones about what had happened back in Rouen and her daughter's role in it, but she was able to summarize enough without completely ratting out Eliza.

"I'm afraid Eliza hasn't shared anything about your situation with me since she's been back. As you can imagine, it's been an interesting adjustment for all of us to get used to living with each other again. I gave the Army my little girl and they sent me back a grown, independent woman who, like her father, doesn't like to tell me anything."

"Does that mean she hasn't told you about Noah?" Grace might not tattle on Eliza about almost getting her court-martialed, but she wasn't going to miss out on the chance to dish about Eliza's personal life with her mother.

"Well, let's just say he made himself known to us before she had a chance to keep him a secret from me. But enough about that. It sounds like the two of you have some talking to do. And I need my child on the seven forty-five P.M. train tonight that's heading down South."

Mrs. Jones pulled out a piece of notepaper from her desk. On it, she wrote down an address in the neatest handwriting Grace had ever seen. "Here's the house address and the directions to get you there. Hurry up, and don't make her miss that train!"

Luckily, the Jones home was within walking distance of the newspaper office. From the outside, the Jones family's brownstone looked like a palatial estate compared with the cramped apartment Grace shared with her own family.

"Well, this explains her Miss Priss attitude when we first arrived at Fort Des Moines," Grace muttered to herself as she pressed the buzzer. She expected a maid in uniform to answer the door. But it was Eliza herself who opened it.

"Grace," Eliza gasped, her eyes widened in shock. "How did you find me? What are you doing here?"

"I saw your mother down at the paper. She sent me."

The corners of Eliza's mouth turned down into a frown. "Of course she would. And this would also be the one time she wouldn't call ahead to let me know you were coming."

"Why does it matter? Were you trying to avoid me?"

"No. I've been wanting to reach out to you. I just didn't know how."

"I guess I never got around to giving you my address."

"It wasn't that. Some mail arrived for you right after you left Rouen. I took the liberty of writing down the permanent address on your directory card when I processed it to come back to the States. What I meant was, I didn't know what was the best way to salvage our friendship."

"I've known for a while that you came back with Charity in December. I just wasn't ready to see you until now."

"Well, come on in. I'm afraid I'm on my way out of town, though. I leave in a few hours."

Eliza led Grace into a lavish sitting room with plump furniture that looked like it belonged in a museum. She did notice, however, one well-loved chair that had a worn spot on the seat cushion. It looked like even the rich had to make do without certain luxuries as well while the war was on.

Grace sat down on the sofa at Eliza's direction and cleared her throat. "I know you're short on time so I guess I'll just get right to it. Jonathan told me it was you, and not him, who cleared my name in France."

A trace of the innocent woman-child Grace had first met almost four years ago flashed across Eliza's cheeks. "He did, did he?" She said the words carefully, as if she was deliberately not going to confirm or deny whether it was true.

"He did." Grace nodded. "What I want to know is how. You busted me in a way that no one could get me out of, not even Charity with all of her connections."

"Oh, that." Eliza waved her hand flippantly. "That was easy. You forget, Captain, we were the ones who controlled the flow of mail coming in . . . and going out."

"Go on."

"So, what if, say, Jonathan had written a resignation letter to his superiors *before* you and he saw each other? As you know, letters get lost in the mail and then turn up miraculously all the time . . ."

Grace finished the thought for her. "Then it would mean that he couldn't have been 'fraternizing' with me because he no longer worked for the government. Oh my goodness. That was a genius move, Eliza."

Eliza grinned at her like the cat that got the cream. "Exactly."

"But why?"

"Because I was wrong. It was my big mouth that got you in trouble. So I did what I had to do to get you out of it."

A stunned Grace stood up and threw her arms around Eliza.

"Thank you, thank you, my friend. I was able to keep my benefits for school. I'm now living my dream, and it's because of you."

"Let's just say I owed you one."

GRACE LEFT SOON after, citing Eliza's impending train trip as an excuse. Eliza had been reluctant to let her go. She had missed her friend. Reconnecting and clearing the air had been everything. Eliza would have to thank her mother for her scheming ways today.

The top of the steps creaked. Eliza looked up to see her father attempting to come down the stairs.

"Daddy, no! You'll hurt yourself. Let me help you." She rushed to cradle his arm. She pretended to ignore how much thinner he had become in the week since he'd injured himself at the golf course.

"Let me go, Eliza. I wasn't going to risk it. I just wanted to catch a glimpse of your visitor."

"Who? Grace?"

"Yes, her. That's your Army friend that your mother was telling me about. The piano whiz. I believe we saw her play at Adam Clayton Powell's church a few years before the war. I hated that she stopped. That girl there had talent."

"Yeah, she's pretty amazing. But enough about that. Let's get you back to bed, Daddy." Luckily, her parents' bedroom was only a few steps away from the top of the stairs. She led him to his bedside. He flapped his arm until she removed her hands from his elbow.

"Let loose of me. I can do this."

Eliza's arms tensed at her sides. She made herself not reach out as she watched him gingerly lower himself back into bed.

"That's a fine girl there. If they were letting girls like that into that Women's Army, then I guess you were in good company."

"Yes, Daddy, I was."

"Then I guess I owe you an apology. I was wrong to put up a fuss when you first told me that you wanted to sign up."

Eliza went still. She didn't think she had ever heard her father apologize to anyone, for anything. "Daddy, I don't understand. What are you saying?"

"I'm saying that since I've been laid up in this damn bed that I've been doing a lot of thinking and a lot of listening to what all goes on around here. I see now that I've been a real hardhead to the two people who mean the most to me. And in doing so that I've been standing in their way."

Eliza's mouth fell open. There was no way that she was hearing him correctly.

"I'm getting too old to lead this paper by myself. Normally, I would have found a man to take my place, preferably a son-in-law." He stopped to give her a pointed look.

"Now, Daddy, don't you start that again. Noah and I are just friends. Yes, I like him a lot. But with him still in the military and stationed back in Alabama, we've decided to take things slow."

"Yes, yes, I know. But he's such a fine young man. And a doctor too."

"Exactly. Doctors don't stop doctoring to run newspapers, Daddy."

"That's why I'm going to ask your mother to take over. I've seen the changes she's put in place in my absence. I like them. Even better, circulation is up. And this trip down South she's sending you on to cover meatier stories . . ."

"Now, Daddy, don't you start."

"Let me finish now. I was going to say that I like it. It's not like you're going down there ignorant. You went to school down there for four years, after all. Besides, I know that doctor and his family are there to look after you. It doesn't hurt to get to know your future in-laws better before you all, you know, take the next step."

"Daddy . . ."

"And when you get back, we'll see about getting you on some even better beats. Maybe even a foreign one."

"Are you serious? Daddy, do you have a fever?"

This time, Eliza didn't hold herself back from reaching out to palm his forehead. He swatted her hand away.

"Back up, girl. I told you I feel fine. A bad back don't cause no fever. But there's one condition. I won't have you running wild all over Europe by yourself. You might be grown, but you still need someone to look after you. Someone trustworthy. Like a chaperone. Someone with some sense."

Eliza thought back to what Grace had said about Jonathan setting her up on a jazz tour through Europe that coming summer once her spring classes at Juilliard ended. Eliza looked at her father again. Just how long had he been listening to their conversation?

"Let me get this straight. When I get back, you are going to send me back to Europe, with pay and expenses covered, to write stories for the paper. But only if I have someone else tag along with me?"

"Yes, baby. The letters you wrote to your mother while you were away overseas, that was some mighty fine writing. But only with the right person."

Eliza fingered the notepaper that Grace had given her with her phone number on it and smiled.

"Okay, fine. I think I know the perfect girl . . ."

ACKNOWLEDGMENTS

THEY SAY IT takes a village to raise a child. Well, it took a whole lot of people to help me "raise" this book.

I humbly thank God for blessing me with whatever it is that wouldn't let me give up on writing this story. Even when life gave me reasons to set it aside numerous times. Especially on those nights when I tried to tell myself that nobody wanted to read this "stuff" anyway. And my thanks for putting people in my path who believed in this project and in me.

To my editor, Tessa Woodward, and my agent, Kevan Lyon, thank you for wanting to read this "stuff." And for your understanding when my life became chaotic. I appreciate you and everyone on your teams for their contributions to this project.

To my partner in crime Heather, who tolerated me for hours as I droned on about Black women's history before politely suggesting that I shut up and write the book already.

To my husband, Diallo, for being my sanity in general and for holding it down so I could write.

To my daughter and my angels, you are the reasons why I do this. Each of you inspires me to be a better version of myself.

To my sister, you are amazing.

To my mom, who passed away while I was finishing this book. Because of you, I do fearless things despite being scared as hell.

To my dad, if not for you putting that Black history book in my hands, none of this would have ever happened. You're the best thing that has ever happened to me. I love you.

A special thank-you to my high school honors English teacher Judy Legenhausen. When I wanted to drop your class, you lectured me about quitting. That has always stayed with me. Yours was one of the voices that kept me going when I wanted to give up on this book.

I must also shout out my Destin Divas for having my back, front, and sides; the Lyonnesses for your kindness and encouragement; the Cooper family; Rosemarie Harris; my Depressed Elephants crew; my VONA Popular Fiction cohorts; Marita Golden, gurrrrrl, you saved me for real; my sister in WWII nerddom Stephanie Baker; Mat Johnson; Marjorie C. Liu; Kevin Powell; Beverly Jenkins, I stand on your blood, sweat, and tears; Nathasha Brooks-Harris, you gave me my start in this writing game, I'll never forget it; the Anointed 2 Fly Spelman College Class of 1998; Aunt Pam; Myrna Scott Amos; and Cheryl Day.

Thank you to Jack Porter of the Fort Des Moines Museum in Iowa and Elizabeth Skrabonja of the Orangetown Historical Museum & Archives in New York for opening your museums and archives to me.

I am also grateful to Colonel Edna Cummings, Ret., and the Lincoln Penny Films team for sharing your resources. All of your assistance was invaluable to my research for this project. I hope the remaining 6888th veterans have their Congressional Gold Medals in hand by the time this book goes to print.

Last but not least, to the ancestors on whose shoulders I stand. I do this because of you and to honor you. But mostly because I miss you all so much.

About the author

About the book

Insights,
Interviews
& More . . .

Meet Kaia Alderson

Jillisa Hope Milner

KAIA ALDERSON is a women's historical fiction author with a passion for discovering "hidden figures" in African American women's history. Her specific areas of interest are women's military history, popular music, women in sports, upper-middle-class African American society, and women's international travel. She holds a sociology degree from Spelman College and a master's degree in education from the University of West Georgia. ∾

Behind the Book

This book started more than thirty years ago as a middle school social studies assignment. I was tasked with interviewing an older relative about her experiences during World War II. I called Aunt Carmen, my grandmother's cousin. She told me that she worked as a civilian Army clerk in Manhattan during the war. A shocked fourteen-year-old me asked, "They let Black women work in the military back then?"

"Ha!" She laughed into the phone. "The only reason my supervisor hired me was because he had 'never seen a Colored girl with a college degree before.'"

That "Colored girl with a college degree" line came back to me the first time I saw a World War II–era picture of Black female soldiers. They were turning the corner of a French cobblestone street. I knew Black women had served back then, but the location in the background was a surprise. I didn't know any had served overseas. Thanks to Google, the story of the 6888th Postal Battalion—the Six Triple Eight—became a part of my life.

Because the true stories of the African American female military experience ▶

Behind the Book (*continued*)

during World War II aren't commonly known, I tried to stay true to the facts while writing *Sisters in Arms*. Grace and Eliza are fictional characters, but many of their experiences are based on true events, including the encounter with the Nosy Nellie on the train who thought they were imposters and, unfortunately, Eliza's train station assault.

Many of the named secondary characters were real people, including my heroine Major Charity Adams. She really did tell that general, "Over my dead body, sir." It is my favorite moment in the Six Triple Eight's story.

PFC Mary Bankston, PFC Mary Barlow, and SGT Dolores Browne are three of the four women buried in the American cemetery in Normandy, France. I found very few details about the circumstances of their fatal jeep accident. I hope that I have honored their memories and their families with my fictionalized account of that tragic event.

The Jonathan Philips character was inspired by Truman Gibson Jr., who served as a civilian aide to War Secretary Stimson during World War II. Gibson led a fascinating life that included a stint as a boxing promoter, as well as representing Lorraine Hansberry's father in *Hansberry v. Lee*, the landmark Chicago civil rights racial housing case on which the play *A Raisin in the Sun* is based.

Dr. Noah Roberts is a fictional character based loosely on the Six Triple Eight's medical officer, Captain Thomas M. Campbell. Captain Campbell was the brother of Captain Abbie Noel Campbell, the Six Triple Eight's executive officer, and of decorated Tuskegee Airman Colonel William A. Campbell.

Below are the books I read to learn more about the Black women who served in the Women's Army Corps during World War II and to reconstruct the world in which they lived, both on the U.S. home front and abroad.

Beyond the Beach: The Allied War Against France by Stephan Alan Bourque

Birmingham at War: 1939–45 by Julie Phillips

Bitter Fruit: African American Women in World War II, edited by Maureen Honey ▶

Behind the Book *(continued)*

Double Victory: How African American Women Broke Race and Gender Barriers to Help Win World War II by Cheryl Mullenbach

Glory in Their Spirit: How Four Black Women Took On the Army During World War II by Sandra M. Bolzenius

Juilliard: A History by Andrea Olmstead

Knocking Down Barriers: My Fight for Black America by Truman K. Gibson Jr., with Steve Huntley

Mighty Justice: My Life in Civil Rights by Dovey Johnson Roundtree

One Woman's Army: A Black Officer Remembers the WAC by Charity Adams Earley

Our Mothers' War: American Women at Home and at the Front During World War II by Emily Yellin

Standing Up Against Hate: How Black Women in the Army Helped Change the Course of WWII by Mary Cronk Farrell

To Serve My Country, to Serve My Race: The Story of the Only African American WACs Stationed Overseas

During World War II by Brenda L. Moore

When the Nation Was in Need: Blacks in the Women's Army Corps During World War II by Martha S. Putney

World War II Love Stories: The True Stories of 14 Couples by Gill Paul ❧

Reading Group Guide

1. How did "playing it safe" help or hinder Grace?

2. Should Grace have responded differently to the woman who assumed she was an errand girl at the WAC recruitment office?

3. Were Grace and Eliza running away from their problems when they joined the military, or were they taking control of their lives?

4. Was Lieutenant Rogers prejudiced against his African American female trainees, or was he just doing his job of preparing new recruits for military life? What do you think he got right, and what could he have done better?

5. Was Eliza's anger toward Grace over the Kentucky incident justified?

6. Was Grace's anger toward Eliza over the Rouen incident justified?

7. Do you think Grace and Jonathan should have fought harder to continue their romantic relationship once they had returned to civilian life?

8. If you had been in Major Charity Adams's shoes, how would you have responded to the general's order stop working in order to participate in the parade?

9. Given what you now know about the African American WAC soldiers' World War II experiences, how would you have responded to the German POW's excuse that he had been "just following orders"?

10. Do you think Grace and Eliza are on their way to becoming lifelong friends by the end of the book?

11. Did the surprise that was waiting for Grace upon her return from Europe add to or take away from her journey and the decision she had made for herself prior to coming home? ▶

12. Should Eliza's mother have undermined her husband to help Eliza join the military?

13. Did Eliza's father have valid reasons for not wanting his daughter to join the military, or was he just a bully?

14. In what other way could Eliza have dealt with her father besides joining the military? Would another option have been as effective in getting him to respect her as an adult?

15. During World War II, the Army refused to allow women to carry arms or receive weapons training. What other weapons did the 6888th Postal Battalion and other Black female soldiers have at their disposal at that time?

16. How would you have responded to the woman on the train who refused to believe that Grace and Eliza really were WAC officers?

17. Do you think Grace suffered from a "not like the other girls" mentality? ∾

Discover great authors, exclusive offers, and more at hc.com.